The Home at Cedar Creek Series

ABBY FINDS HER CALLING
ROSEMARY OPENS HER HEART
AMANDA WEDS A GOOD MAN
EMMA BLOOMS AT LAST

Amanda Weds a Good Man

HOME AT CEDAR CREEK

Naomi King

JOVE
New York

A JOVE BOOK
Published by Berkley
An imprint of Penguin Random House LLC
penguinrandomhouse.com

Copyright © 2013 by Charlotte Hubbard
Excerpt from *Emma Blooms at Last* by Naomi King
copyright © 2014 by Charlotte Hubbard
Penguin Random House supports copyright. Copyright fuels creativity, encourages
diverse voices, promotes free speech, and creates a vibrant culture. Thank you for buying
an authorized edition of this book and for complying with copyright laws by not
reproducing, scanning, or distributing any part of it in any form without permission.
You are supporting writers and allowing Penguin Random House to continue to
publish books for every reader.

A JOVE BOOK, BERKLEY, and the BERKLEY & B colophon are registered
trademarks of Penguin Random House LLC.

ISBN: 9780593198384

New American Library trade paperback edition / November 2013
Jove mass-market edition / September 2020

Printed in the United States of America
1   3   5   7   9   10   8   6   4   2

Cover design by Judith Lagerman
Cover photography by Claudio Marinesco

*In memory of my father, Addison Parry,
a good man to his family and a good
and faithful servant to his Lord.*

*And to Neal, the good man I wed more
than thirty-eight years ago.*

Behold, I will do a new thing, now it shall spring forth; shall ye not know it? I will even make a way in the wilderness and rivers in the desert.

—ISAIAH, 43:19

Have not I commanded thee? Be strong and of a good courage; be not afraid, neither be thou dismayed: for the Lord thy God is with thee whithersoever thou goest.

—JOSHUA, 1:9

Weeping may endure for a night, but joy cometh in the morning.

—PSALMS, 30:5

Courage is fear that has said its prayers.

—AMISH PROVERB

Chapter 1

Amanda Lambright paused outside the Cedar Creek Mercantile, clutching her basket of pottery samples, and prayed that Sam would carry her handmade items in his store. She had also come to share some exciting news: she stood on the threshold of a brand-new life in a brand-new family, and the prospect thrilled her. But it frightened her, too.

When Amanda stepped inside, the bell tinkled above the door. As her eyes adjusted to the soft dimness of the store, she saw her teenage daughter, Lizzie, and the four-year-old twins making a beeline to the craft department while her mother-in-law, Jemima, ambled behind her cart in the grocery aisle. Several shoppers, English and Amish alike, lingered over their choices of cheese, locally grown apples, and other household and hardware necessities, but she was in luck: the bearded, bespectacled man at the checkout counter didn't have any customers right now. She approached him with a smile.

"And how are you on this fine September day, Sam?"

When Sam Lambright looked up from the order form he was filling out, his face lit up. "Amanda! How gut to see you. Things are going well at your farm, I hope?"

Amanda gripped the handle of her basket. Should she break her big news first? Or make her request? "The work never ends, that's for sure. The last hay's ready to cut, the garden's gone to weeds, and Jerome's training several new mules." Jerome was her nephew by marriage, the boy she and her late husband, Atlee, had raised after his parents died in a fire.

"Your girls are growing up, too. I had to look twice to realize it was Lizzie, Cora, and Dora waving at me."

"They change by the day, it seems. And, well . . . I'm making a few changes myself."

Sam gazed at her in that patient, expectant way he had. He was Atlee's cousin, and his expression, his manner, reminded her so much of Atlee that at times she'd not shopped here because she couldn't deal with the resemblance. *But that sadness is behind me now . . . and nobody will be happier than Sam*, she reminded herself. "Wyman Brubaker has asked me to marry him. And I said jah."

Sam's smile lit up the whole store. "That's wonderful! Abby"—he gazed up toward the upper level, hailing his sister as she sat at her sewing machine by the railing—"Abby, you'll want to come down and get the latest from Amanda. She's getting hitched!"

"That's so exciting," Abby called out. "Don't say another word until I get down there."

Amanda noticed several folks in the store glancing her way, enjoying this exchange. It made her upcoming marriage seem even more real now that it had been announced so publicly. She and Wyman had kept their courtship quiet, because they wanted to be very sure that a marriage blending two households and eight children was a wise decision.

"Months ago I suggested to Wyman that it was time he

found another gut woman," Sam said, "and I'm so glad he's chosen *you*, Amanda. I can't think of two finer folks with so much in common."

"Well, we hope so. It'll be . . . different, raising eight kids instead of just my three girls," she replied quietly. "But Wyman's a gut man."

"And with his grain elevator doing so well, it means you won't have to worry about money anymore," Sam replied in a lowered voice. "You haven't let on—haven't let me help you much—but even with Jerome's income, it couldn't have been easy to keep that farm afloat after Atlee passed."

As Abby Lambright rushed down the wooden stairway to hug her, Amanda forgot about her four long years of scraping by. She felt lifted up by the love and happiness this maidel radiated. Rain or shine, Abby gave her best and brought that out in everyone around her, too.

"What a wonderful-gut thing, to know you've found another love," Abby gushed. "And who's the lucky man?"

"Wyman Brubaker."

"You don't say!" Abby replied. "I couldn't have matched up a more perfect pair myself—and as I recall, his Vera and your Lizzie first met while both families were shopping here. And that started the ball rolling."

"Jah, as matchmakers go, they were pretty insistent," Amanda replied with a chuckle.

"And when's the big day?"

"We haven't decided, but it'll be sooner than I can possibly be ready," Amanda admitted. "What with Lizzie still in school, I've hardly packed any boxes—not that I know where to stack them if the wedding's at my house," she added in a rush. "And with Jerome training a team of mules now, we can't clear out the barn for the ceremony. And I can't see me driving back and forth, cleaning Wyman's house in Clearwater—"

"Or keeping it wedding-ready until the big day. His Vera's a responsible girl, but looking after her three brothers and Alice Ann is all she can handle," Abby remarked in a thoughtful tone. She looked at her older brother. "Sam, what would you say to having Amanda's wedding at *our* house? What with preparing for Matt and Rosemary's ceremony next week, and then for Phoebe and Owen's that first Thursday of October—"

"Oh, no!" Amanda protested. "I didn't mean to go on and on about—"

"That would be just fine." Sam gazed steadily at Amanda. "We're setting up the tables for the meals in Mamm's greenhouse—leaving them up between the two weddings, anyway. So if you pick a date in the first few weeks of October, it would be very easy to host your ceremony, Amanda. And I would feel like I'd finally given you some real help when you needed it."

Amanda nearly dropped her basket of pottery. "My stars. That would solve a lot of my problems . . ."

"And with Wyman living in Clearwater and your house being on the far side of Bloomingdale, Cedar Creek would be a more central location for your guests," Sam reasoned.

"And it'll be gut practice for Sam, delivering another wedding sermon," Abby added mischievously. "Right after he was ordained as our new preacher last spring, Rosemary asked him to preach and then Phoebe insisted on him, too. So he should be pretty gut at it by the time you and Wyman tie the knot!"

Sam flushed. "Jah, but if you want the preachers from your district to—"

"It would be an *honor* to have you and Vernon Gingerich officiate for us." Amanda squeezed Sam's arm, her excitement mounting. "Wyman will be so glad you've settled our dilemma, because if we choose one preacher and one bishop from our own districts, we'll still be leaving out the other bishop and three preachers."

"And you don't want them *all* to speak! Six sermons would make for a very long day," Abby added wryly.

As their laughter rose toward the high ceiling of the mercantile, Amanda relaxed. Wasn't it just like these cousins to offer their home when she would never have asked another family to host her wedding? What a relief, to be free to concentrate on moving her three daughters, Atlee's mamm, and herself into Wyman's home rather than also having to prepare for a couple of hundred wedding guests.

Abby leaned closer to Amanda, watching Lizzie and the twins fingering bolts of fabric. "So how are your girls taking the news? And what of Jemima?" she asked quietly.

Amanda smiled. "It'll be a big change for the three of them, but they seem excited about having a new dat—and brothers," she said. "And, bless him, Wyman said from the first that he had a room for Atlee's mamm. It won't be easy for her, living in a home other than her son's. But we'll all be together."

"One big happy family!" Abby proclaimed as she hugged Amanda's shoulders again.

"And what of Jerome?" Sam inquired. "He's lived with you since he was a boy, but he's what, twenty-two now?"

"Twenty-four," Amanda corrected. "And with him being so established with his mule breeding and training, I've asked him to stay there on the home place. It's what Atlee would've wanted for his nephew."

"A gut decision," Sam agreed. "One of these days he'll be finding a wife, and a whole new generation of Lambrights can live there."

Amanda nodded, feeling a flicker of sadness. Her Atlee had passed on before they knew she was carrying the twins . . . but cogitating over the other children they might have had together—or which ones might have taken over the Lambright farm—wasn't a useful way to spend her time. A little gasp brought her out of her woolgathering.

"What's this in your basket?" Abby asked as she reached for the handle. "My stars, these are such pretty colors for pie pans and cream pitchers and—" Her brown eyes widened. "Did *you* paint these, Amanda?"

Amanda's cheeks prickled. "I make the pottery pieces on my wheel and then I glaze them, jah," she said. "I was hoping that—rather than packing away my finished pieces—you might want to sell them here."

"These are pieces any woman could use," Abby said excitedly. She was carefully setting items from the basket on the counter so that Sam could get a better look at them. "A pitcher . . . a deep-dish pie plate . . . oh, and look at this round piece painted like a sunflower!"

"That's a disk you heat in the oven and then put in your basket to keep your bread warm," Amanda said. "I sell a lot of those at the dry goods stores north of home. Seems English tourists like some little souvenir when they visit Plain communities."

"I can see why," Sam remarked. He was turning the pitcher this way and that in his large hands. "I don't believe I've ever seen kitchen pieces with such bold colors. And if *you* make them, Amanda, I'd be happy to take them on consignment. Folks hereabouts would snap these up."

"You've got several pieces with you, I hope?" Abby asked.

"This is such a blessing," Amanda replied. "I've got three boxes of this stuff in my wagon, along with an inventory list. I figured that if you didn't want it, I'd stash it all in Wyman's basement until we get moved in."

"Don't go hiding these in the basement!" Abby insisted. "We'll set up a big display down here, and I'll arrange the rest of them up in the loft."

Sam started for the door. "I'll help you carry in your boxes, Amanda. You can decide which items might sell better over at the greenhouse and work that out with Mamm."

"Jah, I will. Denki so much, you two. Let me show you what I've brought." Amanda's heart skipped happily as the bell above the door tinkled. This trip to Cedar Creek was going even better than she'd dreamed, and she was eager to set her wedding date with Wyman now that they had such a wonderful place to hold their ceremony.

As they stepped outside, however, an ominous *crash* rang out, followed by a yelp and another crash.

"*Simon!* Get your dog out of that wagon!"

Amanda's face fell. Oh, but she recognized that authoritative voice. And there could be only one Simon with a pet who had stirred up such a ruckus . . . and only one wagon full of pottery with its end gate down.

As she rounded the corner of the store with Sam and Abby, the scene in the parking lot confirmed Amanda's worst fears: the Brubaker family had gathered around her wagon and was coaxing Simon's German shepherd out of it while Wyman lifted his youngest son onto its bed. When the five-year-old boy grabbed his basketball from the only box of her pottery left standing, the picture became dismally clear.

"Oh, Amanda," Abby murmured as the three of them hurried toward the Brubakers. "This doesn't look so gut."

Amanda's stomach clenched. How many days' worth of her work had been shattered after Wags had apparently followed Simon's ball into her wagon?

"Gut afternoon to you, Wyman," Sam said. "We just heard your exciting news, and we're mighty happy you and Amanda are hitching up."

Wyman set his youngest son on the ground and extended his hand to the storekeeper. "Jah, I finally found a gal who'll put up with me and my raft of kids. But I can't think she's too happy with us right this minute."

Amanda bit back her frustration as her future husband lowered one of her boxes to the ground so she could see inside it. The other boxes had been overturned, so some of her pie plates, vases, and other items lay in pieces on the wagon bed. She had considered padding her pottery more carefully, boxing the pieces better, but who could have guessed that Simon's energetic, oversize puppy would follow a basketball into her wagon? A little sob escaped her.

"And now, Simon, do you see why you should always

check the latch on the dog's pen when we leave?" Wyman asked sternly. "Not only was it dangerous for Wags to come running up alongside our buggy, but now he's broken Amanda's pottery. What do you say to her, son?"

The little boy, clutching his basketball, became the picture of contrition. Simon's brown eyes, usually filled with five-year-old mischief, were downcast as he stood beside his father. "I . . . didn't mean to break your stuff," he murmured. "I bounced my ball too high, and Wags had to play, too. I'm real sorry."

Chastising this winsome boy wouldn't put her pottery together again, would it? "Things happen," Amanda replied with a sigh. "I was hoping to sell my ceramics here at the mercantile, but . . . well, maybe we can salvage some of it."

"Tie Wags to the wagon, Simon, before he causes any more trouble," Wyman murmured.

Abby had stepped up beside Amanda to carefully lift the contents of the box onto the tailgate while Wyman set the other two boxes upright. Amanda was vaguely aware that the other Brubaker kids were nearby: his teenage sons, Pete and Eddie, went on inside the mercantile, while seventeen-year-old Vera came up beside her, cradling little Alice Ann against her hip.

"See there, all is not lost," Abby remarked as she set unbroken dishes to one side of the wagon bed. "Still enough for a display, Amanda—"

"And look at these colors!" Vera said as she fingered some of the broken pieces. "Dat told me you worked on pottery, Amanda, but I had no idea it was like this! So, do you paint ready-made pieces, or do you make everything from scratch?"

Amanda smiled sadly as she held up two pitchers that no longer had their handles. "I form them on my pottery wheel, and when they've dried I glaze them and fire them in my kiln."

"Would you mind if I take the broken stuff?"

Surprised, Amanda considered the request. Vera's eyes were lit up with interest, as though she truly loved the pottery even though it was shattered. "I don't know what you'd do with it," she murmured, "but it's not like I can sell repaired plates and pitchers, either."

"I'm sorry this has happened, Amanda. I'll pay you for what Simon broke," Wyman offered as he squeezed her shoulder. "At least you won't be needing the income after we marry, jah?"

"Denki, Wyman. That's generous of you."

As much as she had come to love Wyman Brubaker during these past months of their courtship, a red flag went up in Amanda's mind. He—and most men—didn't understand that her pottery was much more than a way to earn money. It had been her salvation after Atlee had lost a leg to gangrene and then lost his will to live . . . a way to focus her mind on cheerful designs and colors instead of becoming lost in the darkness of her grief after he died.

Wyman ran the only grain elevator in the area, so he was able to provide quite well for a large family. Yet as she considered mixing her Lizzie and the twins—not to mention her opinionated mother-in-law—with the three rambunctious Brubaker boys, Vera, and toddler Alice Ann, Amanda wondered what she was getting herself into. Everyone seemed amiable enough now, but what if their good intentions went by the wayside once they were all together in one household?

Would they be one big happy family, as Abby had predicted? Or had she let herself in for more major changes than she could handle by agreeing to marry Wyman Brubaker?

Chapter 2

Wyman gazed around the vast interior of the Cedar Creek Mercantile as he stood beside its owner. He and Sam Lambright had been good friends since they were boys, when Wyman's parents had come here from Clearwater to shop and Sam's dat had run the store. "So what did you think when Amanda told you of our wedding plans?"

"High time," Sam replied smugly. "Wasn't it last winter that I suggested her as a potential wife?"

Wyman shrugged. "Took me a while to get over losing Viola. And with Vera to keep the house running and watch after Simon and Alice Ann, I . . . I wasn't in a hurry to hook up again, at my age."

"At your *age*?" Sam punctuated his question with an elbow to Wyman's ribs. "Are any of us getting any younger? I can't think you'd want to raise five kids alone—especially since Vera will be starting a family of her own soon."

"Let's not rush things, Sam. She's only seventeen."

"And what of Alice Ann?" his friend asked quietly. "Is she talking yet?"

Spotting his toddler in the seat of Vera's shopping cart, Wyman sighed. Alice Ann had been only a year old, snuggled against Viola's shoulder that fateful day when they'd been hurrying to bale the hay before it rained. His wife had been walking alongside the mules when a thunderclap spooked them. Viola had grabbed their harness and then slipped in the wet grass . . . had let go of the baby just as she got crushed beneath the hay baler. It was a scene Wyman would never forget, or forgive himself for. His sweet, orderly world had ended in seconds, and a speech therapist believed the shock of witnessing her mamm's death had rendered their youngest daughter mute.

"No, she's still not talking. Looks ready to blurt something out every now and again—and she understands everything we say," he murmured. "We pray on it a lot."

"And I'll keep praying with you," Sam replied. "It'll be gut for all of you to have Amanda there, and an improvement for her and her girls, as well. It's a match made in Heaven, I'm telling you."

Wyman caught a movement on the opposite end of the store and excused himself. He'd just reimbursed Amanda for her broken pottery, and he had no intention of allowing Simon to do more damage inside Sam's store. And what had gotten into Pete, that he'd put a hook on a fishing pole and was trying to snag Lizzie Lambright's kapp with it?

"You're asking for trouble, son," Wyman called out as he hurried toward the tackle boxes and lures. Several shoppers followed his gaze to where a rod was angled over a section of shelves and its line dangled just above unsuspecting Lizzie's head. And who could miss the way Eddie was chatting with Lizzie, holding the end of her cart, so his brother knew where to ease the hook lower . . . lower . . .

Lizzie's shriek rang out. Wyman winced, hoping she

didn't snag her hand when she clutched at the white kapp that floated a foot above her head.

"Pete! Eddie!" he snapped. "Enough of your foolishness."

His teenage sons had sense enough to look penitent when he reached them, but the prank had accomplished what they'd hoped: poor Lizzie appeared mortified while her sisters, Cora and Dora, giggled at her. Wyman grabbed the clear fishing line, unhooked the starched white kapp, and handed it to the young lady who would soon be living under his roof.

"Pete, you know where you need to be, and right this minute," Wyman said, aiming his voice over the top of the shelf. He sighed. Had living two years without their mother turned his older boys into such troublemakers? As Lizzie hastily replaced her prayer covering, he noted the bags of chicken feed she had probably been looking at when Eddie had waylaid her.

"Sorry, Lizzie," Pete said as he strolled toward them. "I didn't mean to—"

"Jah, you did!" the girl retorted. Her cheeks turned bright pink as she tied the strings of her kapp beneath her chin.

"You boys are old enough to know better," Wyman muttered. "Not only was your prank unspeakably rude, it wasn't smart, either. What if that hook had caught Lizzie on the cheek? Or in her eye?"

"Just give me a sack of that chicken feed," Lizzie muttered. "And turn loose of my cart, Eddie Brubaker!"

A few moments later both boys had apologized and Lizzie had moved on, but Wyman could only shake his head. Thank goodness Amanda hadn't witnessed this little scene while she was helping her mother-in-law across the store, but she would certainly hear about it. He told Vera to finish her shopping quickly and then made his way toward the checkout counter, where Sam was loading a customer's order into her cart.

"Sorry about that," Wyman said quietly. "I should've followed Vera's suggestion and left the boys at home."

Sam's smile was kind. "Eddie and Pete were flirting with a pretty girl. No harm done, really."

"But they're fifteen and thirteen!"

"And you didn't exasperate your folks when you were that age?" Sam teased. "Why, I can recall when you and I unscrewed the caps of the salt and pepper shakers at Abe and Beulah Mae's wedding—"

"Shh! My boys don't need any more ideas." Wyman let out the breath he'd been holding. Maybe he *was* blowing this incident out of proportion, but he'd overheard folks saying his kids needed a mother's firm hand and watchful eyes. "This hasn't been Amanda's best shopping trip. I hope she won't change her mind about marrying me."

"She's patient and kind, the very definition of love," Sam replied. "Everybody's getting the prewedding jitters, I suspect. It'll all work out as God intended, my friend."

"I hope you're right." He looked at the tall, slender fellow with the graying beard, grateful that Sam had displayed such understanding. The Cedar Creek district was blessed to have him for their new preacher. "Did you and Amanda set a date? Abby was saying you'll be performing the ceremonies for your Matt and Phoebe soon, as well."

Sam lifted the page of the wall calendar that hung behind him. "Here in the Cedar Creek district we always hold weddings on Thursdays . . . so how's the second Thursday of October work for you? That'll be the eighth."

"Can't thank you folks enough, Sam. I'll be there."

"It's always a better start for a marriage when the groom shows up," Sam teased. He picked up the pencil beside his cash register. "I'll write you in, Wyman. No wiggling out of it now."

Vera was pushing her loaded cart up to the counter, so Wyman rounded up his three sons. The four of them went outside to fetch a pair of buggy wheels from his wagon and then crossed the blacktop to Graber's Custom Carriages, with Wags circling them excitedly. It was a fine autumn day, so Wyman tried to enjoy the crunch of fallen leaves beneath his feet and the panorama of farmland . . . woolly sheep grazing in nearby pastures, and the deep green cedars that swayed in the breeze along Cedar Creek. "I hope you boys have gotten your shenanigans out of your system," he warned as he opened the door.

Inside the carriage shop, the heavy smell of paint and the tattoo of pneumatic drills filled the air. By the looks of it, the buggy business was keeping James Graber and his men very busy.

"Hullo there, Wyman! Gut to see you Brubakers on this beautiful day," a familiar voice called out above the racket. James had lifted the front of his welding mask and was smiling at them from beside the nearest workbench. "What can I do for you?"

As Wyman showed James where his wheels needed some repair, his boys started toward a young redheaded fellow who was brushing deep green paint on a nearly finished wagon. Noah Coblentz had apprenticed with James a while back. Wyman wondered if Eddie shouldn't be looking for a place to learn a trade, as well, since he showed no interest in working at the elevator.

"We can have these ready in a few days," James said. He attached a tag to one of the wooden wheels before leaning them against his bench. "So how've you been, Wyman? Busy at the elevator now that the harvest has started, jah?"

"The corn's coming in," Wyman said with a nod. "English fellows with bigger, fancier combines are always the first, and this year they haven't had much of a crop. The drought's going to hit us all right in the pocketbook, I'm afraid."

"Makes me grateful to work in a business where Plain folks need vehicles, rain or shine," James replied. He glanced over to where Wyman's sons were chatting with Noah. "Your boys are growing like weeds. Has Simon started to school?"

"Next fall," Wyman replied, and then he couldn't help smiling. "Meanwhile, he'll be keeping Amanda Lambright busy, because she and I are getting hitched in a few weeks."

"You don't say!" James clapped him on the back. "That's mighty gut news for all of you."

On impulse, Wyman chucked James's clean-shaven chin. "Time for *you* to be sporting a beard, the way I see it. You and Abby have been a pair forever, haven't you?" he teased. "Better take notes at our wedding. We'll show you how it's done."

James's cheeks colored a bit. "Matter of fact, Abby and I are moving in that direction. We'll tie the knot in our own gut time."

"Ah. Sounds like I'd better stop kidding you about it, then."

"Emma and my parents do plenty of that, jah," James replied.

"And your sister's well? And how about your folks?" Wyman inquired. "Haven't seen them for a long while, now that Carl Byler farms your dat's ground and hauls his crops to the elevator."

"Our family's fine, all things considered," James replied. "And with the two Lambright weddings and yours coming up, maybe Emma will find herself a beau. She's being a gut daughter, looking after our parents, but she deserves a home of her own, with a husband and children to love her."

Wyman thanked James and rounded up his sons again, realizing how fortunate he was. He had a home, he had children, and soon he would have a wonderful new wife to complete the picture of domestic satisfaction James had described. Like a jigsaw puzzle, his life would again have all its pieces in place when Amanda joined her family with his.

A sense of completion filled him. He'd set his wedding date and the Lambright family was hosting his ceremony, so maybe this exasperating morning had served a higher purpose after all.

Chapter 3

"Glad you could come out with me on this fine fall afternoon," James said as he helped Abby up into his rig. "It's too pretty a Saturday to spend all of it in the shop."

When he was in the driver's seat, Abby scooted just close enough that their arms brushed. "Jah, and I've had about all I can handle of working at the mercantile for the week. Three busloads of English tourists came in today, so I've had to straighten the shelves again and again," she said. "Some of those folks chattered on their cell phones the whole time they were in the store. That makes for a lot of racket!"

James lightly clapped the reins on his gelding's back. "Jah, I see that a lot, too. Makes you wonder what-all they find to talk about."

He could think of several topics to discuss with Abby, however—such as asking how the preparations were going for her nephew Matt's wedding on Thursday, or whether her niece Phoebe's new house would be completed before she married Owen Coblentz the following week. This flurry of weddings made him very aware of the important things he wanted to say to the woman beside him.

How fresh and vibrant Abby looked, in a butterscotch-colored dress that complemented a face made rosier by the autumn breeze. He wasn't surprised that she'd brought along a lidded container for the Brubaker family, because no matter how busy Abby was, she always made the time and effort to share her goodness with others.

"Going to show me what's in your pan?" James hinted.

Abby smiled as though she'd been waiting for him to ask. When she popped off the lid, the aroma of cinnamon and other spices teased him. "When you mentioned you were delivering Wyman's wheels," she said, "I packed some of the pumpkin whoopie pies I'd made for the meal after church tomorrow. I don't suppose you'd want to taste one—to be sure they're all right for the Brubaker kids, of course."

"Oh, we shouldn't take the chance that your goodies aren't perfect," James teased.

When he bit into the treat Abby held in front of his mouth, he delighted in the moistness of the pumpkin cookies . . . the sweet tang of cream cheese filling as it covered his tongue. "Oh, my," he murmured. "This treat's *almost* as wonderful-gut as you are, Abby."

"Oh, James, you say the sweetest things." Abby nibbled at the whoopie pie before holding it in front of him again. "Pumpkin's one of my favorite flavors. What flavors do *you* like?"

At that moment, with her face mere inches from his and her lips slightly parted, James couldn't think rationally about food or anything else. He leaned toward Abby and met her mouth with his, searching . . . tasting a deep sweetness that went beyond sugar and spices. "You, Abby," he whispered. "You surely must be the best flavor there is, and I'm glad God's brought us together in time for me to realize that."

Abby looked so pleasantly surprised that James knew he'd remember the expression on her face forever. "We have the rest of our lives to share, James," she replied quietly. "And now that you've finally caught up to my feelings, it's my mission to learn as much as I can about what you like and don't—"

"You can't go wrong, Abby. As long as I'm with you, I'll be a happy man." James glanced at the road to ascertain their location, because Abby's presence often made him lose track of where he was and what he intended to say. He gazed into her eyes again, hoping he got his words right. "Do . . . do you want to court for a while, then? What with so many folks tying the knot—"

"With all these weddings in the next few weeks, I'm glad I don't have to get ready for my own," she insisted. "Mamm and Barbara are spending every spare moment baking bread. Or they're updating Beulah Mae Nissley about more folks coming from out of state, so she can figure out how many chickens to roast for the two big dinners. It would almost make more sense if both weddings were on the same day."

Abby paused to inhale the fresh air. "But then, that would deprive each couple of their special celebration, wouldn't it? I still have wedding dresses to make for Mamm and Phoebe, along with my usual sewing for other folks," she went on. "If you and I are going to hitch up, James, I'd like it to be at a time when we're not so busy."

Will that day ever come? While he felt relieved that Abby didn't think other couples were getting a head start on happiness, James also realized that Abby's Stitch in Time and Graber's Custom Carriages weren't going into a slack period anytime soon—or at least he hoped they weren't.

And then there was the matter of actually proposing to her. While he and Abby had reached an understanding that they intended to court and marry, it was only fitting to ask her properly. James wanted to leave nothing undone when it came to giving Abby everything she deserved, everything that could possibly make her as happy as she made him.

But when the tall grain elevator buildings came into sight on the horizon, he filed away all thoughts of romance. Even though he and Abby both enjoyed Wyman's kids, it would be more like a circus than a date once they got to the Brubaker farm. Sure enough, as they turned in at the long lane, James spotted a boy racing around in the yard, tossing a neon yellow tennis ball for his boisterous dog. Wags was part German shepherd and part something else, and even though he was still a pup, he was nearly as tall as Simon.

"I vaguely recall having that much energy at one time," James remarked.

"Ah, but you still have plenty of energy, James. You've just learned how to focus it on the jobs that need doing." Abby waved as a young woman stepped out of the Brubakers' large white farmhouse with a toddler on her hip. "And someday when you're a dat, you'll figure out how to spend time with your kids, even when you think you couldn't be any busier at your shop."

James considered what his woman had just said. It tickled him that she was thinking about starting a family, even if the Brubaker bunch would give any woman pause. Wyman had five nice-looking, well-intentioned kids, but it seemed they raised a ruckus everywhere they went— probably because their dat couldn't keep after them the way Viola had. "Let's hope Amanda can establish herself as the mamm of this big, blended family before they overwhelm her," he said as they pulled up beside the house.

"She's got her work cut out for her," Abby agreed.

The huge gray dog bounded toward the rig with the tennis ball locked between his front teeth, managing to bark with his mouth full.

"Wags—whoa, boy!" Simon hollered as he ran toward them. His straw hat had blown off, so when he stopped alongside the buggy, he gazed up at them with windblown hair and a grin full of mischief. "Whatcha doin' out this way, James Graber? And whatcha got in that box, Abby? Treats for *me*?"

James hopped down from the rig to assist Abby. "You'd best make your dog behave, son," he said, "because if he knocks those whoopie pies out of Abby's hand, there won't be any left for you, ain't so?"

Without missing a beat, Simon snatched the ball from between his dog's teeth and lobbed it as far across the yard as he could. When Wags ran after it, the boy stood before them with a hopeful expression on his face. "Whoopie pies? Those are my favorite! Are they chocolate ones with marshmallow filling, or—"

"Simon! Mind your manners!" Vera stepped down from the porch, balancing Alice Ann on her hip. "Matter of fact, you'll sit in the swing until Abby offers you a goody."

Simon's face fell. He turned and made quite a display of walking toward the house to wait.

"We're working on him," Vera went on in a lower voice, "but he's been kind of wild since Mamm passed."

"He couldn't have been much older than this little punkin when that happened," Abby said as she patted Alice Ann's bottom. "And are you excited about getting a new mamm, sweetie?"

Alice Ann slipped her thumb into her mouth, gazing wide-eyed at Abby.

"I'm thinking Amanda will be gut for all of us," Vera replied as she shifted her little sister onto her other hip. She looked at James. "If it's Dat you need to see, he'll be at the elevator a while longer, by the looks of those wagons lined up to unload their corn."

"No need to bother him." James took the two repaired wheels and a toolbox from the back of his buggy. "If you'll point me toward the rigs these go on, I can have them remounted in just a few."

"I know where they go! I can help!" Simon, who hadn't yet reached the porch swing, jogged toward James again. His face glowed with the need to be useful.

"And you're just the sort of helper I'm looking for, too," James replied. "No need for the girls to stand around while we do the work, ain't so?"

"Jah! You and me, we can do it, James."

James's pulse sped up with an unexpected thrill. It wasn't often he got to spend time with kids, as his older sisters and their families lived a couple of hours away. He'd forgotten how much fun it was when a five-year-old got excited about being his right-hand man. "How about if you carry the toolbox and lead the way, Simon. I'll handle these heavy wheels."

When the boy grabbed the box's metal handle, he flinched at its weight, but then he hurried ahead to the nearest outbuilding.

"You folks have a lot of rigs," James remarked when they'd stepped inside.

"Jah, this one's Eddie and Pete's," the boy pointed out as they walked the length of the narrow building. "And this is the big one we take to church or—"

"And let's put one of these wheels on that back axle that's sticking out. We'll use your dat's jack," James said as he took it from a peg on the wall. When the back end of the buggy was raised and steady, he smiled at Simon. "Can you slip this wheel onto the axle while I find us a linchpin?"

Simon grabbed the wooden wheel, which was nearly as tall as he, by its spokes and carefully lined up the hole in the center. "Got it!" he crowed.

"Gut job, Simon. You're a mighty strong young fellow."

"So now what're ya doin'?"

James smiled at the boy's enthusiasm. "I'm lining up the holes just right, and then you can steady the wheel while I drop the linchpin in place. Hold it for me riiight . . . *there*."

Simon put his whole body into this task as James slipped

the metal pin into its slot. "Are you ready to have three new sisters move into your house?" he asked as he tested the spin of the repaired wheel.

Two brown eyes studied him intently. "You mean Cora and Dora? And Lizzie?"

"Jah. Along with their mamm and their mammi Jemima." James pumped the jack until the buggy was sitting on the ground again. "That's a few weeks away, though."

Simon's brows knit. "Does that mean Cora and Dora'll be sharin' my room?" he whispered doubtfully. "Playin' with my wagons and trains?"

James laughed and rumpled the boy's thick brown hair. "The twins are more likely to room with Alice Ann, but it's whatever your dat and your new mamm decide. There'll be a lot of changes after they get married, but you'll help them out just like you're helping me, ain't so?"

Simon looked around to be sure no one else was listening. "Does that mean Wags won't get to sleep with me no more?" he whispered near James's ear. "He's not s'posed to be there, ya know, but I let him in at night so he don't get lonely. You won't tell nobody, will ya?"

"Cross my heart," James replied as he drew an X on his chest with a fingertip. "Now where's this other wheel go? We'll be finished here before two shakes of your best friend's tail."

"And then we can have one of Abby's whoopie pies?"

"Sounds like the perfect pay for a job well done," James replied.

About ten minutes later, James had replaced the wheel on one of the smaller buggies. As he and Simon reached the shed's doorway again, the boy let out a whoop and raced toward the porch. Vera and Abby had settled on the swing to enjoy the last rays of afternoon sunshine, with Alice Ann on Abby's lap, but they were ready for Simon: as soon as he stopped and asked politely, his older sister offered him the pan of treats.

Again Simon's excitement touched James. The boy spun in circles in the yard as he ate, barely keeping his treat away from his eager dog. When James focused on Abby, however, his heart stilled.

It was rare to see her sitting, for she usually bustled about, helping with whatever tasks needed doing. Such a pleasure it was to watch Abby cuddle a little girl on her lap, sharing her shawl. As the swing went forward and back in a lazy rhythm, the two women talked. Abby was focused on Alice Ann, smoothing the blond wisps that had escaped her braids.

She'll look this beautiful holding your children, too.

James inhaled deeply, watching from a distance until Abby caught his eye and waved. He really, really needed to ask this woman for her hand. *Soon.*

Chapter 4

The following Thursday, Abby felt so giddy she could have skipped across the road to her mamm's greenhouse like a schoolgirl. What a wonderful wedding she'd witnessed! Her nephew, Matt Lambright, had just married Rosemary Yutzy in a traditional yet touching Old Order service. Rosemary had radiated with love as she repeated her vows, completing her transformation from being a young widow to becoming Matt's bride. Her toddler, Katie, hadn't made a peep, sitting in her mammi's lap, and Sam had preached his first sermon so well that the guests were now clapping him on the back as heartily as they were congratulating the newlyweds.

As one of Rosemary's sidesitters, Abby had been seated on the front row of the women's side—directly across from James, who had served in the same capacity for Matt. James's flirtatious gazes had distracted her often, making her believe that soon *she* would be a bride, at long last. As much as she loved weddings, however, Abby was eager to help Mamm and Sam's wife, Barbara, with the feast and to visit with friends and family for the rest of the day.

And what a fine September day it was for these festivities! The pasture, dotted with Matt's sheep, shone a radiant green in the sunlight. The sumac bushes blushed with their first hint of autumn color. The garden alongside Sam's white farmhouse still had some ripe tomatoes on the vines, and several acorn and butternut squash were nearly ready to pick. The glass walls of her mother's greenhouse sparkled from their recent cleaning. When Abby stepped inside, the aroma of the traditional "roast," made with chicken and stuffing, filled her soul.

The long white-draped tables looked dreamlike, set off by small potted mums and plants from her mamm's store. On the eck—the raised corner table where the wedding party would be seated—a white tiered cake gave the entire room a festive air. Because Treva's Greenhouse had no cooking facilities, they were blessed that neighbor ladies had prepared a lot of the wedding feast in Beulah Mae Nissley's café, while Lois Yutzy and others had baked the pies and bread in her bakery.

Abby's sister-in-law, Barbara; her mamm, Treva; and other women were setting the catering pans on the serving table, but when Abby saw Emma Graber cutting pies, she hurried over to help. "We have quite a variety here," she said as she picked up a clean knife.

"Jah, I've seen peach and rhubarb and apple, along with cherry and blackberry," Emma replied as she slipped cut pieces onto serving plates. "With Beth Ann Yutzy and Ruthie setting them on the tables, it's all I can do to keep up!"

Abby laughed. "Those two remind me of us when we were that age, Emma. Never able to sit still—"

"Always together, laughing and chattering, too." Emma emptied another pie pan, her expression more serious. "It was so gut to see you and my brother sitting up front for the wedding. Nice of Matt to ask his aunt and his best friend to witness for him."

"Well, since Matt has no brothers—" When Abby noticed Emma's quivering chin, she slipped her arm around her best friend's shoulders. "I'm sorry, Emma. It's probably been a tough day, watching Matt marry somebody else after all the years you had your heart set on him," she murmured.

"Jah, well . . . I thought I'd gotten over it. Rosemary's a gut match for him, and he's crazy about her little Katie."

"God's got somebody special in mind for you. I believe that with all my heart," Abby insisted. "But the waiting's never easy when we can't see into the future like He does."

Emma sighed. "You're probably right. And now's not the time to be sniffling. Folks will pester me about being down in the dumps while everyone else is celebrating."

"Better to put on a smile," Abby agreed. "Maybe as the day goes along, you'll feel better. No doubt the food's going to be gut! And there'll be singing later, and out-of-town folks we don't often get to visit with."

"And if I keep myself too busy to fret about being the only gal hereabouts without a beau, the time'll go faster."

As Abby ran her knife through a few more pies, she realized that today's groom wasn't the only source of her friend's heartache. Emma was also feeling left out because James was with Abby every chance he got—and even the best of friendships changed when one girl was courting and the other wasn't. Not that long ago Abby had agonized as other girls in her buddy bunch got hitched, and she'd been thankful to have Emma as a steadfast—and single—friend. Abby had gotten past that disappointment, though, when she'd started her Stitch in Time business and built her own home.

As her niece Ruthie raced Beth Ann Yutzy to their cutting table, however, it was impossible to remain downhearted. "I'm gonna finish *my* side of the table before you do!" Ruthie challenged as she picked up a tray filled with sliced pie.

"Puh! I might just *eat* some pieces from your side so you'll have to put more out," Beth Ann countered.

"Jah, I'm ready for dinner, too," Abby chimed in as she cut another pie. "It's a gut thing folks are crossing the lane to take their places for the first sitting."

"And once Rosemary and Matt get here, you and James will be sitting up front, where all of us can watch how moony-eyed you get," Ruthie teased.

As the two girls hurried to set out more pie, Abby wondered about that. Were she and James really moony-eyed? Were they too affectionate in public? Or was her youngest niece playing things up?

A little while later, as Abby savored her plateful of chicken roast, creamed celery, mashed potatoes, green beans, and several kinds of salads, she shared an occasional glance with James while making sure to sit so they weren't touching. Neither of them had ever been seated on the eck as a member of a wedding party, and it seemed a lot like being on a stage.

"Feels kind of funny eating with an audience, ain't so?" he murmured.

"We can hope everyone's watching Rosemary and Matt—especially with little Katie sitting between them as though *she's* the reason for all this celebrating."

James glanced toward the center of the table and chuckled: Katie had sprung up with her fork in one hand and her spoon in the other, as though she was about to lead everyone in singing. "It *is* her celebration, when you think about it. It's not every day a girl gets a new dat, and another family to go with him," he said in a thoughtful tone. "That's a gift she'll appreciate more as she grows up, I'm thinking."

"It makes me grateful that Dat lived to see me grown

up . . . helped me build my house a couple years ago," Abby replied quietly. "I feel him with us in spirit today, sharing our happiness for Matt."

"I miss your father." James looked deeply into Abby's eyes. "While my dat and I are close, and he's ecstatic that I'm courting you, I looked up to Leroy Lambright as a fellow I wanted to be just like when I grew up."

Abby gripped her napkin, caught up in a poignant moment . . . and in this handsome man's undeniable admiration. "That's a fine tribute to him, James," she whispered. "Your dat has always been one of my favorite fellows, too. He seems especially dear now that his memory's not so gut."

James flashed her a grateful smile. "With Dat, every day's a new day because he's forgotten things he messed up—along with the sharp remarks Mamm probably made about it. Not a bad way to live, really. Forgiving comes easier when you've already forgotten what the problem was."

And wasn't that an interesting insight? "I think you just gave me the idea for a *Budget* column," Abby murmured. She glanced at the long, crowded table in front of them and forked up another bite of her potatoes. "My word, most folks are already eating their pie! I'll need to help clear the tables soon."

James, too, refocused on his dinner. "That's just one of the things I love about you, Abby," he said. "You put other people first, and you're glad to jump in and help. Especially since, as a member of the wedding party, you could sit up here all day."

"You could, too, James. But I don't see that happening."

"So you think you've got me all figured out." James set his pie on his empty dinner plate. "Guess I'll have to find different ways to do things—just to surprise you. Sharp cookie that you are, that might take some doing."

Abby's heart fluttered. Wasn't it good to know that such a wonderful man thought she was worth some extra effort?

* * *

That night after supper Amanda slipped into the barn to wait for Wyman's call. During harvest, when he had no time to drive all the way to Bloomingdale, they had agreed to keep in touch by phone. It gave her something to look forward to after each busy day of packing and preparing for the move . . . a few moments to just sit. The big old barn filled with peaceful shadows as the sun dipped below the horizon. The sound of animals chewing their hay—mostly Jerome's mules, and the donkeys and horses he kept for breeding them—soothed her.

As she inhaled the earthy scents of manure and hay, Amanda again felt grateful that she didn't have to have her wedding here. The celebration for Matt and Rosemary would still be going strong at Sam Lambright's place . . . *and I thank You, Lord, for surrounding me with family and friends to help me through so many changes—*

The phone on the wall trilled. "Jah, hullo?" she said.

"Amanda. It's gut to hear your voice after a busy day, my love."

She closed her eyes to savor Wyman's endearment, for most Amish fellows didn't wax romantic when they spoke to their women. As her intended's low voice seeped into her being, she relaxed on the old wooden bench. "We've been scurrying like squirrels, too, Wyman," she remarked. "The girls washed jars and chopped the vegetables while Jemima and I canned a big batch of chowchow, along with the last of the tomatoes for the season."

"Mmmm. We'll all enjoy those this winter," Wyman said. "Vera does her best with the garden, but keeping food on our table from one meal to the next occupies most of her time. We haven't had much homemade jam or chowchow lately."

"She's very capable for a girl of seventeen." Amanda rested against the barn wall, soaking up Wyman's pleasant conversation. "And how about you? Did you fellows unload a lot of wagons today?"

"Jah, and what with the drought, several of the locals have already cleared their fields. Some of them will have to live mighty tight this winter." He sighed, a sign that he was both weary and concerned. "It's not gut when Plain fathers with large families talk of taking on a job in town. Makes me thankful that the elevator is just across the road from home, and that English farmers bring their crops to us, too, so Ray and I can support our families. But enough about business."

Amanda could feel his gentle smile coming through the phone line as she anticipated more intimate conversation. Once their courting phase was over, private time together might be hit-and-miss, so she was enjoying every moment of it while she could. "And what else is on your mind tonight, dear man?"

"You."

Oh, but that single word made her feel alive. Ready to emerge from her cocoon of grief. "How so?" she asked, hoping for more of this enticing talk.

"I've been thinking how much easier it is, falling in love this time around," he replied. "When I was courting Viola, I was a bundle of nerves, wondering how I'd pull everything together. Ray Fisher and I had been friends all our lives, but we hadn't been in business long, so we were both worried about getting the elevator off to a profitable start as we took wives," he explained. "With you, Amanda, it's like wrapping myself in a cozy old sweater. We've both been through the newlywed jitters—and we've known our share of trials and tragedy, too. So we can just be who we already are for each other."

"And who you are, Wyman, makes me feel gut about who I am . . . who I can be from here on out, too," Amanda murmured. "But I'm hoping that when I wrap myself around you, it's not an old sweater you'll be thinking about."

Wyman's low laughter sent shivers up her spine. "I can't wait to be with you . . . in our room," he murmured. "I crave you like a ravenous man who's arrived at a feast. But food—and *jah,* old sweaters—will be the furthest things from my mind once we're man and wife."

Amanda hugged herself, barely able to contain her longing—her need for both emotional and physical affection. "Just a couple more weeks now, and we'll make it all come true."

"I wish I could drive over there tonight," he whispered. "Twenty years ago I wouldn't have given a second thought to being out at all hours to spend time with you."

"Twenty years ago we might not have liked each other," Amanda pointed out. "Our first marriages have molded us into different people."

"You've got a point there. And before I completely forget to tell you, I hope it'll be all right if the kids come over for the day on Saturday?"

Amanda's eyebrows shot up. She still had so many things to pack—

"It was Pete's idea that he and Eddie could help Jerome bale your hay, as a way to make up for tormenting Lizzie in the mercantile," Wyman went on. "Vera's hoping to help you pack boxes, or she'll watch the kids while you and Jemima work, or whatever you need her to do. I think she'd like to spend time with you and Lizzie, maybe to talk about how things will be when you folks move in with us."

"Ah. Well, that'll be fine—"

"And Simon's leaving his dog at home," Wyman added. "We're all very sorry about your pottery getting broken."

Although Wyman had paid her for her shattered pieces, he had no idea how it had pained her to see her pie plates and pitchers lying smashed in her wagon. "Well, I could have put my end gate up before I went in to speak with Sam," she murmured. "Could have padded my pieces with newspaper, or—"

"It was a lesson for all of us about being more careful," Wyman summarized. "But I wanted to be sure it was all right for my gang to show up, so you'd be prepared to feed them. Eddie and Pete can eat their weight in food."

"We'll plan for that," Amanda said. "Jerome will be glad for the help, too. Denki for thinking of us, Wyman."

"Anything for you, Amanda."

Oh, but she could make the most of *that* unexpected sentiment. But if she teased him she might not hear it again. *Anything for you, Amanda* . . .

"I'll be sure to thank Pete for thinking of us, as well," she said. "I suspect he's coming as much to be around Lizzie as to make up for his trick with the fishing pole. They're at an awkward age."

"Jah, and since they're not blood relations, we might have to watch how they take to each other as they get older," Wyman remarked. "But it'll all work out. All in God's gut grace."

After a few more moments of banter, they exchanged kisses and hung up. Amanda wished she could rest out here in the peaceful barn for a bit longer, running the more romantic moments of her courtship through her mind, but it wasn't fair to Jemima and Lizzie that she'd gotten out of some kitchen cleanup during these calls. And with the five Brubaker kids coming the day after tomorrow, there was no time to waste. Feeding that crew would require some advance preparation.

Get used to thinking bigger when it comes to meals, she reminded herself as she brought jars of pie filling up from the cellar. *It's a gut thing you'll have Jemima, Vera, and Lizzie to help every day.*

When her mother-in-law saw the quarts of apple, rhubarb, and cherry filling, however, she raised her eyebrows. "Having a pie frolic, are we?"

Amanda heard the weary edge in Jemima's voice and chose her words carefully. "Wyman just told me his kids want to come over on Saturday—"

"Now isn't that just like a man, thinking we want his wild bunch here when we've already got more work than we know what to do with?" Jemima removed the kapp from her silvery gray hair, looking every bit of her seventy-two years. "I'm headed for bed. Too tired and down in the back to think about all that cooking right now."

Amanda set the jars on the counter, not surprised at Jemima's grumbling. Atlee's dat had died nearly twenty years ago—before Amanda had married into the Lambright family—and Jemima's widowhood, along with her bad back and feet, often weighed her down like a dark, heavy cloak.

"Jah, get your rest and we'll figure it out tomorrow." Amanda put out the two lamps by the sink and stood in the dark kitchen for a moment, gathering herself. What would it be like when they cooked for eight kids and three adults as a matter of course? And how would it be to move into a kitchen that had belonged to Wyman's first wife . . . the mother of children who outnumbered hers?

You can figure that out tomorrow, too. Maybe.

Chapter 5

"Ach, here comes the Brubaker bunch, and us not even finished with the breakfast dishes," Lizzie said Saturday morning. "They must've started out in the dark."

"That means I'll get a full day's haying out of Eddie and Pete," Jerome replied. He rose from the table and grabbed his straw hat from its peg by the door. "What're your thoughts about Simon going with us, Amanda? It would be a gut thing for him to work with us fellows. He'll no doubt be underfoot if he stays here with you women."

"Is there any danger of him getting hurt?" Amanda asked. "Those kids lost their mamm to a baling machine, remember."

Jerome considered this as he watched the Brubaker kids out the window. "Comes a time when every boy needs to pull his weight. I was working with my dat at Simon's age, and so were Eddie and Pete," he pointed out. "It'll be their responsibility as big brothers to keep him on task—and I'll watch out for him, too."

"That settles it, then," Jemima said from her sink full of dishes. "That boy will only make more work if he's here leading the twins astray."

Cora and Dora giggled. They began stacking the dirty plates while Lizzie put the leftover sausage and hash browns in containers. "Oh, Mammi, *we* wouldn't let Simon get us in trouble," Dora said.

"Nope, we'd tell him what's what," Cora chimed in. "He's mostly just showing off—like most boys."

"Jah, boys are pretty stupid sometimes," her twin continued.

"That's enough of such talk," Amanda said sternly. "These are your new brothers and sisters, coming to help us today. They're showing us they love us, and we should do the same."

Jerome grabbed the handle of the picnic hamper Amanda had packed for them and opened the door. "See you for dinner. Thanks for these snacks."

Amanda stepped out onto the porch with him, waving at the kids who had hopped down from their wagon. "Gut to see you!" she called out. "Awfully nice of you to come help us today."

"And we menfolk have a full day ahead of us, too," Jerome spoke up. He pointed to a big ceramic water cooler on the top step. "Pete and Eddie, if you'll fill this at the pump over there, Simon and I can hitch up the mules."

Simon's eyes lit up. "I get to go with you guys?"

"Oh, you betcha." Jerome set the basket down to swing the boy up so they were eye to eye. "You're too old to be hanging around with the *girls*, ain't so? We've got a lot of jobs for you, Simon, so there can't be any squirreling around, got it? No fried pies or brownies for those who don't do as I tell them."

"Fried pies? Like, cherry ones?" the boy asked, looking toward Amanda for an answer.

Amanda shrugged, pleased to see that Jerome had taken this matter in hand. "You'll have to pull your share of the load and find out. No telling what might be in that basket for fellows who work real hard."

As Jerome led Simon to the barn, Vera came up the porch stairs holding Alice Ann's hand. She wore a kerchief over her dark brown hair, and she carried a large basket. "What a blessing that Jerome wants Simon to help with the haying," she said in a low voice. "He's been wound tighter than a top ever since he jumped out of bed an hour earlier than we intended."

"That comes with being five," Amanda replied. She held out her hands, but Alice Ann clung to her big sister's leg. "And we girls will be just fine working together, won't we, sweet pea? Cora and Dora have been waiting for you to get here today."

Alice Ann nodded shyly and looked toward the open kitchen door.

Vera set down her basket and let her little sister toddle inside. "I brought along some fresh bread and a bowl of snack mix the kids like, and another box, too. I'll be right back."

Whatever might Vera be so excited about? Amanda watched the teenager jog gracefully to the Brubaker wagon and lift a box from the back end. Lizzie stepped outside then, wiping her hands on a dish towel. As though Eddie and Pete had been awaiting her appearance, they waved from the pump, but Lizzie just rolled her eyes. When she saw Vera hefting the cardboard box, however, she loped out to help her carry it.

"Oooh! What've you got in here, Vera?" she asked. "This looks like Mamm's pottery."

"I hope she'll like what I've done with her bits and pieces," Vera said. "They were just too pretty to toss out."

When the girls set the box on the seat of the swing, Amanda peered inside. Vera carefully lifted something wrapped in an old towel, and when she revealed it, Amanda's eyes widened. Dangling from the bottom of a broken pitcher were strings of various lengths that held other pieces of pottery in reds, blues, and greens. "Wind chimes! What a clever idea."

"Listen to the tinkling sound they make!" Lizzie held the handle so that the breeze caught the shards of pottery.

Vera's cheeks turned pink. "I smoothed the rough edges and reinforced the pieces with a coat of shellac. Then I used some of Pete's fishing line to string them," she explained. "They won't withstand a heavy wind, but if they get hung someplace a little more sheltered—or inside, over a furnace vent—they should be all right."

As Amanda fingered a pitcher's spout, a handle, and some fluted pieces that had once been on a pie plate, something inside her swelled. What a blessing, that this young woman had salvaged the broken pieces of her work—like shattered dreams—and fashioned them into something new. "I would never have thought to do this, Vera. Denki so much for showing me."

"I made some necklaces and bracelets, too," Vera said as she lifted other pieces from her box. "Plain gals won't wear them, of course, but maybe the English folks who shop at the Cedar Creek Mercantile will buy them."

"Wow, these are so *cool*!" Lizzie lifted two more necklaces from the box, gazing raptly at them as they shimmered in the sunlight.

"I'm thinking Abby would display these for you, too," Amanda said as she admired the necklace Vera had slipped over her head. The pieces alternated in color and size, with flat shards separated by tubular chunks that had come from handles or spouts. "You have a fine eye for arranging the shapes and colors, Vera. And you've spent a lot of time smoothing them off and drilling those holes to run the line through, too. That was delicate work."

Vera shrugged modestly. "I didn't think about it much. Your bright colors just inspired my hands to put the pieces together," she said. "After I made the first necklace, the others went fast. Do you really think Sam would carry them in his store?"

"I would certainly take them in," Amanda insisted. "Treva might sell your wind chimes in her greenhouse, too. She carries a lot of gift items to go along with her pumpkins and plants."

"I decorated this pot, too, hoping Treva might want more." From the bottom of her box, Vera lifted a ten-inch terra-cotta flowerpot. She had glued pottery pieces all over the outside of it, similar to a mosaic design but more dimensional.

"Wouldn't that look nice with a mum in it? Or a geranium, in the summer," Jemima said as she came out to see what was going on. "It's even prettier because you used cast-off pieces to make something new and useful . . . just like the Lord takes us all as broken vessels and fits us for His service here on earth."

Amanda blinked. Seldom did her mother-in-law make such touching remarks, and Jemima's attitude boded well for what they might accomplish today. "Amen to that," she murmured. "What a gift you've given us, letting us see your pieces, Vera. The fellows are leaving for the hayfields, so let's start dinner and decide what we'll work on today."

As the Brubaker girls joined them in the kitchen, Cora and Dora took Alice Ann into the front room to play. Even though Vera was four years older than Lizzie, the two teenagers were chatting excitedly about the wind chimes and necklaces as they went to the cellar for jars of chowchow and tomatoes. After they had peeled potatoes, carrots, and onions to put in the roasting pan with two large meat loaves, Jemima took the three little girls to help her pick the last of the vegetables in the garden.

Amanda was glad she had told her mother-in-law she wanted to pack her ceramics today, because Vera's eyes widened when they entered the room where she worked on them. "Back in the day, this was the dawdi haus for Atlee's grandparents," Amanda explained. Wyman's daughter was gazing raptly at the kick wheel, situated near the two windows, and the cylindrical gas kiln in the far corner. "This was the sitting room, and there's a bathroom—where I can run water for preparing my clay and cleaning up. Since we had plenty of bedrooms if more kids came along, Atlee let me set up in here rather than in the basement, where the light's not so gut."

"And when Dat got really sick at the end," Lizzie added, "he stayed in this bedroom, so Mamm could keep an eye on him while she worked. That was before Cora and Dora were born."

Sad compassion clouded Vera's face, but as she ran her fingers around the unglazed pie plates and bowl sets on the shelves, she brightened again. "It's so neat that you start with clay and shape each piece on your wheel," she murmured. "It means that no two pieces are exactly alike."

Amanda brought a stack of old newspapers to the worktable and they began to wrap the dishes. "It's as you said when you made those wind chimes and necklaces," she replied. "If I don't think too much about what I'm doing, my hands just *take over*. I make so many of each item—and I glaze them with my favorite colors and designs—that I don't have to concentrate very hard. I've not thought about it, but jah, I suppose each piece is unique."

Just as God has created each of us with different abilities . . . and different needs, Amanda thought as she watched her helpers. Vera was taller than her Lizzie, with darker hair and a quieter way about her, yet the two girls had taken to each other as if they had been close friends all their lives.

Vera carefully tucked the ends of newspaper around a teapot. "Do you suppose someday you could teach me to make pottery, Amanda? I do okay at cooking and sewing, but I've never taken to quilting like other girls . . ."

"I'm with you there," Lizzie remarked. "Mammi Jemima's tried to work with me, but my stitches are too big and uneven to suit her. I'd rather bake or crochet."

Amanda's pulse quickened. As Vera declared her love of creating, she evoked Amanda's own deep need to continue crafting her colorful dishes, even if the Clearwater elders declared them *art* and therefore unacceptable as a Plain pursuit. She felt a fierce desire to share her skills with this young woman, sensing that Vera was a kindred spirit in ways her Lizzie would never be.

But this could lead us both down the path to perdition . . .

Yet Amanda didn't have the heart to squelch Vera's curiosity, or the important bond they might share as they became part of a new, blended family.

"So you'd rather work with clay than fabric? I started out by helping my mamm's uncle Mahlon in his pottery shop when I was a wee girl for that very reason." Amanda thought about the rest of her answer as she wrapped her paintbrushes and added them to the box they were packing. "I'll warn you, though, that in a lot of districts, this would be considered too worldly. My great-uncle made dishes, using muted blues and browns—but only when he got too old and lame to farm did their bishop allow him to earn his living that way."

Vera reached for another sturdy cardboard box and began to wrap plastic bottles of colored glazes. "Our bishop, Uriah Schmucker, is really old-fashioned. He *still* doesn't like it that Dat partnered with a Mennonite before he joined the church, and that the elevator is on the Fishers' land," she remarked. "He says having electricity and their computer makes the business too English, even though it gives our Plain farmers a place to sell their corn."

Amanda listened as she packed. Wyman had once told her that to compensate for his worldlier way of doing business, he often made extra donations to his district's relief fund—just because he felt it was the right thing to do.

"I probably should've asked the bishop about making those necklaces." Vera sighed ruefully as she met Amanda's gaze. "But I got so excited about using your broken pieces that I didn't think about it."

Amanda had met Clearwater's bishop when Wyman had announced his intention to marry her. She, too, sensed that Uriah would frown on her bright colors, even if the pieces she made were useful. "I've been praying on that very subject," she said. "Lamar Lapp, our bishop in Bloomingdale, allowed me to sell my pottery when Atlee got too sick to work, and he understood that colorful pieces sold better. I'll be awfully busy getting adjusted to our new family anyway, so it might be a while before I can work at my wheel again."

"Oh, but I hope you won't give it up." Vera cleared her throat, as though considering whether to mention something. "My mamm enjoyed drawing and painting, you see. Made the prettiest note cards . . . but when one of the preachers heard Eddie saying she'd painted some canvases of wildlife and flowers, the bishop came for a visit."

Amanda's heart sagged. She could guess what had happened next.

"He made Mamm throw away her paints. And he got after Dat for allowing her to have such a sinful pastime," Vera went on. "Mamm obeyed, of course, and she never spoke of her painting again. But it was like a piece of her heart went missing after that."

Amanda sighed. "Denki for telling me that, Vera. We'll keep this matter in our prayers as well, all right?"

Had Uriah's attitude toward Wyman's first wife's painting prompted him to insist she wouldn't need the money from her pottery? It wasn't a subject Amanda wanted to get into with Vera, because it was such a pleasure to discover the girl's interest in colors and clay. But maybe, since Wyman seemed drawn to artistic women, he would understand her need to create . . . an inner longing to interpret her life using the vibrant palette with which God had made the world. Even if she didn't sell her pottery, it satisfied her soul to make it. *Maybe I can tuck my wheel and kiln into a corner of the basement at the Brubaker place . . .*

She and the girls worked for several minutes in silence, and it wasn't long before they were taping their packed boxes shut. "We've done a gut morning's work here," Amanda said. "Let's see how Jemima and the girls are doing. It'll soon be time for our fellows to show up for dinner."

"Jah, that meat loaf smells *so* gut. Nice to be eating something I didn't have to cook myself." Vera entered the kitchen and immediately went toward the voices coming through the screen door. "And what's going on out here? We haven't heard a peep out of you girls."

"We've been busy bees!" one of the twins piped up. "Look at all the tomatoes and green beans we brought in. And cabbages!"

"And Mammi says it's time to dig the carrots and taters, too," her sister said.

As she followed Vera out to the porch, Amanda relaxed. Wasn't it a good sign that Vera and Alice Ann got along so well with her three girls? Buckets of ripe tomatoes sat on the porch table alongside a wheelbarrow of fat green cabbage heads and at least a bushel of green beans. She and Jemima had a lot of canning ahead of them . . . their last harvest from this garden on Atlee's farm. It was a bittersweet thought, even though Jerome and their expanded family would be eating these vegetables all through the winter.

As Amanda sliced bread for their dinner, she looked out the window. It was satisfying to see Eddie and Pete washing up at the pump, with Simon following their example. The twins were setting the last of the plates on the table when Jerome came in, tossing his hat onto its wall peg. "And how'd it go this morning?" she asked.

Her nephew's easy grin lit up his swarthy face. "Gut help, those Brubaker boys. Made a lot of progress, even if

Simon had to chase a few grasshoppers," he added. "The hay's dry enough that after dinner we're going to bale it and get it into the barn."

Simon burst through the kitchen door. "Jerome says I worked so gut that I get to *drive* when we start balin'! Let's eat *now*, so we can get back out there!"

Amanda's eyebrows shot up. "That's quite an important job, being the driver," she remarked as she looked to the older boys.

Jerome winked at her. "Jah, the fellow holding the reins— and his assistant—have to *stay put* to keep the mules on track."

Eddie and Pete hung their straw hats beside Jerome's and glanced eagerly toward the table. "The snack hamper you packed us was mighty fine," the older boy said.

"But I'm sure ready for whatever smells so gut for dinner," Pete added with a grin, smoothing hair that was still damp from being splashed at the pump.

"Take a seat and we'll get everything on the table," Amanda said. As Vera poured cold water and lemonade, Jemima was taking the blue enamel roaster from the oven. With Lizzie spooning up the hot vegetables and the twins carefully carrying the bowls to the table, they were seated within a few minutes.

As they bowed silently for prayer, Amanda thanked God for how smoothly this group effort was going. When Jerome picked up the platter of steaming meat loaf, they began to pass the carrots and potatoes along with a bowl of slaw, a crock of baked beans, and a gelatin salad loaded with fruit.

Eddie gazed at his heaped plate and smiled at Jemima. "Awfully nice of you to make us such a fine meal."

"Jah," Pete chimed in. "And those fried pies in our basket hit the spot, too."

"I ate three whole ones all by myself!" Simon gushed. Then he stuck a large chunk of carrot into his mouth, letting part of it stick out as he chewed—mostly to entertain the twins.

"Well, now," Jemima murmured. "I reckon it's the least I can do, cooking so you boys can work out in our hayfields all day. We're blessed to have your help, and happy to have your sisters here, too."

And isn't that a fine surprise, coming from Jemima? Amanda gazed around the table, which hadn't had this many folks gathered at it in a long while. The two teenage boys took seconds as they chatted with Jerome about which field to bale first, while Lizzie and Vera talked quietly like two longtime friends sharing secrets. As she cut up Alice Ann's potato, Amanda thought that maybe—by the grace of God—the Brubakers and the Lambrights could blend into one big happy family after all.

"So how is it that this little angel's not yet talking?" Jemima asked. "She follows every word we say." She buttered a slice of warm bread and laid it on Alice Ann's plate.

The Brubaker kids got quiet. Amanda realized that while Wyman had told her about his wife's tragic death, Jemima had heard only the sketchiest details.

Eddie took a deep breath. "When we were out haying a couple of years ago, it started to rain," he recounted somberly. "Pete and Dat and I were across the field raking up some rows so the baler would pick up the cut hay. Mamm was helping us so we could get it in the barn before it got too wet . . ."

Pete cleared his throat as though the memory still felt raw. "Mamm was holding Alice Ann when thunder made the mules bolt. She grabbed at their reins and then she . . . she slipped in the wet grass. Tossed the baby aside as she fell underneath the baler."

Vera nodded gravely. "The doctor believes Alice Ann got such a shock, seeing our mamm get crushed, that she went mute. She wasn't but a year old, not yet forming words, you see."

Jemima's face fell. "Oh, my, I . . . I didn't mean to upset you all over again about how your mother died. Please forgive me if I've been impatient and cantankerous with you. I—I had no idea."

Amanda reached around the high chair to squeeze her mother-in-law's shoulder. "We've all had losses in our lives," she said quietly. "The way I see it, we can help one another bear those burdens and come out the better for it. Are you kids with me on this?"

All eyes focused on her for a solemn moment, and then everyone nodded. Amanda felt as though they'd taken a vow together: their earnest expressions gave her hope that they could carry this moment of understanding forward, through whatever trials their new life presented.

"Gut," she murmured. "Your dat will be pleased. Meanwhile, we've got much to be grateful for—and happy about! Like those pies and brownies on the counter, ain't so?"

The boys' wide smiles made Amanda laugh. Raising three sons would be a challenge—much different from dealing with her girls—yet she had the sense that she'd found her new purpose in life. The place God had prepared for her.

Chapter 6

That evening as Wyman closed the door to the office in the grain elevator, he heaved a tired sigh. He and Ray had taken in truckload after truckload of corn, recording the number of bushels of each farmer's harvest to date. Meanwhile, Ray's son Tyler kept everyone abreast of current prices on the grain exchange with his computer. The summer's drought meant yields weren't as high all over the country, but the short supply also increased the per-bushel price. With the livelihoods of his neighbors on the line, Wyman was keenly aware of how the community of Clearwater depended on him and Ray Fisher.

Why on earth had he decided to get married during the busiest month of the year? There was a good reason many Old Order couples waited until November to wed . . . *But how much longer can you wait for order to be restored in your home, your life? Admit it: you're more desperate for Amanda than she is for you.*

It was a startling thought. And he certainly couldn't express such an idea to anyone—especially not to Amanda— if he wanted to remain the head of his expanding household. It was his responsibility to provide for the five additional people he'd have under his roof, while his new wife relieved him of overseeing the day-to-day business of living. Such a division of duties had kept Plain communities stable for centuries, so there was nothing to gain by deviating from that plan.

As Wyman crossed the county blacktop to stride down Brubaker Lane, the door of his sprawling white house flew open. Simon raced toward the road as fast as his five-year-old legs could carry him.

"Dat! Dat, I got to *drive* today! Four mules!" his son cried. Wags ran circles around Simon until they were close enough that the tousle-mopped boy launched himself.

Wyman caught him, laughing. Simon's joy made him forget all about droughts and family dynamics. "And how did that happen?" he asked as he swung the youngster into the air.

"Me and Jerome, we hitched the mules to a cart and hooked the baler to it—and then a big flatbed wagon behind that," Simon said. "Jerome put the first bale down so's I could stand on it! And then he stood right behind me, showin' me how to hold the reins and get the mules to go where they was s'posed to!"

What a fine young man Amanda's nephew is, Wyman thought as he held his son to his shoulder. He hadn't spent much time with Jerome Lambright, but any fellow who had kept Simon focused, learning a vital skill, deserved respect. "So that means Eddie and Pete were on the back wagon, stacking the bales as they shot out of the baler?"

"Jah. And we had a treat basket!" Simon exclaimed. "I ate five fried pies and four big brownies today!"

Wyman laughed, dodging the circling dog as they reached the house. "How did you have room for dinner, after so many goodies?"

Simon's eyes resembled dark brown buttons. "Dat, we were workin' *hard*," he insisted. "Pete and Eddie ate way more than me. And we had meat loaf, and taters with carrots, and Jell-O with lotsa fruit—"

"All your favorite things," Wyman remarked as he set Simon down on the porch. "Sounds like you all had a fine day at Amanda's."

He let Simon enter the house ahead of him. Filling the dog's water pan gave Wyman a moment to wish *he* had been working in Amanda's fields with his boys and eating such a robust meal . . . The sandwiches and potato salad Vera had packed in his cooler had abandoned his stomach hours ago. After harvest, however, he would again walk home for dinner each day instead of eating his noon meal at his untidy desk between truckloads of grain. And in just a short time, when he married Amanda, his life would be complete again.

As Wyman stepped into the kitchen, he eyed the table. The platter of cold sliced ham and the bowl of the same potato salad he'd had for lunch made him nip his lip. He didn't expect seventeen-year-old Vera to put on a spread that compared to Amanda's when she had been away from home all day, but he was ravenous for a hot, filling meal. As though his daughter could read his thoughts, she smiled apologetically.

"Supper's almost ready, Dat," she said, scrambling to place the silverware around their six plates. "We stayed at Amanda's long enough for the boys to stack the bales in the barn. We got a lot done—Alice Ann even helped the twins and Jemima pick the last of their vegetables. Amanda sent us home with a rhubarb custard pie and a plate of wonderful-gut brownies, too."

The sight of the pie on the sideboard made his stomach growl. "And what were you helping with, Vera? It sounds as though going over there was one of Pete's better ideas."

"Lizzie and I helped Amanda pack her pottery. And you

know those broken pieces I was playing with?" she asked eagerly. "Amanda thinks Treva Lambright might carry my wind chimes and flowerpots in her greenhouse shop—"

"Don't count your chickens before they're hatched," Wyman warned. "I can't think the bishop will go along with that idea. You'd be better off going to more Singings with the young people, finding a fellow to pair up with. You'll have more time for that once Amanda's here, after all."

When Vera's face fell, Wyman regretted being so blunt with her. She had taken on the huge responsibility of minding her younger siblings while keeping up with the cooking, laundry, and gardening, and he couldn't have managed without her these past two years. But there was no sense in allowing daydreams about colorful dishes to distract her from finding a mate. Fulfilling her purpose.

"Do you understand where I'm coming from?" he asked as he took his seat at the head of the table.

"Jah, Dat."

"I see no reason to get your hopes up, after your mother was told to throw away her paints." While Wyman believed he'd given his daughter the correct advice, being right didn't keep Vera from turning toward the sink so he wouldn't see the tears streaming down her face.

The screen door banged. Eddie and Pete's banter about the day's activities filled the kitchen, and soon his children were in their places, bowing in prayer before their evening meal.

Wyman took two large slices of ham and passed the platter to his boys. He glanced at Alice Ann, who sat between him and Vera in her high chair. She was kicking her legs in anticipation of the bread her sister buttered for her. "So you worked in the garden with Dora and Cora today?" he asked in a light voice.

Alice Ann nodded happily. She looked so ready to talk about her busy day, but no words came out.

Wyman gazed at the young faces around his table. "I'm

pleased that you could be so helpful at Amanda's," he said. "We've talked about how . . . challenging it might be to have Jemima here—"

"She makes the best meat loaf and fried pies!" Simon declared. "Can we go there to work *every* day?"

The older boys were nodding as they wolfed down their cold ham and potato salad. It seemed that spending time with Amanda's crotchety mother-in-law had given his kids a new perspective on her—another plus. "In just about two weeks, Jemima, Amanda, and your three new sisters will be living with us," he reminded Simon. "It would be a fine thing if you spoke so kindly about them once they're here, because we'll all have some adjusting to do."

When Vera cut the rhubarb custard pie and brought it to the table, Wyman placed a creamy pink wedge of it on his dessert plate along with a dense, dark brownie. "I'll be back in a while."

"Going out to sweet-talk his girlfriend," Pete mumbled to Eddie as he took a slice of pie.

Wyman turned before he got to the door, raising an eyebrow at his middle son. "After the way you've tormented Lizzie, you could probably take notes from your dat about how to treat a girl right. I don't want to hear any more disrespectful talk about Amanda or my feelings for her. Understand?"

Pete looked down at his plate. "Jah, Dat. Sorry."

Wyman strode outside and down the lane, crossed the road to the elevator office, and punched in Amanda's phone number. As it rang, he settled into his desk chair and took the first big bite of his pie.

"Jah, hullo?" Amanda asked softly.

"Mmmm," he replied, savoring the tartness of the rhubarb and the sweet, creamy custard.

"Wyman? It's you, jah?"

He laughed. "You were expecting another fellow to call?"

"Well, *no*, but—"

"I'm teasing you, my love. I've escaped from the supper table with a slice of the pie you sent," he said as he forked up another bite. "It's the only piece I'll see, so I intend to enjoy every morsel of it."

"Ah." Her low chuckle sent little tremors throughout his body. "Jah, your boys can tuck away the food, but it was gut having them here. They finished the haying—got it all put up in the barn, too. It would've taken Jerome a couple or three days if he'd worked by himself."

"Glad to hear they made themselves useful. I need to encourage Eddie toward an apprenticeship of some sort, as he's not inclined to work here at the elevator." Wyman eased the pie into his mouth, closing his eyes to better appreciate its blend of flavors. "But enough about my boys. What did *you* accomplish today?"

"Oh, Vera, Lizzie, and I packed up my pottery—"

Rather than ruin Amanda's mood with another warning about Uriah Schmucker's intolerance of art, Wyman enjoyed the sound of her voice as he ate his dessert.

"—and Jemima's changed her tune about living with your three boys, too. They won her over with their gut manners and the way they devoured her cooking."

"See there? It's all working out, this blended family thing." Truth be told, he wasn't looking forward to having Atlee's mother live with them, for she had a sour disposition and a sharp tongue. But Jemima was part of the package . . . and maybe she would decide to stay on at the Lambright farm to keep house for Jerome. Or she might move back there after a week or two of living with eight kids. "Packing aside, are you . . . ready to become my bride?"

When Amanda exhaled, he pictured her with her head tilted back and her eyes closed. He wanted to kiss the soft column of her neck . . .

"I am," she stated. "Whenever I feel overwhelmed by

what's still left to do, I remind myself that this packing and upheaval shall pass. I love you so much, Wyman."

He gripped his plate to keep from dropping it. "When you say that, it does funny things to my insides, Amanda."

"Hmm. Gut funny or . . . odd funny?"

"You make me feel like a man again."

She sucked in her breath, as caught up in these intimate whispers as he was. Wasn't it wonderful that they both craved the sexual side of marriage? Many of his friends hinted that their wives merely gave in to their needs rather than respond with any sign of passion.

"And I'm looking forward to being your woman, Wyman, instead of being a single parent."

"I understand *that* feeling. The Lord knew what He was doing when he created men and women to be together." He rubbed the tines of his fork across the plate to capture the last crumbs of his pie. "I should let you go. Something tells me Simon will be too excited about driving those mules to settle down before bed."

Wyman hung up, feeling immensely satisfied. It was peaceful, sitting in the shadows of the office as the sun went down. As he thought ahead to his wedding day, he prayed that this serenity would carry him through the difficulties of combining two broods under one roof.

But mostly, Wyman gave thanks for rhubarb pie and for the woman who had baked it.

Chapter 7

When the greenhouse door opened, Abby glanced up from placing Mason jars filled with celery—the traditional wedding centerpiece—in the middle of a table set for the day's noontime feast. "Emma! Gut of you to come over so early," she said. "Even though this is our third wedding in the past three weeks, Barbara and Mamm and I still can't manage it all ourselves."

Emma picked up another tray loaded with centerpieces and began to set them out. "Jah, but you did it up right for Matt and Phoebe. Amanda's lucky that you offered to help with her big day."

Abby glanced around to be sure they were alone in the glass-walled greenhouse. It was seven in the morning, so folks would soon start arriving for the wedding. "Wyman gave Sam a check that more than covered the dinner and desserts Beulah Mae and Lois have cooked up, plus a donation to our district's emergency fund," she said in a low voice. "He seems so happy that Sam'll be preaching, too."

Emma cleared her throat purposefully. "Speaking of *happy*—did you know Amanda asked me to be her newehocker?"

"Jah? Who's the lucky fellow she's paired you with?"

The way Emma rolled her brown eyes warned Abby that her best friend was in no mood to be teased. "Jerome Lambright, of all people. I've only seen him a couple of times, but—"

"If you ask me, Jerome's a fine-looking fellow."

"Abby! You sound just like Mamm, trying to match me up with him." Emma set a celery centerpiece on the table with a *thunk* that might well have broken the jar. "When we were at Mrs. Nissley's Kitchen cooking the chickens for today's roast, the women went on and on about what a fine catch Jerome would be—"

"Sam says he's doing very well at training and selling the mules he breeds," Abby remarked. "And what with him taking over the farm after Amanda moves into Wyman's—"

"You obviously haven't heard about how he's asked two girls to marry him, and then backed out both times!" Emma blurted. "Jah, he's got the looks and now the farm, but why do I want to get mixed up with a—a bounder like that? Why, he's twenty-four and not even joined the church yet!"

Abby returned to the sink area, where she'd been filling the jars with water and celery. As much as she loved Emma, she wondered if her friend's habit of jumping to negative conclusions might be standing in the way of her happiness about *anything*.

But this was no time to discuss it. Through the glass-paned wall, she saw buggies pulling in, and Amanda Lambright was stepping down from one of them. "Here comes our bride," Abby announced. "Try to tolerate Jerome for today, just because Amanda asked you to stand up with her."

"Jah, but only because she has no sisters or—"

Abby gave her friend a bewildered look. Was it her

imagination or was Emma sounding more like her fussy mother these days?

"You're right," Emma murmured. "I'm making a mountain out of a molehill. It's just for a few hours. I don't have to pretend I'm interested in him."

Here came Lois Yutzy with a pull cart full of bread, and her husband, Ezra, followed her with a similar cartload of pies. As other folks carried in food and serving utensils, Abby rushed to hold the door for James, who was carefully balancing the two-tiered wedding cake Lois had baked in her shop.

"Gut thing you've got strong, steady hands," she said as he brushed past her. Dressed in his crisp black trousers and vest, with a fresh white shirt, he looked so handsome . . . and so much like a groom it made her thoughts wander.

James gave her a lingering look. "These hands are gut for handling things besides cake, too, Abby-girl," he murmured. "But we'll save that thought for later."

Oh, but he was in a romantic mood! Abby had to admit that hosting three weddings had put her in a state of anticipation, too, and yet . . . it concerned her that James seemed eager to show his affection in front of everyone. While she had nothing to be ashamed of, courting this fine man, she felt more comfortable about kissing and such when they were alone.

But first they had to get Wyman and Amanda hitched. Abby had a long day ahead of her and not a moment to stand idle until the dishes were washed after this evening's supper.

Neighbor ladies bustled around the big, airy greenhouse to unload the baked goods for Lois. When Abby turned to watch James arrange the wedding cake on the eck just so, someone tapped her on the shoulder.

"Now there's a fellow who looks ready to sit up front with his own cake and his own pretty bride."

Abby turned and threw her arm around Rosemary's

shoulders. "We thought you and Matt were going to Queen City to visit and collect your gifts."

Rosemary watched her Katie toddle behind Matt as he went up to help James. "Mamm and my sister caught a stomach bug, so we'll go when they're well. And besides," she added, gesturing toward another high-sided wagon loaded with pies, "this is my chance to repay you folks for the feast you prepared for *our* wedding."

"It was our pleasure to help out," Abby insisted. "Especially with your Mamm and family living a couple hours away."

"And here you are hosting Amanda and Wyman's wedding, too," Rosemary continued as they set her pies on the cutting table. "Honestly, Abby, you and Barbara and Treva make the rest of us look like slackers! Besides, this gave me a gut trial run with my new oven before I start up my baking business."

"You and your oven did a fine job, too. These apple pies with the streusel topping smell *so* gut." As Abby inhaled their sweet cinnamon scent, she watched her nephew talking with James as they set up the chairs at the eck. "Matt looks mighty happy these days, too . . . even if his new beard isn't quite filled in yet."

Rosemary blushed. "He says if I'd quit tugging on it, and teasing him about it, the hair would grow in faster. Katie loves to rumple it when she sits in his lap of an evening."

Oh, but that was a picture . . . big, burly Matt with a blond toddler in his lap, chattering at him as she ran her curious fingers over his face. Abby hoped she would see such a sight in her own home, lit by the glow of oil lamps, when she and James were winding down after a busy day.

When James scooped Katie into his arms, the little girl's giggles echoed in the high-ceilinged greenhouse. Abby held her breath, savoring the sight of the man she loved holding a wee one . . . much like Jesus had paid special attention to children. Her heart throbbed with an urgent longing. If her courtship with James would just move a little faster, she might be holding their firstborn next year at this time . . .

"Now, Merle—*Merle!*" Eunice Graber's voice rang out. "No need for you to be in here pestering these gals. We should be getting to the house before the service starts!"

Abby turned to see James and Emma's dat coming toward her with a sweet smile on his face. Behind him, their mother Eunice's thick heels thunked on the floor, and her eyes were wide behind her pointy-cornered glasses.

"Fiddlesticks!" Merle muttered. "I've come to get a hug from Abby. It'll get my day off to a better start."

How could she not adore a fellow who felt that way about her? Abby met Merle with open arms. Bless him, he was getting shorter, but he still had a lot of strength in his embrace—and he needed to know he was a fine person despite how his wife groused at him.

"Merle, gut morning to you," she murmured. "Are you ready for yet another wedding?"

"I'm ready for *your* wedding, Abby," he replied as he hugged her. "I keep telling that boy of mine that time's a-wasting, but he's slow to catch on."

As Eunice caught up to them, Emma came their way, as well. "James will figure it out in his own gut time," Abby replied, hoping her confidence would make the statement come true. "But for today, we've all got our jobs to do—"

"And your job, Merle, is to stop making a spectacle of yourself!" Eunice slipped her arm through her husband's, as though he needed her guidance. "If you're wanting our James to propose to Abby, *you* can't be hanging all over her, ain't so?"

Oh, but Eunice's reedy voice filled the room, to the point that other folks got quiet and turned to gawk. Abby's face prickled as she eased away from poor Merle. She didn't dare look toward James, for he had surely heard his mother's outburst. Emma, too, seemed embarrassed as she came over to assist her elderly parents.

"Mamm, Dat," she said in a tight voice. "I'm thinking plenty of folks we know from Clearwater and Bloomingdale are here. Shall we head to the house to visit?"

"Jah, Dat, let's mosey over to where the menfolk are gathered," James suggested as he stepped in to assist his sister. "I just saw Wyman's brother Otto drive in, and he's always gut for a story and a laugh, ain't so?"

Merle turned to go with his son, but then he wiggled his fingers at Abby. "See you later, alligator."

"After a while, crocodile," she replied as the four Grabers headed for the door. When she returned to the table, Rosemary was taking the last pie from her wagon.

"Where did that come from, the part about the alligator and the crocodile?" she asked. "I thought Merle was getting confused again, except you answered him right off."

Abby chuckled. "Merle used to love eating in a diner close to the auction barn. He took James and Emma and me to a horse sale once, and when that song was playing on the diner's jukebox, we all got a big kick out of it," she explained. "He probably can't tell you what he ate for breakfast this morning, but he still recalls stuff from years ago."

"Merle's come over several times, asking Matt if he needs any help with the sheep," Rosemary replied. "He's such a sweet old fellow."

"Jah, there's nobody nicer than Merle." Abby smiled as she made sure all the tables were properly set. *And James couldn't have missed the way his parents want him to pop the question, either*, she mused.

Filled with a serene happiness, Amanda stood before more than two hundred guests, confidently repeating her vows after Bishop Vernon Gingerich. Standing beside Wyman as he gazed into her eyes, she felt cherished . . . adored by this man whose breathing matched hers as they promised themselves to each other for the rest of their lives.

"Are you confident, Sister, that the Lord has provided this our brother as a marriage partner for you?" Vernon intoned.

"Jah," she replied.

A brief memory of her first wedding flitted through her mind. She had been so nervous the day she married Atlee—sick to her stomach to the point that some of the women had speculated she was already in the family way. But that was a lifetime ago. Surely this surge of strength and assurance was a sign from above that her union with Wyman Brubaker would be a blessing beyond her wildest dreams. He was so handsome, with his dark hair and deeply tanned skin . . . so intent on following her every word, with utter love written all over his face as the ceremony continued.

"Do you both promise together that you will with love, forbearance, and patience live with each other, and not part from each other until God will separate you in death?"

For a moment Amanda got so lost in Wyman's gaze that she forgot to respond—but it was all right because Wyman, too, seemed speechless. "Jah," they whispered in unison.

"Mamma! Hi, Mamma!" a familiar little voice cried out.

Vernon's blue eyes twinkled, and low laughter surrounded the wedding party. Lizzie, near the back of the women's side, hastily grabbed Cora to make her sit down.

"Such a blessing it is to be surrounded by your children as you and Wyman become man and wife," the bishop said, beaming at the congregation. "And as we come to the final part of these sacred vows, I wish to offer up a prayer that this newly formed family will soon be woven together seamlessly," he intoned. "Not like the delicate organdy of Amanda's kapp but like the Triblend denim she will sew into pants for Wyman and his sons . . . sturdy enough to survive years of wear and tear without fading or splitting or unraveling when it's stretched to the limit. Shall we bow for a moment?"

Amanda's soul stilled during the silent prayer. The best blessing this morning was having this eloquent leader of Cedar Creek performing their ceremony rather than Uriah Schmucker. The crusty old Clearwater bishop had preached during an earlier church service about absolute obedience to God and the *Ordnung*, forsaking all individual needs for the higher good of their collective faith. While it was proper Old Order doctrine, his message had sounded harsh and inflexible. Intolerant and unforgiving.

But we'll work it out with Your help, Lord, she prayed as Vernon's "amen" ended the silence.

Moments later the Cedar Creek bishop pronounced them man and wife. When the roomful of guests rose from the benches to congratulate them, the noise level grew deafening, so Wyman led her outside to accept everyone's best wishes. They had barely crossed the threshold before he grabbed her up for a long, exhilarating kiss.

"I thought church would never end," he murmured. "This day will live forever in my heart, Amanda. I'm so happy that you're finally mine."

Their friends and family members spilled out into the large yard, soaking up the warm October sunshine. Children raced around the trees, glad to be making noise and moving after the double church service. As Wyman introduced many friends and family from out of town, Amanda got lost in the blur of faces and names. Out of habit she glanced around to check on her kids. Lizzie and Vera had their little sisters with them as they clustered with other teenage girls, while the boys gathered near the white plank fence to look out over Matt Lambright's flock of sheep. Two Border collies were allowing Simon to pat their black-and-white heads . . .

"All ready for the big move?" Eunice Graber adjusted her thick glasses, peering up at Amanda as she stood beside

Emma. "How's your nephew going to fare in Bloomingdale all by himself?"

Amanda detected Emma's impatience with her mother's question, but it deserved an answer. "We're leaving Jerome with plenty of food and furniture and whatnot," she replied loudly, sensing Eunice didn't hear very well. "He's a busy fellow these days. He'll have his mules—"

"And once I finish training this team I'm working with now," Jerome cut in as he joined them, "I can spend the winter finding somebody to court. Emma, shall we make our way to the greenhouse? I can smell the roast, and I'm ready to eat!"

"Jah, you young folks go along now," Eunice insisted, shooing them with her hands. "And you newlyweds, too! They won't serve the rest of us until you're at the eck with your plates loaded!"

Amanda shared a smile with Wyman. He wasn't used to being told where to go, or having an older woman give him instructions . . . but he'd be putting up with that when Jemima joined them, too, wouldn't he? They made their way across the green lawn, now strewn with colorful autumn leaves.

As they stepped inside the greenhouse, the helpers' applause and congratulations rang around the high glass walls. "Oh, but this room looks like something from a storybook," Amanda murmured as Wyman pulled out her chair. "Such a pretty cake . . . and Treva's potted mums . . . and all these folks seeing to the food . . ."

"The Lambrights have done us a huge favor," Wyman agreed. "All of these Cedar Creek folks have gotten us off to a gut start, and I believe it's a sign of our life to come."

Once again Amanda met her new husband's gaze, praying he was right. Her fondest wish was that this affection between them would blossom into the kind of marriage that—

"Hah, hah! Can't catch *me*!" a familiar voice rang out.

Amanda looked across the room to see Simon ducking behind one of the long set tables, hidden by its white tablecloth. Cora, Dora, and Rosemary's Katie entered the greenhouse in his wake, giggling. As Wyman rose to reprimand his son, Amanda cringed in anticipation: the boy had grabbed the tablecloth's corner, and when he took off r nning again, he didn't think to let go of it. Simon had darted about ten feet down the narrow aisle between tables before the loud crash of china and the horrified cries of the servers made him realize what he'd done.

"*Simon!* Stop!" Wyman ordered as he hurried from the eck.

The boy froze, but the damage was done. Water glasses and celery centerpieces lay shattered on the concrete floor, while plates of pie were cascading down the side of the tablecloth. Amid the clatter of falling silverware and the toppling of potted mums, Abby and Barbara Lambright ran for brooms. Rosemary snatched up her little girl while Emma herded Cora and Dora away from the shattered glass. Amid the cries of alarm and scurrying to clean up the untimely mess, Wyman grabbed his youngest son by the back of his suspenders and steered him outside.

Amanda sat speechless, stunned at the chaos Simon had created in mere seconds. She was his mamm now, so it was her place to clean up after him, but Abby held up her hand when Amanda stood up to help.

"Don't you worry about a thing," Abby said with a wave of her dustpan. "No sense in any more of us stepping in this glass."

"Seems to me we should just pick up the corners of the tablecloth and let everything fall to the middle of it," Barbara suggested. "Treva, if you and Lois could fetch twelve place settings from the house and a couple of tablecloths out of my buffet, we'll be set up again in no time."

Twelve place settings . . . two whole pies wasted . . . potting soil and mums mixed in with all the broken glasses and silverware that would have to be sorted out later. While indeed the dinner plates were stacked on the buffet table, and the glasses and pie plates had come from a wedding wagon that circulated among families in the district, rather than from the Lambrights' kitchen, those items would need to be replaced. In the blink of an eye, her wedding had turned into a disaster.

"My stars, but that Brubaker boy came through like a tornado," she heard one of the Cedar Creek helpers remark. "A boy that age should know better."

"He's had no mamm to train him up," Lois Yutzy replied. "He wasn't but three when Viola died."

"Going to be another sort of storm altogether when all those kids get thrown together at Wyman's place." Beulah Mae Nissley lifted her corner of the tablecloth as the women heaved the heavy, wet mess into a wagon Abby had wheeled over.

The women's voices sounded an ominous warning . . .

But the sight of twin kapps and purple dresses near the buffet table brought Amanda out of her momentary daze. Maybe she didn't need to help with the cleanup, but it *was* her place to discuss this situation with Cora and Dora. Carefully stepping around Emma and the Lambright women, who were resetting the table, Amanda strode to the other end of the room, where her three daughters stood beside Jemima.

"So what's the story here?" Amanda asked in a low, purposeful voice. She crouched so she was at eye level with her twins. "You said you knew better than to let Simon get you in trouble."

"I'm sorry, Mamm. I should've been paying closer attention," Lizzie gushed, while Dora and Cora burst into tears and grabbed each other's hands.

"Let this be a lesson learned," their grandmother remarked. "You girls don't know all these folks, but they certainly know who *you* are. And they'll be *watching* you now. So will you follow your new brother's bad example? Or will you lead Simon to behave the way your mamm has raised you?"

Wiping their faces on their sleeves, the twins looked from Jemima to Amanda with wide, solemn eyes. "We'll be gut now," Cora said with a loud sniffle.

"Jah, we don't want no more of Simon's trouble." Dora gazed toward the back door. "Did he get a *spankin'*?"

Amanda bit back a smile. Her girls had been easy to discipline with warnings and stern looks, so the prospect of getting their backsides warmed seemed like the ultimate threat. "You'll have to ask him. Meanwhile, your new dat and I must sit up front with the wedding party. It's your job to be perfect girls for Lizzie and your mammi now."

"Jah, we will," they said, bobbing their heads. They each reached for Jemima's hands, the picture of contrition.

Amanda rose to her full height again when she saw Wyman coming inside, alone. Guests were forming a line at the buffet table, and because the Lambright women had made quick work of resetting the ruined table, the celebration continued as though nothing had interrupted it.

What a blessing, to have such gut friends, Amanda mused as she returned to the eck. As Wyman pulled out her chair, Amanda studied his face for signs of how his session with Simon had gone. The furrow in his brow disappeared as he held her gaze.

"I've put Eddie in charge of his little brother." As Wyman sat down beside her, a secretive smile lit his face. "I've been keeping a surprise for later, but maybe now's the time to let you in on it, Amanda."

She folded her hands and remained quiet.

Wyman chuckled. "I take it you've had enough surprises for one day? Like I have?"

Amanda felt the joy of their celebration returning. "I'm ready for whatever you've got in mind, Wyman. Your surprises are always the best kind."

"Well, then——" He flashed Sam a thumbs-up when the

preacher waved at him from across the large, noisy room. "Rather than you and me returning home, we'll be staying here with the Lambrights tonight—"

Amanda's pulse raced with all sorts of practical objections. "But—"

"Abby has seen to all the details," Wyman insisted. "She's letting us stay at her house. Meanwhile, Vera will be in charge of the Brubaker bunch, and Jerome and Jemima will be taking your girls home tonight. This also puts us here for the cleaning up in the morning," he pointed out. "That's our part of the bargain as the bride and groom."

"Jah, of course it is. But I don't have a change of clothes—"

"Lizzie packed you a suitcase," he replied, obviously delighted that these details were taken care of. "She and Vera were behind this idea, and everyone else agreed it was the perfect gift. Just the two of us . . . alone together on our wedding night."

Amanda's heart pounded and her mind spun with a hundred questions. "But how did they all keep such a secret? Cora and Dora didn't let out a peep about—"

"Just the older kids and adults know," he clarified. "Sam and Matt have also offered to be at your place early Saturday morning with stock wagons to help move your belongings to Clearwater. James and Abby are in on that, as well. So, once again, God and our gut friends are getting us off to a fine start, Amanda. Don't you think?"

Tears sprang to her eyes. She *couldn't* think. "Oh, my," she whispered. "I—I didn't see any of this coming."

Amanda was vaguely aware that Jerome and Emma were taking their seats beside her while Wyman's brother Otto and his wife, their other sidesitters, sat down at the other end of the eck.

"Here's the first plates for the bride and groom," Barbara Lambright said as she set the steaming meals in front of them. "Not that you newlyweds look the least bit concerned about food."

It was true. With Wyman's hands enveloping hers as he gazed at her, Amanda lost all track of everything except how wonderful he was and how happy he had made her. Never in her wildest dreams had she figured on having her husband all to herself tonight—not with so many last-minute moving details, and eight kids, and—

My grace is sufficient for thee, for my strength is made perfect in weakness . . .

As the verse about Christ's power sprang to mind, Amanda knew the words to be true. Weakness, helplessness, a sense of being overwhelmed . . . hadn't she known all those feelings these past few minutes—and for the past several weeks? Yet with God's help—and her friends pitching in—her new life as Wyman Brubaker's wife would be a witness to the Lord's ability to make everything come out just right, wouldn't it?

Amanda exhaled. She set aside her misgivings and the women's negative musings about Simon. The first bite of the savory "roast"—a combination of baked chicken and stuffing—made her realize how ravenous she was. The voices around her attested to the friends in her life, while the tall white cake displayed on the table stood as a tribute. This was indeed the day to celebrate her love for Wyman Brubaker, and he was seated beside her with desire and affection written all over his handsome face.

That's all she needed to know.

Chapter 8

James waved Sam and Matt ahead of him in their wagons, and then clapped the reins on his Belgian's back to fall in line behind them. The sturdy *clip-clop, clip-clop* of the draft horses' hooves on the county blacktop cut through the early-morning fog and accentuated his own heartbeat, for Abby sat on the seat beside him. As they passed the Ropps' dairy farm to turn onto the highway, she wrapped her shawl tighter and smiled at the black-and-white Holsteins milling around in the misty barnyard.

Who needs sunshine? he mused. *I've got this woman beside me . . .*

James reached for Abby's hand. "And how did the newlyweds fare, staying at your place Thursday night?"

Abby's cheeks turned bright pink. "And how would I know about that? I was busy setting Mamm's greenhouse to rights, and— Well, it's not like I was peeking in the windows!"

James chided himself for phrasing his question that way, yet Abby's spin on it tickled him—he hadn't been thinking about Amanda and Wyman's intimate relations, particularly, but she had. While Abby's modesty pleased him, he was also glad she wasn't upset about this turn in their conversation. Just flustered, she was . . . and it wasn't often he saw her that way.

"Of course you weren't peeking." He elbowed her playfully. "I put in a full day at the shop Friday, so I didn't get to see them, while *you* were clearing away the wedding mess."

"Ah." Her smile returned as she considered her answer. "Let's just say they hardly noticed the rest of us were there. It's gut of you to take time off from your shop to move them," she remarked. "Over and over, Amanda and Wyman said how they appreciated receiving so much help from their Cedar Creek friends."

"I tried to convince Emma to come along, but she wanted Dat to dig the last of the carrots and potatoes while we've got this warm weather."

Abby's lips twitched. "She's avoiding Jerome. But from what I could see at the wedding, he thinks your sister's the sweetest thing since whoopie pies."

James smiled at this turn of phrase. "My sister has a way of throwing up her defenses, ain't so? Doesn't help that our parents keep quizzing her about why she's so dead set against Jerome. Reminding her that all the fellows hereabouts are getting claimed."

Once again Abby's expression wilted. "Nobody likes to feel she's being left behind, without anyone gut to choose from. It was hard on Emma, helping with weddings three weeks in a row."

James gazed ahead of them into the fog, to be sure he saw where Sam's wagon turned off the highway to go toward Bloomingdale. Once again he'd managed to be alone with Abby, yet somehow the conversation had taken anything but a romantic turn. He searched for a happier topic, hoping to put the smile back on his best friend's pretty face. Wasn't this hour-long drive the perfect time to discuss their future? "Abby, now that those other weddings are behind us—"

"Watch out for those deer!" she blurted.

He tugged on the reins, peering ahead. Sure enough, a huge buck sprinted out of the heavily misted woods where she was pointing, to cross the highway not ten feet in front of them.

"Whoa there, Karl." James pulled harder on the traces when the horse began to stomp and shake his head. His Belgian was a levelheaded animal, but the buck's large rack and sudden appearance were enough to startle any creature. James didn't want to think about the nasty wreck they might've had if Abby hadn't warned him.

"I see a couple of does," she murmured. "Waiting to follow their boyfriend, no doubt."

James held steady on the reins while the horse nervously paced the same few inches, forward and back. At last the other two deer bolted across the road, and Karl settled down. When they started up again, James let out the breath he'd been holding.

"Glad you spotted that buck," he murmured. "I once saw a car after it hit a big deer. The windshield was shattered and the driver lost control. Hit a power pole, he did. Thank the Lord—and you, Abby—we didn't have the same sort of collision with Karl."

"It might take a while for my heartbeat to get back to normal," she replied in a breathy voice.

They rode in silence for several minutes, peering ahead into the dense fog that obscured the road, as well as watching the woods for more deer. Abby leaned forward, pointing to where the pavement curved around a hilly embankment. "Sam's turning right up ahead. It's been a long while since I've visited Amanda's place—and everything looks different in this fog—so I'm not much help at finding it."

"You know more about where she lives than I do," James admitted. "That's why I let Sam and Matt go ahead of me."

He spotted the one-lane side road then, and watched Matt's wagon turn there. "Gee," he instructed, and as soon as their wagon was safely off the highway, he pulled the horse to a halt.

Abby searched his face. "Is everything all right, James? I'm sorry if I scared you by hollering out—"

"Abby." James framed her dear face with his hands, settling himself by gazing at her wide brown eyes . . . her parted lips and slightly upturned nose. His insides twisted at the thought of her being thrown from the seat to the side of the road had they collided with that big buck. "Where would I be without you looking after me?" he asked softly. "Where would I be without *you*?"

Abby stilled. Then she gave him a tremulous smile. "No need to worry about that, James. I'm not going anywhere. Not without you, anyway."

His heart thrummed. He gave thanks for this wonderful woman and knew that even though they would be working hard, loading Amanda's belongings, the day would seem shorter and less strenuous because she had come with him.

They continued down the narrow dirt road and then turned in between wooden fence posts that had seen better days. As they headed up the rutted lane to Amanda's farmhouse, they emerged from the fog.

"Glad to see you fellows—and Abby!" Jerome called out from the porch. "We're ready to load the furniture Amanda's taking, and the boxes are packed. The girls are chasing down Jemima's chickens while the women round up the last-minute stuff."

"Got our work cut out for us," James remarked as he helped Abby from the wagon. He sensed a nervous energy in the air as three lithe, kapped figures darted toward the outbuildings. Jerome paced as he talked with Sam and Matt.

Abby said, "This might be a tough gut-bye, even though Amanda and the girls are moving for a happy reason. Let's go lighten their load." She grabbed her picnic hamper and headed for the propped-open door.

James noted how tired the old white farmhouse looked in the sudden brightness of the morning sun, another sign that Amanda and Jerome hadn't been able to maintain the place after Atlee died. From the gambrel-roofed barn, a mule brayed and another one joined in. Lizzie and the twins chattered shrilly, swishing their skirts to shoo the chickens into the henhouse, where they would be easier to catch.

"So how's it all going?" James asked as he and Jerome entered the house.

"We've had our *moments*," Jerome replied. "Comes with the territory, when you've got little ones and a teenager, along with a hobbling grandma and a new bride. But don't get me wrong. I'll miss them."

With Matt and Sam on one end of a heavy walnut sideboard, James took the opposite corner alongside Jerome. In one fluid motion they lifted it and started for the door—and from there the loading continued through the morning. James saw Abby and Amanda taping boxes . . . discussing what to leave for Jerome and what might be useful at the Brubaker place. More than once Abby slipped her arm around Lizzie's and Amanda's shoulders, encouraging them with her smile.

By noon the wagons were loaded and secured for the trip to Clearwater. After they ate a quick dinner of sandwiches, salads, and the pumpkin cake Abby had brought, the three girls clambered onto Matt's wagon, while Jemima and Amanda rode with Sam.

Jerome took a quick look around in the house and cellar. He tethered a horse to the back of James's wagon, and then slid onto the seat beside James and Abby. "They can always come back if they forgot something," he said. "It's not like I won't ever see them again."

James gave Karl his head, allowing the Belgian to take his time going downhill with their heavily loaded wagon. The wistful note in Jerome's response wasn't surprising, for he'd lived here with Atlee's family since he'd been orphaned as a boy. "Will you get by, out here all by yourself, Jerome?"

"It'll be mighty quiet without Amanda and the girls," Abby added. She sat between him and Jerome, and James was enjoying the way he brushed against her each time the wagon swayed.

Jerome laughed. "Well, the mules are gut at bossing me around, telling me when to feed them. But jah, it'll be different. Jemima's been pestering me to find a gal to court, before the laundry and cooking get the best of me."

James waited, sensing what might come next. Abby smiled serenely, as though watching for more deer instead of waiting for Jerome to elaborate.

Sure enough, Jerome leaned forward to catch James's eye. His dark brows and the hair blowing back beneath his straw hat set off a lean face with a strong chin that gave him a determined, outgoing air. "How's Emma? I was hoping she'd come today."

"She and the folks are digging the last of the root vegetables. Watching out for them keeps her busy," James replied. "What with Dat in the early stages of Alzheimer's, we don't like to leave them alone for too long."

"Ah. That's a big concern." Jerome focused on Abby then. "Something tells me you know what Emma thinks of me, but you're not going to spill it."

Abby's laughter rang out in the treelined road. "Anything you want to know along that line, you'll have to ask Emma."

"Might just do that on my way back from Clearwater."

As they rode in silence for a while, James considered his conversational options. He was Emma's older brother after all . . . responsible for her, with the same protective love she gave their aging parents. He did *not* want his sister to live out her life as a maidel, sacrificing herself to care for the folks—but he knew that down deep, Emma was getting desperate. It would be worse for her to make a bad match than no match at all.

"Is it true, what we're hearing, that you've been engaged twice and backed out on those girls?" he asked.

Leaning his elbows on his knees, Jerome let his head drop. "My reputation's made the rounds on the Cedar Creek grapevine, has it? Guess that's to be expected, what with so many Plain folks here having kin all around the region."

"It's a small world," Abby agreed. She, too, seemed intent on hearing Jerome's reply.

"Okay, I got cold feet about three years ago with a gal from Queen City," Jerome admitted in a low voice. "Liked Bess just fine—until I saw the way her mamm said 'jump' and Bess said 'how high?' And her dat expected me to partner in his carpentry shop."

Jerome shrugged, gazing at Abby and then James. "I work better with mules than with wood. And I just didn't like the feel of that family, the day Bess introduced me and said we were getting hitched. So, jah, after a lot of hard praying, I backed out."

James considered this as he checked for traffic and then let Karl go through the intersection of the highway. "Better to realize that before the wedding than after," he agreed. "Sometimes our Plain way of courting in secret—especially if we don't meet the girl's family until she's said jah—isn't such a gut tradition."

"You and Abby have the ideal situation," Jerome said. "You've grown up across the road from each other, with your families being friends forever. No nasty surprises that way."

Beside him, Abby just kept smiling.

"So what about the other girl?" James insisted. "And folks are wondering why you've not joined the church, too."

"Mattie set her kapp for me when we were sidesitters at my best friend's wedding," Jerome replied. "When we got serious, she told me she hoped to jump the fence and join the Mennonites. Wanted electricity and a car. I said I was sorry, but my faith meant more to me than such modern conveniences."

Abby's eyebrows rose. "You made the better choice, Jerome. Your uncle Atlee would be proud that you kept to the Old Ways."

"Jah, that's what Amanda said, too. But it sounds bad that I've jilted two fiancées," Jerome said with a sigh. "Much as I'd like to find a nice girl—like Emma—sometimes it seems easier to stick with my mules. They don't tell tales on me, and they don't believe all the gossip they hear."

James believed that Jerome was being open and honest. He wasn't saying negative things about the girls he'd courted, or placing blame on them. "Here's a hint about my sister," he said quietly. "She doesn't like fellows who come on like stampeding horses. And you may have to spend time with our parents to be with her, on account of how Emma will use Mamm and Dat as her reason for not getting out."

"Is that so?" A slow smile spread across Jerome's face. "Denki for sharing that, James. Give Emma my best when you get home—but don't tell her I'm stopping by this evening. She won't give me a lot of chances, so I'd best get my strategy straight before I approach her again."

James chuckled. He'd heard Jerome's story firsthand, and he had a more favorable opinion of this mule trainer now. Everyone knew his sister could be just as hardheaded as those willful creatures Jerome worked with . . .

So as they came within sight of Wyman Brubaker's place, James figured this road trip had more than repaid the effort he'd put into helping with Amanda's move. If he could foster Jerome's cause and get Emma out of the house on a date, he'd done a good day's work, hadn't he?

Chapter 9

As the men hefted the final piece of her furniture off the wagon, Amanda watched with mixed feelings. In a few minutes they would eat Vera's hamburger soup, along with the sandwiches Jemima had packed in the cooler and the apple bars Abby pulled out of her seemingly bottomless picnic basket. Then James and the Lambrights would return to Cedar Creek. And Jerome would go home.

Home. For a few confused moments, Amanda wondered where her home was.

Wasn't she supposed to feel buoyant and blessed because she and her girls were now part of a whole new family? Wasn't it wonderful that Wyman had vowed to take care of them? What a relief that she and Jemima wouldn't spend another winter watching their home-canned food supply dwindle, wondering if Jerome was eating less than he should to help them get by.

As she watched the men enter a shed with Jemima's pie safe, however, Amanda's spirits sank even lower. Eddie and

Pete had hefted her heavy gas kiln and then dropped it a while ago, which meant it might not fire hot enough—or be safe to use—anymore. Would she ever find a place for the rocking chairs, sewing machine, and other family pieces now stashed on the screened porch? She had brought only the furnishings and dishes that truly meant something to her, leaving most of the household items behind for Jerome. Wyman had assured her they would make room for her belongings, just as his kids had shifted around in the bedrooms so that her girls' beds and clothing had their places.

Still, this ranked as a very difficult moment in her life . . . almost as low as coming home from the cemetery after Atlee's funeral. Why was that?

"Mamma! Whatcha doin'?"

"Supper's ready, Mamma!"

As her twins rushed out the front door, Amanda blinked and put on a smile. To Cora and Dora, this move was a big adventure. They were excited about sharing a room with Alice Ann, and more eager to spend time with Simon than they would admit. Amanda stooped to hug them close. "You girls have been such gut help today," she murmured. "Soon as supper's cleared away, we'll make up your beds in your new room, all right?"

"Jah, it'll be fun having a little sister," Cora said.

"Maybe we can teach Alice Ann how to talk!" Dora chimed in.

We could use a miracle like that about now, Amanda mused as she grasped their tiny hands. Then she sighed tiredly. *I need to quit feeling sorry for myself.*

Supper proceeded quickly, for their helpers had to drive home and tend to their animals. Even with sixteen of them around the long table, the meal was quiet, for it had been a long day of lifting and riding and deciding where to put everything. Jemima's face was drawn with fatigue, and no doubt her ankles were bothering her. Pete and Eddie spoke in low voices with James and Jerome. Sam, Matt, and

Wyman discussed the rising price of livestock feed as they chose brownies, pumpkin cake, and apple bars from the dessert platter.

From across the table, Abby smiled at her. "All this will feel better after a gut night's sleep, Amanda. You'll soon be settled into your new place, feeling like you've lived here forever."

Oh, how Amanda wished she could believe that. She came out of her dismal thoughts, however, when Abby stood to scrape plates. "You've done so much for us, Abby," she protested. "We'll clean up these dishes and let you folks start home."

Even as she said that, Amanda felt torn. Why did she wish Abby, with her sunny disposition, could stay into the evening—and longer—to help her with this transition into Wyman's family? How could she doubt that everything would work out the way her new husband had promised?

Soon the Lambrights and James were walking to their empty wagons. With her heart in her throat, Amanda followed them across the yard. "Denki so much for all you've done," she said as the men hitched up their draft horses.

Abby hugged her. "Many hands make light work. If there's anything at all you need, you'd better well let me know!"

As the three wagons pulled out onto the road, Jerome slung his arm around Amanda's shoulders. "Feels funny going back without you, Aunt Amanda," he murmured.

"Jah, tell me about it." She gazed up into his angular face. "If it gets too quiet there, you can always come visit us. Never a dull moment here amongst us Brubakers." Her new name sounded strange, after so many years of being a Lambright.

"I'll get tired of my own cooking pretty quick." Jerome's smile looked tight. "But you and Jemima left me lots of food in the freezer and notes about washing clothes and warming leftovers, so I'll be fine. Gut practice for me."

The nervous edge to Jerome's voice brought to mind the early days of when he'd come to live with her and Atlee, at ten, after his parents had died in a fire. How far he'd come since then! Amanda hugged him fiercely and then let go. The longer she held him, the harder this parting would be.

"Call if you need me," he said. "You're letting me live on the farm, but it's still yours. Don't be a stranger."

She watched him mount his horse, then waved until he was well down the road. When Amanda turned, she saw Wyman standing on the front porch watching her. What must he be thinking, if she acted so reluctant to let go of her nephew and her friends? Amanda composed herself and started for the house.

Through the screen door she heard Lizzie's and Vera's voices over the sound of dishes being washed. Out in the yard, Simon was throwing a tennis ball for Wags and his three younger sisters clapped gleefully when the dog caught it. Eddie and Pete were headed for the barn to do the evening chores, tussling with each other. Everyone else seemed to be fitting in just fine . . .

Wyman opened his arms. Amanda rushed up the porch stairs and into his embrace—and then, to her horror, she burst into tears.

"Ohhhh, what's wrong, my love?"

Why did she suddenly want to fling a long list of fears and misgivings at him, the man who had provided her with a more secure, prosperous future? It would *not* be a good idea to reveal how lost and frustrated she felt right now. "I'm just tuckered out," she murmured.

"Jah, you've moved heaven and earth, as you know it, to be here with me," Wyman whispered. He kissed her cheek. "What with no church service tomorrow, we can get you settled in. Everything will look better after a night's rest."

There it was, an echo of Abby's earlier words.

Why was it so difficult to believe the words of those she trusted most?

* * *

Wyman woke up with a gasp. After lying awake, listening to Amanda muffle tears with her pillow, he'd finally drifted off. So why was there a child climbing into bed with them?

"Mammaaaaa," a little girl wailed as she clambered across him. And from Amanda's side came an echo as another body made the mattress sink and shift.

"What's wrong?" he muttered.

"Cora? Dora?" Amanda murmured as she gathered them in her arms. "You should be in your new room—"

"Waahhhhh." Beside Wyman, Alice Ann was smacking the mattress, trying to find him in the darkness. With a sigh, he hooked an arm around her and hoisted her up. "Jah? What's the matter?" he whispered, desperately wishing she would talk to him instead of making him guess.

"We—*hic*—we was sleepin', Mamma—"

"And there was this scary noise."

"Jah. Like a wolf clawin' at our wall."

Wyman wanted to point out that their bedroom was on the second floor, well beyond where any wild animals could get them, but girls this age believed what their imaginations told them. Alice Ann had picked up on the twins' fear and followed them, and she was now snuggling against him as though her young life depended on it.

"Shh," Amanda murmured. "Let's not wake everyone up. You're fine, babies . . . probably just a bad dream."

"But I *heard* it—"

"Shh!" Amanda whispered more insistently. She had a daughter in each arm, lying against her sides. "If you can't be quiet, you'll have to go back to your room. All by yourselves."

The twins' fearful talk stopped immediately, and Wyman smiled in the darkness. Soon Alice Ann's breathing deepened, while Cora and Dora settled against their mother. It had been years since any of his kids had come to bed with him . . . Alice Ann had previously slept in Vera's room, while Simon was always deep asleep as soon as his head hit the pillow. Awakening in a strange house had probably spooked Amanda's girls, and their minds were still wound up from such a major transition.

But this bed wasn't intended for five of us. We can't allow this nighttime drama to continue if Amanda and I are to get any sleep or . . .

When Wyman woke again, Amanda was tucking the quilt around the twins . . . slipping out of the room to dress and start her day before the sun rose. He thought back to the night they'd spent in Abby's house after the wedding. Would that blissful night be the last private time he would have with his new wife?

He savored the warmth of the blankets until the clock on the dresser chimed five and played a delicate tune, as it had since he'd given it to Viola as a wedding gift. Carefully easing Alice Ann's limp, warm body over to the center of the mattress with her new sisters, Wyman got up and slipped into his clothes. As he made his way down the shadowy hall, boots in hand, he heard the older boys stirring in their room and saw a girl—Lizzie, for she was too short to be his Vera—slipping into the bathroom. So far, the morning routine wasn't all that different. More people to account for, but the same chores: the guys would head outside to the barn while the girls cooked breakfast.

The rich aroma of coffee made him close his eyes in gratitude, because Vera didn't always have a chance to make it for him. Wyman looked forward to entering the kitchen and slipping his arms around Amanda for a hug and a long kiss before anyone could interrupt them—

But his wife was kneeling in front of Jemima, tugging her mother-in-law's black stockings to her knees. Then Amanda tied her sturdy, thick-soled shoes.

"Ah. Gut morning, you two," he said. "Did you sleep well in your new room, Jemima?"

Her frown could have curdled milk. "I heard the grandfather clock downstairs strike on every hour and chime each quarter hour in between." She sighed as though she were a hundred years old. "Takes a body a while to get used to new noises, I suppose. Gut thing there's no preaching service today."

"Amen to that," Wyman murmured.

He stood by the stove, waiting for the percolator light to signal that the coffee was ready. It occurred to him that his earlier thoughts about Jemima had been all wrong. If Amanda's mother-in-law needed assistance with dressing, she wouldn't be returning to the farm to stay with Jerome.

He glanced at his wife, who was opening drawers, searching for something. "Any idea what spooked the girls last night?" he asked. "We should nip that in the bud before coming into our bed becomes a habit."

Amanda's stricken expression made him wish he hadn't spoken so bluntly. In the light of the oil lamps, the dark shadows beneath her eyes told him that he and the girls had slept a lot more than she had.

"Jah, Wyman, you're right. But I didn't know how else to handle it. When the twins were born, a few months after Atlee passed, it was all I could do not to sleep in their room," she murmured forlornly. "But after they were weaned, I closed their door. They did fine because they shared a crib. They had each other."

And you slept alone . . . as sad and lonely as I was, his thoughts taunted.

"I'm sorry," Amanda went on, still hunting for something in the drawers. "I'll talk to them about it."

The fragile edge to her apology stung worse than a paper cut. Wyman felt the weight of Jemima's glare as he poured his coffee. "Guess I'd best get on out to the barn. I'll be back in a bit."

"Where *are* the knives?" Amanda blurted, slamming a drawer.

Her desperate tone gave him pause. "What kind of knife do you need?" he asked carefully.

"Serrated! To slice bread for toast."

Wyman gestured toward the wooden knife holder in the corner, beside the bread bin. It seemed like a good idea to leave his coffee behind and put on his coat. The horses and cows could probably suggest better ways to deal with the new females in his life than he could devise himself, if these past few minutes were any indication of how their first day as a blended family would go.

Chapter 10

Abby sat at her little table, gazing out the back window of her house as she sipped a cup of tea and enjoyed a fresh sticky bun. These Sundays when they didn't have church gave her a welcome rest after a six-day week of helping Sam run the Cedar Creek Mercantile. Even with Amanda and Wyman's wedding preparations, she had kept up with her Stitch in Time orders and delivered the draperies for a newly remodeled bed-and-breakfast in Kirksville.

From a large remnant of olive green crepe she'd used for the B and B's valances, she had sewn a dress for Emma, as well. Jerome Lambright might come calling at the Graber place any day, and her best friend had no time to sew. Not that Emma gave much thought to dressing for a date.

Abby tapped her cheek with her pencil, ready to draft her next column for the *Budget*. As the local scribe for the international Plain newspaper, she sent in the week's news, along with insights she hoped readers would find uplifting.

*The leaves are taking on their prettiest colors, but
nothing compares to the blush on a bride's cheeks.
We Lambrights hosted our third wedding, this one
for Sam's cousin Amanda, who married Wyman
Brubaker of the Clearwater district. Their eight children now have new brothers and sisters as well, and
we wish them all the best as they form their big,
happy family. Your congratulations and gifts may
be sent to—*

A loud knock at her kitchen door made Abby look up as
someone stepped inside. "Jah, who's there?" she called out.

"Abby! What's going on with Jerome Lambright?" Footsteps clattered on the kitchen floor as Emma rounded the
corner.

When her best friend took the chair across the table,
Abby fought a grin. "What do you mean? How would I
know anything about—"

"You can't fool *me*, Abby! You and James worked with
him all day yesterday," Emma ranted. "Last night he left a
phone message for Dat that he's coming over this morning,
around ten. And he called you, too, Abby. Something about
being ready to *ride*."

Abby focused on Emma's flustered expression, hiding
her delight as best she could. "So he's coming to see your
dat, then? Maybe it's about his mules, or—"

"James says the same thing, but I don't believe it for a
minute! After the way that man pestered me all during
Amanda's wedding, he's got something up his sleeve."

"Hmm. His arm, most likely." As she offered Emma the
other sticky bun she'd warmed for her breakfast, Abby considered this news. Because the answering machine in their
phone shanty recorded messages for the mercantile and
James's carriage business, as well as for everyone in the
Lambright and Graber families, it was common for each of

them to know whom the other had heard from—and then to either relay the new messages or write them down on the tablet in the shanty.

"There's more tea in my pot. Get a cup if you want some," Abby offered as questions whirled in her head. "So what else did Jerome say in his message to me?"

"Puh!" Emma pinched off a short section of her sticky bun. "He says you and Gail might want to come along, and if Ruthie invites Beth Ann, that's fine, too."

Abby watched Emma jam the piece of glazed pastry into her mouth as she took another bite of her own roll. Oh, but this little mystery tickled her! "So let me get this straight. Jerome's coming to see your dat, and he's offered to take the girls and me for a ride?" Emma hadn't mentioned her own name. Had she left herself out on purpose, or had she not been invited? "Something tells me Jerome doesn't want to spend Sunday by himself."

Abby set aside her pencil and paper to formulate her plans. "Gut thing I made this batch of cinnamon rolls last night," she thought aloud. "And if I warm the leftover fried chicken and . . . I bet Barbara's got some sliced ham in her fridge—"

"Who said anything about feeding the five thousand?" Emma demanded. "Jerome just said he was stopping by to see Dat! And your message told about taking a ride."

So Emma *had* noticed that she wasn't on Jerome's guest list, and she was peeved about it. Abby rose from the table. "I'm guessing Jerome doesn't want to heat up the food Amanda left for him. So if he's offered to take us girls for a ride, it can't hurt to have a few things ready, ain't so? Might be our last chance for a picnic this fall."

"This is so—exasperating!" Emma ripped off another section of her sticky bun. "James is grinning like the cat that ate the canary, and the folks are in a dither. Mamm's saying Jerome can eat dinner at *our* house, and now *you're* packing a basket—"

When Abby held up her hand, Emma went silent. "Before you go, remind me to give you something," she said. "Matter of fact, I'll fetch it now, before I handle that chicken or wrap those gooey rolls."

Abby went to the hall closet and took out the new dress. "I overestimated the fabric I needed for making some curtains," she called toward the kitchen, "and I thought this shade of green would look nice with your complexion."

Emma was already striding toward her—and then her mouth dropped open. She got a funny look on her face, as though her thoughts were racing faster than she could catch them. "Abby, when on God's gut earth have you had time to sew?" As she fingered the textured crepe, she looked ready to cry. "Here I've been carrying on about how Jerome—And you've fed me a warm roll and made me a new dress. Oh, Abby, you're being a lot better friend than I am these days."

When Emma rushed at her, Abby opened her arms. Emma released a long sigh as they hugged.

"I've never thought that for a minute," Abby said softly. "There's nobody else like you, Emma. It's been that way since we were wee girls."

"For me, too, Abby. And denki for reminding me." Emma ran her hand down the front of the dress. "I *suppose* you figured I'd have this in case I actually went out on a date someday."

Abby shrugged nonchalantly. "It's up to you when you wear it. There's always church, or the holidays—"

"Puh! I'll not be waiting for Thanksgiving to—and I'll not let Mamm hang it in *her* closet, either."

"That sounds more like the Emma I know."

Her friend's dark eyes glimmered as they walked to the front door. "It's been a morning of surprises," she said, "and not even eight o'clock yet. I guess I'll just see what else comes our way today and be happy with it."

"Sounds like a gut plan." Abby walked down the gravel drive with Emma as far as Sam's tall white house to tell

Gail and Ruthie about their possible outing. "Give your folks my best."

"I'll do that. Truth be told," Emma said, "it's gut to see them excited, looking forward to something. Dat doesn't let on, but I suspect his days feel awfully long now that Preacher Paul's gone. So many of his other longtime friends are passing on, too."

As Emma crossed the blacktop with the dress she carried flapping beside her, Abby was pleased to see that the spring had returned to her step. Whatever Jerome was up to, he had indeed stirred the pot at the Graber place. She couldn't wait to see what other surprises he brought to Cedar Creek when he arrived in a couple of hours.

James held the door for his dat as they went out to the front porch to watch for Jerome. The morning-glory sky was dotted with occasional cotton candy clouds, and for a moment the two of them stood at the railing, taking in this perfect October Sunday.

"Peaceful out here," James remarked.

"Jah, it's gut to get some fresh air. Your mamm and sister are wound up pretty tight about Jerome coming by," his father remarked. His face was alight with anticipation as he gazed down the county road. "What do you suppose he's got in mind, saying it's me he wants to see?"

"I've learned not to second-guess Jerome," James replied with a chuckle. Then he pointed over his dat's shoulder. "But look there! Isn't *that* a sight to see!"

Around the bend from the Ropps' dairy farm came an eight-mule hitch hauling a long black wagon trimmed in red. Jerome sat in the seat with traces in each hand, encouraging the mules into a quicker gait.

"My word, I don't recall ever—Let's go to the road for a better look, son!"

Down the steps they hurried. James offered his arm as support, knowing his father had forgotten how his legs didn't always cooperate these days. It had been a long time since Dat had shown so much spunk, and despite the ruckus between Emma and Mamm over Jerome's phone message, James was grateful for this burst of energy.

"Let's cross to the Lambright side, so he can pull off the road without us being in his way," he suggested. "It'll take him some room to maneuver a hitch that big."

"And boy howdy, would you look at those matched-up mules and that fancy wagon? Reminds me of the draft horse competitions I watched at a big livestock exposition, long time ago." His dat waved and waved, and then Jerome waved back from about fifty yards away.

"He's going to bring them in with a big flourish, too." James felt his pulse speed up as he watched the tall, dark mules thunder toward them in perfect cadence, moving as a flawless, synchronized unit. "Better than a Fourth of July parade, ain't so?"

"Oh, jah!" his dat crowed. "You don't see the likes of *this* in Cedar Creek every day!"

The pounding on the pavement brought Gail and Ruthie rushing down Lambright Lane, with Abby and their family close behind. Matt, Rosemary, and Beth Ann stepped out to their porch to see what was coming up the road, as well. The first pair of mules was so close that their upright ears and eyes were clearly visible. The silver accessories on their collars and harnesses glistened in the sun, a shiny-bright contrast to their black coats.

"Haw!" Jerome called out as the lead pair approached the Grabers' lane.

With seamless precision, the mules turned left to enter the drive, each pair flowing effortlessly into the curve so that Jerome's black-and-red wagon rolled smoothly behind them. As if guided by some unseen hand—although James knew Jerome was controlling each mule with the eight sets of reins woven between his fingers—the animals made an impressive serpentine curve around the parking lot of Graber's Custom Carriages before heading toward the front of the house.

"Whoa, now!"

After the hitch came to a faultless halt, Jerome jogged up one side of the team and then down the other, to pat each mule's shoulder and praise it. Then he came around from behind the wagon. "What do you think, Merle? I've spent the past several weeks training this team for competition at the National Western in Denver, come January, and then at the Calgary Stampede next summer. This owner really wants to strut his stuff."

"And strut they do!" James's dat hurried toward Jerome like an eager child before stopping to take in the entire spectacle again. "What kind of mules are these? Don't believe I've ever seen such tall ones, and with a black coat."

"They're a Percheron cross, so they're draft mules," Jerome explained. "They'll compete in pulling exhibitions as well as in the showy driving events. Their owner has invested a chunk of change in these animals, and in the parade wagon and the fancy tack, too."

"Well, he certainly chose the right trainer." James stroked the muscular shoulder of the nearest lead mule, which stood several hands taller than he was. "It's one thing to train a pair of draft animals to work together instead of each one going their own way. It's another thing altogether to form a team of eight mules that know exactly how to perform in their spots."

"Do you switch the mules around?" Abby asked as she approached the hitch. "Or do they always have the same position?"

James slipped his hand around hers as Jerome gestured toward the mules nearest the big wagon. "These wheelers have to be the biggest and the strongest, because they start the wagon—and they have to be able to slow it down and stop its weight," he explained. "The next two pairs, the body and the swing, have to be agile and quick to adjust to wherever the leads go. The leaders are the fastest, and usually the ones that respond best to commands during their training."

"So we get to *ride*? In this wagon?" Ruthie piped up. As the youngest of Abby's nieces, she wasn't a little girl, but she wasn't yet a teenager, either.

"Jah, it's time for these mules to handle noisy crowds and little kids that run up to them," Jerome replied with a chuckle. "I figured to pick up anybody here wanting a fine, fun ride, and then head over to the Brubaker place. Those eight kids and Simon's dog will be a better test of these mules' training than they'll get from being around just me."

Jerome stepped up beside James's dat then, gesturing toward the wagon's seat. "I figured you for a gut judge of these critters, Merle, on account of how you've had the longest time in a driver's seat. You want to ride up there with me?"

"*Me?* Well, I'll be—" He turned toward the porch, flabbergasted. "Did you hear that, Eunice? Jerome wants me to check out his mule team!"

"It's your lucky day, for sure and for certain," James's mother replied as she gawked at the spectacle parked right in front of her.

"You can ride along, Eunice," Jerome added. "I've got a real sturdy bench there behind the seat, fastened on so it won't shimmy and shift. Got hay in the wagon for the kids—"

"A hayride!" Ruthie crowed. "I'll fetch Beth Ann."

"Jah, you betcha! Sundays are made for visiting, and that's exactly what we're going to do," Jerome replied. "James and Abby, you can join us if you want, and—"

Jerome focused on Emma then, who stood beside her mamm on the porch. "Emma, I'd be pleased if you'd ride along, too. But I'll understand if you'd rather not."

James squeezed Abby's hand to keep from laughing out loud. Before Emma could reply, Jerome was lowering a ladder so Dat could climb to the high seat. Gail followed him, stepped into the wagon, and grabbed the picnic basket Abby handed up to her. Then up the ladder Abby scrambled, nimble as a monkey, while Ruthie and Beth Ann came running over from Matt and Rosemary's place.

James watched the indecision play on his mother's face. She was hesitant to go, yet she didn't want to let Dat out of her sight . . . or let him have all the fun, either. James didn't say a word. This was a chance for his mamm to decide how she preferred to spend her day, and for his sister to either accept Jerome's invitation or be left behind. James settled against the wall of the wagon beside Abby in the fresh, sweet-smelling hay. He knew an opportunity for adventure when he saw one. And how often did he get to enjoy being driven in such a fine rig behind eight magnificent mules?

"Jerome, I'll ride along on one condition," his mamm called out over the kids' voices. She pushed up her glasses, shifting from one foot to the other with anticipation. Emma got a strange look on her face.

Jerome smiled up at the two women. "And what might that be, Eunice? I'm having a fine time with my mules today, and I'm in the mood to do anything you'd ask."

Mamm's face lit up. She leaned over the railing like a girl being courted. "You've got to join us tonight for the supper I've fixed. And we've got some things to bring along for a picnic, too."

"Hoo-*wee*!" Jerome cried as he lifted his hat in a salute. "Now how can a fellow say no to that? Come on down here, Eunice, and I'll help you up the ladder. From the bench, you can see for miles in every direction, just like a queen."

"I'll get my shawl and pack the basket and be right back!" James felt his heart flutter as his mother disappeared into the house with Emma. "I tell you what," he murmured to Abby. "Jerome's got a real special way about him, especially with my parents. If Emma hangs behind, she's missing out."

"Jah, but she's got to figure that out," Abby replied. "I'm not going to coax her anymore."

"Me neither."

When his mamm returned, James helped her up over the last step from the ladder. He was glad to see his mother in such a fine mood—and happier yet to see Emma ascending the ladder behind her, even if she refused to look at Jerome. Winking at James, Jerome handed Emma's basket up to James and then joined Dat in the driver's seat.

"Are we all here, Merle?" he asked as he wove the eight sets of reins between his fingers.

James's dat looked back into the wagon bed, counting with his finger. "Seems to be nine of us, including you and me, Jerome."

"Nine it is, then. Off we go!"

Everyone in the wagon cheered as the mules started toward the road. From beside the phone shanty, Sam, Treva, and Barbara waved them off. Rosemary and Matt had joined them, with Katie sitting on her new dat's shoulders.

"You folks can ride when I get back this afternoon, if you want," Jerome called to them. "I'll be putting these mules through their paces all day."

When they got past the mercantile and Treva's Greenhouse, to where the blacktop ran straight and flat for a few miles, Jerome urged the mules into road speed. James looked up from his seat in the wagon bed and held his breath.

Mamm had tied her kapp tight beneath her chin. She was gripping the edge of the bench to steady herself, but her smile was that of a woman fifty years younger as she watched the countryside pass by. Directly behind her, Dat clutched his black hat in his lap. He raised his face and closed his eyes to revel in the autumn sunlight as the breeze blew his silvery hair back over his ears like wings.

What a picture the two of them make, having such fun they've forgotten their age. James's throat tightened. Who could know how much longer either of them might live? He captured this moment in his mind, a memory he would cherish forever.

The young girls were surprisingly quiet, kneeling on hay bales as they clung to the wagon's side. They, too, gazed out over the farmsteads as if fascinated by the sight, even though they knew every family who lived out this way.

"I'm glad you came along, Emma. It wouldn't be the same without you," Abby said.

James leaned forward to smile past Abby at his sister. Emma was a tough one to figure out these days, touchy about every little detail—especially if a man was involved.

"How would it look if I was the only Graber who stayed behind?" Emma countered. "Mamm knew I'd have to come along if she went."

James considered this. Did Emma believe he wasn't capable of looking after their parents on this outing? Or was she once again using Mamm and Dat as a convenient excuse not to get out more often? She had stopped attending Singings, saying everyone else was so much younger, and he couldn't recall the last time Emma had gone out on a date. James hoped she hadn't resigned herself to the fate of being a maidel—

Hopefully Emma will come around. After all, Abby had consciously chosen to remain unmarried, and look at her now.

James glanced at the winsome young woman beside him. Was it his imagination, or had Abby gotten prettier? Had the girl from across the road changed, or had his vision of her altered with his love for her? James slipped his arm around her and leaned contentedly against the side of the swaying wagon. As the *clip-clop! clip-clop!* of thirty-two mules' hooves beat out a loud, steady tattoo on the black-top, James realized that he experienced *everything* differently now that he was with Abby.

He hoped that someday Emma would feel the same wonderment in her heart when she met the right man, the same joy of living with which Abby had blessed him.

Chapter 11

Amanda peered into the fridge, overwhelmed again. She saw a couple of covered containers, a jug of milk, bacon grease, condiments in the door . . . and empty shelves. What did these people *eat*? Why was there no cheese, or cold cuts, or other foods most folks fell back on?

"This being Sunday, we're not supposed to cook," she remarked to Vera and Jemima. "But with the move taking all day yesterday, it's not like we had time to prepare to-day's dinner, either."

Vera smiled apologetically. "When the time gets away from me, I fry up bacon and eggs and potatoes. Everybody likes that. Or pancakes. Or French toast."

"Do you suppose my hens have made friends with yours yet?" Jemima peered out the kitchen window toward the chicken house. "Might take a while to get eggs, while they decide on their new pecking order."

"I did make a big batch of mac and cheese," Vera said, pointing at a covered pan. "Shall we put that in the oven?"

"That sounds gut," Amanda replied. "Then you can show me where everything is, so I don't scare your dat again, looking for knives."

Once the casserole was in the oven, Amanda followed Vera around the large kitchen, opening cabinets and drawers. She stifled a sigh, wondering if she would ever get past feeling like an outsider. Vera, bless her, was being very helpful—and grateful that Amanda and Jemima were willing to do most of the cooking.

But this was still Viola Brubaker's kitchen. And while basic functions like making bread, setting the table, and preparing food from the deep freeze and the cellar shelves didn't vary much from one Plain household to the next, each wife had her own way of doing those things. And each woman arranged her kitchen to suit the way she worked. Amanda and Jemima had always stored basic baking ingredients in the pie safe, where they made pies and bread. She'd kept the heavier crocks and equipment down low, where they wouldn't fall on her. But Viola had arranged things differently . . .

As Vera showed her the old pots and roasters, Amanda realized that Wyman's first wife had probably cooked with items belonging to his mother. While that wasn't unusual in families where several generations lived in the same home—she had moved into Jemima's kitchen when she'd married Atlee—it made Amanda long for her familiar pans and utensils. Jemima's perplexed expression said she was having the same thoughts.

But this wasn't the time to suggest major changes. Even if it wasn't the Sabbath, they would have to consider Vera's feelings before they could shift her mamm's cookware out to make room for their own.

Wags began barking outside, and then the younger children let out whoops.

"Lookie *there*!" Simon cried. "Sounds like thunder comin' down the road!"

"It's like a parade! Mamma—come quick!"

Amanda stepped out to the porch. Tired as she was, she wondered if those distant black horses and the matching wagon were somebody's funeral procession. Then her mouth dropped open. "Why, that's Jerome and his mules."

"He was saying they were almost road-ready," Jemima murmured. "But I had no idea about the fancy tack and wagon. Must've kept them under tarps in one of the sheds."

"My stars, what a sight!" Vera smiled at the approaching spectacle. "We can go out for a better look, kids, but only if you stay right beside me, out of the road."

"We're doin' it!" Simon bolted down the lane while Wags bounded ahead of him. Vera scooped up Alice Ann to follow him, and the twins jogged along on either side of her.

"Now, what do you suppose Jerome's up to?" Jemima asked. "We've not been gone from the farm but a day."

"He's got riders, too." Amanda couldn't yet distinguish who those other folks might be. "Hate to say this, but I hope he doesn't think he'll be getting a Sunday dinner like we would've fixed him at home."

"He'd best put that notion out of his head pretty quick," Jemima remarked. "But look at that fancy rig and those mules trotting along so perfect-like. He's a sight for sore eyes, ain't so?"

"He's that, all right," Amanda said with a wistful laugh. "Let's get a better look."

First, however, she stepped back into the house. "Wyman! You and Lizzie and the boys might want to step outside!" she said loudly. "We've got company."

By the time she and Jemima had walked halfway to the road, the eight-mule hitch was slowing down to make the turn into the Brubaker lane. Vera had grabbed Simon's hand and was standing well off to the side in the grass. As the children called out their greetings, the occupants of Jerome's wagon popped up to reply.

"Why, that's Ruthie Lambright and Rosemary's Beth Ann," Amanda remarked.

"Jah, and isn't that Merle Graber sitting alongside Jerome?" Her mother-in-law shaded her eyes with her hand. "Still don't know what our Jerome's cooking up, but he's in gut company."

The tall black mules thundered along the hard-packed dirt lane, kicking up quite a cloud of dust in their wake. "Whoa there!" Jerome called out. His grin was nearly as wide as Merle's as he gazed at Amanda. "What do you think about *this*? Didn't I tell you I was into a bigger project than I've ever handled before?"

"Now *that's* a mule team," Wyman said as he and the older boys joined them. "And you've picked a fine day to run the roads with them, too."

Jerome shook Wyman's hand, and then hugged Amanda and then Jemima as though he already missed them more than he would admit. "I'm giving these mules a workout. They need to be around noise and crowds, so— Now don't take this wrong, Wyman, but your kids came to mind first thing."

Wyman laughed as he helped Merle and Eunice Graber down the wagon's ladder. Eddie was cautiously holding his palm out to one of the lead mules while Pete corralled Wags and Simon to keep them from spooking the whole team. The twins rushed over to greet Ruthie and Beth Ann—and here came Abby, Gail, James, and Emma out of the wagon, as well.

Amanda's heart thumped harder as Lizzie came up beside her. "Isn't this a fine surprise, seeing Jerome and our friends from Cedar Creek?" she murmured.

Lizzie grabbed Jerome around the waist. "I want to ride, too! You never told me you were training your new mules to haul this *awesome* wagon."

"Their owner brought the tack and the parade wagon that Saturday you girls were at the Lambrights' getting ready for the wedding," he said as he hugged her. "I figured it might make for a nice surprise sometime, so here we are. And isn't this a perfect day for a picnic?"

"Jah, we've brought a basket along with ham and slaw and fried pies," Ruthie piped up.

"I packed chicken and sticky buns," Abby said.

"Emma and I made up a batch of applesauce last night, along with corn bread and cupcakes," Eunice chimed in. "Plenty enough for everybody."

Amanda's mouth dropped open. "We've put a big pan of mac and cheese in the oven, and were just wondering what else to have for our dinner," she murmured. "And along came a feast, with our favorite people. It's an answered prayer."

"You have no idea," Jemima added under her breath. Then she found her smile. "We can set the food on the countertop for a buffet line. Won't take but a minute to get out plates and silverware—"

"We brought along that sort of thing, as well," Emma said. She glanced at her parents and then winked at Amanda. "Might be easier to fill our plates, like you say, and then folks can sit on the porch, or on quilts in the yard, or at the table, if they like."

"I'm for that!" Jemima declared as she started toward the house. "These old knees aren't much gut at getting up and down from the ground anymore."

Thank you, Lord, for the unexpected turn this day has taken, Amanda thought. She and the other women set up the impromptu meal while the fellows helped Jerome unhitch his mules so they could drink from the horse troughs. The buffet was soon arranged, and after they gave thanks, happy conversations filled the kitchen as everyone loaded their plates. The men and boys gravitated toward the porch. Vera and Lizzie had spread quilts in the yard so that Gail and the three younger girls could eat with them and keep track of the kids.

Amanda, Abby, and Emma were the last to go through

the line. The kitchen seemed a good place to sit and visit, so they settled into chairs at the table with Eunice and Jemima. As Amanda gazed at her plate, filled with chicken, slaw, applesauce, corn bread, and Vera's mac and cheese, her heart welled up.

"This is a fine surprise," she murmured. "We were just wondering how we'd get any sort of dinner together—"

"When glory be, our friends from Cedar Creek showed up with this wonderful spread." Jemima glanced toward the screen door and lowered her voice. "It's been rough around the edges this morning, let me tell you. Nothing we won't adjust to, but it's . . . different here."

"I'm glad we've brightened your day." Abby smiled at Amanda over her chicken leg. "Jerome's taking the kids on a hayride after we eat, so maybe we girls should have a hen party while they're gone. We won't unpack or move anything, as it's Sunday, but we could help you decide where to put the furniture you moved here."

Oh, but that idea brought sunshine to a cloudy day. Amanda had loved the clean simplicity of Abby's little house—and so had Wyman—so hearing Abby's suggestions about furniture placement might convince her new husband to move a few old things out and clear away some clutter that had accumulated since Viola's death. This thought made Amanda feel so much better that she dared to dream further. "It might be a while before I have time for my pottery, but I'd like to decide where my wheel will go," she said in a rising voice. "It's downstairs with my boxes of glazes and—"

"Was that your kiln I saw behind the house?" Emma asked as she buttered her bread.

Amanda sighed. "Jah, the boys dropped it getting down from the wagon. The lid won't close now . . . It was my great-uncle Mahlon's, and I have no idea how I'll pay for a new one—"

"But the Lord provides—and where there's a woman,

there's a way," Abby insisted. "So for today, we'll concentrate on what we *can* accomplish. How's that?"

The lilt in Abby's voice convinced Amanda that somehow, someday, she *would* be making her dishes again. "Denki for reminding me, Abby. You're such a gut friend."

"And if we have specific places to put things, we're off to a stronger start," Jemima murmured. "Don't wait too long to tell Wyman you're ready for your furniture to come in out of the machine shed, or he'll forget it's there. And if I'm to help with the cooking, we've got to put the flour and shortening and whatnot where I can reach them. Preferably in the pie safe we brought."

"I can wash the dishes if you girls want to work on that," Eunice said. Her eyes looked magnified behind her thick glasses. "Always more fun to clean up at somebody else's house, you know."

"Jah, and I'll grab a towel for drying," Jemima added. "Not my place to say what should go where in Wyman's house."

Amanda's heart beat faster. Surely if she established her pottery-making space and had a placement plan for furnishings on the main floor, Wyman would get the hint. She needed to make this house *her* home as well as his.

As they rose from the table, however, Jerome and James stepped inside to get more dessert. "Everybody's wanting to go for a hayride when we've finished our dinner," Jerome announced. "The kids are really excited—"

"And if the rest of us go along," James joined in with a purposeful look at Abby and his family, "the newlyweds can have some quiet time together. Wyman said things were in an uproar last night with Amanda's kids getting settled into their new rooms."

Amanda sighed. It seemed her plans for arranging the house had just been hitched to a mule team and hauled off. Then her cheeks prickled with embarrassment. It was one thing to talk about quiet time, but it was something else altogether that every adult in the room knew why Jerome and James were insisting they all go on the hayride. She suspected Wyman had told the young men about his unsatisfying night for that very reason.

Merle cleared his throat loudly. "I can ride around on that wagon all day if it means I'm helping more little Brubakers come into the world."

"Honestly, Merle!" Eunice said sourly. "We could've gone all day without hearing that."

Emma glanced apologetically at Amanda. Abby looked ready to say something about their afternoon plans, but then Wyman came inside and set his dirty plate in the sink. "Jerome says his mules need practice at stopping and starting with a lot of weight in the wagon," he remarked. "We've got enough hills around Clearwater to give them a challenge, too."

"If all of you fellows ride along, that team will get a gut test, then," Abby insisted playfully. "We girls can clean up these dishes and get in some visiting—"

"Plenty of girls in this house to visit with every single day," Wyman pointed out. He slipped a possessive arm around Amanda's shoulder. "And my wife will have all the dishwashing help she needs, too, with Jemima, Lizzie, and Vera. There's a time and a place for everything."

Especially for everything YOU want. Amanda blinked at the bitterness of that thought, which had come at her from out of nowhere. Wyman was right about the additional kitchen help she had now, but it galled her that he'd convinced Jerome and James to leave the two of them alone for some *quiet* time . . .

Am I out of line here, resenting the way the men have overruled my wishes? Or do I need to learn how to submit to a husband again, after four years of living without one?

A few minutes later, the Grabers and Lambrights were heading toward the shiny black wagon, with Jemima shuffling along beside them. The kids scrambled for places in the straw, while Jerome, James, and Wyman made short work of hitching up the mules. Merle sat on one end of the driver's seat, and Simon was in his glory on Jerome's other side. The two older women claimed the bench, and the younger adults squeezed in among the children in the wagon bed.

Two little heads popped up over the side of the wagon. "Mamma, come on!" Cora exclaimed. "It's gonna be real gut fun!"

"Jah, we've got a space right here for you!" Dora chimed in.

Amanda's heart fluttered. How sweet of her little girls to think of her in the flurry of their excitement . . . and truth be told, a ride in Jerome's wagon would lift her spirits. When she stepped off the porch, however, Wyman gave her a purposeful gaze from across the yard.

"Go have your fun," Amanda said, hoping she sounded cheerful. "I'll want to hear all about it when you get home."

As Jerome clucked at his team, the silver trim on the tack glistened in the sunlight with each spirited step they took. Everyone called out their good-byes, waving happily.

Amanda raised her hand, chiding herself for feeling so out of sorts. After all, she had just eaten a wonderful meal with good friends, and she had been blessed with a fine man. She loved Wyman deeply . . . felt lucky that such a strong, successful, attractive man had wanted her for his wife. Her husband of three days cut a fine figure coming toward the porch, his broad shoulders blocking out the team and wagon as they headed toward the road. The unmistakable glimmer in his eyes was for her alone.

Why did she feel so cranky? Why was a nap—by herself—what she craved most right now?

Chapter 12

James took Abby's hand beneath the loose straw, secretly glad that so many folks had come on this ride. What with Emma, the Brubaker brood, and Gail, Ruthie, and Beth Ann all crammed into the wagon, he and Abby couldn't avoid rubbing against each other as the vehicle swayed along behind the mules. Ordinarily such close physical contact would be considered improper, so James wanted to enjoy every moment of this delicious friction—right here beneath the watchful eyes of his mother and Jemima, from their perch on the bench.

"Do you have enough room, Abby?" he murmured. "I can scoot over if you—"

"You're fine, James."

Her response echoed in his soul, taking on a much deeper meaning. Even though Abby inched away from him for the sake of propriety, she kept hold of his hand beneath the straw. For a moment James imagined himself in Wyman's place. What would it be like to finally become

Abby's husband? To become one with her in body the way their hearts and spirits were already growing closer?

James inhaled her clean scent, mingled with the aroma of warm chicken and sticky buns. He wanted to kiss away the dab of frosting on her white apron. In his mind he let those thoughts flow toward their natural conclusion, as though he and Abby were totally alone . . . the way Wyman and Amanda were. A surge of longing made him suck in his breath and look away.

His mother's expression sent his randy thoughts flying; the eyes behind those old-fashioned glasses had missed little while he was a kid, and even now Mamm seemed to be reading his mind.

James shifted on the hard wagon bed, looking around to put his imagination in a safer place. Ruthie and Beth Ann were entertaining the twins and Alice Ann with a clapping game . . . Lizzie had ended up between Pete and Eddie and looked none too happy about it, while Vera, Emma, and Gail were discussing the recipe for the mac and cheese casserole everyone had devoured. In the driver's seat, Jerome was explaining to Simon how he'd woven the eight sets of traces between his fingers to control each of the mules. The ecstatic look on Dat's face made James grateful for the way Jerome had paid his father such special attention today.

But even surrounded by so many folks, James felt acutely aware of Abby . . . her breathing, and the pulse of her fingers in his, and the solidity of her warm, slender body.

Stop thinking about her body!

James cleared his throat. He couldn't help but smile at Abby even as he sensed a troubling thought behind her subdued brown-eyed gaze. Women were such complicated creatures—he certainly recalled that from when he was courting Abby's younger sister, Zanna. Now *there* was a girl who had provoked him almost beyond his ability to curb his urges.

A year ago this week you were to marry her. What a

miracle that God had turned Zanna's betrayal into the blessing he now shared with Abby—a steadfast love that would see him through the ups and downs of their life together.

"Is everything all right?" he murmured. "You seem quiet."

"I'm fine."

James considered this. When a woman said she was fine, it generally meant she was not. But he had no idea what to do about that, or how to draw out her troubles while they were surrounded by so many people.

"I'm concerned about how . . . *overwhelmed* Amanda's feeling by all the changes in her life," Abby clarified in a low voice.

Wasn't it just like Abby to be worried about a friend's welfare? James squeezed her hand. "Amanda's kept body and soul—and her family—intact through four difficult years," he pointed out. "She'll figure out how everything fits together again. God didn't lead her to Wyman by mistake, after all."

"That's true."

Once again James sensed an undercurrent beneath Abby's too-short reply. He kept hold of her hand, hoping he'd get better at gauging her moods. He relaxed with the steady rhythm of the wagon and the bold staccato of the mules' steps . . . drifted in the warmth of the afternoon sunshine and the pleasant chatter around him. All too soon they were rolling down the last stretch of blacktop, toward the towering Clearwater grain elevator. The wagon bumped and jostled as it passed over the railroad tracks.

"End of the line," Jerome called out. "I'd best head back to Cedar Creek to feed and water my team—and to share the supper Eunice invited me to," he added with a lift in his voice. "I hope everybody's day has been as wonderful-gut as mine has."

"Jah, this was great fun, Jerome!" Pete replied.

"Denki for taking us!" Eddie chimed in.

"Don't forget the picnic hampers and dishes you left in the kitchen," Vera reminded them as the wagon came to a stop about halfway down the lane.

The Brubakers scrambled down from the wagon, scattering after they said their good-byes. Simon let out a whoop as Wags bounded out to greet them, which in turn gave the mules a start. Jerome, however, spoke to his team in a low, confident voice and settled the huge animals quickly.

"Emma and I can fetch the dishes and baskets," Abby volunteered as the two of them scooted toward the end gate. "Sit tight, Eunice. We'll be right back."

James guided Jemima toward the ladder, steadying her as she turned to plant one foot on the top rung and then the other. Jerome waited for her at the bottom, guiding her safely to the ground. Gail and the younger girls had hurried behind Abby and Emma to help gather up their pans, so James stood in the wagon bed watching them. It made a pretty autumn picture as they climbed the porch steps of the rambling white Brubaker house with the breeze rippling their dresses of bittersweet, evergreen, and butternut.

Once again his thoughts wandered toward Wyman and Amanda. Had they enjoyed their time alone? Had they gotten themselves dressed in time to—

None of your beeswax! his conscience warned. And again his mother's pinched lips reminded him to keep such ideas from leading him astray.

"How'd you like that ride, Mamm?" He eased onto the bench beside her.

"Fine."

James considered her tone. Once again, a one-word answer seemed to indicate something to the contrary.

"Oh, *fine* doesn't nearly cover it!" his dat crowed. "But my backside's ready to be at home in the recliner after so much bumping along."

"I'm surprised the fellow who owns this rig didn't opt

for a padded seat," Jerome remarked as he resumed his place.

"Jah, it's been like sitting through church, except being bounced around." Mamm stood up to stretch her stiff legs. "Of course, in church the young people aren't flirting and getting . . . *ideas*."

James decided not to respond to his mother's remark. The girls were coming back down the lane, swinging their baskets—and wasn't it good to see Emma and Abby with their kapps together, sharing a laugh as only longtime friends could do? He was glad Abby's mood had improved. And when she smiled up at him, James felt as though the afternoon sun had warmed him through to the bones.

The ride home went quickly. Abby had chosen to sit across the wagon from him so she and Emma could visit, which suited him fine—he could watch her facial expressions as she talked. Gail, Ruthie, and Beth Ann joined in on their chat about how Thanksgiving was next month. Their discussion of pumpkin pies, roasted turkey, and corn bread stuffing made with dried cranberries and pecans made his stomach rumble.

Jerome slowed his team as Treva's Greenhouse and the Cedar Creek Mercantile came into view, and then expertly directed the mules up into the parking lot of James's carriage shop. "Here we are, folks," he called out. "Sure glad you all could ride along today."

"Wouldn't have missed it for the world," Dat replied.

Emma headed into the house as though something was burning on the stove—ducking Jerome's attentions, most likely. And indeed, Jerome had all but ignored Emma today. Maybe that was his strategy, to keep his distance until Emma became more accustomed to him, much as he gained the confidence of the mules he trained.

James chuckled as he helped Mamm down the ladder. He could see some similarities between his sister and mules, but it wouldn't do to say such a thing out loud.

"See you at school tomorrow!" Beth Ann said as she headed to Rosemary and Matt's place.

"I'll be there," Ruthie hollered back as she and Gail crossed the road.

Dat had gone to fill the horse tanks, so James helped Jerome unhitch his team. They led the mules into the barnyard two at a time, to drink and munch on fresh bales of hay. As the three men strode toward the house, James was pleased to see Abby coming out the side door from the kitchen.

"I'll be along in a few, fellows," he said.

Jerome shot him a knowing look, steering James's father into the house. "Don't do anything I wouldn't," he teased.

When the door had closed behind them, James grabbed Abby's hand, intending to walk her to the road. "While I was in that wagon, bumping up against you, I was wishing we were all alone, Abby," he murmured.

Her eyes widened. "I enjoyed the ride, too, James," she replied quietly. "But . . ."

The pinkness in her cheeks—that expression of a shy, wary deer—reminded James again that he loved this woman more than life itself. Everyone in Cedar Creek knew that, too, so he needed to make it official between them. "But what, honey-girl? Something besides Amanda's situation was on your mind during the ride, ain't so?"

Abby closed her eyes and leaned back against the side of the house. Was she thinking about what to say? Or was this the invitation—the opportunity—he'd been looking for all day?

Marry me, Abby . . . Abby, would you do me the honor of . . . I love you so much, would you be my wife? Dozens of times the words had circled in his heart, like a dog chasing its tail. Her sigh, her uplifted face, surely must be signs that she was waiting to hear what he so desperately needed to say.

James kissed her lightly, but it wasn't nearly enough. He

took her face between his hands to kiss her more urgently. When she placed her hands on his shoulders, James eased away, his emotions driving him toward the moment they had both awaited. "Abby, will you—"

"Sorry to interrupt, but it's best that I have," a deep, familiar voice announced.

James jumped and Abby let out a gasp. Sam Lambright was halfway up the lane and he looked none too happy. "I—I was just about to—" James stalled, not wanting to turn his proposal of marriage into a confession, for such a moment was far too special. Something he and Abby should share alone.

"Abby, you're the last person in this world I would call a bad example to your nieces," Sam stated sternly. "But Gail and Ruthie could easily have seen you and James kissing so . . . *intently.* That sort of behavior's not allowed in public for gut reason—"

"I'm so sorry, Sam," Abby murmured as she lowered her eyes. Her face turned five shades of red.

"—and truth be told, the both of you would be expected to make your confession before the church in a more conservative settlement," her brother continued. "Now that I'm a preacher, I can't pretend I didn't see you."

James's heart hammered in his chest as he eased farther away from Abby. "It's all my doing, Sam," he said. "I got carried away—"

"Jah, that's what I was seeing, too." Sam sighed as though this situation felt as uncomfortable to him as it did to James. "While I believe your feelings for my sister are true and honorable, that's the sort of affection that belongs behind closed doors, between a man and his wife. Otherwise it becomes lewd and lascivious, as the apostle Paul tells us in his letter to the Galatians."

A sob escaped Abby. She looked so miserable that James wanted to kick himself for being careless about kissing her. He heard a shuffling near the side door and suspected that

Emma—or Mamm—had come to call him in to supper but had remained silent when she'd heard Sam's lecture.

"After the way Zanna disgraced us with her unwed pregnancy last year," Sam murmured, "I'm not up for handling another scandal. Nor do I want to put our mamm through it again, Abby."

Abby swiped at her eyes. "If it's a confession you want, I'll be there next Sunday to kneel—"

"And I'll be there right beside her," James insisted. "It wasn't my intent to shame your sister. And you know that, Sam."

Sam exhaled. He removed his black broad-brimmed Stetson and then replaced it, as though handling the new hat he'd bought for his ordination gave him the wisdom to make a sound decision. "I believe this matter can remain between the three of us," he said. "I'll trust you not to let your affections get out of hand again—until you're married, of course."

James sensed that the lightening of the preacher's tone was intended to make them feel better, but it only served as a reminder that he should have asked Abby for her hand long before this. "Denki, Sam," he murmured. "You have my word on it."

"Jah, I . . . I'll get on home now." Abby gave James the saddest look he'd ever seen before turning to walk across the road.

James's heart clenched. He longed to escort her to her house, apologizing every step of the way. But he would have to stew in the juices of his regret for a while, and unfortunately, so would Abby. If only he hadn't gotten so caught up in Wyman's request for some private time with his new wife . . .

"So how was the ride? That's an impressive team Jerome's been training."

James blinked, brought out of his woolgathering by Sam's question. Getting caught kissing Abby made for an awkward situation between him and her brother. "A gut time was had by all," he replied in a subdued voice. "We're just sitting down to supper with Jerome, if you'd like to join us. He'll be happy to tell you whatever you'd like to know about those mules."

Sam laid his hand briefly on James's shoulder. "Maybe another time. After the way Jerome was following Emma around like a puppy at the Brubaker wedding, I think we'll be seeing more of him, ain't so?"

James managed a smile. "Might depend on who you ask."

"Jah, there's that. Take care now, James."

"You, too, Sam."

Take care now. A word to the wise was sufficient—and James wished he'd been wiser sooner. As he watched the sturdy, erect preacher cross the blacktop, he trusted that this unfortunate episode would indeed remain between the three of them.

But one of us got her feelings hurt . . . and was so mortified that she cried. You've got a fence to mend before you can even think of asking for her hand now.

Chapter 13

Later that evening, as Abby sat working on her weekly piece for the *Budget*, she realized she was staring out her back window more than she was writing. The deepening dusk made the cedars by the creek appear like dark flames swaying in the evening mist. She lit the lamp on her table, still unsettled by the afternoon's kissing incident. Her article had to be in the mail tomorrow morning, so there was no setting it aside in hopes that inspiration would come later. She reread what she had written yesterday and kept going.

> *Here in Cedar Creek we have celebrated the third wedding in as many weeks, this one of Wyman Brubaker to Amanda Lambright. As the both of them were widowed single parents, two families have become one that includes eight kids. We wish them all the best. What a wonderful way for God to show us that if we open our hearts to His heavenly love, we*

*will surely find more opportunities to love one an-
other here on earth.*

*Many of us were also treated to a fine ride this
afternoon, compliments of Jerome Lambright and
the impressive eight-mule hitch he's been training.
Jerome drove us over to the Brubaker place with our
picnic baskets, and after a potluck dinner we gave
his team some practice at controlling a heavy wagon
on hills and curves. Wyman and Amanda are also
learning how to maneuver their larger family . . .*

The *clip-clop! clip-clop!* of an approaching buggy prompted
Abby to look out the window of her front room. Barbara
was coming up the lane. She had been called to deliver a
baby, for otherwise she wouldn't have been working on the
Sabbath. Sam kept insisting that Barbara give up her mid-
wifery, as befitted a minister's wife, but she hated to refuse
treatment to the dozens of mothers she'd assisted over the
years.

Abby hurried outside, driven by an uneasiness she
couldn't discuss with just anyone—the cause of her writer's
block, no doubt. "Do you have a few minutes for a cup of
tea and a visit?" she asked as her sister-in-law clambered
down from the buggy. "I—I've got a question for you
about . . . men and women."

Barbara's eyebrows rose. "Let's unhitch the buggy and
sit for a bit," she murmured. "Hannah Hartzler just had a
miscarriage. It'll be gut to unwind before I put supper on."

Abby sucked in her breath. "I had no idea she was in the
family way again. And so soon after their Polly was born."

"Jah, that's part of the problem," Barbara replied with a
sigh. "I'd warned her it was best to give her body several
months' rest after Polly's difficult birth in May, but . . .
well, husbands don't wait very well."

Abby's heart thudded. Here it was, the topic that had

been bothering her this afternoon as she'd witnessed the emotions playing tug-of-war on Amanda's face.

The two of them went in Abby's back kitchen door. As they sat down at the table with their tea, Abby's throat tightened around a subject that was seldom discussed in Plain households.

Barbara leaned forward. "Does it bother you that your friend Hannah has birthed three babies while you've remained a maidel?" she asked gently. "Your time for mothering will come, now that James realizes he loves you. And even though Sam wants me to set aside my midwifing, I wouldn't for a minute miss out on helping with your babies, Abby," she insisted. "No matter what the elders say, I believe my skills are a gift that God intends for me to keep using."

Abby's cheeks burned as she gripped Barbara's fingers. "Denki ever so much," she whispered. "But we need to back up a bit . . . to the part about husbands not wanting to *wait*."

Barbara squeezed out her tea bag. She took a sip of the steaming brew in her mug. She'd had practice at waiting out her kids and patients, so there was nothing for Abby to do but blurt out her concerns. She couldn't expect Barbara to read her mind.

"Today when Jerome drove us to the Brubakers', it was almost as though . . ." Abby paused, wondering how best to word her question. "While I believe Jerome had the best of intentions, taking all of us for a ride so Wyman and Amanda could have some time together, it felt like he and Wyman and James were plotting . . . without any regard for Amanda's feelings. I was embarrassed for her."

Barbara's lips quirked. "One thing we women don't realize until *after* we get hitched," she began, "is that men look at love and sex differently from the way we do. Seeing's how Wyman has gone a couple of years without a wife, I suspect he's making up for lost time."

Abby took a long drink of her tea, considering this. "Amanda didn't look all that happy about what he had in mind," she murmured. "Is . . . is it a husband's right to have relations with his wife no matter how she feels about it? Do you think Amanda doesn't *like* to—and what if I find out that, as much as I love James, I don't enjoy the physical side of being his wife?"

Oh, but it had cost her something to say that. Most Plain women considered such mysteries unmentionable. And because she had declared herself a maidel, her mamm hadn't discussed the facts of life with her, beyond explaining the basics of becoming a woman. Barbara, however, didn't seem the least bit dismayed about her question.

"I suspect Amanda has had her hands so full, what with the wedding and moving and getting her girls and Jemima situated, that she's too tuckered out to care much about sex." Barbara smiled at Abby. "It's quite a different thing, hitching up with someone who's been married before. Especially with so many kids in the family."

"Jah, it seems the three little girls heard scary noises and climbed into bed with them last night," Abby replied with a chuckle. "Understandable, since they're sleeping in a new room with new sisters."

"I'm sure Wyman didn't like it, though. That sort of interruption will cause problems if they don't convince those girls to stay in their own beds." Barbara stirred her tea, a thoughtful expression on her face. "Amanda—like all Plain wives—walks a tight line, because our faith teaches that we should submit to our husbands. And just as I suspect Hannah Hartzler has gotten caught in the consequences of such submission, I hear the same story from a lot of women. They can't talk about their feelings—their needs—with their men because a lot of husbands don't believe there's anything to discuss."

Abby set her mug on the table. Was this the sort of relationship she would endure once she married James? He had sat closer to her than usual in Jerome's wagon, even in front of his family and the kids . . . as though he had been thinking about what Wyman and Amanda were doing. James's kisses exhilarated her when they were alone together, yet Abby had no idea how she would react when her hair came down and her clothes came off. What if she wanted to hide in the bathroom? What if it *hurt* to become one with a man?

"I believe, however, that James will be more understanding than most Amish men," Barbara remarked. "We discovered how compassionate he was after Zanna accused him of getting her pregnant. Not to speak unkindly of your sister, but Zanna was freer with her affections than she should have been. No doubt James's honor was tested to the limit while he was courting her."

"And even as devastated as James was when Zanna betrayed him and then lied about him, he controlled his temper. Forgave her and went on with his life," Abby said.

"You've hit on something, talking about *control*." Barbara's lips twitched as though she was about to reveal a secret. "For some fellows, sex is a way to maintain control of a marriage—keeping themselves satisfied and keeping their wives with child. They see it as a sign of manhood—and figure other men will think they rule the roost—if the kids stack up like stair steps."

Abby frowned. Would James expect her to have a baby every year? She sensed that another child was the *last* thing Amanda wanted right now . . . and while she liked Wyman Brubaker, Abby suspected he wasn't a man who negotiated with women.

"Part of the imbalance in a marriage comes from the way men and women look at love," Barbara continued. "We females tend to follow our hearts, our emotions, while males are driven by their bodies, much like stallions and bulls are. Husbands can be terrified of showing their feelings because they think it's a sign of weakness—a lack of ability to maintain *control*. So a woman's best strategy is to train her man early and often. Especially in the bedroom."

Abby's eyebrows flew up. She couldn't imagine her brother Sam being *trained* by anyone. Had Barbara heard these details from her mother before she married? Or was there a grapevine between married women that Abby hadn't been privy to? She could name a handful of her friends who seemed contented with their men as their marriages progressed beyond the rosy haze of being newlyweds, but she also knew women who seemed pinched and restrained . . . as though they had been yoked with wifely duties that chafed at their souls.

Maybe she should ask what Barbara meant by *training*. James had reminded her more of a stallion this afternoon than the patiently affectionate man she had adored for most of her life. And while his kiss still tingled on her lips, it was frightening how quickly she had forgotten where she was— and how other folks could have witnessed the way she had given in to James's persuasion.

Barbara was smiling across the table at her, as though sensing her hesitant curiosity. "It's nothing more than the Golden Rule, applied with a firm hand—so to speak," she added with a little laugh. "If you show your man, in no uncertain terms, how you expect to be treated, and then give him the same affection and respect, you've got a head start. But the woman has to establish this pattern right off, because once her man believes he's in control, her cause is lost."

Abby blinked. This wasn't the juicy secret she had been expecting. She'd been taught to follow the Golden Rule since she was a wee girl, after all.

Barbara leaned toward her, her face lit by the lamp's light. "It's like the old saying, 'what's gut for the goose is gut for the gander,'" she continued in a low voice. "Or, I've heard the men say it another way, too. 'If Mamma ain't happy, ain't nobody happy.'"

Abby laughed out loud. "I can't imagine saying that to—"

"Ach, but you can't *tell* a man you're training him. That's got to be your little secret." When Barbara gripped her wrist, Abby felt her sister-in-law quivering with pent-up laughter.

"You've never seen a woman confessing in church that she didn't submit to her husband's desires, ain't so?" she continued. "That's because no man will admit—to his friends, much less to his preacher—that he doesn't have the upper hand in the bedroom, or in his marriage. Yet you don't have to think twice to name fellows who don't get every little thing their way."

Indeed, when a few men around town came to mind, Abby chuckled right along with Barbara. "I think I see what you mean."

"You'll figure it out quicker than most, Abby, because you've had time to assess what you want in your life—what your gifts are, and how you should use them," Barbara assured her. "And as for Amanda and Wyman? They're both dealing with old habits and memories of their first spouses, to be sure. But if she's not going to submit to Wyman's every little whim, she'll have to show him that right off. Nothing we can do for her but pray."

Abby cleared her throat. "That seems an odd thing to pray about."

"God already knows what goes on between husbands and wives. He won't be the least bit embarrassed if we ask Him to bless our women friends with happiness and fulfillment."

Abby considered this carefully. While she believed in God's all-powerful love, she had never considered how He watched over folks even during their most intimate moments. "I guess this whole matter of men and women isn't really all that scary."

"I'm so glad to hear you say that, Abby," Barbara murmured. "Too many women live their lives shackled by fear—fear of the unknown, mostly, because they can't ask the questions that really matter. While we believe that everything in our lives is God's will, I don't agree that God wants us to be slaves to abusive husbands. But you can't tell Sam or Vernon I said that."

Abby sucked in her breath. While her sister-in-law sometimes hinted at personal beliefs that didn't match their faith's doctrine or the *Ordnung*, this concept gave her something new to think about. "It's like that verse in the Bible, 'God is love,' jah?" she murmured.

"Exactly. And if we train our men to love us more, aren't we showing them how to love God more, as well?"

Oh, but saying such a thing in public would bring the bishop to counsel Sam's errant wife . . . or would it? Wasn't Vernon Gingerich the image of heavenly love come down to earth?

The clatter of an empty mug on the table brought Abby out of her deep thoughts. "I won't keep you from your supper, Barbara," she murmured. "I can't thank you enough for what you've shared with me tonight."

Barbara hugged her warmly. "No matter what's gone wrong with my patients, I always feel better after I've visited with *you*, Abby," she murmured. "You have such a special gift, a light about you that inspires me to keep going even when I'm frustrated by attitudes I can't change."

Abby closed her eyes, absorbing these words . . . such a balm to her soul after her embarrassing encounter with Sam. "We do what we can with what we've got, ain't so?"

"Exactly. And James is one lucky fellow to have you— just as I'm blessed to have a fine man like Sam," Barbara said as the two of them started for the door. "The trick is to keep reminding ourselves of our blessings. Gut night, Abby."

"Jah, thanks again," she replied as they stepped onto the porch. Then she gasped. "James! I had no idea— How long have you been sitting in my swing?"

Barbara smiled knowingly. "You two have a gut evening, now," she said as she started for the white house down the lane.

James stood, looking nervous as he curved the brim of his hat in his hands. "Didn't mean to startle you, Abby," he murmured. "But when I realized you had company, well . . . I just couldn't leave until I said how sorry I was for upsetting you earlier. I—I got so caught up in my feelings for you that I couldn't control myself."

Abby pressed her lips together. It wouldn't do to chuckle at James while he was apologizing and baring his soul, but it made for a humorous twist that she and Barbara had just been discussing men and . . . control.

"It was my fault, Abby." James stepped closer, gazing into her eyes. "As I've been thinking back over the wagon ride and that kiss when Sam caught us, I . . . I realize that you've been trying to remind me how to properly behave in public—scooting away in the wagon, and then pressing your hands against my shoulder to *stop* that kiss—but I wasn't paying attention. Too caught up in my own ideas, I was. And now I've shamed you in front of your brother."

His words had tumbled out in such a heartfelt rush that Abby couldn't remain upset with him. And maybe this was a chance for some of that *training* Barbara had talked about. She leaned against the doorjamb, crossing her arms so she wouldn't be tempted to grasp his hand. "Jah, even though we're courting, I've tried to keep my distance—"

Oh, but his face fell when he heard that. When James swallowed, his Adam's apple bobbed. "Does this mean . . . you don't *want* to kiss me, Abby? Maybe . . . maybe I *really* haven't been paying attention—"

"No, I didn't mean it *that* way!" she blurted, grasping his arm. This *training* wasn't as easy as Barbara had made it out to be. "I was just aware of—nervous about—how much *touching* we've done with other folks around. I didn't know how to tell you," she confessed in a whisper. "I was about to say something when you were kissing me at your place. But Sam beat me to the punch."

James let out a long sigh. "Jah, well, I should've taken

my cue from Mamm during the wagon ride. She was giving us the eye, you know."

Abby smiled. Had there ever been a more considerate, contrite suitor than James? Maybe he didn't come across with the commanding, stern presence Sam or Wyman or other Plain men possessed . . . but she appreciated his gentler manner. And she knew James loved her as no other man ever would. "Well, we got through Sam's lecture, and we both offered to confess. So it's behind us now. But, James?"

"Jah?"

Abby *almost* suggested that they not kiss again until they were married—but she caught herself. As she gazed into James's eyes, she saw nothing but love, for no one but her. And what would such a restriction prove? That she could say *jump* and he would say *how high*? He already dealt with a mamm and a sister who tested his patience, and Abby didn't want to be like either Eunice or Emma.

And whom would she be fooling? Now that she was courting James, after so many years when he'd had no idea she loved him, Abby *adored* his kisses. She just didn't like being called out for them.

She let out the breath she'd been holding. "Never forget that I love you," she said as she gripped his hands. "But the Old Order ways are clear about what's permissible for unmarried couples in public, and we should respect them . . . at least until we're in our own home, behind closed doors. Together for always."

His smile came out to play like the sun after a rain. "Together for always. I like the sound of that," he whispered. "And jah, for you, Abby, I can follow the rules."

They stood for a moment in the day's last rays of sunlight. James looked so ready to embrace her, but instead he squeezed her hands and then released them. "Consider yourself hugged and kissed, honey-girl," he murmured.

"You, too, James."

Abby watched him walk down Lambright Lane, waving when he turned to gaze at her as he reached the blacktop. With a contented sigh, she went inside and sat down at her table again. She raised the lantern's wick and then reread the piece she'd started for the *Budget*. Her head was full to bursting with ideas to pray over. A new confidence about becoming a wife filled her, and she picked up her pink eraser. The last line she'd written, about Wyman and Amanda maneuvering their large family, seemed to point a finger at the newlyweds rather than opening arms to all who would read her column. As she brushed the eraser shreds from her paper, she got a better idea about how to finish her column.

> . . . *after a potluck dinner we gave his team some practice at controlling a heavy wagon on hills and curves.*
>
> *Most of us would live and love better if we, too, practiced controlling the loads—the burdens—we've hitched ourselves to. Like Jerome's mules, we must learn how to keep pulling steadily uphill when our lives feel heavy, just as we must hold our own when our troubles threaten to weigh us down and run us over. Mules are wiser than we give them credit for. They know their places—their individual jobs—in the team. They trust their driver and depend on him for guidance.*
>
> *Christ tells us that His yoke is easy and His burden is light. Surely we'll serve Him best if we let Him hold the reins, if we listen for His still, small voice, and if we love one another the way He loves us.*

Abby smiled. Finishing her column on an uplifting note always gave her a sense of satisfaction. When the words flowed so effortlessly, she believed God had been whispering in her ear. And wasn't that a fine way to end an evening?

After she recopied her piece and tucked it into an envelope, she doused the lamp. All things considered, her Sunday had been a gift . . . a day of exploring emotions, accepting responsibility for her actions, and gaining new insights into becoming a wife. Abby put on her nightgown and let down her hair. As she brushed it, she gazed out her bedroom window into the clear, starry night.

Across the road at the Graber place, the light burned in James's upstairs room. It made her smile to know that he, too, would look her way before he turned in. Even though their kissing in public had gotten them in trouble today, it tickled her that James loved her so much he couldn't always control himself. And after they married, she would continue to show him *how* she wanted to be loved.

Chapter 14

Wyman watched the train chug away from the grain elevator on Thursday afternoon with an enormous sense of satisfaction. "Thanks to Tyler's savvy with the computer and the markets, we made our neighbors a nice profit on their corn today. My bishop's peeved that I'm in business with you worldly Mennonites," he teased his partner, "but he can't argue with the way we help the locals support their families—and the church."

Ray squinted into the late-afternoon sun. "Our partnership is one of the biggest blessings in my life, Wyman," he replied. "Don't see any more grain trucks on the road, so what say we close up a little early?"

"You don't have to ask me twice. See you fellows tomorrow, Ray."

"Jah, you betcha. Hug that new wife of yours. It's gut to see you happy again, my friend."

As Wyman started home, it seemed this October day had been created solely for his pleasure. He paused before crossing the county blacktop, taking in the glorious blaze of the red-orange sweet gum trees against the brilliant blue sky—his favorite backdrop for the sprawling two-story white house that had been a haven for three generations of Brubakers.

Perhaps his grandparents and parents could have planned the added-on wings so they appeared more symmetrical and proportionate to the original structure, but Wyman believed the true measure of a home was reflected in how well it served its family. His house remained a sturdy structure, well maintained and surrounded by the stalwart red barns and sheds that bespoke the prosperity God had blessed him with.

And a week ago today, his marriage to Amanda had restored order to his life . . . had brought him new energy for the years of parenting that lay ahead. Wyman smiled. If he had his way about it, Alice Ann wouldn't be his youngest child for much longer. And with new life would come new growth, new purpose. New love. *More laughter.*

Wasn't that what a man lived for?

He crossed the road, pleased to see that Eddie was nearly finished cutting the grass with the reel mower while Pete was raking the multicolored leaves. The home place appeared neat and tidy—except for the screened porch. Even from the road, the china hutch, sewing machine, and chairs they had stashed there looked tacky and out of place. Until Amanda decided where those pieces would go, it seemed best to store them with the rest of her furniture.

"Dat! Dat, watch this!" Simon called to him. His son tossed a stick with amazing skill for a five-year-old. When Wags caught it and ran in a gleeful circle around the boy, Wyman laughed.

"You'll be pitching for the ball games at recess on your first day of school next fall!" Wyman grabbed his son and hefted him into the air. "And what did you do today, Simon?"

The boy let out a joyous shriek as he went airborne.

When Simon landed against Wyman's shoulder, his smile brought back a delight Wyman recalled from his own boyhood, right here in this yard.

"Me and the twins—"

"The twins and I," Wyman corrected.

"Jah, the three of us kids, we played hide-and-seek and I ate *two* grilled cheese sandwiches for dinner!"

As Wyman considered this, his stomach rumbled. The sandwiches, fruit, and goodies Amanda had packed in his lunch pail had left him hours ago. He looked forward to the end of harvest season, when he could eat his noon meal at home again. "And what about Alice Ann?"

Simon looked away, camouflaging his guilt with a mischievous grin. "When it was her turn to hide, we, um, didn't find her right off. Jemima called us in to eat, and then sent us back out to fetch her. She had cow poop all over her legs from falling in it."

"But she was all right?" Wyman quizzed. "You *know* better than to let your little sister wander amongst the animals, Simon."

"Jah, that's what Amanda said, too," he said with a sigh. "And then dinner was late because they had to clean her up, and then Alice Ann was too busy poutin' to eat. That's why I got her grilled cheese sandwich."

Wyman set his squirming son back on the ground. "You're Alice Ann's keeper, Simon. I expect you to do better than that."

"Jah, I know it." The boy raced across the yard full tilt to throw himself into the leaves Pete had raked into a deep pile.

"Hey there, Dat. Lawn look all right?" Eddie stopped pushing the mower to wipe his sweaty forehead with the sleeve of his green shirt.

"Jah, and I appreciate the way you and Pete took on the yard work without me having to ask you to." As Wyman waved his other son over, Pete dropped the blue tarp heaped with leaves.

"Truth be told, working out here seemed like the better option," Eddie confessed with a glance toward the house. "We fellows are outnumbered now, you know. And the hens have been squawking all day—"

"So we've stayed out of their way," Pete finished. He looked up at the sky, shrugging in his exasperation. "There's just no figuring out women, you know? Say or do one wrong thing and the *drama* starts up. Sheesh."

Wyman suspected there was more to this *drama* than his boys were saying, but they made a valid point. Tempers and tensions were bubbling a lot closer to the surface now that five new females had moved in. But that was bound to happen, wasn't it?

"Let's clean up the clutter in the screened porch real quick," Wyman remarked, nodding toward the enclosed room on the side of the house. "Won't take us but a minute to carry that furniture out where the rest of Amanda's pieces are. She can take her time deciding where it'll go."

The boys exchanged a glance but then propped open the porch door. Eddie and Pete hefted the treadle sewing machine between them while Wyman grabbed a cane-seated rocking chair in each hand. The china hutch was easy to separate into two sections, and when they had carried out an old dry sink in need of refinishing, they found tarps to drape over Amanda's pieces.

"Hmm, smells like supper might be turning into a burnt offering," Eddie murmured as they approached the porch again.

Wyman gripped his eldest son's shoulder. "Don't say a word," he warned. "The quickest way to ruin a meal is to upset the cooks."

As they entered the kitchen, Vera was dashing out the back door with a pan of black, smoking biscuits. Alice

Ann, already in her high chair, was coughing and waving her little arms. Jemima swished the air with a tea towel as Amanda opened the windows. It was not the picture of domestic bliss Wyman had imagined before the wedding, but baking disasters happened, didn't they?

When Simon came in, however, his exaggerated coughing did nothing to help the situation. "Fire! Fire!" he cried. "We've gotta get buckets of water and—"

"Son, *stop*." Wyman grabbed the boy before he scrambled between the women. "We're going to be sure everyone's all right, and then we'll get out of the way. Amanda?"

His wife sent him a harried look from the haze surrounding the oven.

"Is there anything we can do?"

She shook her head, slamming the oven door. "Give us a minute. You're early today, jah? Supper will be on shortly."

"That gives these fellows time to wash up out at the pump. Let's go, boys." Wyman, clutching a wiggling Simon against his hip, steered Eddie and Pete ahead of him. On the way outside he whipped open a drawer and grabbed a handful of towels.

While his boys splashed water on their faces and cleaned their hands, the voices coming from the kitchen window provided a few clues to the havoc he had walked in on.

"Now we've got nothing to spread the creamed chicken on," Vera fretted.

"It's too late to peel potatoes. Got a bag or two of store-bought noodles?" Amanda asked. There was a pause before she said, "Do you need to sit down, Jemima? You look pale— Ach! Don't run into that drawer, sweet pea!"

A loud wail, like a siren, announced that one of the twins had banged her head . . .

Wyman winced. He hadn't considered the consequences of leaving that drawer open. Alice Ann joined in the lament, and the two little girls made more racket than seemed humanly possible for their tiny size.

"Just another day in paradise, jah, Dat?" Pete remarked as he toweled his hair.

Wyman bit back a retort. What they needed was order restored, not smart remarks. "It's best to solve a problem rather than becoming a part of it," he reminded his sons. It was wisdom passed to him from his father, which he had often shared with his kids—and he grabbed Simon when the wailing drew the boy toward the kitchen door like a magnet.

"That means," he insisted in a low voice, "we don't keep stirring up trouble by running and yelling in the house. Your sisters are upset, Simon. What can you do to make them feel better?"

Simon's eyes lit up. "Can I tell Vera that Wags likes her biscuits? Except he's tossing them around like balls because he can't bite into them."

"Burned his tongue, most likely," Eddie said as he refilled the dog's water bowl. "Not the sharpest pencil in the pack, that mutt."

When it seemed the commotion had died down, Wyman waved the boys inside. "Let's sit at the table, out of the way. And not a *word*, if the food's not quite as you like it. Understand?" Eddie, Pete, and Simon filed in ahead of him and slipped into their seats. The smoke had cleared, a large pot was bubbling on the stove, and Alice Ann, still in her high chair, was stuffing a piece of buttered bread into her mouth. Cora sat beside Dora, who held a damp cloth against her forehead—or perhaps it was Cora who had run into the drawer. He couldn't yet tell the twins apart.

Wyman knelt beside the two girls in their matching blue dresses. "I'm really sorry I left that drawer open," he murmured. "Can I kiss your boo-boo and make it better?"

The injured girl's eyes, so much like her mother's, widened as though she might start crying again. She quickly shook her head.

Disappointment stabbed him, but Wyman contented

himself with stroking her shoulder. By the time he took his seat at the head of the table, Amanda and Vera were setting on bowls of creamed chicken, noodles, peas and carrots, and sliced peaches. When Jemima shuffled to the table from the bench where she'd been resting, he noticed that the skin around one of her eyes had turned purple.

It seemed like a good time for prayer. As they bowed their heads in silence, Wyman asked God for guidance and words of wisdom. Without clearing his throat—his usual signal to start the meal—he opened his eyes. While it was a satisfying sight to see his newly expanded family praying around his grandparents' table, he couldn't miss the tight line of Jemima's lips . . . the way Vera's chin quivered . . . the dark circles on Amanda's pale face.

Wyman cleared his throat and reached for the bowl of noodles. He noticed an empty seat near the end of the table. "Where's Lizzie?"

Vera let out a testy sigh. "She locked herself in the bedroom after school. Won't let me in."

Amanda sprang from her seat. "I had no idea. We can't have that sort of thing—"

"She had a rough first day with Teacher Elsie, and I was trying to give her some advice," Vera went on in a strained voice. "But she's not of a mind to listen, it seems."

Wyman decided not to delve into the sisters' squabble—at least until Lizzie was present. He spooned up a clump of sticky noodles and passed the bowl to Eddie. Wyman was almost afraid to mention it, but he couldn't ignore Jemima's distress. "And what happened to you?" he asked gently.

"Jah, how'd you get that shiner?" Simon piped up.

Wyman gripped his boy's shoulder and glared him into silence.

The elderly woman looked up from the bread she was buttering. She seemed to weigh her words very carefully. "I was reaching up into the cupboard for the flour and the can of baking powder fell in my face—and then the flour bag, too," she replied. "I'm used to working at a pie safe, you see. Everything's right there in reach, not way above my head."

Wyman sighed ruefully, thinking about the dilapidated old piece out in the shed. A glance around the crowded kitchen made him wonder where they could possibly put it. "You cooks are going to have to work that out amongst yourselves," he said. "If you want some major changes made, you'll have to let me know so we can consider them." He suspected from the way Vera was blinking rapidly that rearranging the kitchen was a sore subject. And what could he do about so *many* topics that were making every female in the house cranky? As Lizzie entered the kitchen ahead of her mother, her red-rimmed eyes and downcast face told of yet another troublesome situation.

Amanda sat down, her forehead furrowed. "It seems Lizzie's having trouble at her new school," she murmured. "She says Pete has been pestering her to the point that she doesn't want to go back. Teacher Elsie assigned him sentences to write on the blackboard, but still he teased her all during recess."

Wyman scowled at his thirteen-year-old son. Bookwork came easily enough to Pete that he was often bored by school, as Wyman had been at his age. But that didn't give him license to cause problems in the classroom. "It seems my warnings and extra chores haven't convinced you to behave properly."

"So that's why you were late coming home?" Eddie challenged. "Writing sentences on the board for flirting with Lizzie?"

Pete's nostrils flared. "I wasn't flirting—"

"Enough, both of you!" Wyman's temples were beginning to pound, and the devastated expression on Lizzie's face . . . the way everyone at the table was looking to him to solve these problems—well, it was wearing him thin. He longed for the days when his kids had caused him no such trouble—

Before Viola died.

But that time would never return. His active children had given their mother some headaches, but back then they were all of an age when she could discipline them before he got home. Wyman wondered how much time Viola had spent keeping the three older ones in line and the two wee ones out of harm's way . . . but such mental meanderings accomplished nothing.

"Apologize to your sister, Peter," he insisted. "And assure me, in front of your family, that you will never again cause Lizzie such embarrassment."

Pete's fork clattered to his plate. Lizzie's face turned red and tears streamed down her cheeks.

"Your pranks make you look like a love-struck puppy, Pete," Wyman went on. "And now that she's your sister, it doesn't look so gut for you to be *interested* in her, even if she's not a blood relation."

"I'm *sorry*," Pete blurted to no one in particular. "Can we please move on?"

Eddie smirked as he piled peas and carrots on his plate. "Might want to do that yourself, little brother. After your trick with the fishing rod, didn't I tell you to give it up?"

Wyman gazed purposefully at his second son. Pete was beyond the age of being escorted to the shed, where the paddle used by generations of Brubaker dats still hung. But what would make the boy leave Lizzie alone? "I need your assurance that your behavior at school—and around your sister in general—will not require my attention, or Teacher Elsie's, ever again."

"All right, I'll leave her alone," Pete muttered. He scooted back his chair, but Wyman grabbed his arm.

"You're not excused. Running from situations that bother you solves nothing, Peter Calvin."

"Jah, Peter Rabbit," Simon said under his breath. "You've been a bad, bad bunny."

Wyman closed his eyes, exasperated. Why was it that

everything he said inspired such a reaction tonight? How had his kids turned into such hellions right under his nose? He'd never dreamed of testing his parents this way . . . nor did he recall such discord in this kitchen when Viola had begun preparing the meals with his mother and his grandmother.

"We're going to eat our supper now," he announced in a low voice. "And we're going to say nothing further unless it's positive and uplifting."

Silence. Lowered eyes. Only the subdued clattering of forks against plates.

Wyman gazed down at the rubbery noodles swimming in chicken gravy that had congealed on his plate. He'd lost his appetite, but if he was to be an example to his sons, he had to eat every bite of it, didn't he?

Chapter 15

As Wyman settled into bed Thursday evening, he prayed once again that a night's rest would restore his family's imbalance. Jemima had gotten irritated about the younger kids being underfoot in the kitchen, to the point that Alice Ann and the twins had been in tears at supper—so now Amanda was exhausted and frustrated, too. While he longed to talk quietly with her or to console her by cuddling, she lay facing away from him . . . throwing up a wall he sensed he shouldn't climb. The clock on the dresser played its delicate tune at nine thirty . . . nine forty-five.

"Amanda," he murmured. "How can I help you through this transition, my love? What can I do differently to—"

A little cry came from the room across the hall, followed by another cry and then a wail. As he heard the pitter-patter of little feet, he sighed. Once again the twins crawled into their mother's side of the bed while Alice Ann whimpered for him to help her up, to protect her from whatever had frightened them in the night.

"Now what?" Amanda demanded in a tremulous whisper. "You girls should sleep in your own bed—"

"We heard those scary noises again," one twin wailed.

"Jah, that wolf was scratchin' on our wall, howlin' out in the yard," her sister joined in.

Alice Ann burrowed against him, wiping her wet face against the sheet. This could *not* continue. "I'm going to go see about that wolf," Wyman muttered. "And then you girls can return to your own room." Cradling Alice Ann in the crook of his arm, he rolled out of bed and padded into the shadowy hall. The three girls shared a corner bedroom, so two of their walls were inaccessible to any scratching, even if that "wolf" could reach the second story. Because Simon's room adjoined the girls', he had a pretty good idea where those noises were coming from.

Yet when Wyman stood in his youngest son's doorway, the sound of deep, even breathing suggested that Simon had been asleep since Amanda had tucked him in nearly an hour ago. Wags raised his head but he remained silent, curled up on the bed to fit the curve of Simon's bent legs and backside. When Wyman crept close enough to lean over the twin-size bed for a look at his son, Simon didn't stir. He didn't grin in the darkness or muffle chuckles beneath the covers, either.

At least SOMEONE'S sleeping. Best to quiz him about these animal noises another time. Perhaps Wags had let out a *woof*, or maybe one of the twins had yipped during a nightmare and her sister had imagined it to be an animal. No doubt they were still upset about Jemima's cross words and not sleeping well because of them.

As he went back into the hallway, Wyman realized that Alice Ann was asleep on his shoulder, so he settled her back into her own small bed. He intended to tell Cora and Dora that the wolf was gone for the night, yet the sounds of their deep breathing—and Amanda's—seemed reason enough to leave them be. It made a touching sight, the three of them nestled together so peacefully, so Wyman eased under the covers again, careful not to wake them. He'd spent a lot of time being *careful* this week, it seemed.

Tomorrow will be better. Someday we'll look back on these incidents and laugh.

When Wyman rose before dawn the next morning, he was pleased that Amanda and the twins were already up and about—but his hopefulness for a better day was short-lived. Vera stood outside the bathroom door in her robe, hugging herself, waiting her turn, so Wyman went on downstairs. He could shave later . . .

Amanda accepted his good-morning kiss on the cheek. "Feeling better?" he murmured.

She shrugged, struggling with a smile. "At least the twins are helping Alice Ann dress, as though nothing happened last night—"

"Sounded to me like *plenty* was going on," Jemima remarked. She lowered herself to the bench beside the kitchen door with a loud groan, holding her stockings and her sturdy black shoes. "But then, I was up and down all night with a cranky stomach and these achy old feet . . ."

Wyman decided it was a good time to slip upstairs and shave, for listening to Jemima's complaints would do nothing to improve his day. "Gut morning, daughter," he said, squeezing Vera's shoulder as she reached the bottom step.

"Jah, we'll see about that."

With a sigh he ascended the wooden stairs, only to find one of the twins outside the closed bathroom door, shifting from one foot to the other in an unmistakable dance of desperation. "Do you want to go outside?" Wyman asked. "I'll help you open the outhouse door—"

Was this Cora or Dora? Her eyes widened, and she shook her head even as she recrossed her little legs.

"Ah. What if Vera or your mamm takes you out there?" he asked.

After a moment's consideration, the little girl nodded and

went down the wooden stairs with a rapid tip-tapping of her shoes. By the time Wyman reached the kitchen, Vera was grabbing their wraps and hurrying outside with the little girl, so he decided to start the livestock chores. Amanda had helped Jemima finish dressing, and they seemed to have breakfast under control. The salty-sweet aroma of sizzling bacon soothed him. Perhaps the day would right itself now . . .

He'd barely gotten to the barn door before he heard a little voice cry out, "Oh, but I can't go *here*! I'll fall right down that big ole hole!"

Wyman kept his chuckle to himself as he saw the four-year-old dart back to the house, with Vera a few steps behind her. How could it be that Amanda's girls had never used a privy? That was something she should help the twins get accustomed to, because while everyone in Clearwater had indoor plumbing, most families had kept their outhouses for when they hosted church services and other events.

Eddie and Pete came out to help with the horse chores, and then the three of them went inside for breakfast. As the women put on the scrambled eggs, sticky buns, and bacon, the boys steered Simon to the table and sat down, out of the way . . . doing their part so that the morning meal would go smoothly. Wyman was slipping Alice Ann into her high chair as everyone else took their seats. He sat down at the head of the table just as Lizzie hurried in with her kapp strings fluttering back over her shoulders.

"Took forever to get my turn in the bathroom this morning," she said breathlessly. She slid into her chair and bowed her head for the prayer.

Beside her, Vera cleared her throat. "Maybe if you hadn't been reading my diary, you would've gotten here sooner."

Amanda dropped the spoon she'd been putting into the bowl of fried potatoes. "Elizabeth Louise! You know better than to—"

Lizzie's face turned red as she grabbed the table's edge with both hands. "It was out there on your bed," she protested feebly. "How was I to know it was your—"

"It says DIARY on the front," Vera countered, glaring at her. "Is that what you're doing when you lock yourself in our room? Snooping in my stuff?"

"Girls, let's stop right here." Wyman couldn't imagine the two of them coming to blows, but then he'd never guessed they would speak with such animosity, either. The other kids sat in stunned silence, wide-eyed, waiting for this drama to play out.

"And why would you read someone's private diary, Lizzie?" Amanda asked as she went to stand behind her. "At the very least, you owe your sister an apology."

When Lizzie hung her head, the dam burst. After a few moments of hiccuping and trying to control her tears, she blurted, "I wanted to see if—if Vera was writing anything about *me* . . . saying she didn't like me or she thought I was *different*, or stupid, or—"

Wyman's eyes widened. Of all the kids, thirteen-year-old Lizzie was having the toughest time adjusting to their blended family and her new home, but he'd never expected to hear her talk this way. "Why would Vera say such things?" he asked cautiously. "You two girls seemed to be such gut friends when you were getting your mamm and me together."

Sniffling miserably, Lizzie shrugged. "Nobody else likes me . . . or wants to be my friend at recess or—"

"Oh, Lizzie, *I'm* your friend—and I'm happy to be your sister, too." Compassion replaced Vera's anger as she grasped Lizzie's wrist. "I'm sorry the kids are being mean, and— Well, Teacher Elsie can be . . . a pill sometimes."

"I'm your friend, too, Lizzie—if you want me to be," Pete murmured.

Amanda draped an arm around Lizzie's trembling shoulders. "Maybe I should come to school and talk with the teacher about—"

"Oh, please don't, Mamm!" Lizzie blurted. "Then the kids will think I needed my mamma to make things all better for me." She gazed at Vera with red-rimmed eyes. "I'm sorry I snooped in your diary. That's not a gut way to treat somebody who's been trying to help me figure things out here and fit in at school."

Wyman pondered Lizzie's words as she and Vera continued to make up. What did she mean by *figure things out here and fit in at school*? The very reason Plain folks dressed alike and followed the *Ordnung* was so that everyone belonged and no one stood out as different. He suspected his troubled daughter was keeping some of her trials and tribulations to herself—or exaggerating them in her frustration—even as he knew Elsie Schmucker could indeed be difficult. But speculating aloud that Elsie had landed her teaching position because she was the bishop's daughter wouldn't improve this situation for Lizzie. "Shall we pray over this fine breakfast now that you girls are getting along again?" he asked.

As everyone bowed their heads, Wyman gave silent thanks for order being restored. The meal proceeded without any further disruptions. When Pete and Lizzie left for school, Eddie went out with Simon to feed and water Wags. Amanda, Jemima, and Vera began clearing the table, so Wyman offered to assist Cora and Dora with the chicken chores before he went to the elevator. It seemed like a good way to spend some time with them, and to become more familiar with any mannerisms that might help him tell the twins apart—and it was a chance to discuss the "wolf" that was pestering them at night.

He helped the three little girls with their jackets and then they headed outside. His heart fluttered when each of the twins took one of his hands as they walked out to the chicken house. Alice Ann toddled along happily behind them, and as the sun brightened the horizon, Wyman felt hopeful that the day's difficulties were behind them. As they stepped inside the chicken house, however, he stopped.

The white bucket they used to fill the chickens' water tank had pale yellow liquid in the bottom . . . with a little wad of white tissue floating in it.

Wyman noticed that the twins walked quickly past it, to scoop feed out of the bin in the corner. "Chick, chick, chick!" they called out. The feeders were made from gallon plastic milk jugs with sections cut away, hanging along the wall so that the cracked grain was off the ground yet easy for the birds to reach. As Cora and Dora filled each feeder, the hens scrambled around them. Alice Ann laughed, not one bit afraid of the clucking birds.

For a moment Wyman wondered if Amanda should handle this matter of where the girls went to the bathroom. *But there's no time like the present. And YOU are present.*

Which twin had dashed away from the outhouse earlier this morning? He'd gone into the barn, so he hadn't seen a desperate little daughter dash in here, probably with a tissue from the box in the kitchen. But it made sense to him that she would have come here as a last resort.

"Girls, we need to talk about what's in this bucket," Wyman said, beckoning them with his finger. "The chickens will get very sick if someone uses it for a toilet and then we pour their water from it. Cora, did you come back out here instead of using the bathroom upstairs—or the outhouse?"

The girl to his right shook her head emphatically. "No, not me."

"Me neither," Dora insisted from his other side. Then she gasped, clapping her hands to either side of her face. "The wolf! What if it was that scary ole—"

"Jah!" Cora chimed in, also clapping her hands to her face. "It must've been the wolf."

Two identical girls were gazing at him with such wide, innocent eyes that Wyman had to clench his teeth to keep from laughing. He'd just been outfoxed by four-year-olds, who surely looked exactly as their mother had at that age. Yes, he should correct them and insist that lying was wrong. But after enduring the breakfast-table drama between Lizzie and Vera, it was nice to have something to chuckle at . . . and maybe he could still work this situation into a lesson about taking responsibility for their actions.

Wyman crouched so that he was at the twins' eye level. "Can you two be big, brave girls for me?" he asked in a serious tone.

Cora and Dora glanced at each other and then back at him. As one, they nodded, caught up in the challenge.

"Next time that wolf scratches on your wall at night, tell him in no uncertain terms that he is *not* to use the livestock buckets for a toilet. Will you do that for me?"

The twins considered this. They nodded solemnly despite their apparent doubts about confronting their spook.

"And then, will you get back into your own bed?" Wyman continued with a gentle smile. "Alice Ann will see that you're being brave, so she won't be scared, either. Your mamm and I will be so pleased that you're staying in your room like big girls," he continued earnestly. "And once that wolf knows you're not afraid of him anymore, he probably won't come back."

As Dora and Cora gazed at each other, Wyman sensed they were communicating in that inexplicable way twins had . . . silently deciding how they would carry out his request. The one he'd decided was Dora looked him in the eye. "If the wolf says *no*, will you come to our room and talk to him?"

Wyman's lips quirked. "Jah, I can do that for you."

Their faces brightened with relief, and their sudden hugs made Wyman tingle with an overwhelming love. Alice Ann crowded in, too, and the four of them enjoyed a moment of rare sweetness—a blessing he wouldn't have known had he not married Amanda.

Wyman sighed as he gave his girls one more squeeze. "How about if Alice Ann and I gather the eggs," he said as he stood up, "while you twins empty the bucket in the outhouse and ask your mamm for some bleach so we can disinfect it? Then we'll fill the chickens' watering tanks and be done here."

Dora and Cora scampered off with the bucket, eventually to have their mamm ask them why it needed a special cleaning. Wyman smiled at the way this little incident had played out. Perhaps it would be a reason for Amanda to chuckle with him this evening when they reviewed the day's events.

He took an egg basket from its hook on the wall, smiling at Alice Ann. "How about if you find the eggs and I carry them? There's a job to fit every hand, ain't so?"

Alice Ann's laughter rang around the ceiling beams as she hurried toward the nearest nesting boxes on her short legs. While the chickens were gathered around their feeders near the doorway, she pointed eagerly to the eggs in the lower row of nesting boxes, gazing up at him with irresistible eyes. Viola's eyes.

No, they're Alice Ann's eyes. She's my child and Amanda's now.

It was a startling thought. And a little later, as Wyman walked across the road to the grain elevator to begin his workday, he felt subtle inner shiftings that signaled major changes—for himself and for his family.

Chapter 16

Amanda settled on the crowded pew bench Sunday morning and let out a sigh. Not yet eight o'clock in the morning and she was exhausted . . . frustrated . . . feeling anything but worshipful. It was a blessing to have Cora and Dora on either side of her, for she hadn't met many of the Clearwater women yet. And here in Bishop Uriah Schmucker's home, she felt all eyes were on her and her children as the newcomers—the grafted-on family that would be closely observed to see if they followed the faith the way folks in this district did.

"I'm Mildred Schmucker, married to Bishop Uriah," the woman to her left murmured. "You must be Wyman's new wife. And who are these girls in the *pink* dresses?"

"This is Dora and Cora." Amanda sensed Mildred was about to say something else about the girls' attire, so she kept talking. "Nice to meet you, Mildred. I'm Amanda, and my daughter Lizzie is sitting farther back. At thirteen, she's in her final year of school."

"Jah, Lizzie. I've heard about her, too."

A hush fell over the houseful of people. The bishop, the deacon, and the two preachers strode to the center of the huge, crowded room. Amanda took the twins' hands, the signal that they were to quit wiggling and whispering. Was it her imagination, or had the women on all sides of her looked at her girls as though they disapproved of them? How could two quiet, well-behaved four-year-olds possibly be cause for such downturned mouths?

Amanda prayed for the patience, wisdom, and strength to adjust to this new district full of strangers and different ways. She asked God for a solution to having one main bathroom, and for Jemima's inability to get out of it in a timely manner. She petitioned for restful nights and restoration of the friendship Lizzie and Vera had enjoyed before they shared a room as sisters. She had so many concerns that she was just getting warmed up, ready to pray for Wyman's sons—*her* sons now—when a man on the far side of the room sang out the beginning note of the first hymn.

The familiar words should have soothed her, for Amanda had sung this slow, steady song all her life, yet doubts pricked at her as though cockleburs had crept into her clothing. When Preacher Isaac Yoder began the first sermon, Amanda immediately missed Lamar Lapp and the ministers who served her congregation in Bloomingdale. She recalled how Sam Lambright and Vernon Gingerich had so lovingly preached her wedding service, too.

Isaac's low monotone sounded less than inspiring as he preached about absolute obedience to God. Amanda tried to focus on his message, but the room was too warm . . . the minister droned on and on . . .

She sat up with a gasp. Had someone pinched her arm? Amanda looked over to find Mildred glaring at her. *My stars, I fell asleep—and with church not even half over.*

She rubbed her forehead, putting on a smile when Cora

and Dora gazed at her with such endearing expressions. She was glad Vera was tending Alice Ann while Simon sat with his dat. Amanda wondered if Lizzie was being stared at by the girls with whom she was sitting, but she didn't dare turn around to find her daughter's face.

Going to her knees for prayer brought Amanda's attention back to the service, and singing another hymn kept her awake. But when the bishop stood to deliver the second, longer sermon, she felt as though Uriah Schmucker had singled her out for a lecture.

"'Wives, submit yourselves unto your own husbands, as unto the Lord,'" he quoted from the book of Ephesians. "'For the husband is the head of the wife, even as Christ is the head of the church . . . Therefore as the church is subject unto Christ, so let the wives be to their own husbands *in every thing*.'" Uriah then gazed right at her with his piercing eyes.

Amanda soon realized that the bishop intended to concentrate on those verses alone, rather than include the following verses about how husbands should love their wives as Christ loved the church. Hadn't the deacon read to them about how a man that loved his wife loved himself? The ministers in Bloomingdale had often preached on this passage from Ephesians, but they had held husbands as responsible as wives in keeping the faith as Christ had intended.

Oh, but this bishop and this district were going to test her before she found a way to fit in . . .

When at last the service ended, Amanda rose with the rest of the women. The twins stood on the pew bench to hug her as they waited for the women behind them to disperse into the kitchen, and Amanda's heart thrummed gratefully. Such a blessing it was to have little girls of this age, this innocence.

"I'm hungry, Mamma!"

"Jah, me, too! Church just went on and on and *on* today!"

Amanda almost chuckled—until a woman in the row behind them plucked at Dora's dress.

"You're not from around here, are you?" she demanded.

Amanda blinked, startled by her tone. "Matter of fact, I married Wyman Brubaker just a week and a half ago—"

"Your girls shouldn't be seen in this color. Pink's too bright and showy—"

"Jah, and in *church*, no less," Mildred joined in with a shake of her finger. "You'd best be sewing up *appropriate* clothes for them. And your Lizzie ought not to be wearing her dresses so short, either, or showing so much hair in front of her kapps," she went on in a sharp voice. "My daughter is Teacher Elsie, you see. She's instructed your girl about these matters, yet Lizzie refuses to obey her. That'll lead to trouble down the road. Just you wait and see."

Cora's chin was quivering. "But Mamma says we look perky in pink, like the zinnias in her garden."

"And Lizzie's my sister," Dora spoke up boldly. "We love her, and you should, too!"

The women around them could have flown to the ceiling, the way their eyebrows arched up like wings. "Ach, but that's no way for you girls to talk," Mildred chided, again shaking her finger at them.

Amanda nearly grabbed that accusing finger, even if it belonged to the bishop's wife. "They're four, you know," she replied in a strained voice. "We're adjusting to a new home, and new siblings, and—"

"As the branch is bent, so grows the tree," another woman behind them warned.

Something inside Amanda snapped. Had there ever been an unfriendlier bunch than these biddy hens who pecked at her precious daughters? She helped Cora and Dora hop off the bench into the aisle and then steered them out the kitchen door, thinking some fresh air and quiet time would be the only thing that got her through the common meal.

And there stood Lizzie. While the other young people buddied up beneath the red and gold maple trees, her daughter leaned against the house by herself, the picture of misery. As Amanda strode closer, she saw the wet tracks streaming down Lizzie's cheeks. Would they ever reach a time when this girl stopped crying?

"So, they've been picking at you, too?" Amanda murmured. The twins grabbed Lizzie and hugged her between them. "I hear the teacher's told you to wear your kapp farther forward—"

"That's just the half of it," Lizzie rasped. "Seems my dresses are too short—even though they're below my knees. It's not like we've had time to buy fabric or sew anything, even if I knew where we were going to set up the sewing machine! I've *had* it, Mamm! My stomach's in such a knot I'm going to throw up—and this *stink* isn't helping."

"Well, we can't have you getting sick." Amanda knew exactly how distraught her daughter felt, and there was no ignoring the aroma from the bishop's hog houses as she searched the crowd for her husband. When Wyman emerged from the other end of the house with the men, she slipped her arm around Lizzie's shoulders. "Come on, girls. We can't do this ever again, but we're heading home to deal with what these women are saying."

Amanda nodded at Vera, who was chatting with her friends, and walked on by without an explanation. "Wyman," Amanda said when they reached him, "Lizzie's got a stomach bug, it seems. If you'll hitch up one of our rigs, please, you and Vera and the boys can stay for the meal."

Aware that the other men were observing how he handled this situation, Wyman looked ready to challenge her—especially considering today's topic of a wife's submission. When Lizzie clutched her stomach, however, Amanda marched the girls on toward the stable and the corral. Wouldn't be the first time she'd hitched up a buggy, after all.

Her husband caught up to them, keeping his voice low. "What's this about, Amanda? I saw how upset you looked when a couple of the women were—"

"*Upset* doesn't nearly cover it," she replied tersely. "Seems we newcomers don't measure up to your district's standards. Seems I have a lot of rethinking—and sewing—and *praying* to do before the next preaching service."

Wyman's eyes widened, but he said no more. He called Dottie from among the dozens of horses and then hitched the mare to the smaller of the Brubaker rigs. When she heard a peculiar sound behind them, Amanda turned to see Jemima lurching toward them, favoring a leg.

"Grabbed your coat and mine," the older woman huffed. "Don't even *think* about leaving me here. Lord a-mercy, I'd rather be dead on the road for the buzzards to pick at."

Wyman scowled. "I can see we have some things to talk about when I get home," he murmured. "I had no idea . . . Viola never let on about these women being difficult—"

"Well, I'm not Viola. *Obviously*," Amanda retorted more vehemently than she'd intended. "Denki for not making us stay. We won't ask you to do this again."

Wyman helped Jemima into the back of the buggy while Amanda grabbed the reins. As the mare clip-clopped down the Schmuckers' long lane, she felt the other members' curious stares . . . sensed that she and her girls and Jemima would be discussed during the common meal.

But she had no control over what these people said about her and her family. Vera and the boys would have a full report when they returned home, but for the next few hours Amanda just wanted to regroup—to bind herself, her girls, and Atlee's mamm together with love so they could move forward in this difficult new district.

Once they got home, she and Lizzie unhitched the rig while Jemima took the twins inside to find something for dinner. Amanda thought glumly about the big bowl of chow-chow and the sliced ham she'd left in Mildred Schmucker's refrigerator . . . nothing fancy, but with laundry to catch up on yesterday, she hadn't had time to cook anything but their three regular meals. Would she ever reach a point where mothering this huge family felt normal?

Amanda slung her arm around Lizzie. "I had to bite my tongue when the women around me insisted the twins' pink dresses were inappropriate," she muttered. "And when Mildred Schmucker said Teacher Elsie was her daughter—"

"Oh, *jah*, I've been warned we'd be getting a visit from the bishop if I didn't *cover* myself with my kapps and dresses," Lizzie interrupted. "You'd've thought I wasn't wearing anything at all."

Amanda steered her daughter around to the front of the house. Why was it that on such a glorious autumn day, the five of them who'd lived in peace in Bloomingdale now felt so attacked? And so at odds with the world?

"This place looks lived in and loved," Amanda remarked as she gazed at the tall white house with its additions sticking out both sides. "It's been painted and kept up so well, anyone would realize that generations of Brubakers have lived *gut* lives here. Surely there's a way for us to make it our home, too. When Wyman and the rest of them get back, we need to talk about . . ."

Amanda blinked. She walked closer, focused on the screened porch as another wave of dismay washed over her. "Where's Mamm's china hutch? And the chairs Uncle Lester built? And—"

"The sewing machine!" Lizzie blurted. "How am I supposed to make new dresses if— And I don't *want* to use Viola's machine!"

"Well, those pieces have to be here somewhere. They'd *better* be!" Amanda stalked toward the machine shed, her heart throbbing uncomfortably. *Why would Wyman do this without telling me? Or is it another one of the boys' tricks? Do they despise me already?*

Into the shadowy shed she went, with Lizzie on her

heels. It smelled of the kerosene stored there. The stench of filthy rags tossed into a corner made her wrinkle up her nose, as well. Along the wall, a row of uneven shapes lurked beneath an assortment of old tarps. Lizzie gasped as a mouse scurried past them and out the open door.

Amanda yanked at the nearest tarp. As dust flew around her head, she beheld the dresser and headboard of a bedroom set Atlee had made from bird's-eye maple, the first year they were married.

She burst into tears. How was she supposed to talk to Wyman about moving her pieces into his household—*her* home now—if she had no words for yet another disappointment that cut right through to her soul?

Chapter 17

So why are the Schmuckers following us home?" Eddie murmured as the buggy rolled out of the bishop's lane and onto the blacktop.

Wyman reconsidered an answer Simon would repeat at exactly the wrong moment. "Most likely he and Mildred are . . . *concerned* about Lizzie and your mamm leaving before the meal was served," he replied carefully. He glanced at Pete and Vera in the backseat. "What can you two tell me about how Lizzie's doing? Why is she so upset all the time?"

Brother and sister exchanged a glance, neither wanting to respond first. Alice Ann, the only cheerful one among them, wiggled her fingers at him from where she sat on Vera's lap.

"I warned her that Teacher Elsie would call her out for her short dresses," Vera replied in a tight voice. "And Lizzie wants so much time to herself in the room, and— Well, it's my room, too! Even though she apologized for reading my diary, she still sniffles and looks out the window as though she'd rather be anywhere except with me!"

Pete let out a rueful laugh. "She doesn't earn any points with Teacher Elsie when she rants about how her dresses and kapps were just *fine* in Bloomingdale—and how much nicer the kids were," he said. "Lizzie doesn't come out and say so, but she liked her other teacher a lot better, too."

Wyman didn't doubt that. Elsie took after her mamm, pointing out *improvements* other people should make. Most folks speculated that Elsie had been chosen over other girls qualified for the teacher's post because she was the bishop's daughter. It seemed the young men weren't eager to court her, either, so she might remain the teacher in Clearwater for many years.

"Jah, Lizzie's a bawl-baby, all right," Simon murmured. "Doesn't like *anything* we—"

"Enough, son. That's not helpful," Wyman warned. How could he explain Lizzie's situation without seeming to condone her attitude or favor her? "Lizzie's in a difficult position. Everything in her life changed this week—her home, her school, her church, her friends," he pointed out. "And frankly, I hadn't noticed that her hemlines are any higher than yours, Vera."

Truth be told, he liked it that Amanda wore her dresses slightly shorter than Viola had. He loved her energy and admired the way she had overcome so many obstacles as a woman alone supporting a family, too. His new wife had been extremely upset when she'd left church, however, and he longed for some time alone with her before Uriah and Mildred arrived.

But there was no negotiating when the bishop of Clearwater tended his flock, and Wyman had a feeling that a few of the newer sheep were about to be chastised. He could only hope that during their time at home, Amanda, Jemima, and the girls had settled their ruffled feathers and that Lizzie wasn't sick to her stomach anymore . . . if indeed she had been physically ill. Girls that age were hard to figure out. He decided not to remind Vera of her own moods and complaints about Teacher Elsie when she'd been thirteen.

As they turned in at the lane, Uriah's rig was only twenty feet behind them. Wyman would have no time to prepare Amanda for guests . . . He recalled with a sigh that the kitchen sink had been piled high with their breakfast dishes when they'd left home, because Jemima's lengthy stint in the bathroom had made them late.

"I'd appreciate it if you boys would tend the horse and rig, and the evening chores," he said as they pulled to a halt by the barn. "And Simon, this would be a gut time to stay outside and run off Wags's energy, all right?"

"Jah, he's always ready to romp after being in his pen so long." The boy sprang down from the buggy and ran full tilt toward the backyard.

"Vera, do we have anything to offer the Schmuckers if they stay to supper?" Wyman asked.

His daughter's horrified expression confirmed his fears. "I'll try to scare something up while they're visiting with Amanda." She glanced toward the couple that was climbing down from the rig parked alongside the house. "Since we're not to be working on the Sabbath, calling for pizza delivery seems like a real gut idea. But I won't do that, of course."

Wyman laughed in spite of his misgivings about this visit. There had been times after Viola died when they'd relied on the sub and pizza place down the road for hot meals. "We'll believe that the Lord will provide," he murmured. "And we'll pray for His help with Uriah and Mildred, as well."

This was no time to mention the murmurings among some of the members about how difficult and unyielding their bishop was compared to Vernon Gingerich and the leaders of other nearby settlements. Over the past few years, while they were delivering their corn crop, a few fellows had confided that they were looking for land elsewhere—and some had moved—because Uriah had lit into them about one problem or another.

Be with us, Lord, Wyman prayed as he waited on the porch for the bishop and his wife. *After all, You caused the lot to fall upon this man, choosing him to be our leader. It's not my place to defy Your will.*

As he held the door, he saw Vera running hot water to wash the dishes. "It was a hectic morning. The eleven of us are still figuring out our get-ready-for-church routine," he explained as their guests entered the kitchen.

"You should assign everyone a time to be dressed and at the table to avoid rushing around. Especially on Sunday," Mildred stated as she scowled at the messy kitchen. "And now that you have more women here, there's no excuse for chores to go undone at the last minute. Amanda—and you, as the man of the family—need to set your house in order, Wyman."

Wyman remained silent. He felt badly for Vera, who hunched over her work at the sink. Had Abby or anyone else from Cedar Creek been visiting, they would have grabbed towels and helped his daughter rather than finding fault—but pointing that out to Mildred wouldn't improve her disposition.

"Seems mighty quiet," the bishop remarked as he peered into the front room.

"Could be that Amanda and the others are napping, as none of them were feeling well this morning," Wyman replied. "It *is* a day of rest, after all—and they didn't know you folks would be visiting."

When Uriah raised one shaggy eyebrow, Wyman realized his reply might have sounded flippant. It *was* highly unusual that the house seemed deserted at this hour, and except for the swishing of dishes in the rinse water, the only sound was Alice Ann banging together two pots she'd grabbed from the open cabinet beside the stove.

"Not now, sweet pea," Wyman murmured as he pried

the pan handles from his daughter's tiny fists. "How about if you find your dolls—or stay here to help Vera—while Dat talks to Bishop Uriah?"

As he put away the pans, Wyman desperately hoped Alice Ann's screwed-up face didn't turn into a crying fit. Where *was* everyone? Surely Amanda had heard them coming inside—

A loud *crash* downstairs, followed by his wife's voice saying, "Fine! Just fall on the floor and break, then!" answered his question about her whereabouts.

Mildred made a beeline for the basement stairs. "That didn't sound like an empty Mason jar hitting the floor—or a full one, for that matter," she remarked. "We should be sure your wife's all right, what with that broken glass to contend with."

Wyman closed his eyes. He could guess what Amanda was doing, just as he knew she would be anything but all right when the Schmuckers descended upon her. But there was nothing to do except follow the bishop and his wife into the corner of the basement where he had set her potter's wheel and the shelves for her ceramics.

"And what would these paints be for? These pots and pie plates?" Mildred demanded in a shrill voice.

"Didn't I see some of these items for sale in the Cedar Creek Mercantile?" Uriah demanded. "Couldn't believe Sam Lambright would carry such gaudy pieces in his store, and him a Plain preacher, too."

Wyman's heart sank as he caught Amanda's eye from the bottom of the stairs. *I'm sorry*, he mouthed, shrugging and shaking his head behind the Schmuckers.

Amanda stopped sweeping the colorful shards of the piece she had dropped. She gripped the broom handle, a determined expression on her face. "And gut afternoon to you, too," she said in a strained voice. "Before I married Wyman, I supported myself and my three girls by selling my pottery in shops around Bloomingdale. My first husband's lingering illness and death drained all our cash reserves."

Uriah picked up a pitcher that was painted bright red with yellow and white flowers on it. "Gut thing the Lord led you to Wyman, then," he remarked archly. "You'll have no reason to continue with this *artwork*, which is far too fancy for those of the Old Order."

"Colorful to the point of being sinful." Mildred turned to address Wyman. "Didn't Viola make a kneeling confession about her painting? Note cards and framed likenesses, as I recall."

Wyman felt his temperature rising with his temper. Why were the Schmuckers being so rude and hard-hearted? "She did."

"You should have instructed Amanda to dispose of her paints and pots before she moved them—and their worldly influence—into your home," the bishop said sharply. "I feared you were straying from the path when you married in Cedar Creek rather than in your home district, Wyman. It seems I was right. Never mind that I felt slighted when you chose Vernon Gingerich to conduct your vows."

Wyman nearly bit his tongue, keeping his retort to himself. Wasn't Uriah expressing his pride, his envy? "Preacher Sam offered us his home as—"

"And you listened to him rather than consult your own bishop?" Uriah turned sharply to glare at Amanda again. "And *you* are yet another example of how progressive ideas slither into our lives just as the serpent—the Devil—beguiled Eve in the garden. You know better than to be unpacking on the Sabbath, Amanda."

Amanda stood still, not even breathing. Her knuckles turned white on her broomstick. "You're absolutely right, bishop," she murmured. "Will you please forgive me?"

The silence in the basement nearly smothered Wyman as the seconds ticked into minutes, marked by the clock on the wall. He wasn't sure how his wife was holding her composure, but he had never loved her more or felt so in awe of her inner strength. He wanted to suggest that they all go upstairs to talk, but until the bishop responded to Amanda's plea, it wasn't anyone else's place to speak.

"Consider yourself warned, Amanda," Uriah finally stated. "Mildred and Elsie have pointed up other shortcomings concerning your daughters' clothing, I believe."

"Jah."

Mildred's eyebrows shot up, as though she expected Amanda to go down on her knees, thanking her for such constructive criticism. Amanda, however, said nothing more.

Uriah cleared his throat loudly. "We'll be watching for the recommended improvements, as a sign of your sincere effort to cleanse your soul from the influences of sin—and as the assurance that you, Wyman, are steering your wife toward her salvation, and that she has submitted to your guidance."

Wyman merely nodded, to keep from spewing out his true feelings. While he knew he should welcome the bishop's correction, it galled him that the Schmuckers had treated Amanda so harshly on her first Sunday in a new church district. "Shall we go upstairs, then?" he asked when it seemed Mildred was looking around the cellar for something more to criticize. "Maybe you'd like some coffee—"

"We wouldn't want to keep you from praying on these matters as a family," Uriah insisted, "so you can amend your attitudes and rectify these matters immediately. Next time I'm in the Cedar Creek Mercantile, I hope to see that Amanda's pottery has been removed from the shelves, as well."

Again Wyman nodded, and then followed Mildred and the bishop upstairs. It was only proper to see the Schmuckers to the door, but he wasn't surprised Amanda didn't accompany him. He stood on the porch as they stepped up into their buggy, waving briefly as they pulled away. When he entered the kitchen again, Vera was drying the last of the dishes, a distressed expression on her face.

"Well, at least it's over and they're gone," she murmured.

"And they didn't tell Amanda to make a confession next preaching Sunday," Wyman said.

"*Yet,*" his daughter replied. "Remember how it was with Mamm? They told her to put away her paints, and not two days later Uriah was back to inform her she'd be on her knees at a members' meeting."

"I'd forgotten that part. He came when I was at the elevator." Wyman sighed, feeling drained and exhausted, but there was a lot of talking to do yet. "We Brubakers will have to pull together. Can you help Lizzie make some new dresses in the next couple days? And lend her some of yours in the meantime? Tall as you are, your dresses should be long enough, ain't so?"

"I can do that, *jah*. Should have thought of it myself." Vera draped the wet dish towel over the drying rack. "I'll go upstairs and have her try some on."

"Denki, Vera. I appreciate your help."

She held his gaze for a moment, looking so much like her mother that it clutched at his heart. "If we put Jemima's pie safe over on that far wall, can we leave the rest of the kitchen as it is?"

While he was pleased his daughter wanted to prevent any further injuries, Wyman knew a loaded question when he heard one. "That's between you and Amanda. You three cooks need to figure out where things will go," he said. "As long as gut meals are put on and the room's set to rights afterward, I'm satisfied."

Vera nodded, not entirely happy but accepting his answer.

"After you help Lizzie try on dresses, get together with the boys and call in an order for pizza and some hot subs," he suggested. "We've got a lot to discuss, and having food delivered means none of us has to *work*, jah?"

Her grin lifted his spirits. Wyman wished something as simple as a store-bought supper would make Amanda feel better, too. As he returned to the basement, he prayed that his new wife would willingly comply with the bishop's wishes instead of burying her resentment where it would fester. Few folks realized how much of herself Viola had sacrificed, for she had put on a faithful face at church and among her friends. The last thing Wyman wanted was for the same dark cloud to settle over Amanda—and therefore over him and the entire family.

Where does a man draw the line between following his faith and fostering the welfare of his family? The question weighed heavily on him as he went downstairs to find Amanda sitting on the old couch, muffling her sobs.

What have I done to her? Was I wrong to believe Amanda would be the solution to my problems?

Wyman drew her into his arms. At least she didn't push him away but instead cried out her frustrations against his shoulder. This wasn't how he'd envisioned Amanda as she ran his household and raised his kids, but he'd witnessed such deep disappointment before . . . and felt grateful for his experience with Viola's low moods. He couldn't have handled this emotional overload as a new groom of twenty.

"I'm sorry, Amanda," he murmured, wishing his apology could wipe away the pain the Schmuckers had inflicted. "I couldn't say no when Uriah insisted on a visit. I should've warned you that he'd object to your pottery before you brought it here."

Amanda raised her head, sniffling. "But I knew about Viola's pictures," she rasped. "And when I met Uriah and suspected he'd tell me to put away my work . . . I took my pieces to Sam's store, thinking I'd find them homes rather than packing them away forever."

Wyman held her until her crying subsided. What a fine woman she was, not to whine or make excuses. Amanda deserved his understanding, even as he reminded her that he was responsible for the Brubaker family—and was its chief decision maker. In that sense, Viola had been easier.

She had never been the breadwinner, and had never tasted the independence that came from living without a man.

"The kids have ordered pizza and subs," he murmured, hoping this would ease her most immediate concern. "I have a solution for our bathroom problem, as well, I think. Shall we discuss it over supper?"

Amanda mopped her blotchy face with her apron. "Jah, that would be fine."

"And Vera's going to lend Lizzie some dresses until they can sew her some new ones," Wyman continued in an upbeat voice. "So, see? We'll figure it out, my love. We'll shed our tears, but our joy *will come*. Do you believe that, Amanda?"

She peered at him through swollen, red-rimmed eyes. Again, it wasn't the vision Wyman had imagined for his wife of a week, but at least she was looking at him. "Jah. We'll make it work."

"I love you, Amanda."

She nodded, straightening her kapp and smoothing her crumpled apron. "Jah, there's that. Let's go upstairs."

It wasn't the response he'd hoped for, but then this wasn't the sort of Sunday he'd figured on, either. Days like this had their purpose, however. *When you're down and out, the only way to go is up.*

Chapter 18

Early Monday morning Abby entered the mercantile's back room and shivered. A cold front had blown through in the night, so she turned on the furnace to take the chill off the large open rooms of the store. She made a mental note to ask Sam about getting the propane tank refilled, and realized it was time to order the jimmies, spices, and baking supplies for the upcoming holidays. So many things to remember, now that she often ran the store while her brother tended to his duties as a preacher.

About an hour before opening time, the bell above the door jingled. "Merle, gut morning to you!" she called out from the freezer case she was stocking. "You're up before the sun today."

He scratched his head, looking around as though he'd forgotten why he'd come.

Abby tucked her box of bagged fruits into the freezer and went over to help him. James's dat loved to shop—sometimes to get away from Eunice's watchful eye—so it was Abby's mission to be sure he didn't buy items they wouldn't use. "Does Emma need something for your breakfast?" she asked.

"What Emma needs, I can't give her," Merle teased as he reached for Abby's hand. "But *you* can help me. Eunice has a birthday coming up, and I don't have the foggiest notion what to give her. It's not like I can make her some little surprise, because she'll see me working on it."

Abby squeezed his gnarled hand. It was always a fine day when Merle's memory and sense of humor were working at the same time. "Gut thing you reminded me. I'd feel awful if October twenty-ninth went by and I didn't have a little something for her, too." As she gazed around the store, a splash of color caught her eye. "How about a piece of Amanda Brubaker's pottery? Something new and cheerful for the kitchen—"

"Jah, *new* and *cheerful* would be improvements."

"—or we have some of Zanna's braided rugs. Or maybe a dress," Abby suggested. "I could sew up a couple before then, if you'd like."

"I'll take a quick look at that pottery before anybody realizes I'm not tending the horses," he whispered, as though his absence was a secret between him and Abby. "Might have to come back a few times to finally decide, you know."

Abby smiled at his wily idea. "I can wrap your gift and keep it in the back room for you. That way Eunice won't find it."

"Gut idea. If she thinks I'm not getting her anything, she'll be madder than a wet hen, saying I *forgot* again."

As Merle ambled toward the pottery display, Abby hoped that, come time for presenting his wife's gift, he would remember that he'd bought her one. She went back to stocking her frozen food, occasionally glancing Merle's way. It was something to see, the way his face lit up as he lifted each pitcher, bowl, and pie plate. Amanda had a true gift for raising peoples' spirits with her bright colors, and several of her pieces had already sold.

"I've narrowed it down to three," he called to her a few minutes later. "I'd best get on home now, Abby. Denki for your help."

"Have a wonderful-gut day, Merle."

Abby went upstairs to her Stitch in Time nook to do some sewing before any more customers came in. It felt good to focus on the easy straight stitching for the table-cloths she was making for a banquet center in Kirksville. She heard the back door open and close.

"I'm going to fill bags of pasta and spices, Abby," her niece Gail called out. "I'll work in the supply room."

"Is Sam coming in this morning?"

"He went over to Vernon's. No telling how long he'll be."

That was the way of it for Plain preachers, no matter how they made their living. As Abby eased another length of the linen-like fabric beneath the needle of her sewing machine, her body swayed with the rhythm of pumping the treadle. When the bell above the door tinkled, she was focused on finishing the last few inches of a hem.

"Dat! Nobody's in the store!" a child's voice echoed in the high-ceilinged room.

Abby looked over the railing, and then spoke in a spooky voice. "Siiimon Bruuuuubaker! I seeee you!"

The little boy's head bobbed until he caught sight of her. "Whatcha doin' way up there, Abby? Dat and Eddie and me, we came for lumber and pipes to build us boys a new bathroom, out in the barn!"

Abby rose from her chair, not surprised at this news. "That sounds like quite a project, and I bet you're going to help with it," she replied. "I'm on my way down."

"Don't leave your sewing, Abby," Wyman said. "We'll find Sam—"

"Not this morning, you won't." Most men preferred to

deal with her brother, so Abby hoped to show the Brubakers that she was almost as proficient in the hardware and plumbing departments as Sam was. Once downstairs, she found Wyman studying the display of Amanda's ceramics with an odd look on his face. "Your wife's pieces are selling fast. We're happy to have them," she remarked.

"The bishop has told her to stop making her pottery," he said sadly. "Says her pieces are too worldly—and he wants them taken off your shelves, too."

That explained why Uriah Schmucker had been in such a sour mood last time he'd been here. "I'm sorry to hear that," Abby murmured. "We're really blessed that Vernon Gingerich isn't averse to bright colors."

"Could you possibly box up her pieces this morning, Abby? It'll save Amanda the disappointment of having to do it herself."

With a sigh, Abby went to the checkout counter where they kept the inventory notebook. As she'd thought, nearly half of Amanda's pieces had already sold. "I suppose we'd better pack the wind chimes and necklaces Vera made, too, and—"

Abby frowned. What should she do about Merle's birthday present for Eunice? She did *not* want to deprive that dear man of the joy Amanda's pottery would bring . . . even if it meant defying Clearwater's bishop. "May I keep her pottery in the back room until a customer decides on a gift? I'd feel bad for him—and for Amanda—if he couldn't choose what he wants."

Wyman's eyebrows rose. "So, folks really like her pottery?"

"Oh, they're snapping it up! I can't tell you how happy I feel, looking at those pretty pieces whenever I pass the display," she added ruefully. "It's troublesome that God created the flowers and the sky and the rainbow, yet so many Old Order folks believe those colors are too showy."

"You said that just right, Abby," Wyman said. "Meanwhile, I've got a list of supplies so Eddie can start on our new, um, men's room. The upstairs bathroom is a busy place with five extra women."

"I can believe that," she agreed as they walked past the gardening tools.

"We were nearly late to church Sunday," Wyman went on. "And when you consider the bishop's surprise visit after the service, when the breakfast dishes were still in the sink—plus the black marks Mildred Schmucker tallied in her imaginary book about Amanda's pottery and Lizzie's shorter dresses—it wasn't one of our better days."

"Oooh, that's not gut," Abby said with a commiserating grimace. "Let's get you fixed up and on your way."

"I'll tell Amanda what you've said about her pottery. And denkl so much for listening, Abby," Wyman said. "It's gut to have a friend in the faith who understands how folks get pulled in opposite directions sometimes."

"Jah, gut isn't always white and evil isn't always black, ain't so?"

Eddie had loaded pipes, a faucet, and a sink into a pull cart, so it didn't take much longer to find the rest of the items on their list. "This should build us a simple shower stall and a place to wash—"

"Dat!" Simon piped up from the other side of the aisle. "You can't forget *this*!"

Abby fought a grin. She had a feeling Simon was being his busy, curious, funny self—and indeed, he was sitting on the model toilet in the plumbing display, grinning as he swung his legs.

Wyman snatched him off the seat. "Simon, if you can't behave I'm going to—"

"But, Dat! Why would we shower in the barn but then go out to the stinky old privy to—"

As Wyman clapped a hand over his youngest son's mouth, Eddie snickered. "He's got a point, Dat. This winter, we'll be wishing all the fixtures were indoors."

"And that was my intent all along, but I forgot to write it

on the list. I don't have *anything* on my mind these days."
As the two boys hefted a new toilet onto the cart, he leaned closer to Abby. "At least Simon hadn't dropped his drawers to *use* your model."

"Jah, there's that," she replied with a chuckle. "No harm done. Anything else you might need?"

"I'm sure Eddie'll be making another trip for things we didn't think of, but for now we're gut to go."

By the time Wyman paid his bill, other folks were coming in to shop. Adah Ropp picked up a box of granola bars on her way to work at the Fisher Cheese Factory. The Coblentz twins chatted excitedly as they fingered the colorful necklaces Vera Brubaker had made, and both girls decided to buy one.

"Might as well have some fun wearing these while we can," Mary said as she fished money from her apron pocket.

"Jah, our rumspringa won't last forever," Martha replied as she dropped her necklace over her head. "Just you wait. All the girls in our buddy bunch'll be wanting one when they see ours."

Abby smiled at their youthful exuberance. When the twins left, the silence in the store gave her time to think about events at the Brubaker place. What an awful weekend it must have been for Amanda. Abby regretted having to box up the pottery pieces and jewelry, but Uriah Schmucker would make things more unpleasant for the whole Brubaker family if Amanda didn't comply with his instructions.

After she carefully placed the pitchers, bowls, and pie plates in a couple of boxes, she carried them to the back room where Gail was working. "When Merle comes looking for these, we'll let him choose what he wants. Otherwise, we're not supposed to sell them anymore."

"Jah, I heard Wyman talking about that." Gail was seventeen, and she'd gotten to be good friends with Vera lately. She looked up from the barrel of rolled oats she was scooping into gallon plastic bags. "Do you suppose Amanda and the girls will do all right in Clearwater? They're off to a rough start."

Abby sighed. It wouldn't be proper to express her opinion of Uriah Schmucker. "Amanda's made it through a lot tougher ordeals than this, and Wyman's doing his best to help everyone adjust. They'll work it all out."

"But will they be happy?"

Now *there* was a question every woman pondered and few dared to express. While it was the right thing to marry, and obligatory to obey the bishop and one's husband, and to give up personal pleasures for the good of the family . . . was there a point where such sacrifice became more of a burden than a blessing?

What would happen if Amanda reached that point?

And what will you do if Vernon—or Sam or James—tells you to give up your Stitch in Time business after you marry? What if you're no longer allowed to work here in the mercantile? Wives are to stay home and become mothers.

As Abby went back upstairs to sew her tablecloths, these thoughts circled in her mind. She loved James with all her heart, and she yearned to become a mother, but . . . she also wanted to *choose* how she spent her days. The ability to decide her future had been the biggest advantage of remaining a maidel, and it would be the most difficult part of her life to give up when she married.

It's a gut thing James and I made up after Sam caught us kissing, she thought as she pumped the sewing machine's treadle. *Now we have another important topic to talk about . . .*

Chapter 19

James gazed across the county road at the splendor of the maple and sweet gum trees on Sam Lambright's place. Was it his imagination, or did the fall foliage shine with special brilliance this year? As the late-afternoon sun turned the sky a deep morning-glory blue, those trees seemed to catch fire and glow.

Like Abby glows, with a beauty only God could bestow, he thought as he crossed the blacktop. Abby had invited him and Emma over for supper tonight, saying Gail and Sam would work the final shift at the mercantile, so he had declared an early quitting time at the carriage shop. Invitations like this weren't to be wasted; he figured on spending some time alone with Abby while Emma helped their parents with an early supper. Before his sister arrived at Abby's, he hoped to *finally* pop the question—

Jerome Lambright came cantering up the road on a spirited bay gelding with a black mane and tail. "James! Gut afternoon!" he called out.

"And what brings you to Cedar Creek on this fine day?" James smiled despite the urgency of his mission at Abby's.

Jerome's horse pranced as he dismounted. "I've come to ignore your sister while I visit with your folks," he teased.

James laughed. He had to admire this fellow's strategy, because Emma was equally as set on ignoring Jerome—or at least she *said* she had no interest in him. "Between you, me, and the fence post," James murmured, "Emma will be going to Abby's house for supper in about half an hour. I'm sure Abby would be tickled if you'd make it a double date."

"What a fine idea. Your sister would refuse to have dinner with *me*, but she won't back out of Abby's invitation, ain't so?"

"That's how I see it, jah."

Jerome clapped James on the shoulder, grinning. "You're a gut man, Graber. I owe you for this one."

Jah, you do, James thought as he saw his private time with Abby slipping away. But if it meant Emma got out of the house for an evening with friends *and* had a chance to get better acquainted with Jerome, he'd done a brotherly good deed.

"I'll go tell Abby you're coming," he said. "The folks'll be real happy to see you. Dat hasn't stopped talking about his ride on that fancy wagon with your mules."

"It was a great day for all of us," Jerome agreed. "Pass along my appreciation to Abby for setting another place at her table. And thanks for being a gut sport, James. You've got your own courting to do, after all."

"See you in a few, then. But take your time," James added with a purposeful smile. "Dat will be happy to talk your leg off."

As Jerome led his bay up the drive, James jogged past the phone shanty and down Lambright Lane. He hadn't checked for messages today, but this was no time to let business or the phone detain him. It was a rare treat to eat dinner in Abby's cozy little home, and he didn't want to waste a minute he could be spending with her.

Once again the key phrases whirled in his mind. *Abby, so many times I've tried to ask you . . .* but that sounded like he was making excuses.

I love you so much, Abby. Will you marry me? Was that too abrupt? Did he need to lead up to it with some sort of endearment?

Will you do me the honor of becoming my wife? That seemed awfully formal. Abby was a down-to-earth woman. She wouldn't require such a high tone . . .

But he could miss his chance—again—to propose to her if he fussed with the wording. He wanted to hold her close and kiss her first, but after the way Sam had warned them last week about getting too physical, he couldn't take the chance that someone would see them through the window. And he'd be a fool to ignore Abby's plea for less public affection—especially since Emma and Jerome would be coming at any moment.

James knocked on Abby's front door, his heart in his throat. The rapid patter of her footsteps announced her approach, and he braced himself, praying he wouldn't sound like a fool when he bared his soul to her.

"James, you're just in time," Abby gasped as she threw open her door. "A bird's flown down my chimney! I don't dare open the fireplace doors to catch him, for fear he'll fly all over the house."

How was it that *something* always happened at just the wrong moment every time they were alone together? James considered his options as he approached the fireplace, where a forlorn *peep . . . peep* greeted him from behind the glass doors. A sparrow hopped around on the cast-iron grate, probably wondering how he'd gotten himself into such a fix.

"I don't suppose you have a butterfly net," he said. "Dat's fishing net might work, but if the bird got through those holes . . ."

"What about this?" Abby hurried into her kitchen and

then came back carrying a large mesh strainer with a long handle.

"Jah, I think I can make that work," he said as he pictured the maneuver in his mind. "But I'll need you to toss a kitchen towel over the open side of the strainer real quick, just as I bring the bird out between the glass doors. Think you can do that?"

"Let me grab a towel."

As James considered the best way to corner the bird and catch it without any of them getting hurt or more frightened than necessary, he inhaled the aroma of dinner in the oven . . . ham, by the smell of it, along with something sweet and flavored with cinnamon. The homey aromas made him hunger for the time when he would come home each evening to dinner and Abby.

Considering how most Amish couples announced their betrothal and tied the knot a few weeks later, he could be living his dream by Thanksgiving—and what a wonderful thing to give thanks for. It wasn't as though one of them would have to relocate, as Amanda Lambright had done . . . wouldn't take much effort to move his clothes and a few belongings here into Abby's little nest, which would be his preference over living with Emma and his folks. He'd be just minutes away from his parents and the carriage shop—

Abby stopped beside him with the towel, smiling as she anticipated this adventure. "Ready?"

Jah, I'm ready, sweet lady. You don't know the half of it, James thought. But he focused on the bird in the fireplace, praying his rescue effort succeeded the first time. "We'll hope the sparrow knows this is for his own gut and not to scare him," he said. "Once you've draped the towel over the open end of the strainer, I'll be hurrying to the door. You'd best stand to the other side of me."

"Jah, gut idea. We can do this, James."

His nerves stilled as her confident voice soothed him.

James gripped the strainer handle, slowly opening the fire-place doors as he crouched. The bird hopped along the grate ahead of the open side of the strainer, just as he'd hoped . . . and as the sparrow reached the end of its perch, James gently caught him against the inner wall of the fire-place. "So far, so gut. Now for the tricky part."

"I'm praying for the both of you," Abby whispered.

As she stood poised with her towel, Abby's rapt expression was yet another reason James loved her. He eased the strainer to the edge of the bricks beside the hinge of the glass doors. "Okay, now, fold back the other door so it's out of the way. I'm bringing it out . . . jah, just like—"

At exactly the right moment, Abby tucked her towel around the top of the strainer and then covered the entire opening. "Got it?"

James grabbed the ends of the towel with his free hand, grinning. "If you'll open the door—"

Abby sprinted ahead of him, as giddy with victory as he was. When he'd stepped outside, he turned the opening of the strainer away from him, stooped, and let the towel drop near the ground. The bird let out a *peep* and fluttered toward the nearest tree, as though it hadn't been the least bit concerned for its safety.

"Oh, James, that was the best favor you've done me," Abby gushed as she grabbed his hand between hers. "We make a gut team, ain't so?"

The moment begged for him to pop that all-important question, yet as James gazed into Abby's eyes, he temporarily forgot how to speak. What a blessed man he was, having such a caring, compassionate, and beautiful woman at his side. "Abby, I—"

"Abby! James! We've got an idea, and you'll want to be in on it!"

Emma was hurrying toward them, well ahead of Jerome, who strode along with the air of a fellow whose mission was going exactly as he'd hoped. James had to chuckle. "By the way," he murmured to Abby, "I invited Jerome to join us for dinner a few minutes ago. I hope that's all right."

"It's more than all right," she murmured. "We've all got your sister right where we want her." Then she waved gleefully at the oncoming couple. "And what might you two be cooking up? Come inside while I tend to our dinner. We've had a little distraction."

Just that easily, Abby had adjusted her plans. James opened the door and she scurried into the kitchen, swung open the oven, and retrieved the blue enamel roasting pan between two pot holders. She lifted the lid with a flourish.

"Ah, gut. Still enough broth for making gravy," she announced. "And nothing's burnt."

"Oh, your ham loaf—my favorite!" Emma set down the canister she'd brought along. "Let me get that baked pineapple out, and the potatoes. You've got enough for quite a crowd here, Abby."

"Cook once, eat twice—or more." Abby lifted the ham loaf onto a platter and then turned on the burner beneath the roaster. "If you fellows would get our salad out of the fridge and pour some water, we'll be ready to eat in two shakes of that sparrow's tail."

By the time James told his sister and Jerome about rescuing the bird, a fourth place had been set and the meal was on the table. After their silent prayer, James passed the ham loaf, inhaling its savory-sweet aroma. What with a three-bean salad plus fresh cinnamon-swirl bread, the meal seemed like quite a feast for a woman who had spent most of her day at the mercantile.

"Denki so much for this dinner, Abby," Emma murmured across the small table. "Dat's having one of his forgetful days, and Mamm's all the fussier because of it."

"We're glad you two could join us," Abby answered. "So what's the idea you were so excited about?"

Emma brightened, spooning ham gravy over her baked potato. "It's Jerome's idea, truth be told. When Dat men-

tioned that Mamm's birthday was coming up, Jerome took
me aside and whispered that we should have a surprise
party. That's especially true because she'll be eighty."

"And we can't miss *that*," Jerome chimed in. "The trick
will be keeping it a secret. Your mamm's sharp enough to
catch on if she overhears any plans."

"So we're having her party over here—at Sam's place,"
Abby declared. She got up to look at the wall calendar.
"The twenty-ninth is a Thursday, too. How perfect is that?
We can invite the neighbors, and your sisters' families from
Queen City and—" Abby's eyes widened with an inspira-
tion. "The Brubakers, too. If anyone needs a gathering of
friends, it's Amanda and Wyman."

James reached for a slice of the soft, swirled bread.
"Trouble at their place? Already?"

As Abby recounted the incident with Uriah Schmucker,
James recalled being a kid when the lot had fallen to Uriah,
and the Clearwater bishop and his wife seemed to be getting . . . crabbier. While a lot of folks did that as they
aged—and this was God's plan, or it wouldn't happen with
such regularity—James sensed that the crusty old bishop
was making an example of the blended Brubaker family.
Several folks had moved away from Uriah's district over the
years for this very reason . . .

"Jah, we should invite them," Emma was saying. "Could
be Sam and Vernon will have advice about dealing with the
Schmuckers. It's not a nice thing to say, but Mildred is such
a meddler!"

"And if Uriah's telling Aunt Amanda to put up her pottery and let down her girls' dresses—" Jerome raised his
expressive eyebrows. "That's not going to set so well. She's
got bigger fish to fry, convincing all those kids to get
along—not to mention looking after Jemima. I hope Uriah's decree doesn't backfire."

The four of them ate in thoughtful silence for a moment.
When Emma went to fetch the dessert she'd brought, James

noticed how much happier she seemed. Was she secretly pleased that Jerome had come to Cedar Creek this evening? Or was she merely enjoying the company of friends after a difficult day of caring for their parents?

"This party for Mamm is a wonderful-gut idea," James remarked as he caught the last crumbles of his ham loaf in the tines of his fork. "We should probably keep the planning amongst us four—and Sam and Barbara," he added as he glanced at Abby. "If Dat knows, he'll let the cat out of the bag when he gets excited."

"And that way the party will be a nice surprise for him, too." Abby rose to scrape their dinner plates, a smile lighting her face.

As James watched her performing the ordinary task of clearing the table, his heart thrummed. What other prospective wife could possibly love and understand his parents the way Abby did? When he'd planned to marry her younger sister, his biggest concern had been Zanna's youth, because when Emma married, he and his wife might well be taking over Mamm and Dat's daily care. God had indeed been at work when Zanna had run off the morning of the wedding, and James was grateful for the way his life was working out these days.

"Oh, you brought your lemon bars, Emma! They're my favorite," Abby said. "Let me put on water for tea, and we'll take our sweet time enjoying our treats. What a wonderful-gut evening this is turning out to be."

James smiled. He couldn't have said it any better himself.

Chapter 20

As Amanda washed the dishes from Thursday morning's baking session, she stared forlornly out the window. *Lord, I hate to complain, but this cold, drizzly weather—for three days straight—is wearing on all of us.* Wyman was at the elevator, Lizzie and Pete had gone to school, Eddie was working on the bathroom in the barn, and Vera had taken the younger children on her shopping trip, so Jemima was pouring out her frustrations while just the two of them were at home.

"Those older boys should pick up their room every day," she declared as she formed dough into dinner rolls. "And Simon claims he keeps that mutt outdoors, but you can't fool me! I hear those paws going clickety-clack—"

Amanda smiled wryly. She knew Simon sneaked Wags into bed with him, but Wyman had allowed it as a comfort after the boy's mother had died. *She* didn't want to be the one who tried changing such a habit.

"—and if he's allowed to keep fibbing about it, he'll come to no gut end." Jemima gingerly propped one foot on the small stool she kept by the pie safe. "The twins think Simon's the cat's meow, so they're going to copy what he does, Amanda. And Alice Ann follows everything Cora and Dora do. Before long, we'll have quite a problem."

Amanda didn't have the heart to reply. As raindrops trickled down the murky windowpane, she realized they needed to wash all the windows before winter set in . . . but what an overwhelming job, for a house as large as this one. Jerome had always taken on that chore at the other place, easily climbing the tall ladder required to wash the windows on the outside . . .

"And why do you suppose Wyman put the pie safe on the wall farthest from the oven?" Jemima demanded in a rising voice. "It's all I can do to stand on my feet kneading the dough, and then I have to cross this big kitchen to bake it, as well!"

Amanda reminded herself to be kind, because rainy days weren't easy for her mother-in-law. "Have you taken some of your arthritis-strength aspirin?" She opened the oven door when Jemima picked up two pans of caramel rolls that had risen.

"Are you telling me I'm being a pain? I hope you never get the rheumatism, Amanda."

With a sigh, Amanda looked at the older woman. Jemima's kapp was askew and her bun was coming unwound, sure signs she was having trouble with her hands today, as well as her feet. "Why not sit in the recliner for a while and I'll watch these rolls for you? I can bring you some tea."

"So now you want me to be *useless*?" came Jemima's retort. "Bad enough that I feel like a fifth wheel here, amongst these Brubaker kids who don't much like me. Am I supposed to call Wyman's bunch my grandchildren even though they're not related to me? I just don't know what to do anymore!"

I know that feeling. It seemed that no matter what Amanda said, it was wrong, so she kept quiet after Jemima slid the coiled, sweet-smelling rolls into the oven.

"Admit it, Amanda," her mother-in-law muttered. "We might've been watching every dime, but life was a lot easier on the home place. If Atlee hadn't been so dead set against getting his wound tended, he'd still be with us, and we'd have none of these problems to contend with."

"We all make our choices. We all have to deal with change," Amanda replied wearily. "Wyman's a gut man, doing his best to—"

"Shh! Here comes Vera with the kids."

Footsteps clattered on the porch and the kitchen door burst open. Simon led the parade with a tote bag of groceries in each hand and a sucker stick protruding from his mouth.

"We're back, Mamm!" Cora chirped from behind a bundle of toilet paper that was nearly as big as she was.

"Vera let us pick out candy," her twin chimed in. "I got root beer barrels."

"And I picked red-hot cinnamon disks!" Cora said.

Amanda gazed in dismay at Alice Ann, whose entire right side was covered with mud. "What happened to you, angel?" She opened her arms, but the toddler's lower lip quivered as she turned toward her oldest sister instead.

Vera came in last, carrying two loaded tote bags in each hand. "The parking lot at Miller's Market is full of puddles, and Alice Ann found one," she remarked as she set her bags on the table. "I'll clean her up, Amanda. Meanwhile, Dat's gotten a message on his office phone you might want to hear, about a party in Cedar Creek!"

"A party? A message like that might be a gut excuse to pester your dat, ain't so?" Amanda remarked. "I can't think many farmers are hauling grain in this wet weather, so it's not like I'd be taking him away from his work." Even in the rain, a walk to the elevator sounded like a welcome break from Jemima's complaining—and Amanda would rather hear about the party now than wait until Wyman came home this evening.

She slipped into her coat and bonnet before anyone

could detain her. She grabbed an umbrella and then strode along the gravel lane, avoiding the puddles. With everything else that seemed to be going wrong today, the last thing she needed was squishy shoes.

Once across the highway, Amanda went around to the back of the little frame building that sat in the shadow of the elevator's towering grain bins. When she tapped on the door, Wyman smiled and waved her in.

"I *thought* our invitation to Cedar Creek might get your attention," he teased as he rose from his old chair. "It was a plot to lure you over here while Ray and Tyler are running errands, you see. How's your day been, Amanda?"

Why spoil his playful mood by telling of Jemima's aches and pains? When her husband opened his arms, Amanda stepped into them. "It's ever so much better now," she whispered before he kissed her. "Jemima's baking and Vera's done the shopping, so who am I to complain?"

Wyman studied her face as though he didn't quite believe her. But he, too, refrained from ruining these rare moments they had together. "Our message was waiting when I came in this morning, from Abby Lambright."

"It's always gut news when it's from Abby."

"Seems she and Emma and James are planning a surprise party for Eunice's eightieth birthday, and they'd like us to join them," he went on. "It's next Thursday, on the twenty-ninth. I don't have any plans then. Do you? For such a special occasion as that, I can ask Ray and Tyler to handle any grain we get that day."

Amanda's heart fluttered, not only at this invitation but at the expression on Wyman's face. He was such a handsome man, and so eager to please her. "I have plans now," she replied brightly. "Did Abby say what we were to bring?"

"Here—listen for yourself." Wyman handed her the receiver and punched the PLAY button of the phone's message machine.

Amanda listened to Abby's lilting voice and felt her

mood lifting with every word. Wasn't it just like Sam's family to host another gathering, even if it wasn't for one of their own? Amanda was tempted to replay the message for another dose of sunshine on this dreary morning. "What a wonderful idea for celebrating Eunice's birthday," she said as she hung up. "And how nice of them to include us."

"Vera's tickled that Abby asked her to bring a pan of her mac and cheese." Wyman smiled boyishly. "When she mentioned goodies, I thought of those raisin cookies you made when we were courting. Could you bake some for the party, and save some back for me?"

Amanda swallowed a sigh. Those cookies were twice the work, as they required cutting two circles of dough for each cookie, filling them with the thickened raisins, and then crimping all the way around the edge with a fork—and the younger kids didn't like them. "For you, I could probably arrange that," she answered lightly. "I'll bake another kind for the kids. We'll go through a lot of cookies even with a birthday cake there."

"You're the best, Amanda," he murmured as he held her close.

Why can't it be this easy all the time? Amanda lingered in his arms, soothed by the patter of rain on the tin roof. "I'd better get back and start dinner," she murmured. "You and Eddie will want more than the rolls and soup Jemima and I have been making."

"I'll be home in about an hour," Wyman said. "Most of the harvest has been brought in, so I'm catching up on the accounting work—which means I'll have more time to spend with *you* now. And the kids, of course."

Feeling much better than when she'd left the house, Amanda stepped outside with her umbrella. The rain had almost stopped, and with mist hovering in the low-lying areas behind the house, the day had taken on an ethereal beauty despite the clouds. As she crossed the highway, she noticed a black buggy parked at the house. She wasn't yet familiar with the neighbors' rigs, so she walked faster, hoping guests would raise Jemima's spirits. If these folks stayed for dinner, they could add another quart of tomatoes to the soup . . .

As she ascended the porch steps, however, Amanda's heart sank. Through the window she saw Mildred Schmucker, once again pointing that finger of hers—this time at Vera. Oh, but she wished the bishop and his wife would leave them be. She opened the door, praying for a civil tongue and wise counsel from God.

"—so it makes no difference if you're using your rumspringa as an excuse to make necklaces from Amanda's pottery," the bishop's wife was saying in her reedy voice. "You *know* it's not our way to wear jewelry! The larger danger is that your example will influence the way your younger brother and sisters grow up."

As Amanda closed her umbrella, she was tempted—just for an unholy moment—to poke Mildred with its tip, or to splash her with rainwater by pushing it open again. "Hullo, Mildred," she said as she hung up her wraps. "What brings you out on such a drizzly day?"

The bishop's wife pivoted on her heel. "Your pottery," she spat. "You agreed to remove it from the stores in Cedar Creek, but when I was in Treva's Greenhouse today, Vera's wind chimes and jewelry were prominently displayed. So, not only have you defied Uriah's instructions, you have led Vera astray with your artwork, as well."

Amanda glanced apologetically at Vera, who stood by the sink with her hands clasped and her head bowed. Jemima, too, looked flummoxed as she sat on the small bench near her pie safe.

"That was an oversight on my part," Amanda replied in a strained voice. "Wyman had my dishes removed from the mercantile, but I forgot about Vera's pieces at the greenhouse. The blame is entirely mine, not hers."

"Oh, but Vera's seventeen. Old enough to be joining the

church and setting aside pastimes that lead to perdition."
The bishop's wife took a deep breath, as though to launch
into another tirade, but then an ominous *crash* in the cellar
made them all look toward the stairs.

As Wags loped out of the stairwell, Amanda ruefully
noticed the muddy paw prints already on the kitchen floor.
The rapid patter of feet preceded Simon's appearance, with
the twins following close behind him. All three children
wore fearful expressions, which intensified when they saw
her standing there.

"Wasn't our fault—honest." Simon hurried past Mildred
and into the front room, whistling for his dog.

"We only did what the bishop said," Cora added in a
quavering voice.

"Jah, we didn't break a thing," her sister insisted as the
two of them hurried behind Simon.

Amanda scowled. This fiasco would only escalate if she
demanded an explanation in front of Mildred. "You girls
are to sit on the sofa until I say differently," she instructed
in the calmest voice she could muster. "Simon, put your
dog outside. And then you're to sit with the girls, understand me?"

"Jah, Mamma," the twins replied as one.

"I will," Simon murmured.

The children did as they were told, but as Amanda
watched them, her heart pounded so loudly that Mildred
could surely hear it. And of course the heavier, slower footsteps ascending the stairs could only belong to Uriah
Schmucker.

What had he been doing downstairs? Snooping to see if
she'd packed away her pottery, no doubt—and intimidating
the kids in her absence. Oh, but that galled her! Never had
she met a bishop with so much nerve.

Once again Amanda prayed for support. Why had she
again been chosen to bear the brunt of Uriah's vindictive
nature? Jemima's caramel rolls smelled like they were

scorching, but neither Amanda nor her mother-in-law nor Vera dared to move as the bishop stepped into sight.

"You didn't trust me to put away my ceramics?" Amanda asked in a taut voice.

Uriah surveyed the kitchen with a disapproving frown. Then he focused on her with eyes as hard as marbles. "I knew Wyman would carry out my instructions. But because those packed boxes remain in your cellar—with pieces of your work still in Treva Lambright's store—you haven't really given up your art. You have *not* obeyed me, Amanda," he went on in a rising voice. "So perhaps a kneeling confession in the presence of all our members will be the more effective means to rid you of this deeply ingrained sin."

"We can only hope Vera will learn from your mistake—cloak herself in contrition before she falls as far," Mildred chimed in.

Amanda didn't know whether to protest or to cry. She was so tired of crying. And she had seen enough of this self-righteous couple for one day, too. "Denki for coming," she muttered, gesturing toward the door. "I have children to discipline."

"And I'd best be taking my rolls from the oven," Jemima said as she rose stiffly from her bench.

The Schmuckers looked incensed that they were being dismissed, but Amanda was beyond caring what they thought. Her insides were churning, and she couldn't tolerate another minute of their presence in her home.

Or IS this your home? If you stay in Clearwater, you'll never be out from under Uriah's watchful eye. When the bishop realizes you didn't agree to a kneeling confession, he'll be challenging Wyman about it—and if you don't confess next Sunday, he'll shun you without a second thought. Is there no end to this vicious circle, this cycle of blaming and shaming?

The *whack!* of the slammed kitchen door goaded Amanda into action. Without a word to Vera, Jemima, or the kids, she descended the steps to see what had happened in her absence. Had the children been downstairs when the Schmuckers arrived? They were capable of creating quite a mess when they played in the basement, but it was a rainy day, and a little more chaos was to be expected.

She had *not* figured on seeing her pottery smashed all over the floor.

Nor had she anticipated finding Great-Uncle Mahlon's kick wheel on its side, with the wheel and the splash pan detached . . . demolished beyond her ability to repair it. While Simon's mischief at the mercantile had broken some of her pieces, this blatant destruction went beyond anything her kids were capable of. *Uriah fancies himself as Christ overturning the tables of the money changers in the temple.*

Something inside Amanda snapped.

She had figured on taking her boxes of pottery back to Atlee's farm to stash them away. The devastation—the *waste*—scattered across the basement floor was the last straw. And in her despair, feeling as shattered as her pottery, Amanda could think of only one thing to do. One place to go.

Out the basement door she strode, not bothering to fetch her wraps. The cold rain mingled with her hot tears, and Amanda didn't care if anyone saw her enter the stable. "Dottie, let's go home, girl," she called to her mare.

A few minutes later her enclosed buggy was rolling past the pile of furniture covered with ragged blue tarps, then heading down the lane toward the county highway. It was wrong to run from her troubles. She had left soup bubbling on the stove, along with three little children on the sofa awaiting her discipline. But other folks could take care of those things.

Lord knows they don't need me . . .

That thought was the final crack in the dam that had been holding her frustrations and unrealized dreams in check. It was wrong to run away, like a child defying her parents, thinking the grass had to be greener anywhere other than home. She had promised to love, honor, and obey Wyman Brubaker. Willingly, knowing full well what marriage meant, she had entered into a sacred relationship with him until death parted them.

But she hadn't known much about Uriah Schmucker then. Hadn't foreseen the consequences of continuing the craft that had fed her family since Atlee had died. And she hadn't predicted the growing pains of blending two families . . . or the way Wyman had assumed she could bring all those kids together merely by becoming their mother.

Amanda shivered in the buggy, staring at the road ahead through her tears. No one was out in Cedar Creek to witness her shame, her caving in beneath an emotional burden she didn't know how to bear. Abby was probably sewing in the loft of the mercantile and would surely have words of comfort and support . . . Sam could offer advice from the perspective of a preacher who was not *her* preacher . . . She could fetch the rest of Vera's jewelry and her dishes if she stopped . . .

But then she would have to explain why she was leaving Wyman.

Think about what you're doing . . . to your family and your future. Turn around before it's too late.

It was unthinkable to abandon her family, or to forsake her husband of two weeks. She had vowed before God to commit herself to the Brubakers, and if she carried through on these feelings that churned in her heart, she would be excommunicated from Clearwater. Banned from seeing her kids again. And rightly so.

As Amanda rounded the curve by Graber's Custom Carriages, however, she didn't stop and she didn't look back. *Lizzie and the twins will come home, too—because Jemima will bring them,* she reasoned. *I must find a way to set Wyman free so he and his kids can move on, no matter what the awful consequences. Maybe I can join the Men-*

nonites . . . still raise my girls with Plain principles and values . . .

Dottie trotted faster as they approached the turnoff to the farm. Down the gravel road the buggy clattered until the faded white barns and the old Lambright house came into view. Within minutes Amanda was unhitching the mare, and she went right back to the stall where she'd lived for most of her life. *She knows where she belongs, and so do I,* Amanda thought.

As she stepped into the back door of the kitchen, the overheated smell of something on the stove greeted her, as did the clutter of her bachelor nephew. Amanda turned off the burner, barely recognizing the stew she and Jemima had left in the freezer for Jerome on moving day. She heard his footsteps above . . . water running through the pipes as he washed his hands before his noon meal.

What will you tell him? Jerome's a man, with a male perspective. He'll drive you right back to Clearwater if you don't go on your own.

For a few moments, however, Amanda drank in the sight of the familiar worn cabinets . . . the dishes in the sink, the stoneware a gift when she'd married Atlee . . . the table she'd eaten on all during her first marriage, shorter now because Jerome had removed the leaves. Oh, how the walls needed a fresh coat of paint, and oh, how she loved this kitchen anyway.

"Aunt Amanda? Is something wrong?"

She turned to face Jerome, her defenses crumbling. "Jah, you might say that," she rasped. "I can't do it. I can't be a Brubaker or live in Clearwater with those hateful, mean-spirited people."

Jerome's thick, dark eyebrows rose as though he might haul her right back out to her rig. Instead, he took her in his arms. "Better tell me what's going on," he murmured. "You're no quitter. And you would never, *ever* leave your girls behind."

Chapter 21

When Wyman stepped into the kitchen, he immediately knew something was wrong. Vera was in tears as she bustled around Jemima setting their noon meal on the table, while Jemima looked as sour—yet as fearful—as he had ever seen her. Alice Ann sat in her high chair sucking her thumb, her little face puckered with worry.

"Why are Simon and the twins sitting on the couch?" he whispered.

"Oh, Dat, it was *awful*." Vera mopped her face with her sleeve. "While Amanda was at the elevator with you, the Schmuckers came, and—"

Wyman clenched his jaw.

"—after the bishop went downstairs, we heard glass breaking against the floor, and—"

"We didn't do it, Dat. Honest!" Simon called from the front room.

"So where's Amanda now?" Wyman asked.

The kitchen fell silent.

Wyman's heart raced faster. The more questions he asked, the more he didn't like the answers he was getting. "Did she go downstairs to assess the damage, or what?" he demanded.

"That's what we figured, jah," his daughter rasped. "But it got real quiet. And when I went down to see if Amanda was all right, she . . . she wasn't there."

"Can't say as I blame her, after the way that bishop and his wife lit into her," Jemima sputtered. "Now Uriah's demanding a kneeling confession, after they found Vera's necklaces at the greenhouse in Cedar Creek—"

"And—and he smashed all the pottery she'd packed up, and broke her potter's wheel, too," Vera gushed. "How can that be right, Dat? What did Amanda do to deserve such treatment? She put away her ceramics, just like he'd told her to."

Wyman's heart slid into his boots. If Amanda had left without telling him . . . but surely she just needed to let off some steam. He sighed wearily, wondering whether he should first hunt down his wife or go speak to Uriah Schmucker. Jemima was dishing soup into bowls, so he decided that everyone—including Amanda—needed time to settle down. If the twins were here, it meant his wife couldn't have gone far . . . and that she wouldn't stay away long. *Would she?*

Wyman went into the front room, where the younger kids sat in a row, with their hands folded in their laps. "Come to dinner," he said gently. "After we pray, we can talk about the bishop's visit and figure out what to do."

Simon's eyes widened. "I'm real sorry about Wags getting into the kitchen with muddy feet," he whimpered. "Mrs. Schmucker got after me for that, and then she talked mean to Vera, and then—"

"It was so *scary* when the bishop made us go downstairs," one of the twins blurted.

"Jah, I didn't want to," her sister continued. "And when he started throwin' Mamma's dishes on the floor—"

"We were all grabbin' hold of Wags so he wouldn't attack the bishop—or step in that broken glass," Simon exclaimed. "Why did he *do* that, Dat?"

As these images raced in his mind, Wyman felt his temper rising. *Why, indeed?* "I don't know, son," he replied, "but I intend to find out. For now, though, we've got hot soup on the table, and we can think about these things while we eat, all right?"

"I don't *want* to think about it," one of the twins declared, and then she began to cry.

"I don't *like* that man. He's *mean*," her sister added, and then she, too, burst into tears.

"I want Mamma! Where'd she go?" sobbed the first twin.

"Why isn't she upstairs yet?" wailed the other, while in the kitchen, Alice Ann howled in sympathy.

Wyman felt totally out of his depth. He still couldn't tell Dora and Cora apart, and they turned away from him when he opened his arms. Simon's eyes were wide with the belief that he'd contributed to this catastrophe by letting his muddy dog in the house. Vera was in tears, Jemima was sputtering like a drenched cat, and meanwhile Alice Ann and the twins continued to cry inconsolably.

And Amanda was gone. Not an hour ago he'd been embracing her, enjoying a rare moment alone with her. How had so much happened since then?

It occurred to Wyman that this was the first time he'd been with all of the younger children when Amanda wasn't present. *Does she ever feel this overwhelmed? This helpless?* he wondered as he headed back into the kitchen. Thank goodness the three kids on the couch followed him, for he had no idea how to stop their tears. But he was the man of this family, expected to be strong and invincible. Expected to *fix* this situation.

When Eddie came in from the barn, his eyes widened at the sheer racket of the girls' weeping. "What's going on?" he asked as he hung up his coat. "Why did Amanda race out of here like a house afire? I called after her, but she didn't answer."

She's gone. Maybe for good . . . Wyman tried not to act as though he'd lost all sense of control, but that's how he felt. "The bishop stirred things up," he replied beneath the children's din. "And then Amanda went for a ride to, um—settle herself."

Eddie's cocked eyebrow said he didn't particularly believe that. Or condone it. Wyman was grateful that Vera and Jemima were soothing the children, reminding them it was time to give thanks for their food.

And, God, I hope You'll watch over Amanda, wherever she is, Wyman prayed fervently. *Please return her safely here, where we love her and miss her.*

Wyman blinked. While it wasn't unusual for his prayers to flow without conscious thought, he *did* miss Amanda—and not just because she wasn't here to restore order. Mere weeks had passed since the wedding, yet she'd become such a part of him that he hadn't realized how . . . *lost* he felt without her beside him. He stirred the fragrant vegetable soup, smiling at the alphabet letters—surely Amanda's idea. She was good about teaching the kids and making them think. The twins were starting to read, so Simon wanted to catch up to them—a positive step for a boy who couldn't sit still.

"When's Mamma coming back?" one of the twins asked as the sandwiches started around.

Wyman gazed at the two little girls dressed in pink, so like their mother, with their dark braids and beautiful eyes. "I don't know," he murmured. "But she *will* return, girls, because she loves you. And she won't want us to worry about her."

Please make that true, he mused as Cora and Dora thought about his answer.

"She loves me, too," Simon declared as he crushed crackers into his soup. "Even when me and Wags get into trouble, I can tell she still wants to be my new mamm."

Wyman's heart thudded. If his five-year-old son felt so convinced of Amanda's love, surely she would return to care for the boy—and all of them. Surely her devotion to her new family overrode her aversion to the bishop . . .

"She has to come back," Eddie said as he grabbed sandwiches from the platter. "She's married to you, Dat. She vowed to love and obey you, so she's got no choice but to follow the rules."

As Wyman stirred his steaming soup, he came to a startling realization: while his eldest son had stated the truth as Old Amish folks knew it—and while Wyman firmly believed in the tenets of their faith—at this moment he wondered if the rules should be their highest priority. After all, hadn't Uriah Schmucker crossed the line when he had broken Amanda's pottery and her wheel? Bishops were indeed chosen by God, but weren't they also accountable for their actions?

"We have a lot of things to consider, son," Wyman replied. He glanced at Vera, who was breaking a sandwich into bites for Alice Ann. "I didn't realize you had pieces in Treva's Greenhouse, Vera, and I'm sorry I didn't remove them," he murmured. "Maybe the Schmuckers' visit would have gone differently if the bishop hadn't thought we were ignoring his instructions."

Vera sighed. "Jah, well, you told me not to get too caught up in Amanda's pottery. I should've listened."

"Uriah's mind was made up before he got here."

Wyman's eyes widened at Jemima's quiet remark. Women of her generation tended to believe bishops could do no wrong—or they kept their differing opinions under their kapps. Amanda's mother-in-law looked older today, more frazzled, and while her sharp tongue often rankled him, Wyman could see how worried she was—probably because she depended on Amanda for help getting dressed each day.

"Where do you suppose she went, Jemima?" he asked.

Jemima kept stirring her soup instead of eating it. "I think I know. But it's best to leave her be rather than go chasing after her. You have *no idea* . . ."

As her reply trailed off, Wyman sensed the elderly woman had given the most insightful answer of all. He *did* have no idea what might be going through Amanda's mind—about the bishop, about settling into his home and family . . . about being married to him. First they'd had three scared little girls climbing into bed with them, along with Lizzie's troubles at school, and Simon's mischief, and Pete's and Eddie's defiant attitudes, and Vera's struggle to keep her mamm's house the same. Had Amanda known even a moment's peace since she'd married him?

Peace? Viola never complained about keeping your family together—

Guilt stabbed Wyman's heart. His first wife had complied with everything that had been expected of her . . . but had she been at peace? Had she been happy?

You have no idea. He winced inwardly. Viola had been a model Amish wife, never complaining . . . letting him make the decisions and set the course their family followed. But Wyman recalled bleak periods of their marriage when she had withdrawn into depression, too—especially after the bishop had forbidden her to paint.

So what are you going to DO about this? Amanda isn't Viola. And she's not getting a fair shake.

Wyman sighed. He'd been staring into his soup as though hoping the macaroni letters would form a message—a sign from God about how to handle this situation. Meanwhile, the silence at the table meant everyone else was waiting for his solution to this problem.

"Jemima's right," he murmured. "Amanda will come

home when she's ready. We can only pray that it'll be sooner rather than later."

And when had he ever let one woman take off and disrupt his home while another woman told him what to do about it? It went against Wyman's deepest beliefs for Amanda to work out her troubles in her own time, because he so desperately wanted to find her *now*. Would his children think he was weak—or unconcerned about Amanda's welfare and theirs—if he didn't go after her? He knew quite well what Uriah Schmucker would say.

Wyman took his first bite of soup. The situation was out of his hands—not because he liked it that way but because he was letting go of it. He would allow this problem to resolve itself in the way God intended and pray that Amanda behaved the way he wanted her to. He thoroughly disliked not having control over the outcome, but then . . . wasn't that how the world worked for Amanda every day?

Chapter 22

Amanda sat beside Jerome at the table that had been used by generations of Lambrights. They were eating bacon, eggs, and potatoes she'd fried after they'd agreed his leftover stew was beyond saving. While it was a comfort to sit in this kitchen again, using dishes that had been here when she'd moved in as Atlee's bride, she'd gotten herself into another pickle. Coming home to this farm satisfied a longing in her soul, but Jerome was adamant: she couldn't stay.

"Does Wyman mistreat you, Amanda?" her nephew demanded. "I'll not stand for him abusing you. But if he's taking care of you and the girls, you've got no cause to complain."

"Oh, we're fed and we have a roof over our heads," she replied in a strained voice. "But you might as well fetch the furniture I moved over there. Except for Jemima's pie safe, it's all out in the shed under dirty old tarps. There seems to be no room for my pieces in the Brubaker house."

Jerome's thick eyebrows rose, but he kept eating his home fries as though they were the tastiest food anyone had ever cooked. Amanda got up to fry him a couple more eggs. How could she state her case without losing his support? There was a fine line between whining and stating a truth that was unacceptable . . . but talking with her nephew forced her to figure out exactly how she felt about her new life as Wyman's wife.

"I don't think Wyman realizes how hard it is to take another woman's place. He assumes I can fit right into Viola's mold," she mused aloud. "And Vera, naturally, wants the kitchen—the whole house—left the way her mamm had it. Eddie and Pete seem to feel the same, so I'm outnumbered."

"So Wyman's not intentionally being cruel? He's just clueless?"

Amanda smiled at Jerome's slangy way of saying things. "Jah, that's how I see it—although the Clearwater bishop is a horse of another color entirely."

As she described her first preaching Sunday, and then the way Uriah had destroyed her pottery and Great-Uncle Mahlon's wheel while she was away, Jerome's brow furrowed. "And he was making the twins and Simon watch while he destroyed your pots? That's a . . . really extreme way to be sure they don't follow your artistic example."

"And dangerous!" she blurted. "Uriah left the floor covered with broken glass. I'm amazed that Simon could keep the dog from attacking him—and then we would've had a wounded animal and blood all over the place, as well."

"Not to mention a bishop who'd been bitten. Denki, Aunt," he said as Amanda lifted the crackling eggs from the skillet onto his plate. "Truth be told, I saw some of this trouble coming. Not sure I could live in Schmucker's district."

"Jah, well, what am I to do about that?" Amanda blurted. "I thought I'd followed his instructions. Yet now he's saying

I'm to give a kneeling confession because my evil paints and clay were in the basement."

"Not a very heartwarming way to welcome a new member to his district."

"Ach, and those women!" Amanda said. "All they could do was point out that the girls' dresses were too showy. Am I out of line here? You can't tell me God would condemn Cora and Dora to hell for wearing pink dresses to church."

Jerome scowled. "Sounds like a pretty conservative bunch there in Clearwater."

"Mean and hateful, if you ask me. But then, no one asks me," she continued in a lower voice. "I'm just supposed to take whatever they dish up, as though . . . as though I have no feelings. Or as though my feelings don't matter, and I should strive to be a better person, even if that means becoming a person I wasn't created to be."

Amanda hated that she was crying again. Yet she had finally made a statement that expressed her exasperation: *Uriah expects me to obey him rather than follow the path God has put me on.* "Sorry," she murmured, clasping her hands in her lap. "I know it's wrong to believe I know better than the bishop. You must think I've become horribly self-centered, whining like a child."

Jerome let out a long sigh. "No, Aunt Amanda, you sound very frustrated. And very sad," he whispered. "This isn't how I imagined you two weeks after you married Wyman Brubaker."

Amanda wiped her eyes. At least her nephew wasn't discounting her emotional outpouring, or declaring that she had to head back to Clearwater and silently accept her new lot in life. "I didn't come here to burden you. I—I just didn't know what else to do. Where else to go."

Jerome laid a gentle hand on her arm. "This farm is still yours, Aunt. You can come whenever you want to. But you know what they say. You can run, but you can't hide."

"Jah, Wyman's no doubt figured out that I'd come

here—and that I wouldn't leave the girls." Amanda let out a shuddery breath. "It's wrong to say this, too, but I can't go back if everything in his house and the Clearwater district will remain the same. I *won't go back* unless changes are made."

Amanda's hand fluttered to her mouth. Oh, but she'd crossed a forbidden line by uttering such words. Jerome's startled expression confirmed that she had overstepped, yet his gaze was filled with love and compassion.

"You'd best figure out how to say that to Wyman and Uriah Schmucker," he said softly. "And before that, you'd better think out your options, in case they don't see things your way."

Options. Amanda sighed. For a Plain wife, there was but one choice: "until God will separate you in death." If she left Wyman, she would be excommunicated. As far as members of the Old Order faith were concerned, such separation would send her straight to hell when she died, and it would make life difficult for her and the girls in the meantime. While visions of returning here to the Lambright farm seemed a sweet, simple solution, Amanda knew the Bloomingdale district wouldn't accept her as a member again if she left her husband. Becoming a Mennonite would be the only way to continue life as she knew it . . .

And if I divorce Wyman, he won't be able to remarry until I die.

That really wasn't fair to him, was it? Wyman was a good man . . . He couldn't have foreseen the bishop's extreme reaction to her pottery, and he'd had no way of knowing how those women in church would berate her, either.

Amanda came out of her thoughts to find Jerome studying her intently, awaiting her answer. "I don't know what to say," she murmured over her half-eaten eggs and potatoes. "It's not my intent to dishonor Wyman or his family—"

"Your family now," her nephew reminded her.

"—but I can't tolerate Uriah Schmucker or his wife," she

continued in a rising voice, "and I won't resume my place in that household until some changes are made." Her stomach was coiling in a knot. Making such statements would surely send her to her knees for another confession, if anyone other than Jerome heard them. But she had stated her case, and there was no unsaying what her heart had declared as the truth.

Jerome sat quietly for a moment. "If that's to be the way of it, Aunt Amanda, you'll need to speak your mind to Wyman, straight out. And then you'll have to accept the consequences."

"Jah, there's that." Amanda swallowed hard, envisioning how her husband would react. Would he listen to her concerns? Would he lash out like a wounded animal? Would Wyman, as the head of the Brubaker family, dismiss her feelings and expect her to put away her misgivings about the Clearwater district as she had put away her pottery . . . as he had stashed her furniture under those musty tarps?

Amanda sighed. Would their marriage be doomed to one of mutual resignation and unrealized dreams if she accepted those terms? Or, if she put her own desires ahead of her allegiance to the church . . . to her husband, would Wyman throw her out? She would be the one breaking her promises, after all.

"I'll go with you," Jerome said in a low voice.

Amanda's eyes widened. "I—I don't expect you to fight my battles, or take my side when I'm asking for—"

"You and Jemima and the girls are my family." He looked her straight in the eye. "What sort of man would I be if I knew you were sinking in quicksand and I didn't throw you a rope? Whatever happens with the Brubakers, Aunt Amanda, you always have a home here. And I will always take care of you."

"Oh, Jerome, I—" Amanda clutched his strong, broad hand, speechless.

"But I have to know you've given Wyman every chance.

This is serious business," he reminded her. " 'What God has joined let no man put asunder' is part of the wedding vows, and I'll not have it on my conscience—or have anyone else believing—that I gave you an easy way out of the promises you made."

"I would never expect you to do that, Jerome."

"All right, then. Soon as we finish our dinner, we should head on over there," he said. "I know some little girls—and one cranky old girl—who'll be worried about why you left them and when you'll be back."

Amanda nodded, again wondering if she was wrong to insist on her own way. Wyman, eight kids, and her mother-in-law were depending on her to do the right thing. She smiled at her nephew. "Since when are you such a wise man, Jerome Lambright? Seems like only yesterday you were a kid helping Atlee with the chores, keeping track of Lizzie when she was a toddler," she said in a faraway voice. "And now you're advising me about my commitments. Way ahead of your years."

"Telling you what to do and where to go," he teased. "Seems my experience with contrary mules might be paying off."

Laughter bubbled out of her as she swatted his arm. "I suppose your old aunt resembles a mule in more ways than—"

"Oh, but you're not old, Aunt Amanda," Jerome countered quickly. "And I don't want you getting that way before your time, either. Of course, it's easy for *me* to say how Wyman ought to run his household and treat his wife. If I ever get hitched, you can't hold me to such a liberal view of a woman's power and privileges."

Amanda almost asked him how his pursuit of Emma Graber was going, but this wasn't the right time. She picked at her lukewarm potatoes, waiting until Jerome scraped his plate clean. "Let's do these dishes and be on our way," she suggested. "I don't know what I'll say to Wyman, but the words won't come any easier if I stay around here, stalling."

Half an hour later, Amanda took a long last look around the kitchen and the front room. Empty, slightly darker spots on the faded walls marked where pieces of furniture had been. It struck her that this home was showing some wear and tear, whereas the Brubaker rooms had been painted recently . . . perhaps as Wyman had prepared for his new wife and her kids?

After Jerome tethered a horse to the back of her buggy, they took off down the county road. While Amanda feared she would muddle the things she wanted to say to Wyman, she sat taller in the seat, filled with the conviction that her concerns were worthy of attention.

After all, didn't the whole family agree that Uriah and Mildred Schmucker had behaved improperly? Wasn't it everyone's place to give and to receive, to speak and to listen—to *share* and to cooperate as they became a new family? As Amanda thought more about it, she realized that as the mother of this Brubaker bunch, she was second in command . . . which placed her wishes above the children's as she encouraged them to get along as sisters and brothers with different last names.

Still, as Dottie started down the lane to the large white house across the road from the grain elevator, her insides tightened. Even with Jerome taking her part, she had no guarantee that this situation would be worked out to her satisfaction. She had defied Wyman's authority, after all. She had left him without a word of explanation, like a child running away from home. He didn't have to understand that. He didn't have to forgive her without first demanding penance . . . and the bishop would stand by him if Wyman made an example of her in front of the entire membership. Her sins were mounting up . . .

"Whoa, Dottie," Jerome said as the buggy halted beside the house. He gazed at her, his dark eyes intense. "Ready for this?"

Amanda squeezed his sturdy knee. "What happens will be God's will, ain't so?"

"Remember our Plain proverb, Aunt," Jerome murmured with a last pat of her hand. " 'Courage is fear that's said its prayers.' "

Chapter 23

Through the glass in the kitchen door, Wyman saw Amanda coming up the porch stairs. His first impulse was to jump up from the supper table, but when the kids heard her footsteps, they beat him to it.

"It's Mamma! Mamma's here!" one of the twins cried.

"She's come to take us home!" her sister exclaimed as the two of them ran for the door.

Wyman winced at this sentiment as he watched Simon hurry out to the porch. "I *told* ya she'd miss us!" his boy crowed.

Lizzie, too, rushed outside. "Mamm! When I came home from school and you weren't here, I was afraid—"

As Amanda hugged her eldest, rocking side to side, Wyman realized it would be a while before her children felt like a part of his family. The emotion on their two faces, mother and daughter, illustrated a love such as this woman would never feel for him . . .

Better to let the kids express their feelings first . . . soften her up, Wyman thought. Vera glanced at him, as though wondering whose side to be on. When Alice Ann squawked to get out of her high chair, however, his oldest daughter grabbed her up and followed the younger children out to where they were clamoring around Amanda.

"Praise be to God," Jemima murmured at her end of the table. "Jerome's come with her, I see. Figured that's where she went."

Eddie raised an eyebrow as he stabbed another hot dog from the platter. "What do you suppose Uriah will say about her leaving us?" he asked in an edgy voice.

"Jah," Pete chimed in, "if the bishop was mad enough to smash her pottery—"

"This is not the bishop's concern." Wyman leaned closer, forcing his two teenage sons to meet his gaze. "And if Uriah hears of this incident, I'll know who the tale-tellers were, won't I? This is between Amanda and me, understand?"

Eddie glanced toward the porch, where Amanda was hugging the twins and Simon in one wiggly, giggly huddle. "If she's run back to her farm once, what's to keep her from going back there every time some little thing—"

"Mind your mouth, Edward. And mind your own business, too," Wyman added. "I don't need your advice about how to handle my marriage."

He rose from the table. Better to greet Amanda before she came inside, to set the tone for her return. Even though he yearned to hold her close and kiss her, Eddie hadn't been totally off the mark: as the head of this family, Wyman was to establish the boundaries . . . state what sort of behavior was acceptable and what he wouldn't tolerate from his new wife. He longed to have this conversation with her alone, but that luxury wasn't possible while the kids and Jemima— and Jerome—were within earshot.

He stopped halfway across the kitchen, his breath catching. Amanda was holding Alice Ann on her shoulder, and his wee blond daughter was clinging to her neck. This was the first time he'd seen his youngest allow anyone other than him and Vera to cuddle her. Witnessing this little miracle, he could easily imagine his wife cradling a baby—his baby—in her arms as she cooed to it and rocked from side to side, as she was doing now.

Truth be told, the kids might be the reason she'll stay, he thought. *She owns a farm. And she already knows she can get by without a husband.*

Opening the door, Wyman nodded at the dark-haired young man who stood off to the side, observing Amanda with the kids. Had Jerome talked some sense into Amanda and escorted her home? Or did he see her side of this complicated situation? Wyman couldn't tell. Amanda's nephew was keeping his feelings off his face, leaning against the porch pillar as though he was in no hurry to leave.

Wyman focused again on Amanda, who hadn't yet met his eye. Although she belonged to him legally and by virtue of the *Ordnung*, she wasn't a woman whose heart followed the rules—and the dire consequences of leaving their marriage hadn't kept her from running away, either.

Making her stay was his right . . . but it wasn't a good strategy. How could he persuade her to remain here because she *wanted* to? How could he convince Amanda to love him so much that she could overlook the ties that bound her to him?

As though Amanda finally realized he'd stepped outside—or was she waiting him out, making him sweat?—she looked at him full-on with her deep, dark eyes . . . eyes he dreamed of at night and in his spare moments at the grain elevator. The pain and hesitation he saw there gave him pause, for he suspected he'd caused some of it.

"Amanda," he murmured.

"Wyman."

He waited. But his wife didn't look ready to burst into an apology or an explanation. And the way she swayed with Alice Ann on her shoulder suggested that she knew her power all too well. *The hand that rocks the cradle rules the world.*

Wyman felt torn between following the Old Ways, reprimanding her and demanding her allegiance, and wanting to engage her . . . to woo her. He knew what the bishop would expect of him, but Uriah Schmucker wasn't here. And for that, he thanked God.

"Come in," he suggested, gesturing for everyone to come inside. "We're eating our supper—"

"I'll set on a couple more plates," Vera said. "We're so glad you're back, Amanda!"

Amanda's smile made Wyman wish he'd said that first. Why was he making this harder than it had to be? "We've been mighty concerned about you . . . where you went, and why," he said, gently grasping her arm. "We have a lot to talk about."

"Jah, we do."

As Amanda stepped into the kitchen ahead of him, Wyman observed the way the younger children shifted their plates to make room for Jerome and their mamm . . . how the twins insisted she sit between them rather than in her place at his left . . . Eddie's and Pete's expressions as they assessed Jerome's presence . . . Jemima's relieved smile as she opened her arms and Amanda hugged her.

Would nothing ever be *simple*, now that three adults and eight children lived under his roof? Again Wyman longed for time alone with Amanda, but he sat down to handle this moment, the rest of this meal, as best he could.

"Let's bow for a word of thanks," he said quietly. "God has blessed us, and we ask for His guidance as our family comes together again."

The moments of silence gave Wyman a chance to gather his thoughts and to peer at Amanda from between his eyelids. The kids were settled in their places, their heads sweetly bowed—except for Alice Ann, who wiggled happily in her high chair.

When he saw that Amanda was also secretly looking at him, Wyman's pulse quickened. Her expression told him she wouldn't surrender, but at least she had come back to work out their problems.

"Amen," he murmured to bring their prayer to a close. Before he could say anything more, Jerome looked purposefully around the kitchen and then into the front room.

"I see you've found a place for the pie safe," Amanda's nephew said, "but otherwise, I understand that all of Amanda's furniture is out in the shed. It's difficult for her to use it out there, ain't so? And harder for her to feel welcome if nobody else is willing to make the same sort of changes *she* made to become a part of this family."

The room got so quiet, it seemed the entire house had sucked in its breath. Wyman opened his mouth to reply, but again Jerome jumped in.

"And what's to be done about Uriah Schmucker destroying Amanda's pottery and her wheel?" he asked in a more insistent voice. "While Plain folks aren't to become worldly artists, we must still acknowledge how the Creator has gifted some of us in special ways. If it wasn't God's will for Amanda to make such colorful, useful dishes, He wouldn't have granted her that ability, ain't so?"

Where had these sentiments come from? Jerome Lambright hadn't impressed Wyman as such an eloquent sort, but he had just addressed two important issues that Amanda must have taken to her nephew . . . instead of to him, her husband. "Points well made," he said. "And they will be addressed—"

"Jah, they will," Jerome remarked with a firm nod of his head. "Not my place to tell you how to run your house, Wyman, but had Amanda and Atlee not taken me in when I was orphaned, I would be *nowhere* today. Probably would've left the Plain faith altogether rather than sticking with an order that demands our highest and our best, without room for compromise. So if you folks won't give this gut woman the home she deserves, I *will*."

Retorts whirled in Wyman's mind. "You're trespassing on sacred ground, Jerome. I—"

"Jah, but I'm going to speak my mind anyway." Jerome set down his fork. "The way I see it, you folks are clinging to the way things were when Viola was alive. Jah, you'll always feel bad that she died when your mules spooked in that thunderstorm, believing somebody else should've grabbed those reins instead of her. But you know what?"

Wyman blinked. He had no answer for the earnest young man who had nailed him with a pointed question and a gaze to match it. Why on earth would he be talking about Viola, when it was Amanda who—

"Maybe I'm as much to blame for your first wife's death as anyone else." Jerome's sibilant whisper rang in the silent kitchen. "After all, I trained those mules. Many's the time I wondered if I should've done better with them."

"Nobody can predict how an animal will react in a storm," Wyman murmured, feeling the weight of his children's gazes from around the table. "If we truly believe that God's will prevails—"

"Then we let go of our guilt, because guilt means we've not accepted God's will or His forgiveness," Jerome insisted. "And we let go of the past, because dwelling there—feeling bad about things we couldn't control—doesn't allow us to enjoy God's blessings now and in the future."

Wyman sat back in his chair, speechless. The amazement on Amanda's face told him she hadn't expected her nephew to speak out this way . . . and that she, too, felt overwhelmed by such a profound baring of his soul.

"That's a better sermon than I've heard in a long while," Wyman murmured. "Part of me wants to tell you to mind your own business, Jerome, but you speak a truth none of us in this room can afford to ignore."

Jerome smiled cautiously. "Denki for hearing me out, Wyman. You're a gut man—Amanda says so herself—and

I want the best for you and your family. Amanda *is* the best, you know."

Wyman couldn't argue with that. During the remainder of the meal, the conversation was lighter, and even if Amanda spoke mostly to the kids, she at least looked ready to stay. Ready to fix what was broken.

But then, that was his job, too, wasn't it?

As Amanda listened to the children's prayers and then told her teenagers good night, her exhaustion made her feel heavy and slow. But there was no slipping away from the inevitable discussion with her husband. All evening, she and Wyman had exchanged tentative but meaningful glances that told her he intended to have his say . . . and then go beyond talking. Amanda saw lovemaking as a sign that Wyman had forgiven her in ways he couldn't always say with words. And truth be told, she craved his affection after this tumultuous day.

After she helped Jemima out of her clothes and into her nightgown, Amanda went downstairs. In the kitchen, her husband was warming milk in a small pan. He poured it into two mugs and then stirred in a liberal amount of hot chocolate mix.

"I've never outgrown my love of cocoa. How about you?" he asked as he handed her one of the steaming cups.

Amanda inhaled the rich fragrance. "It hits the spot like nothing else, jah."

"Shall we sit on the couch in the basement? Our voices won't carry up to where other ears will hear us."

Amanda nodded, preceding him downstairs. Her stomach fluttered with nerves, for this was the moment the whole day had been leading up to. She was grateful that someone had swept up the shattered glass and removed her broken potter's wheel, so the room held no reminders of the bishop's visit. She and Wyman entered the sitting area, where a square of old carpet, some game tables, and a sofa were set apart from the storage area and shelves.

Had Uriah and Mildred been here just this morning? Amanda felt as though she'd traveled more than the miles and time between here and her farm today. And who could have anticipated Jerome's challenging words after he'd driven her back?

But her nephew wasn't the only one who needed to speak. Wyman had been trying to engage her all day, and she'd kept quiet until they could be alone.

"I'm sorry I took off," she murmured as they sat on the old sofa. The corduroy showed signs of kids' drinks being spilled here, and she picked a couple pieces of popcorn from between the cushions. "I should have gone to the elevator to talk with *you* about the bishop's—"

"You did what seemed best." Wyman sat apart from her, but wrapped his hand around hers. "Hearing about your frustrations from Jerome made me listen closer. I realize now that I've not paid enough attention to how . . . we Brubakers have expected you to change, while we're still surrounded by our favorite, familiar furniture. It was never my intention to hurt you, my love."

My love. At least Wyman was inclined toward endearments instead of exhortations about following their faith . . . namely, being more submissive and obedient.

"I'll go to Uriah's first thing tomorrow," he continued earnestly. "I don't appreciate the way he came into our home and destroyed your pottery and your wheel while our little ones looked on. But if Uriah refuses to back down or apologize, I don't know what recourse we'll have. He's the leader God chose for our district."

"I understand that." She could predict how Uriah would react to Wyman's visit, too. "But as I've told Jerome, I can't tolerate the Clearwater bishop, and I won't resume my place in this family until some changes are made. I'm going to stand by what I've stated."

The flash in Wyman's eyes told Amanda she'd gone too far. She had challenged his old habits and the Old Ways, and at first impulse, he intended to put her in her place—to make her submit to *his* will. But he held his tongue . . . sipped his cocoa as he considered her words and his response to them.

"Jah, that's the idea I got from listening to Jerome," he finally said. "But I'm in a bind here, Amanda. It's one thing for you to not get along with the bishop and his wife, but it's another matter altogether that our home is in the Clearwater district. If we live here, we worship here."

Her throat constricted. "I know that," she said in a strained voice.

A tense silence surrounded them as they each gazed straight ahead. Then Wyman set his empty mug on the old end table. "I was ready to come after you, Amanda, to lash out about how you made me look bad in front of the kids—"

"And you had gut reason to do that."

"—but when I behaved that way with Viola, asserting my rights as the man of the family," he went on, "nothing was gained by it. We all felt bad. The kids were afraid of me—Eddie and Pete were still young enough that they didn't know everything—"

Amanda couldn't help but smile. Jerome had gone through that know-it-all phase as a teenager, too.

"—and Viola's resentment festered below the surface for days. Took us way too long to clear the air," he murmured ruefully. "So maybe I'm catching on, jah? Maybe this time around I know what I stand to lose, even if holding my tongue—considering your requests—goes against the grain of everything I've believed as a man raised in the Plain faith."

Amanda let out the breath she'd been holding. That was quite a statement for Wyman to make. And if she hoped to honor her husband, her marriage, she had to give—and give in—at least as much as he had. *Courage is fear that's said its prayers*, she reminded herself. She had prayed fervently about this matter since her wedding day. Did she have the faith to face her husband with her true feelings?

"I love you, Wyman," she said quietly. "I was wrong to be afraid of you. Wrong to run away rather than trusting you with my troubles."

His lips quirked. "Oh, maybe not," he said as he squeezed her hand. "Your instincts about people are pretty keen. You were smart to bring Jerome—"

"Oh, coming here was *his* idea. There was no keeping him away."

"—because after that day he drove his eight-mule hitch over so I could have time alone with you, I had him figured as a fellow of like mind," Wyman said with a short laugh. "Guess he told *me* a thing or two today. I believe it when he says he'll be keeping close watch over how I treat you, too. I'm not wild about that, but I *am* crazy in love with you, Amanda. So I'd better act like it, ain't so?"

Amanda sighed, releasing the tension she'd held for too long. Her whole body relaxed. How could she remain upset with a man who said such loving words? Wyman had taken her troubles to heart rather than forcing her to back down . . . or to fit into the empty space Viola had left in his life. "Do . . . do you want to go upstairs?" she whispered.

Wyman smiled and softly kissed her cheek. "Let's stay right here," he murmured. "When I was Simon's age I wondered why the cellar door had a sliding lock—and a time or two I got in trouble for using it. But now I realize why my parents—or maybe my grandparents—put it there. Jah?"

Amanda nodded. Her body thrummed as her husband slipped up the stairs to slide the bolt into place. What a relief it was that Wyman had agreed to consider her emotional needs . . . that he was offering his affection rather than insisting she accept it. And what a blessing, that together they would somehow resolve her problems with the bishop.

Chapter 24

As James surveyed the scene in the Lambrights' front yard, his heart swelled. Despite a few distant clouds, they were enjoying a sunny autumn day—Indian summer, folks called this final warm spell before winter, when most of the leaves had fallen and the fields were bare. Emma, Jerome, and Abby had pulled together quite a surprise: what with his two sisters' families from Queen City plus the Brubaker bunch, Vernon, and the neighbors, nearly forty people had come to celebrate his mamm's eightieth birthday. A dessert table was set up with the cake and punch, as well as trays of other treats and freezers of homemade ice cream. Mamm was seated at a gift table, with Emma to help her, while everyone else sat in lawn chairs or on quilts spread on the lawn.

His mother was grinning like a kid as she opened her gifts—embroidered kitchen towels, a pack of blank recipe cards, new kapps and black stockings . . . useful items for around the house, mostly. When she tore the paper from the next box, however, her eyes got nearly as large as the lenses of her glasses.

She held up a bright red pitcher painted all over with white and yellow daisies. "I was eyeing this pretty piece at the mercantile a while back—but there's no name with it! Who was so nice as to get it for me?"

The guests looked eagerly at one another until finally James's dat raised his hand. "I'm glad you like it, Eunice," he said. "Happy birthday eighty times over—and you know that's one of Amanda's pieces, ain't so?"

James held his breath. Such a pleasure it was that Dat had chosen a gift for its cheerful beauty and that Mamm had been so tickled to receive it.

"Jah, I recognized it right off." His mother held up a matching pie plate and two mugs, which had been in the same box. "Amanda, I'm real glad Merle latched onto these before you had to take your pieces out of the store. I'll think of you every time I see them, and it'll brighten my day."

Amanda flushed modestly. "Denki for saying that, Eunice. I hope you'll enjoy using those dishes as much as I liked making them."

As the folks around them murmured their agreement, James leaned close enough to his dat that the arms of their lawn chairs bumped together. "You did real gut, Dat," he murmured. "Mamm loves the pottery you got her."

"Jah, sometimes I get lucky," his father said with a chortle.

As his mother opened more of her gifts, James let his gaze wander over the crowd. He was glad to see that Gail, Ruthie, and Beth Ann Yutzy were whispering with Lizzie on their quilt—but Wyman's and Amanda's expressions gave him pause. As was the custom, Amanda sat among the women while her husband had situated himself with the men, but both of their faces bespoke a tight-lipped determination to keep their troubles to themselves.

And wasn't that a regrettable state of affairs for newly-weds? When Abby had removed Amanda's pottery from the mercantile shelves, word had gotten around about the Clearwater bishop's reaction to it. Still, James sensed other matters were causing this handsome couple to appear so . . . preoccupied. It was one thing, the way his parents groused at each other after more than sixty years of marriage. A couple in the prime of their lives, however, with a large house full of healthy children, had so much to be thankful for now that they were together.

One big happy family, Abby had predicted when Wyman and Amanda had announced their engagement. Yet their faces told a different tale, not a month after they'd tied the knot.

"And would you look at this?" his mother crowed. "Another piece of Amanda's pottery, in blue with those same daisies! Thank you, James."

"You're welcome, Mamm," he called over to her. "Happy birthday!"

His heart thrummed as he observed the joy on his mother's face. And who could have guessed as she opened the next presents, from Emma and Abby and Jerome, that each of them had also chosen colorful platters and serving bowls with Amanda's distinctive daisies on them?

"My word," his dat remarked. "I think we must have bought nearly every piece from that display."

"Jah, we did!" Emma chuckled as she stood beside her mother. "And, Mamm, I see this as a sign we can get rid of some of your old, stained pie plates and—"

"Puh! I'm saving these pretty pieces for gut," Mamm informed her. "Think how they'll brighten up the china hutch and the plate rail—and, Vernon?" she added as she peered at the crowd through her old-fashioned spectacles. "You're not going to make me hide these away because they're too fancy, are you?"

Their bishop chuckled until his white beard quivered. "Eunice, it's a wonderful day indeed when these dishes have brought you such joy," he replied. "And just as we've been blessed by Amanda's pottery—every piece with its own useful beauty—I believe God has found the perfect home for them. I only wish I'd seen her display before Abby took it down, so I could've bought some for my aunts. Maybe if there's an item or two left—"

"You're too late," Abby chirped. "We've sold every last dish and pitcher, as well as several wind chimes and necklaces from the greenhouse. Now *that's* a witness to how much local folks appreciate your talent, Amanda and Vera."

Amanda appeared amazed and gratified, and James was pleased that word of their pieces had gotten around Cedar Creek before Uriah Schmucker had banned them. Each church district tended to reflect the personality of its bishop, and he was grateful to Vernon for being more understanding—and less conservative—than many of the leaders in neighboring Plain communities.

When Matt's Rosemary cut the big birthday cake she'd baked and decorated, and everyone had eaten a generous square of it with ice cream, the adults settled into smaller groups to visit. His sisters' youngsters were playing tag with Ruthie, Beth Ann, and the Brubaker kids, while Matt's Border collies frolicked with them. It was a fine afternoon, indeed, and James figured on spending some of it with Abby. She and Emma were circulating in the crowd, pouring more punch, however. When his dat began to chat with Jerome, James moseyed over to where Sam and Vernon were talking with Wyman.

"I sense there's trouble at your place, son," the white-haired bishop was saying. "Uriah was at our regional bishop's meeting this past week, telling us he'd visited your place twice in a few days. I was sorry to hear he *broke* things in his zeal to put Amanda on the higher path—"

James leaned against the nearby tree, hoping his presence wouldn't make Wyman uncomfortable.

"—and I'm wondering how she's handling that," Vernon went on in a sympathetic voice.

Wyman seemed torn between dodging the truth and sharing only part of it. "Amanda . . . well, she ran off," he admitted. "Went back to her farm to tell her troubles to Jerome."

Vernon's eyes widened while Sam leaned into the conversation. "How long was she away?" the preacher asked with a scowl. "And what did you say to her when she came back?"

"Jerome returned with her and he gave me quite an earful, I can tell you. He thought we Brubakers hadn't made much effort to fit Amanda and her belongings into our home," Wyman replied. "And what with the static the ladies at church gave her about the girls' dresses being too short and too colorful—this before Uriah smashed her pottery and broke her great-uncle's wheel—my wife has declared she wants nothing more to do with him or the Clearwater district."

"Oh, my," Vernon murmured. "It's more serious than I imagined."

"And what're you going to do about *that*?" Sam demanded.

James considered this. Never had he imagined Amanda running off—but then, he could understand how so many criticisms from so many folks could make a new bride feel like an outcast. He couldn't imagine members of the Cedar Creek district being so unfriendly.

"I . . . don't know what to do," Wyman confessed in a barely audible voice. "Uriah's actions aside, Jerome made some tough points that have me wondering if I've married the right woman but . . . for the wrong reasons," he continued ruefully. "I thought I'd be doing Amanda a favor, providing for her after Atlee's death. I should never have assumed she would take up where Viola left off, as far as managing the house and raising our eight kids—much less dream of us having more."

"It takes time to adjust to a difference in routine, not to mention all that additional responsibility," Vernon pointed out.

"But that's the life of a Plain wife, and Amanda was well aware of that," Sam countered. "Wyman, I hope you've told her she can't have her way just because Uriah's forbidden her to make her pottery."

"Oh, it goes a lot deeper than that." Wyman stared into his punch cup as though he wondered how it had gotten empty. "Jerome pointed out things I'd tried to forget about Viola's passing. And when he said that her death could just as easily have been his fault because *he* had trained the mules that bolted that day, I realized I was still feeling her death was *my* fault. I should have been guiding those mules in the rain, instead of working halfway across the field while my wife walked alongside the baler."

"Survivor guilt," Vernon murmured. "I've seen it eat away at a lot of folks. Since I doubt Uriah will counsel you about this, Wyman, why don't you and I set up a time to discuss it? I've lost a wife, too, you know. I understand some of what you're going through."

"That might be a gut thing. Uriah tells me I've given my wife way too much leeway." Wyman turned in his chair to find her among the women sitting near the cake table. "And meanwhile, what am I to do about Amanda not having her pottery anymore? Viola lost a vital part of herself when Uriah ordered her to give up her painting . . . and even though such artwork goes against our Plain ways, I can't condemn Amanda to the same fate."

"You think she's going to have *time* to make pottery, along with running your home and raising eight kids—or more?" Sam asked.

"That's not so much the issue," Vernon insisted. He leveled a steady gaze at Sam, as though telling the new preacher to ease up a bit. "Even if Amanda can't find the time, having the *choice* to pursue her talent would make an important difference in her outlook. And in her emotional health, as well."

Sam sat back in his lawn chair, pondering the bishop's words. "Sounds similar to Barbara's midwifing," he admitted. "I've told her she's to give it up now that she's a preacher's wife, but she insists it's a God-given skill that serves the community."

"And it is," Vernon agreed. "While we Old Order men have stood by our beliefs about women and their work for centuries, there are times when the blacks and the whites might deserve a second look. Life's often more like that sky over there—a spectrum of grays rolling around us, defying our attempts to define absolute right and absolute wrong."

James glanced behind him, to where the bishop had gestured. "We're in for a storm later today."

"Jah," Sam remarked. "Look at the way the cedars are blowing along the creek."

James caught a movement among the women: Abby was picking up a tray of cookies, heading toward the men, who sat in scattered bunches. As she held his gaze, James's breathing stilled. So kind and thoughtful she was, never idle, and a friend to all. But would he face a challenge like Wyman's after they married? Would her Stitch in Time business become a matter of contention—especially because her brother seemed so intent on the women in his family toeing the Old Order line? Would Abby feel as trapped and desperate as Amanda did if she had to remain at home caring for his elderly parents and then the children as they came along?

"Sweets for the sweet?" Abby murmured as she offered him the tray of treats.

James fought the urge to kiss her, right in front of everyone. Instead, he chose a fried pie she had made—Abby drizzled her glaze in a way he'd come to recognize these past months. "Pineapple lemon, jah? My favorite."

"That's why I made them."

James closed his eyes as the tart-sweet filling covered his tongue. Such a simple delight, yet it made his concerns about marrying Abby float away. If God had brought the two of them together, surely He would bless them with every happiness.

That's what Wyman thought, too, when he married Amanda.

Even so, James lost himself in Abby's brown-eyed smile and then watched her move among the other fellows with her tray. Later today—*today*—he would find the right moment, the right words, to make this wonderful woman say *yes*. After all, he had to ask before she could answer.

Chapter 25

As Abby returned to the dessert table with her nearly empty tray, a gust of wind whipped at her skirts. The ladies sitting near the gift table hopped up to catch the wrapping paper from Eunice's gifts.

"Looks like a rain'll be blowing in soon," Emma said as she stuffed a handful of paper and ribbons into one of her mother's boxes. "Let's get your presents into the house, Mamm."

"Jah, and I'll be going with them," Eunice replied. "No need to get wet and then catch my death of cold."

"I'm with you there, Eunice," Jemima Lambright said as she struggled up out of her lawn chair. "But in my case, I don't want to melt, you know. That's what happens when hard candy gets wet."

As the women around her chortled at Jemima's old joke, Abby stacked the trays. Eunice fussed over the least little thing, healthwise, and she'd soon be hounding Merle to come inside, too—but then, maybe the two of them had reached their eighth decade by taking care of themselves and watching out for each other. It was a blessing that they were still enjoying birthday parties and life's simple pleasures, even if they bickered a bit.

Amanda tucked wrapping paper between the pottery pieces so they wouldn't chip, while the other women started into the house with the remaining desserts and Eunice's other gifts. Once inside, Barbara ran dishwater while Amanda and Abby took up towels. While the others put the leftover food into containers, the three of them chatted at the sink.

"So what's this I've heard about Uriah breaking your pottery in your basement?" Barbara asked Amanda. "Do you think he's made his point now?"

"That had to scare the little ones half to death, if you weren't there when he did that," Abby remarked. All afternoon she'd noticed the weariness etched on Amanda's face. She sensed that Uriah and Mildred Schmucker had upset the entire Brubaker family—and if Amanda had felt compelled to run off, the situation was indeed serious.

"I don't see Uriah as a man who will let up on me or my girls—or Wyman," Amanda replied with a sad sigh. "Trouble is, he's expecting me to be on my knees Sunday, and I . . . I just can't go. I've told Wyman I can't abide that bishop, and while he understands my misgivings, I've put him between a rock and a hard place."

Barbara's eyebrows rose. She carefully rinsed a glass tray and handed it to Abby. "Jah, there's no ducking a bishop's order to confess," she murmured. "And no way to avoid him and his wife unless you move to another district."

"That's not likely to happen, what with the grain elevator being there," Amanda pointed out. "I've prayed on it and prayed on it. It's a tough thing to discuss with the kids around. What sort of example am I setting if I refuse to obey the bishop—and if I expect their dat to go along with it? Pete and Eddie are of an age where they'll think that if *I* can defy Wyman's and Uriah's orders, they can, too."

As Abby listened, her heart went out to this new wife. More than Amanda's fear of retribution from the bishop she heard a longing . . . a need for private time and a heart-to-heart talk between two bewildered adults who hadn't foreseen so many obstacles on their path to happiness.

"What if you and Wyman came to stay at my place for a couple of days?" As soon as the words popped out of her mouth, Abby knew this was the best idea she'd had in a long time. "While you're here in Cedar Creek, you could visit some more with Vernon, and— Why, James and I could go out to your place to help Jemima and Vera keep an eye on the kids! What do you think?"

Amanda's eyes widened. "Oh, I couldn't ask you to—"

"You didn't ask," Abby pointed out. "I offered."

"And what of the work James has lined up in his carriage shop?" Amanda protested. "Wyman and I couldn't expect him to—"

"I think that's a wonderful-gut idea," Emma joined in as she, too, grabbed a towel. "James has an apprentice and other fellows to carry on when he's not there. It'll do him gut to get away—and maybe he'll finally propose to Abby! We've all been waiting for *that*!"

Abby's cheeks prickled with heat, yet she chuckled with the rest of the women. "If James agrees, and Wyman goes along with it, you can work out these matters before they get any more serious, Amanda. I'm concerned about you," she added in a lower voice. "I don't like to see you and Wyman looking so unhappy."

Amanda's eyes welled up. "Oh, Abby, what a friend you are, to make such an offer. I suppose it won't hurt to ask James and Wyman what they think."

"Gut!" Abby replied. "Let's go out and talk to them right—"

The kitchen door flew open ahead of Jerome, who was urging Merle inside. "It's raining," the younger man announced. "What with the wind whipping around, the other fellows are stabling the horses and putting away the chairs and tables. Gut thing we started Eunice's party earlier in the day."

"My word, would you look at those nasty clouds," Rosemary remarked. "We'd better gather up the children. My Katie's afraid of storms."

"Simon gets as wound up as a toy monkey when the weather changes," Amanda remarked as she followed Rosemary toward the door. "If we bring him inside, the girls will follow."

Abby marveled at how Amanda was already so familiar with the ways of Wyman's children. A look out the window, to the expressions on their wee faces as they ran toward Amanda, gave Abby hope for the Brubaker brood. Alice Ann reached eagerly for her new mamm while Simon grabbed the twins' hands, and the three of them skipped in a ring around Amanda's wind-whipped skirt. At Amanda's suggestion, the trio raced toward the porch—then challenged one another to see who could stomp the loudest on the wooden stairs.

"Whoa there, you wild horses!" Abby declared as she met them at the door. "We've got dishes in our hands here. Time to put your bridles on and behave in the house."

Simon pantomimed slipping a bridle over Cora's and Dora's heads as they did the same to him, giggling. James's older sisters steered their youngsters inside, with Rosemary and her daughter close behind. Little Katie's huge eyes bespoke her fear of the impending storm as Rosemary went into the front room to cradle her in a rocking chair.

"The fellows are moving the buggies into the shed," Barbara remarked. She and the other gals gazed out windows that were being splattered with fat raindrops, which pinged with a hint of hail.

More loud footfalls pounded on the porch stairs. The men shook the rain from their hats before stepping into the kitchen. Their dark shirts were soaked, and while Jerome and the Brubaker boys laughed with the exhilaration of racing inside ahead of the weather, the older men's faces showed concern.

"Thank the Lord none of us were on the road home," Vernon said. "This is blowing into a lot more than the shower we were expecting."

A loud rumble of thunder punctuated his statement, and with the darkening sky came a burst of wind and a lightning bolt that made everyone gasp.

"Ach, the wind just snapped the swing's chains," Gail cried.

"Let's head for the basement," Sam instructed above the startled chatter that filled the kitchen. "Take the lanterns and matches—and you men be sure your family members are accounted for. Can't have any kids playing hide-and-seek outside or thinking they should stay in the barn."

Wyman, Matt, Sam, and Jerome immediately began finding faces in the crowd, as did James and his brothers-in-law. Barbara lit a lamp and paused at the top of the stairs. "What with nearly forty of us, we won't all fit in the root cellar," she said. "Those with scared kids can sit in there, and those who don't like to be crowded into small spaces can gather in the back corner, where there aren't any windows."

Abby lit more lamps for the folks heading down the dark stairs, pleased to see that everyone was proceeding without undue panic. *Thank you, Lord, for Your protection*, she prayed as another clap of thunder rattled the windows. Her faith, and the way this old home had withstood storms for more than four generations, kept her calm. As she handed the last of the lamps to Emma, who had her mamm's arm, Abby motioned to James.

"Sit by Wyman if you can," she whispered. "Amanda and I have an idea for you."

James chuckled as he escorted his dat to the basement door. "Why do I suspect you girls have been plotting?"

"Because we never stop," Abby teased. Once the Graber men began their descent, she and Sam were the last two upstairs. "I'm going for some towels and afghans. No telling how long we might be downstairs."

"I'll grab some cushions from the couches," her brother said. "Those older folks shouldn't be sitting on a concrete floor."

Moving quickly through the shadowy house, Abby soon had an armload of towels, afghans, and the shawls from the door pegs. While Barbara held the lamp high to illuminate the stairway, she and Sam descended to where their guests sat huddled in the two safest areas. Even though the afternoon had been unseasonably warm, the basement felt damp and cool—especially in the darkness of the storm. The men dried themselves as best they could, and when everyone was settled on the cushions and with the coverings, Abby headed for the spot James had saved for her.

How sweet to see those three little girls cuddled in Wyman's lap, while Simon has chosen Amanda's, she thought as she smiled at them. Abby deftly lowered herself to the floor, scooting as close to James as she dared. At last she got to spend some time with him, after a busy day of helping with his mamm's birthday party. If disaster did strike, it was a fine thing that all the people she held dearest were gathered here in Sam's basement, weathering the storm together.

"Shall we douse the lamps and pray? It might be best to save Sam's wicks for tonight, after this weather passes." Vernon's serene voice filled the basement, and as the flames flickered out, everyone took a collective breath.

So what have you been cooking up, missy?" James asked. With his parents, Jerome, and most of the Brubakers in this corner of the basement, they were all sitting close enough that pressing his arm against Abby's seemed acceptable. He noticed that Emma had chosen *not* to sit with Jerome, yet the young man seemed content chatting with their parents, making sure that they and Jemima were comfortable on their couch cushions.

Abby's eyes glimmered in the darkness. "I invited Wyman and Amanda to stay at my house this weekend while you and I go to their place to help with the kids. Would that be—"

"You've done too much for us," Wyman protested. "I couldn't impose—"

"But it's our best chance to decide how we'll handle the situation with Uriah," Amanda insisted quietly. "Just the two of us, Wyman. No interruptions. No little mouths repeating what little ears have heard."

"I can keep a secret, Mamma," one of the twins piped up.

"Jah, me, too," her sister said.

"I don't wanna talk about that mean old bishop anyway," Simon declared.

The adults chuckled at this example of how Wyman and his wife had so little opportunity to speak privately. James's pulse rate picked up. Wouldn't a day or two with the Brubaker kids be a perfect way to find out if he and Abby were suited to having a large family? "I'd be happy to help at your place," he replied. "Especially since Uriah's expecting Amanda to confess at church this Sunday."

Wyman's brow furrowed in thought. "Vernon and I just chatted about how, if the kids' feet are to be planted firmly on the ground, they need some weight put on their shoulders," he said quietly. "Maybe he'd meet with us about that, Amanda, if we spend some time here in Cedar Creek."

The wind whistled fiercely, and then a *ka-boom!* of thunder made everyone jump and start chattering. Lightning flashed, striking a tree near the window, and when a large section of the treetop fell to the ground, the house vibrated. James squeezed Abby, pleased to see that she wasn't afraid of the storm.

"I agreed with Vernon that I've let the parenting slip

since Viola passed," Wyman continued when the wind had died down. "It's time to get my family back on track, to make your job as their mamm easier, Amanda. More fairly balanced."

Amanda's expression touched James deeply. Here was a woman devoted to her family—no slouch at keeping her three girls dressed and fed without a husband's help—and now *hope* flickered on her face, visible even in the shifting shadows of the basement. "I would go along with whatever Vernon suggested," she agreed. "Not just because he likes my pottery but because he listens as compassionately as he speaks."

"That settles it, then," Abby said as she looked around their little circle. "All of us here want you Brubakers to be happy, and we'll do whatever we can to make that happen."

James reached for her hand and squeezed it, proud of the way Abby had once again given of herself to make another family's life easier.

"Will you bring fried pies, Abby? Cherry ones?" Simon asked. "That would make *me* happy!"

James laughed, even as Amanda gently reminded her son to be more polite. James recalled having a mischievous streak much like Simon's at five, being the only boy among three sisters as he was growing up.

"I could probably pack along some treats for a young fellow who'll do as I ask him," Abby replied as she tugged playfully on Simon's pant leg.

Another *whoosh* of wind made everyone gaze toward the windows on the far side of the basement. In a flash of lightning, they could see large trees waving crazily as loose leaves circled in whirlwinds. From in front of the house, beyond where they could see, came another ominous *crash* that reverberated for several moments. This storm was one such as Cedar Creek hadn't seen in a long while, yet James found his attention drawn to Abby's serene smile. Already she was figuring out special things to do for the Brubaker kids, and he looked forward to joining her at their farm. It occurred to him how much richer his life had become these past months—how many surprises he'd enjoyed because this wonderful woman spent her time with him.

Say it now! Ask her! his thoughts urged. *Whisper in her ear. You know she'll say yes.*

James held his tongue, though. He had always envisioned the special moment when he proposed marriage as something private and sacred between the two of them. There had been a time when his skittish heart had held back out of fear of rejection or another betrayal like Zanna's, but now he simply wished to honor Abby with the most important question he would ever ask her. He wanted to do this right.

Conversations remained hushed until the storm finally blew itself out of the area and the sky began to lighten. When Sam and Vernon went to the windows, however, shock tightened their faces.

"Oh, my," Sam rasped. "Several big tree branches are down—not to mention that big maple out front, which blocks the lane. The lawn is littered with fence posts—"

"Looks like we had a small tornado," Vernon said as he pointed toward the road. "I sure don't like the looks of that teetering tree near the greenhouse."

Wyman eased the children from his lap to stand up. "The least we can do is take down that tree, clear your lane, Sam, and assess the damage here before we head home. Could be our places only got a gut soaking of rain."

As the others rose around him, James helped Abby up. "I should take a look at our place before Mamm and Dat start home," he remarked as he saw the concern etched on his parents' faces.

"I'll go with you, James," Jerome insisted. As he helped Eunice up from her couch cushion, he held her gaze. "How about if you and Merle stay here where it's dry until James and I are sure you can cross the road safely?"

"We'll do that," Eunice replied, mostly to make the point to her husband. "Merle and I can find a cart to haul my presents home."

"I'll tag along with you fellows," Abby offered. "Sam's got plenty of help for clearing any blocked lanes and rounding up livestock, so I'll check your house before I see about any damage to the mercantile and Mamm's greenhouse." Without pausing for him to protest, Abby went over to reassure James's parents that she would return soon with a report.

As they stepped outside through the basement door, however, everyone got quiet. James had never seen so much damage, what with tree limbs ripped off, shingles and other debris scattered across the wet grass, and gaping holes in Matt's pasture fence. "It's a miracle that your house wasn't hit and your barn's still standing," he murmured.

"I see a few panels out of Mamm's greenhouse," she replied in a tight voice. "But we can fix those things. God has truly blessed us by sparing the people we love most."

"You're right, Abby." James pointed to the old sweet gum tree Vernon had mentioned, grimacing at the huge roots that protruded into the air on one side as it swayed precariously. "We'll need to deal with that—"

With a loud groan, the uprooted tree listed and then slammed into the ground. The impact shook the earth beneath them. The *crash* reverberated against the back of the mercantile and greenhouse, making a few more panes of glass tinkle as they fell inside it. Several of the women reached for one another, their hands going to their mouths in shock.

Abby grabbed James's hand. They stared silently at the ancient tree, native to the property when the Lambrights had acquired it generations ago. Sam and the others stood frozen in place as they took in the extent of the damage . . . and the fact that some serious sawing and hauling would have to be done before anyone could start home. The men spread out to look at the outbuildings and check on the livestock inside them, here and across the road.

James swallowed hard. A glance at his home place revealed several severed limbs and broken windows in the barn and the carriage shop, along with damage to the front porch posts of the house, but the structures had remained intact—and for that he felt immensely thankful. He inhaled repeatedly to still his racing heart. He reminded himself that their lives would return to normal and that the world had not come to an end despite the force of the fierce winds they'd heard from the Lambrights' basement.

Yet something inside him craved reassurance. His mindset shifted. What if they hadn't gotten into the house in time? What if his parents or Emma—or Abby—had been in the way when the storm had ripped off such huge tree branches and hurled them to the ground?

James felt very insignificant and vulnerable even as he sent gratitude to God for the safety of everyone he loved. The thought of losing Abby stabbed at him, even though she stood stalwartly next to him. A thunderstorm had contributed to the accident that cost Wyman Brubaker his first wife, after all, and even though he was married again, his life—and his children's lives—would be forever altered.

It seemed absurd to wait any longer. Too many times he'd let the chance to speak up pass him by.

"Abby, will you marry me?" he pleaded in a rising voice. "I love you so much I don't even want to *think* about going through another day without you by my side. If something happened to you, I couldn't—"

"James, I'm right here. I always will be." Abby turned to stand before him, taking his hands between hers. Her deep brown eyes held his, so steady and full of love they overflowed. "If it'll make you feel better, I'll marry you this very minute—if Vernon and Sam will perform the service."

James stood transfixed. His mouth opened and then closed before he hugged her fiercely. "Oh—but of course we'll do this up right, Abby. A special day and a big dinner, with all our friends and family," he insisted before a nervous laugh made him shake all over. "I just had to ask—had to know—"

He pivoted toward the other folks scattered about the yard. "I asked her, and Abby said jah!" he cried out. "We'll be getting hitched real soon!"

Everyone within earshot turned to gaze at the two of them. Applause burst out all over the large lawn.

"About *time*, Graber!" Jerome cried out as he sprinted across the wet grass. He clapped James on the back and hugged Abby exuberantly.

Emma and Barbara ran over, along with Rosemary, Vera, and the other young women. "Oh, this is the *best* news!" Emma was laughing and crying as she grabbed her brother and Abby in a hug. "A wedding will be just the thing to heal us all after this storm—"

"Yet another reason to celebrate all the gifts the Lord has bestowed upon us," Vernon agreed as he walked over. His blue eyes twinkled and his cherubic face lit up within the wreath of his snowy beard. "I've waited a long time for this particular joy, James and Abby," he said as he placed his hands on their shoulders.

James felt bubbly and excited yet indescribably at peace. "Jah, so have I," he murmured. "It's going to be a gut life for Abby and me. We'll give it all we've got."

Chapter 26

All the way home, Wyman, Amanda, and Jemima shook their heads over how some farms had escaped the storm's fury while other places had lost buildings, fences, and large old trees. "What does it mean, when one fellow's barn gets blown in while other folks don't have a blade of grass out of place?" Wyman pondered aloud.

"Jerome mentioned a newfangled weather term he heard on someone's television," Amanda said. She shifted Alice Ann on her lap. "Something like *microbust* or *microburst*, to explain a big hit of power in one spot that can crack trees and knock out electrical power. Not that any new name for storm damage helps us clean it up."

Jemima let out a short laugh in the buggy's backseat, where she sat with the twins. "Might take a microburst to get Emma and our Jerome together," she remarked. "Seems like one's trying to outdo the other, far as pretending not to be interested. Maybe James and Abby's engagement will get them off the fence."

"With Jerome, there's no telling what he's up to," Amanda pointed out. "But Merle and Eunice sure are crazy about him."

"Nice of him to stay and help James put plywood in the windows that blew out," Wyman remarked. He sat taller in the seat when the home place came into view, clucking for the horse to go faster. "Let's hope Wags is safe in his doghouse, or we'll have no end to Simon's . . . oh, my. This doesn't look gut."

As they hurried round the last curve, the destruction on the front of the house made Wyman suck in his breath. He halted the horse . . . heard the buggy behind theirs, which Eddie was driving for Simon and the older kids, stop behind him.

"Wags! Wags!" the little boy hollered as he hit the ground running.

While Wyman understood the anguish in that shrill voice, he also knew how dangerous it was for Simon to approach the damaged house. He jumped down from the buggy and ran until he hooked an arm around his frantic son, praying that the dog would bark when he heard Simon's voice.

"But, Dat, we've *got* to see if—"

"And we *will*," Wyman insisted as he lifted his struggling son to his shoulder. He whistled loudly, yet another prayer for Simon to be spared the agony of losing his pet.

Meanwhile, he could only gape at the front of the house: two massive old maple trees had toppled, one into the kitchen and the other into the front room. They had crashed through the roof and upper story on their way down, leaving three bedrooms open to the elements.

Behind him, he heard Amanda's anguished "Ohhhh—"

"What happened, Mamma? Lemme see!" one of the twins piped up.

"There's Wags!" the other one crowed. "Let's get out and—"

"You girls are staying right here," Jemima said as she

grabbed them. "We can't see what other damage might be waiting for us—and what we *can* see is plenty nasty enough."

Wyman stood motionless, unable to process the horrendous sight before him. He set Simon on the ground while Wags bounded toward them. As he watched the boy tussle with his dog in the wet grass, Wyman wished himself back at that innocent age when play was so much more pressing than the responsibilities of parenting . . . when he could depend on the adults to provide his food and shelter without a moment's doubt that they would. With few exceptions, he'd spent every day and night of his life in this old white farmhouse, and that comfort—that eternal sense of security—had just been snatched away from him. The only positive side to the devastation was that somehow Wags had gotten out of his pen and into a safe place.

"Let's think about what we need to do," Wyman said above the children's worried chatter. He gestured for everyone to get out of the rigs and gather around him. "First off, we thank God that we weren't here during the storm, and that none of us are hurt—including Wags."

During their moments of silence, Wyman corralled his racing thoughts, hoping that in his state of shock and disbelief he would take proper care of his family. Never in his life had he thought his beloved home would become uninhabitable, and nothing had prepared him for such an emergency.

"We can't sleep here tonight," he said when the others had raised their heads. "And no matter how badly you want to go inside, we can't enter the house until someone from the propane company checks for leaks. Is everyone clear on that?"

"Why, Dat?" Simon whined. "It's still our house, ain't so?"

"Jah," Eddie replied, "but if gas has been leaking from the stove or the furnace, the whole place could explode when we light a lamp."

The twins huddled closer to their mother, and Alice

Ann's thumb went into her mouth. Four sets of little eyes widened as they gazed at their home.

"Do you understand why we can't go inside now?" Wyman looked at each of the kids until they nodded at him, wishing he could wipe the fear from their earnest faces. "Vera, you and Lizzie go down to the Bylers' roadside motel and see if you can get us three or four rooms. Eddie and Pete, you can check the livestock in the barn while I call for someone to check the gas."

He looked at Amanda then, pleased that she and Jemima had remained calm. "You ladies stay put until I get back from the elevator office," he said. "Have I left anything out?"

"What about me, Dat? I wanna help, too!" Simon hopped from one foot to the other beside his dog. His hair was rumpled and his clothes were streaked with wet grass stains, but his spirits had rallied with the chance to be of assistance.

Wyman was thankful for this son, who made him smile. "You and Wags come to the elevator with me. We need to decide what kind of pizza and subs to order."

"Jah, I can do that!"

Amanda was scanning the branch-strewn lawn and then glanced down the road toward the Fisher place. "You might call Ray and see how his family has fared . . . see if he and his boys can help you haul those trees out of the house sometime soon."

"Gut idea." Wyman stared again at the caved-in section of his lifelong home. It struck him then: the folks in Cedar Creek had been checking one another's places as soon as the storm had passed, sawing the tree in Sam's lane and helping with repairs. While it was true they had no close Amish neighbors, because the Fisher place adjoined Brubaker property alongside the elevator and the railroad tracks—and other folks in their district were probably tending to their own damaged property—Wyman felt strangely . . . isolated.

Was it his troubled imagination, or had church members kept their distance since he'd married Amanda? Friends aplenty had extended their condolences and brought food after Viola's death, yet those ladies—and their husbands—had been absent these past few weeks. He'd been too concerned with the harvest and blending two families to notice it until now.

Maybe he was just feeling desperate and sorry for himself, and he had no time for such useless emotions. His family was depending on his decisions. His direction.

"We'll handle this crisis one step at a time, as best we can. We've got one another, and that means everything," Wyman murmured before he went to make his calls. "God's gotten us this far safely, and He'll see us through to wherever He's leading us."

Within half an hour, Wyman felt that the situation was indeed in the Lord's capable hands: a truck from the propane company had been in the area when he called and was on its way. When he returned from the office, Amanda and the girls were picking up small limbs and litter from the yard. The older boys came back from the barn chores to report that the animals were skittish but safe. The Bylers had rooms for them in the old mom-and-pop motel down the road, and supper would be delivered in about an hour. Best of all, Ray and the two older Fisher boys were coming by first thing in the morning with their chain saws to clear away those fallen trees.

Step by step, one foot in front of the other, Wyman reminded himself—because it kept him from dwelling on the catastrophic damage done to his home. By the time the propane man had turned off the tank and declared the house free of leaks, the sun was sinking in the red-streaked western sky. Wyman saw the curiosity on his children's faces, but he couldn't turn them loose.

"We can't risk having the floor collapse or pieces of the roof falling on you," he told them. "So I want you kids and Jemima to drive on down to the motel, while your mamm and I pack up some clothes for everybody. After we see what damage has been done, wc'll have a better idea of what to do next. Meanwhile, save us a sub and some pizza, all right?"

"But, Dat, I wanna check my room—"

"We've got to get our dolls—"

"Nope." Wyman held up his hands to silence them. "Better enjoy this time off tonight, because plenty of work awaits us until we get our home put back together. Scoot, now. We'll see you in a while."

When the two buggies were rolling down the road, Wyman let out a huge sigh. Worry weighed him down like a wet overcoat as he took Amanda's hand. "I can't stop wondering what this means," he murmured as they started down the lane. "And I can already hear Uriah declaring that God sent the storm here to get me back on the path to salvation. To set me straight about my attitude."

"*Your* attitude?" Amanda murmured. "It's me who's led you astray, with my pottery and my flashy, short dresses."

Wyman smiled ruefully. "I went to see Uriah after he smashed your pottery. Didn't let on about it, because I didn't want to upset you any more," he admitted in a low voice. "The bishop informed me that I was too blinded by my love for you to be focused on God's will. At least he was right about that one thing."

They stopped several feet in front of the porch, which was filled with the top of a huge, uprooted tree. Shattered window glass, broken furniture, and gaping walls were warning enough not to come any closer, and the moan of the sagging upstairs floor sounded like the desolate cry of Wyman's frightened heart. "We'll have to go in through the back. But don't pack anything until I've entered the rooms first," he insisted. "Looks like Vera, Lizzie, and the older boys might have to wear some of our clothes for a while."

"We'll figure it out, Wyman. And you know what?"

The strength in his wife's voice made him pause before they opened the back door. Amanda looked wary about entering the house, but she had remained as solid as a rock throughout their ordeal this afternoon. "What, my love?"

When she smiled, his heart lifted. "I'm not telling you what to do," she said, "but I have a house that'll hold us all, you know. We can live there until this place is put back together. And now that Jerome's returned that eight-mule team to its owner, we can move the animals into my barns, too."

Wyman's breath caught. Wasn't this the most obvious sign of all that God was watching out for him, despite the negative things Uriah Schmucker had said? He cupped Amanda's sweet face between his hands, kissed her, and then pressed his forehead to hers. "You can't imagine what a relief this is—"

"Jah, I can," she whispered.

"—and how many problems you've just solved by mentioning a house I'd forgotten about," he went on. "Denki, Amanda."

"You're welcome. You've had a lot on your mind these past few hours."

Wyman hugged her close and then opened the door to peer inside. The kitchen cabinets and appliances nearest the front had been crushed by the tree, and the room was filled with shingles, wet lumber, and a demolished bed and dresser from Vera and Lizzie's room. He shut the door quickly, before he could dwell on the extent of the damage—and because they were losing daylight. "We'll go in the other way," he said, pointing toward the addition where the dawdi haus was.

And wasn't it true, the adage about God shutting a door but then opening a window? Wyman sensed that Amanda had thrown open more than a simple window for their family. He clung to that hope as he clutched her hand, and together they went inside.

Chapter 27

By the next afternoon, Wyman, Ray, and the Fisher boys had hacked the fallen trees into manageable pieces with their chain saws while Eddie and Pete hauled the chunks off into the yard with the forklifts from the elevator. One of Ray's cousins, who worked for the electric cooperative, was to come with a "cherry picker" truck so they could fasten tarps over the exposed section of the house when they had finished working for the day. The situation was grave and everyone was upset about losing some of their belongings, yet Amanda thrummed with hope. She hadn't pointed this out to Wyman, but because her furniture from Bloomingdale had been stashed in the shed, all her pieces had been spared. Wasn't this God's providence at work?

When Uriah Schmucker pulled into the lane, however, Amanda steered the kids to the side yard to pick up debris, figuring the bishop would rather speak with Wyman than her. When the chain saws stopped, Uriah's reedy voice rang out as he surveyed the damage.

"Time to set your house in order, Wyman," he declared. "If this storm damage isn't God's punishment, what else would you call it?"

Amanda scowled at Uriah's self-righteous tone. She watched Wyman set down the section of crushed kitchen cabinet he'd been carrying to wipe his forehead on his sleeve. "Jah, I see this as the Lord's way of saying it's time to remodel—both our home and our family," he replied confidently. "I'm sure you'll understand why we'll not be at the service on Sunday. We won't be able to live here for a long while, so we'll be staying in Bloomingdale. On Amanda's farm."

Amanda's heart danced. She'd secretly hoped Wyman would consider that angle about church—just as she knew the bishop would get steamed about it.

"That's ducking your responsibility to God," Uriah replied with a glare. "And if Amanda fails to confess, as I've directed, you're both setting a bad example for your children. Not to mention risking your wife's salvation."

"Ah, but God was the first one I talked to about this," Wyman replied quietly. "What a blessing it was to find our Brubaker family Bible unharmed, and to read our evening devotions in the safety of our motel room. Jesus was saying that 'In my Father's house are many mansions: if it were not so, I would have told you. I go to prepare a place for you.'"

Amanda held her breath. That passage had brought them great comfort last night, but Clearwater's bishop discouraged his flock from reading the Scriptures. He believed lay folks were too inclined toward their own interpretations.

"Beware of using God's word to justify your actions," Uriah warned in a strident voice. "You're crossing the line into heresy—"

"But how can that be?" Wyman asked in all sincerity. "While Jesus was referring to making a place for believers in Heaven, in our hour of need we were able to stay at the motel. And because Amanda has a furnished home, our family can recover from this disaster together as we rebuild our lives here. Seems God has provided us many mansions even in this earthly life, wouldn't you say? And for that we are truly thankful."

Uriah's scowl could have made the hens stop laying. "You'd best halt *right there* with your loose interpretation of—"

Wyman crossed his arms. His expression remained calm, but he was clearly not in the mood for Uriah's lecture. "Is it wrong for Lizzie and Pete to keep up with their schooling in Bloomingdale while Eddie and I work with carpenters to rebuild this house?" he asked. "Is it wrong for Amanda to keep our family together, running the household—as you've told her to? While it's painful to see my family in such upheaval, I believe God is working His purpose out during this setback. He's showing us ways to fix what's broken. Ways to amend our lives."

Amanda's heart beat faster, and she wanted to cheer for her husband. She and Wyman had talked late into the night, and his faith—the transformation of yesterday's devastation into today's hope and purpose—was an inspiration for the whole family.

"I can see my words are falling on deaf ears." Uriah glanced disparagingly at the three Fishers, who had quietly continued carrying debris from the kitchen. "You folks have been associating too closely with these Mennonites . . . another topic we'll pray over at the Members' Meeting on Sunday."

"We'll appreciate any prayers you offer in our behalf. And now, bishop, I have work to do," Wyman replied coolly. "Denki for stopping by."

Oh, but Uriah looked ready to pop. Amanda sensed the bishop would soon return with the district's other two preachers to discuss Wyman's *attitude*. And what could they say about her husband's partnering with the Fisher family for all these years? Wyman and Ray had built the elevator before they'd married or joined the church—before Uriah had become the bishop—with help from both families. Amanda couldn't help but notice that Uriah hadn't lifted a finger . . . and that it was Ray's wife, Sally, who brought over a noon meal for them.

As they were finishing their dinner of fried chicken, stewed tomatoes, and cabbage with noodles, Amanda's ears perked up. While it was everyday business for the men to discuss local crops and the farmers who raised them, Trevor Fisher's voice had an interesting edge to it.

"Our uncle's cheese factory is doing such a gut business, they're looking for more local milk," he said as he stood up to gaze over the lower hayfields. "Wyman, I was wondering if I could rent some of your pastureland to expand my dairy herd—next spring, probably, when the grass would be growing to feed the extra cows. I'd maintain the fences, of course, and pay whatever you think's fair."

Wyman's eyebrows rose at this unexpected question. "That's not really such a stretch, since we already sell you a lot of the hay we raise," he replied in a thoughtful voice. "The feed would go directly into your cows without us having to bale it."

"Jah, I was hoping you'd see it that way," Trevor said.

Now there's an interesting turn of events, Amanda thought. As far as she knew, Wyman's land had never been used by anyone except Brubakers. The farm had provided for previous generations, but Wyman had diversified into the grain trade because the acreage couldn't support another growing family. As the men rose to resume work on the house, Amanda helped Sally pack up their dishes.

"We're guessing Trevor has his eye on a certain young lady," Sally murmured. "He's taking his instruction to join the church, and he's suddenly a lot more interested in earning a gut living."

"It usually takes the right girl to convince a young man

to get out of rumspringa and into adulthood," Amanda agreed.

Sally focused on Eddie and Pete, who were shoveling debris into wheelbarrows. "You know, I just made Tyler and Trevor longer pants, and the ones they've outgrown would be about right for your boys. How about if I bring you a box of trousers and shirts? Too bad I don't have any girls—"

"Ach, but you folks have helped us so much already." Amanda grasped Sally's arm, overcome by this quiet woman's generosity. "You have no idea how much your kindness means to us."

Sally's face lit up. "If you need anything at all, just ask us, promise? We've been put on this earth to love one another, after all."

That summed up the very basis of the Plain faith, didn't it? As Amanda waved at Sally's departing buggy, she believed the difficult task of rebuilding the Brubaker house might go better than they'd expected, even if the Fishers' friendship wouldn't ease the situation with Uriah. While she knew it was wrong to dodge the bishop's request for her kneeling confession, she saw their temporary living arrangement in Bloomingdale as a postponement of her moment of truth—not a way to escape it. Disagreeing with the bishop did *not* mean she could ignore his ruling, for God had chosen him to lead Clearwater's congregation.

But look how many solutions have come to us in just a day of trusting the Lord, she reasoned. *Surely more answers will reveal themselves during our stay in Bloomingdale . . . while we solidify as a family.*

That afternoon, Amanda, Vera, and Lizzie were working in the unharmed end of the upstairs, packing the younger children's clothes, when the *clip-clop! clip-clop!* of hooves announced another visitor.

"My stars, when you said the storm hit—" a familiar voice called out.

"Glad you called us, Wyman. Is this a gut time to talk about moving you folks back to Amanda's place?"

Lizzie's face lit up. "It's Abby and James! Let's take a break and visit with them."

"You girls go on down. I'll be there in a bit." Amanda smiled at the rapid patter of their footsteps on the wooden stairs. It pleased her that Wyman had called upon so many friends, rather than believing their family could deal with this disaster alone. She could recall a time when he had remained stoic and self-reliant, as though he believed God was dishing up trouble as punishment for his sins.

Amanda peered into the room she and Wyman shared, where Jemima had been packing for them. "Seems more helpers have stopped by. Sure wish we could offer them more than water from the pump."

Jemima looked up from the suitcase she was closing. "We all take our turn at depending on the kindness of others," she mused aloud. "But I can't say I'm sorry to be going back to the home place. Beats all that folks from far and wide are lending you and Wyman a hand, when members of the Clearwater church—"

"Jah, I've noticed that, too. Just one more thing we have to figure out as we put our household together again." Amanda gestured for her mother-in-law to precede her down the stairs. "I'm hearing a tone in Wyman's voice I've not noticed before. Maybe he's considering bigger changes than he wants to talk about in front of the kids—but it's for him to decide what comes next. You and I can just keep praying he'll do the right thing for all of us."

When Amanda and Jemima made their way around to the front yard, Abby ran over to hug them. "What a horrible mess to come home to," she gushed. "I'll get the gals in Cedar Creek together for a sewing frolic this weekend to replace the clothes you lost. And what about food? Did you lose any canned goods or the meat in your deep freeze?"

"The jars downstairs are untouched, and we've kept the

freezer shut since the gas got turned off," Amanda replied. "We lost all the staples in the kitchen, as you can see, but otherwise—"

"Well, it's mighty handy that my brother runs a mercantile, ain't so?" Abby placed her hands lightly on Amanda's shoulders. "Sam says he wants to help any way he can, so consider your kitchen in Bloomingdale restocked. How about if James and I pack up your frozen foods and get them into a deep freeze at the store until you get shifted? We brought along several knocked-down boxes."

Amanda's mouth opened and then closed as she took in what Abby was saying. "You're a miracle on two legs, walking amongst whoever needs you," she murmured. "Bless you ever so much, Abby."

Within an hour, the deep freeze was emptied and the boxes of meat and frozen vegetables were loaded into James's wagon. Abby had jotted down Lizzie's and Vera's measurements for new dresses, too. Because they were only moving their clothing, some food, and a few other personal necessities, Wyman told the newly engaged couple to stay in Cedar Creek rather than coming to Clearwater for the Saturday morning move. "What with the Fishers helping us, we've got plenty of muscle and rigs to get us into Amanda's place," he said. "It's such a help that you're keeping our frozen food, and we'll stop by for those boxes on our way through town."

James had another idea, however, as he climbed up into the driver's seat. "Don't know if you folks have carpenters in mind, but I could ask Amos and Owen Coblentz to give you a bid," he offered. "What with the way the fellows in Cedar Creek helped them rebuild the Ropps' house after their fire, we can have you folks back in your house pretty fast."

Wyman let out a long sigh as he considered this. He was looking tired after a day of physical labor, but his expression bespoke his good spirits, despite the work and decisions that would fill the coming days. "I'll think on that," he replied. "I've promised God to take this process one day—one step—at a time, so I don't miss out on anything the Lord wants me to consider. Can't thank you and Abby and your families enough, James. See you tomorrow, when we come through Cedar Creek."

Yet another interesting twist, Amanda thought as she waved them off. While a couple of cabinetmakers lived in Clearwater, she was surprised that Wyman hadn't jumped at the offer to have the Coblentz fellows stop by—Amos and his son Owen were well respected for their craftsmanship and the homes they had built all over this part of Missouri.

However, if their friends from Cedar Creek were already seeing to the clothes the kids needed, plus the kitchen staples they had lost, while the Fishers would keep helping with the cleanup after the move, hadn't this day brought more blessings than anyone could count? The sight of the mail car had the kids dashing out to the box, and after Amanda visited with the carrier, she crossed the road to check for phone messages in the elevator office. No doubt word had gotten around about the damage to their house, and other folks might be trying to contact Wyman.

When she pushed the blinking red button, Amanda had to smile. ATLEE LAMBRIGHT showed in the message window, as she hadn't changed the directory listing after her husband passed. It was Jerome's voice that filled the little office.

"Awful sorry to hear about those trees landing on your house, Wyman, but I'm glad you called to say you folks'll be bunking here in Bloomingdale for a while," he said. "Tell Aunt Amanda I'll try to have the place cleaned up before you get here. I haven't changed a thing, so all the spaces for her furniture are just waiting for those pieces to come back home."

A giggle escaped her. Maybe she should erase Jerome's

message so Wyman wouldn't think her nephew was out of line, implying she should be returning to her first husband's farm . . . hinting that all of them might stay beyond the time it took to repair the Brubaker place.

But no, Jerome had spoken his mind to Wyman before. Amanda replayed her nephew's message for the fun of it, and left it for Wyman to hear, as well. Considering all the offers and suggestions they had received since the storm, why should she interfere with anyone who wished to help them? God worked through all His people, and it seemed there was no limit to the blessings He had delivered today.

Chapter 28

What would we do without our friends? Wyman looked at his family and the Fishers on Saturday morning, inter-mingled at the long table in Ray and Sally's kitchen. He swallowed his final bite of breakfast and stood up. "Sally, that wonderful-gut sausage and egg casserole will get us off to a fine start today," he said. "We can't thank you folks enough for helping us through this difficult time."

Amanda rose, too, and began scraping plates. "We'll help you with all these dishes—"

"No, you won't!" Sally insisted. "You folks have a full day of it, getting shifted to your other place. It was gut hav-ing you all here to eat with us."

Wyman discussed a few plans with Ray and his two sons, who were helping with the move, and then the Brubaker and Fisher rigs headed down the road. Wyman grimaced at the sight of his damaged home place, partly covered by big blue tarps, yet he felt happier than he had in a long while. While his body ached from yesterday's physical labor, his mind and emotions were adjusting to this temporary change of residence. Amanda had been kind enough not to remind him that she had gone through the same upheaval when she'd moved from her home in Bloomingdale. And Amanda had sensed his moments of desperation when thoughts of his lifelong home, with its gaping holes and destroyed furnishings, threatened to undo him. Rather than telling him how he should feel, or how grateful he should be that they could move to her farm for a while, she had simply wrapped her arms around him.

What would you do without this fine wife? He could not imagine the chaos his family would be experiencing if the storm had struck their home before he had remarried. And indeed, Amanda's suggestion that she, Jemima, and the girls take the first load of food and clothing, so they could get everyone settled today, made far better sense than his idea of taking the animals first.

When they'd parked the buggies in front of the house, Wyman came out of his deep thoughts to organize their loading efforts. "Pete, how about if you and Tyler take Simon out to the barn with you?"

"We get to gather up the feed and hitch the horses to the wagons, like you said last night, jah?" his youngest son piped up. "Let's go, guys! Last one out's a rotten egg!"

"And speaking of eggs." Jemima smiled at Cora and Dora. "If you twins will take Alice Ann and gather up what the hens have laid, Lizzie and Vera can catch the chickens. It'll take all day if we set the fellows to that job."

Wyman laughed. Jemima was in good spirits about moving back to the Lambright place, even if it was only to be their temporary home. "Meanwhile, Eddie, you and Trevor can help Ray and me carry the canned food upstairs, so we'll be ready to load the first wagon."

"We'll get the suitcases and boxes of clothes outside," Amanda said as she headed toward the back door with her mother-in-law behind her. "Won't take us long."

Where would we be without teamwork and coopera-tion? Wyman thought as he and Ray and their two eldest sons followed the women inside. The men descended the basement stairs and then each of them hefted a box of home-canned vegetables. "Hard to know if we'll need all these jars we packed," Wyman said. "Depends on how long it takes to put this place back together."

"That can't happen soon enough to suit me," Eddie re-marked as he started up the stairs. "Not much goes on in Bloomingdale, from what I've seen."

Wyman put a foot on the bottom step, hanging back for a moment. "Thanks again for your help, fellows," he mur-mured to Ray and Trevor. "That boy of mine's none too keen about leaving his buddies behind. I'm thinking it's time for some good old-fashioned attitude adjustment—meaning, so much manual labor rebuilding this place that he's too tired to care about running with his friends."

"Jah, there's that," Trevor replied. "Comes with being out of school but not yet old enough for rumspringa."

Wyman nodded at this observation as he studied his partner's son. Was it his imagination, or had Trevor Fisher filled out over the summer? The young man was all muscle now, with a clear-thinking mind. How had he changed so quickly from the little boy who had loved to tumble down the mountains of shelled field corn piled at the elevator?

"Trevor, I was thinking last night that you might want to start milking those extra cows sooner rather than later," he began, winking at Ray. "I saw the sale bill for Elmer Riehl's auction—"

"Jah, he's fixing to retire," Trevor cut in eagerly. "Selling off his milking equipment and most of his cows."

Wyman smiled. This young man was eager to start his adult life, and he admired such ambition. "So why not ex-pand your herd now? Not telling you what to do or how to pay for it, understand," he continued, "but that barn we're using for hay storage was a milking parlor in my dat's day.

If you'd care to make the repairs on it, we could shift the hay to other places—"

"You'd let me do that?" Trevor's eyes nearly filled his face.

"That's mighty generous of you," Ray remarked. "Especially since your own boys are coming to an age when they'll decide how to make their way."

Wyman's heart skipped in his chest. This conversation took him back to when he and Ray had first considered going into the elevator business. "For you folks, I would do that," he replied quietly. "And what with having another farm in the family now, Eddie and Pete have more options—although neither of them seems inclined to take up farming as a first choice."

It felt good to offer Trevor a chance to make a go of it, especially because land prices had shot up higher than most young fellows could afford. Truth be told, it would save him a lot of cutting and baling if cows grazed that pasture . . . and the looks Ray and his son exchanged confirmed that they were seriously considering his offer.

By the time they'd made a few more trips with the canned goods, Pete was pulling up alongside the house in a wagon hitched to one of the Belgians. They got the clothing and food loaded in short order, leaving room for the girls to ride in the back. With so much good help, Amanda was climbing into the driver's seat half an hour later, looking serene and capable. Jemima settled on the seat beside her, wrapping an old quilt around their legs.

"Bye, girls. Be gut for your mamm," Wyman called to his daughters.

Alice Ann waved at him from Vera's lap, and he couldn't miss how excited Cora, Dora, and Lizzie looked as they called out their good-byes. They were bundled in their heavier jackets and bonnets, and the crisp autumn air and sunshine made for a perfect day to be on the road.

As the ladies pulled onto the county highway, Wyman

couldn't suppress a grin. "All right, fellows, I haven't told Amanda, but we're taking her furniture with us," he announced. "What with all of us extra folks living at her place, and Jerome saying the house still has all the right empty spaces, it seems like a gut way to make her happy."

Eddie and Pete raised their eyebrows at each other, hinting at their disapproval. Or perhaps they didn't relish reloading old furniture they had no connections to—but to Wyman, it felt like the right move.

Ray clapped him on the back. "Considering how much better off you are these days, my friend, making Amanda happy seems like the reasonable thing to do, jah?"

"Jah, because when Mamma ain't happy, ain't nobody happy," Simon quipped.

Wyman stared at his youngest son as the other fellows laughed out loud. "I don't know where you pick these things up, Simon, but that's a gut thing for *you* to keep in mind, ain't so?" he teased. "You and Wags will have to toe the mark at Amanda's place, or Jerome will harness you up like one of his mules."

Simon's round face lit up. "Mules! I'm gonna help Jerome with those awesome mules when we get there! Let's go *now*!"

What would we do without this boy's energy and enthusiasm? Wyman thought as they headed toward the shed where Amanda's furniture was stored. *Simon might well be the one who gets us through these next weeks with our perspective and sense of humor intact.*

As Amanda let the big Belgian set its own road pace, her thoughts buzzed like bees. She had so many things to tend to, because she wanted the children settled in their rooms by the end of the day. With a preaching service to attend tomorrow, and the Sabbath being a day when no work was to be done, it was important for all eleven of them—plus

Jerome—to be able to dress and eat breakfast with a minimum of fuss.

"So, Mamma, do we get our old rooms back?" Lizzie asked eagerly. "Where will we put the boys?"

"I don't want Simon in our room!" Cora declared.

"Jah, because he sneaks Wags in at night," Dora said. "He wants to help Jerome with the mules, so maybe he should sleep out in the barn with them!"

Amanda turned to smile at her daughters, who were clearly excited about this return to Bloomingdale. "Let's remember that Vera and Simon shifted into different rooms when we moved into their house, so we should share and be willing to change, just like they were," she replied. "And it's not like we're staying for gut, you know."

"I have a suggestion," Jemima said. "It would suit me just fine to sleep in the dawdi haus, which would open up a room for Eddie and Pete . . . and get me out of the main bathroom, too."

Amanda smiled ruefully, for her mother-in-law had felt like she was in the way at the Brubaker place. "If you're sure you'll be all right—"

"A downstairs room is better for me anyway, with these legs acting up," Jemima insisted. "Probably should've moved into those rooms long ago . . . and it'll be quieter there. No pitter-patter of little feet in the hallway at night."

"But, Mammi," Cora said. "We won't need to go to Mamma's room anymore because that wolf doesn't live at our house."

"Jah, he won't be scratching on our wall or howling anymore," Dora chimed in.

"*That* would be an improvement," Amanda murmured. After finding a metal currycomb beneath Simon's bed yesterday, she and Wyman had confirmed where those scratching noises had been coming from, and this change of houses would be the perfect opportunity to stop them. "What do you think, Lizzie? Would you and Vera rather share Mammi's old room?" she asked. "We'll let Jerome stay put, and your dat and I will be in my room, and we could put a bunk in the sewing room for Simon. But I'll put you girls in charge of where Alice Ann and the twins should go, and Eddie and Pete, too."

"Jah, that works!" Lizzie said. "Vera, you and I can go upstairs and figure that out first thing."

"Jerome will help you shift beds or set up the extra ones we've stored in the attic." Amanda checked that chore off her mental list. It would be best for the older girls to arrange their siblings' rooms and clothes anyway, while the boys helped Wyman with the unloading. She and Wyman had agreed that all the kids needed more responsibility, and that they should be held accountable for their decisions, too.

She glanced at Jemima. "Shall we stop by the mercantile? See if they'll load our frozen food and those cooking supplies Abby offered us? You and I could get the kitchen whipped into shape that way and make dinner, along with something to take for tomorrow's common meal."

"Jah, and if I do the cooking, that'll free you up to tell the fellows where to put things as they unload." Jemima was trying to suppress a satisfied grin. "Even if Jerome's left the place looking like a bachelor's hideout, it'll be gut to have my kitchen back . . . if only for a few weeks, jah?"

"We'll know more about that after Wyman talks to the carpenters. He hasn't had time to call them, busy as we've been." Amanda hadn't let on to Wyman or the kids, but she harbored a secret hope that the rebuilding would take most of the winter. Was she being selfish? It would be so good to worship with old friends tomorrow . . . to eat meals cooked in the kitchen she'd known since she'd married Atlee, and to watch autumn ease into winter through the large, sunny windows in the room where she'd worked on her pottery.

It won't be the same without my wheel and clay and glazes . . . but I'll be too busy to notice, she told herself.

And if the girls want that nice downstairs room for themselves, well, I don't have a gut reason to refuse them, do I?

As they rounded the bend near Cedar Creek, Amanda could see that most of the downed trees and broken windows had been cleaned up to the point it didn't look like this little town had even seen a storm. *Neighbor helping neighbor*, she mused. *That's how it's supposed to be.* She had hardly halted the horse in the mercantile's parking lot before Sam stepped outside.

"You gals got an early start!" he said cheerfully. "Let me tell Abby you're here. She and Emma put a few things together for you."

Moments later Sam was pulling a wooden cart toward the wagon, and as he lifted bulk bags of flour and other kitchen staples to the wagon bed, Vera and Lizzie shifted them over beside the other packed boxes. Abby, too, came outside with a cart that was filled with bundles wrapped in brown paper, while Emma walked along beside her, holding a garment bag.

"You ladies have a busy day ahead of you," Emma remarked. "I can't imagine changing houses and having to move your things again so soon. James and the folks send you their best."

"Mamm and Eunice and Emma and I had our own little sewing frolic last night," Abby added as she beamed at Amanda. "We got some dresses made, and then we wrapped up some socks and underthings from the store—"

"And I'd better see a bill for the fabric and the underwear—not to mention for the cooking supplies," Amanda rasped. Who would have believed such generosity? As she helped Abby and Emma hand the packages up to the girls in the wagon, she saw that each one was labeled—and there was a bundle for each member of the family, not just for the kids who had lost their clothes. "Wyman will have a fit when he sees how much you've given us."

"I'll handle Wyman," Sam replied with a chuckle. "Stop

by with the kids who lost shoes and boots, and we'll fix you up with the right sizes. Got a new shipment in last week."

Amanda let out an exasperated sigh. "Wyman will insist on paying you," she repeated, "and we'll just have to have all you Lambrights out for dinner soon—and, Emma, I want you and James and your parents to come along, too. How about a week from tomorrow, when it's a visiting Sunday?"

Emma's expression vacillated, as though she'd really love to come yet she felt hesitant. "That'll depend on how Mamm and Dat are doing that day," she hedged.

Abby glanced quizzically at her friend as she emptied her wagon. "That would be nice, Amanda. We'd love to come," she insisted. "And I've got Gail covering for me in the store today, so if you need help unpacking, I can go with you right now."

When Emma handed up the garment bag, Amanda counted six hangers. How on earth had these busy women found time to sew up that many dresses since yesterday? And now Abby was offering to spend her day helping them, as well. "Denki so much," Amanda murmured, "but you've already gone above and beyond, Abby. I'm putting the kids in charge of setting up their rooms, and with Jerome and the Fisher fellows helping, we'll be settled in no time."

Sam slung his arm around her shoulder. "I'm not supposed to tell you this, cousin, but Jerome has already paid for your groceries and some new pie pans and bowls and whatnot. I suspect he's real glad to have his favorite cooks moving back home for a while."

Up on the seat, Jemima laughed. "Well, what do you think about that? I might just find the time to make that boy a raisin sour cream pie today."

"Jah, he made sure we put in a big bag of raisins." Abby flashed Amanda a grin. "We'll be right back! Don't leave yet."

"Jah, we couldn't carry everything on this last trip," Emma added as she hurried toward the store behind Abby.

Now what were they going to do? Amanda knew better than to protest their generosity any further, even as she surveyed the huge stack of staples and clothing the Lambrights had added to their load. "Looks like the frozen food should wait until the men come through," she suggested. "They're loading the animals into Ray's stock trailer, so they'll have room for it in the buggies and the other wagon."

"That'll work. You'll be settled in no time, and then your Clearwater house will be rebuilt, and all of these inconveniences will be behind you," Sam said. His expression sobered then. "After that, it's a matter of how you work everything out with your bishop. But the Lord will see to that, as well."

"Jah, He will," she said, hoping she sounded confident rather than doubtful. "Uriah's none too happy about us leaving the district when I was to make my kneeling confession tomorrow, but we all have to *wait* occasionally. Even bishops, ain't so?"

"That's one way to look at it, jah. Hope you get these matters—"

"Here you go!" Abby rushed around the side of the wagon with a lidded container, which she pressed into Amanda's hands. "Even though James and I won't be watching the kids for you this weekend, I thought a certain somebody might be tickled to have these."

At that, Cora and Dora peered eagerly over the side of the wagon. "What's in there?" one twin asked, while her sister said, "Let's look now! I bet Abby made us some goodies!"

Amanda laughed. "This pan will ride up front with Mammi and me, so everyone sees this surprise when we eat our dinner," she said. "Denki ever so much, Abby."

"And here's a little something for your breakfast," Emma said as she handed a rectangular pan to Jemima. "You gals have a lot to do today, without worrying about baking for Sunday, too."

Jemima lifted the lid of the pan and chuckled when she saw its contents. "Why do I suspect you made these for *another* certain somebody at our place?" she asked.

As Emma's cheeks flushed, her brow furrowed. "Now don't you go thinking I—I baked anything for Jerome," she stammered. "Matter of fact, if he carries on as though these sticky buns are especially for him, you'd better set him straight right off. He's been nice to my folks lately, jah, but that doesn't mean I'll go out on even one date with him."

Amanda blinked, while Sam and Abby seemed surprised by Emma's declaration, as well. "I still hope you and James will bring your parents next Sunday," Amanda repeated. "Wyman and I want to thank you for all you've done—and it'll be a fine time to celebrate everyone surviving the storm and moving beyond it."

"Can't think of a better reason for getting together," Sam agreed. He reached up to clasp her hand. "Have a gut day with your move, Amanda—and if there's anything you need, you know where to come."

As Amanda drove on down the county blacktop toward Bloomingdale, her mind was spinning yet again. She wasn't sure what to think about Emma's attitude toward Jerome—but was there no end to Sam's generosity and Abby's surprises? If she could make any request at all, she would have her cousin the preacher convince Uriah Schmucker to back down from his hard-line attitude about the state of her soul and its salvation. But as Sam had said, the Lord would see that everything happened the way He wanted it to. Patience and prayer were her best friends . . .

Such concerns disappeared once they pulled into the familiar old farm lane. Oh, but it was good to see Jerome stepping out onto the porch, and it was music to her ears as the girls laughed and jumped down to hug him. Even though Vera hung back, gazing around the yard and at the house as she talked quietly to Alice Ann, Wyman's eldest child seemed ready to accept this temporary home with an open heart.

And wasn't it a joy to watch Lizzie take Vera by the hand, chattering about the different rooms they had to choose from? Lizzie seemed like her former self again—looking forward to school with her friends, smiling and laughing and singing while she'd chased down the chickens this morning. Cora and Dora followed their sisters inside, their faces bright with the excitement of returning to the house where they'd been born.

Jerome helped Jemima down from the wagon and then slipped an arm around the two women's shoulders. "I'm sorry about the circumstances," he murmured, "but it's mighty gut to have you gals home. Hope I haven't left the place in more of a mess—"

"Puh!" Jemima tweaked his nose, a gesture that had irritated him as a kid. "Takes more than a little mess to keep *me* out of this kitchen."

"And *I* will see that Wyman repays you for all that food," Amanda insisted as she playfully jabbed his chest with her finger. "You had no reason to—"

"Ah, but I didn't need a reason," Jerome stated simply. "After all the years you and Uncle Atlee looked after me, it's my turn to do the looking-after, ain't so? And maybe I'm practicing for when I have a wife to take care of."

Amanda's eyebrows shot up, but she kept her comments—and Emma's remarks—to herself. It was no secret that her nephew had his eye on the Graber girl, and she didn't want to be the one to disappoint him.

Jemima, however, let out a grunt. "Don't get your hopes up, far as Emma Graber goes," she remarked. "She might've made us some sticky buns, but she's not sending you any encouragement to go with them. Made that pretty clear, she did."

Oh, but Amanda felt sorry for her nephew when his

smile dropped. He'd been trying so hard to prove himself worthy, but it was best to let him work through his feelings about Emma for himself.

"Jah, well." Jerome adjusted his hat, gesturing toward the road. "We've got company."

The hum of a truck engine and the thunderous *clip-clop! clip-clop!* announced the arrival of the stock wagon and the three other vehicles Wyman had decided to bring over from Clearwater. As the parade entered the lane, a little arm shot up in a wild wave.

"Jerome, hi! Remember me and Wags?"

"Hey there, Simon," Jerome called out. "Gut to see you!"

"Can we go see your mules?"

Jerome chuckled as the Fishers' pickup rumbled in front of him. He directed Trevor and Ray toward the barn, then ambled over to meet Wyman's approaching wagon. When Jerome held up his arms, Simon leaped into them.

"You can help me feed and water those mules later today, Simon," he said as he turned the boy upside down to make him laugh. "Right now, you can help us guys put your animals and all this *furniture* where your mamm wants it."

Once again Amanda was dumbstruck. There on the wagon she saw her treadle sewing machine, her mamm's china hutch, and Jemima's pie safe. The legs of the maple bedroom set Atlee had crafted for her peeked out from beneath old quilts. But what did this mean? Did Wyman *never* intend to find room for her furniture in the Brubaker house? He hadn't said a word about bringing these pieces along for the family's temporary relocation . . .

"Don't look so worried, Aunt Amanda," Jerome murmured as he carried a cane-seated rocking chair toward the front door. "A little bird told Wyman this furniture would feel just as gut in its old home as you would. And he listened! That's progress, jah?"

Amanda's throat tightened, but she refused to cry. She was *finished* with all those tears, because it seemed everyone she loved was conspiring to make her happy. God was bringing joy and love and peace home to roost like pigeons—or like the chickens squawking in their make-shift pen—and she had plenty of room in her heart for all of those emotions.

"Denki, Wyman," she whispered when her husband kissed her lightly. "With all the surprises the Lambrights had for us, seeing my furniture is, well—it's the frosting on the cake."

When Wyman smiled at her, he looked handsome and . . . downright relaxed, as though his recent worries had disappeared. "Let's try for some cake and frosting every day, shall we?"

Amanda smiled. Was it her imagination or had the sky just grown bluer and had the autumn leaves turned even more brilliant in the morning sunshine? "Jah, Wyman. We can do that."

Chapter 29

As Wyman sat among the men of the Bloomingdale district, eating the common meal after Sunday's church service, it struck him: everyone here was so *friendly*. Laughter filled the crowded front room, which had been extended by taking down the wall partitions to set up for church. The Hilty family was hosting today, and the women circulated among the long tables, pouring more water and tea, passing trays of sandwiches. Folks were smiling as though this was a special party to welcome him, his kids, and Amanda's family *home*. Wyman hardly knew a soul—but he wanted to.

"What a difference in atmosphere," he murmured to Eddie, seated on his left.

"Jah, back in Clearwater I bet they're talking of hellfire and damnation, on account of how Amanda's not there to repent," his son replied. "Truth be told, Dat, I've not been inclined to join the church, partly because of the way Uriah treated Mamm—and now the way he and the others are picking on Amanda. It doesn't seem very Christian, you know?"

And wasn't *that* a notable observation from his critical, more rebellious son? At the next table, Pete sat beside Jerome, chatting with several younger fellows . . . Simon had chosen to join Cora and Dora at a table where other youngsters and their mothers were eating . . . Vera giggled loudly at something one of Lizzie's friends had just said. While he had visited other districts for weddings and funerals, it was the ordinary Sunday services that bespoke the true personality of a Plain community. He had felt as though Preacher Dwayne Lehman's sermon on a passage from Joshua had been chosen specifically for him, as well. *Have not I commanded thee? Be strong and of a good courage; be not afraid, neither be thou dismayed: for the LORD thy God is with thee whithersoever thou goest.*

While Wyman wasn't afraid of Uriah Schmucker, he had certainly been dismayed by his bishop's attitude—and now this Bible verse was nudging him to think outside the tightly defined world where he'd lived all his life. He was pleased when Eddie went over to mingle with a cluster of young people who'd finished eating . . . noticed how his son chatted with a couple of the girls, who responded to him with enthusiastic nods and smiles. And when he caught Amanda's eye from across the noisy room, her expression made him hold his breath. She looked so relaxed. So *happy*. She was laughing with her friends as she had done before she met him . . . unaware of the transformation that Wyman could see so clearly.

Amanda looked young and bubbly. *Jubilant*. Wyman wished he had been the one to put such a sparkle in her brown eyes. While, yes, she was glad to be in her former home with her favorite furnishings, today's radiance came from a different place within her. Wyman couldn't recall seeing such bliss, such peace, in her pretty features, even while they'd been courting.

What can you do to maintain this harmony, this happiness?

Wyman pondered his options on the ride back to the Lambright farm and as he and his boys helped Jerome with the livestock chores that afternoon. Clearly, this improvement in his wife's mood had nothing to do with prosperity, for her house, the barn, and the other outbuildings were sorely in need of paint and maintenance. While there were bedrooms enough to go around, they were smaller than the ones he and his kids were used to. He and Amanda had discussed what type of new cabinets and flooring she wanted as they rebuilt the Brubaker house, yet this morning's efficient, effortless breakfast had been a testimony to how well she and Jemima worked together in their care-worn kitchen. Even while spending all day Saturday unpacking and settling the kids into their rooms, they had baked pies for today's common meal. Vera had made a big pan of her macaroni and cheese . . .

"How's this feeling to you, Wyman? You look lost in thought."

Wyman focused on Jerome as the two of them broke up some small, square bales of hay into the horses' mangers. Eddie and Pete had taken Simon outside to see the mules and the donkeys Jerome used for breeding them. "It's been quite a day," he replied. "Not only have I gained more insight into how much adjusting Amanda did when she and the girls moved into our house but . . . well, the service this morning and the people I met have given me a lot to think about as I repair the place in Clearwater."

"I bet that's right. It had to rip a hole in your heart, seeing how much damage those trees did to your home," the younger man remarked. "Now that I've sent that mule team back to its owner, I'd be happy to help with your renovations if you need me."

"I appreciate that. And by the way," Wyman added with

a wry smile, "denki for suggesting that we bring Amanda's furniture with us. I never realized how much it meant to her."

Jerome chuckled. "What man has ever figured out what truly makes a woman happy? That can change from one day—one hour—to the next."

"Jah, there's that." Wyman grabbed a bucket to fill it from the pump and then he paused, listening. "Where's that train I hear? It doesn't sound far off."

"Cuts across the west forty, not far from Cedar Creek. If you followed the creek—and the tracks—through the countryside, you'd eventually end up at your place, you know."

As the water filled his bucket, Wyman mentally tried to sketch the railroad's route from here to Clearwater. "Now why didn't I realize that? Guess I'm so used to taking the county highways or the other side roads, I don't have much reason to travel north—"

"Because it's all hills and trees. Mostly English-owned hobby farms and hunting acreage out that way," Jerome pointed out. "Not even a feed store or any other services we Plain folks would use."

Wyman considered this as he dumped the water into a trough and refilled his bucket. "Could you and I take a ride around this farm?" He had no idea where such a question had come from, but it seemed logical to look around now that he was going to live here for a while. "I didn't marry Amanda for her land, so I have no idea where the boundaries are or what her fields are like," he added with a laugh.

"You betcha. We can saddle up after supper."

The afternoon passed quickly, filled with chores. As Wyman bowed for prayer before their simple supper of soup and sandwiches, he asked God for the words that probably should have been spoken when his extended family had first gathered around the Brubaker table. He could have done several things differently when he'd brought Amanda and her girls into his home . . . yet now he felt prodded by a new motivation. The preacher's words ran repeatedly through his mind: *the LORD thy God is with thee whithersoever thou goest.* He wasn't sure why so many unusual thoughts were occurring to him today, but he took them as gifts from God. Not ideas to be dismissed.

"As I look at all of my children—and all of us adults—gathered at this table, I'm grateful that our family has come through the storm in much better condition than our home did," he began.

Around the long table, spoons paused above soup bowls and eyes focused on him. Wyman slipped his hand over Amanda's, bolstered by the steady beat of her pulse and the love in her eyes. Was he reading his own emotions into her expression, or was his wife still aglow from the fellowship they'd shared with her friends at church?

"Even so," Wyman continued, "this seems like a gut time to discuss remodeling our family as we rebuild our home. As I watched each of you today at church, I saw improvements in our relationships, but as your dat, I need to state some expectations . . . to be sure we're all on the same page now that we're starting a new chapter as a family."

Vera and his boys glanced warily at one another, while Amanda's girls looked apprehensive. It wasn't his intention to instill fear in their young hearts, but children often learned best when they had to account for their actions—a concept he'd let slide after Viola died. He also realized that Lizzie and the twins hadn't had a father's guidance for four years—since before Cora and Dora were born—so he hoped to guide them rather than alienate them as he spoke.

"Eddie and Pete, I was glad to see you joining in with the local folks at church and during the meal today," he began. "Even so, several of your recent remarks—and your attitudes—have suggested rebellion rather than respect. Especially concerning Amanda."

The boys' eyelashes lowered. They listened without comment.

"If you think you're too old to obey Amanda and me, then you're old enough to be out on your own. And while leaving home might sound tempting, be very careful about assuming that you'd be able to support yourselves," Wyman stated firmly. "Amanda's not the mother who bore you, but she's in charge of this family now. I expect you to decide on an occupation soon, Eddie—and you, Pete, are to apply yourself at school here in Bloomingdale, even though it's only temporary. I don't want to hear of any more shenanigans that upset Lizzie. And I hope she'll show you kindness and consideration as you get a taste of being the new kid in the classroom. Understand me, boys?"

Pete and Eddie nodded, while beside them, Simon smiled smugly. "Bad wabbit, Peter wabbit," he whispered.

"And *Simon*." Wyman gazed at his five-year-old until the boy looked up at him. "Stop scratching on the other side of your sisters' wall with a currycomb and making wolf noises in the night to scare them."

As Simon looked ready to deny these escapades, Cora's and Dora's eyes widened. "I *wondered* if it was Simon!" one of them crowed.

"Jah, and we've told Mamma there's no wolf in *this* house," her twin chimed in. Both girls looked triumphantly across the table at their mischievous brother.

"Which means you twins—and Alice Ann—will sleep in your own beds now, like big girls," Amanda added emphatically. "And, Simon, you and I will have a chat about where Wags will spend the night, as well."

"Gut points. I'm glad we've solved that little mystery." Wyman took a bite of his ham sandwich, letting the kids absorb his words . . . and wonder what he might say next, about whom. He was pleased that Amanda had joined him in this discussion about discipline—and overjoyed that their bed would be for just the two of them.

He smiled at Vera then, and at Lizzie. "I enjoyed watching you girls at the meal today, talking and laughing with your friends. I hope this means you'll be more patient with each other about sharing a room—and more considerate about each other's private belongings," he added in a purposeful tone. "Consider it practice for when you get married, because the both of you have had your own rooms for so long it'll be a real eye-opener when you have to share the space with your husbands. And share the bed."

The girls' cheeks flushed but the glance they exchanged suggested they were already getting beyond their difficulties. "Matter of fact," Vera said, "I've decided to buy Lizzie her own diary next time we're at the mercantile. Writing about your troubles can help you sort them out, and when you jot down the gut things that have happened, you can smile about them again when you read through your entries."

Lizzie's grin was a sight to behold. "Denki, Vera. What a wonderful-gut idea," she replied. "I'm lucky to have you for a big sister."

Wyman was so pleased that the girls had reconciled, but there was another matter he needed to address. "Lizzie, I know you feel better now that you're back in Bloomingdale," he said gently. "I hope you'll make every effort to get along with Teacher Elsie and the Clearwater scholars when we return to the other house. Do you think you can do that—especially if Pete stops pestering you?"

Lizzie let out a long sigh. "I'll try to do better. At least I've got longer dresses now, like the other girls."

Wyman nodded. He decided not to press Vera to be more accommodating about Amanda's furniture. She had lost so many of her mother's belongings in the storm—and their kitchen and front room would be totally redecorated anyway . . . He really needed to call Amos Coblentz for a bid, but for some inexplicable reason, he seemed to be dragging his feet about that.

Alice Ann's giggle coaxed Wyman back to his present purpose. She was ecstatically jamming a chunk of ham sandwich into her mouth after Amanda had cut it for her, and his toddler's affection for her new mamm delighted him. There was no point in telling Alice Ann to start talking, though, so he would touch on a couple more points and then let everyone eat in peace.

"Along this same line, I believe we should all show Jemima more patience and respect," he went on as he smiled at Amanda's mother-in-law. "Those four pies on the counter—and all the things you bake for us—are a thoughtful way of sharing yourself. Especially since we can make them disappear as fast as you can bake them."

Jemima's cheeks flushed as she smoothed her kapp over her steely gray hair. "What with my husband and son gone, I'm grateful that you've given me a place . . . and a way to be useful," she murmured. "I'll try to smile more and complain less."

Wyman nodded, pleased to hear this—and even more gratified when Amanda squeezed his hand.

Then he clapped the young man at his right on the shoulder. "And let's also express our appreciation to Jerome, who has restocked the kitchen and the fridge and done so much more for us—even before we took over his house. You're a part of our family now, too, you know."

"Happy to help you folks out," Jerome replied with a shrug. "Truth be told, it's awfully quiet out here with just me and the mules."

The meal continued in silence then, yet Wyman sensed the kids were more pensive than peeved at him. As they finished the main course, Vera rose to cut the pies while Lizzie opened a flat container and began to put other treats on a plate.

"It so happens Abby sent along a little something yesterday—besides our new clothes and underthings," she said as she set the plate in front of Simon.

The five-year-old looked ready to pop, he was so excited. "Fried pies!" he crowed. "Ask and you shall receive! Knock, and Abby will answer."

As the kitchen filled with laughter, Wyman gave thanks for the love this family shared even as they experienced some growing pains. Special moments like this one were what he'd envisioned when he'd courted Amanda. Watching these kids help one another during yesterday's move and socialize at church today had made him believe that they could indeed be one big, happy family if they kept working at it. God didn't make mistakes, after all. He had brought the Brubakers and the Lambrights together for a good reason . . .

And now that you've told the kids how you expect their behavior to change, how will YOU contribute to this remodeling project? If you're all words and no action, it's only hot air. You must follow through. You must do better.

Chapter 30

Amanda shook a damp plum-colored dress until it snapped, and then hung it on the clothesline. Beside her, Vera did the same with a dress of deep green. They bent toward the laundry basket and then pegged the clothes in a rhythm they had acquired during many washings, for nearly every day was laundry day in a household of twelve.

"You looked so pretty at church in your new green dress," Amanda said. "Abby does such a gut job of sewing, and she chose a fabric that's easy to care for, too."

"I enjoyed having something new to wear," Vera answered. "I tend to let the sewing slide, as I'd rather tend the kids or cook."

"Those are important jobs, too," Amanda reaffirmed. "And I'm grateful for the way you've spent time with Cora and Dora in the kitchen. When Jemima's not feeling gut, she gets impatient and shoos them away."

Vera cranked the pulley to send the hanging clothes toward the barn and bring open clothesline in front of them.

Amanda took in the blue sky and the long line of dresses, pants, and shirts flapping in the early November breeze. She worded her next thought carefully, hoping not to upset her new daughter. "It didn't occur to me yesterday, but you probably missed seeing your friends at the Singing in Clearwater," she said. "You'd be welcome at this district's Singings, of course—but I could understand why you wouldn't want to go by yourself. It's a shame Eddie and Lizzie are too young to attend."

Smiling, Vera shook out Lizzie's new maroon dress. "After all the work of moving on Saturday, I was ready for a day of rest," she admitted. "Lizzie was introducing me to a lot of the young people at your church, though. Especially the fellows."

Amanda chuckled. "Jah, I saw a few of them looking you over, too. And now that you're not constantly in charge of the little ones, I hope you'll do more things you enjoy with your friends."

"All in gut time. I've had a lot of new situations to figure out this past month," she replied. "And now that we've all shifted into your house, I understand why you were feeling . . . displaced after you married Dat. I'm sorry about the way I wanted the dishes and furniture just like Mamm kept them."

Displaced? Now, that was a word Amanda had never associated with Plain families. "Don't fret about that another minute, Vera," Amanda insisted as she slipped her arm around the girl's shoulders. "Nobody likes to change their homes, especially after their mamm or a spouse dies. It would feel like we were throwing those folks themselves away if we got rid of all their belongings. This house still looks pretty much as it did even before I married Atlee."

Vera nodded, listening. She wasn't one to let on, so Amanda wondered how Wyman's eldest was handling the destruction of her home. "I'm sorry those trees crashed into your house and destroyed your bedroom and the kitchen," she murmured. "That's a lot to lose—more adjusting than I faced when I married your dat, because it was my choice to leave this place."

When they had hung all the laundry in the basket, the two of them went back into the house. Amanda enjoyed having only the girls here today, as Wyman, Jerome, and Eddie had taken Simon to work at the Brubaker place. After sampling some fresh snickerdoodles, which the twins were baking with Jemima, Amanda and Vera carried buckets of hot, soapy water into the room where the potter's wheel and ceramic supplies had once been.

"I'm afraid we're behind on more than the fall cleaning at this place," Amanda remarked as she gazed at the blank walls. "With the furniture gone, you can see how badly the paint has faded. This must seem like a very run-down old house compared to what you're used to, Vera. But after Atlee passed, I had to be very careful with my money."

As Vera knelt with her scrub brush, a grin flickered at her lips. "Maybe you should set Eddie loose with a roller," she said. "Dat made him paint all our bedrooms when he smarted off about how I wasn't keeping up with the cleaning—how dingy the house was looking—after Mamm passed, and we found out how really gut he is with paint. Eddie won't say so, but he got a kick out of doing it, too. Decided to keep painting until he'd done the whole house."

"Now there's a thought. Eddie seems tired of cleaning up at the other house, so we could put him to work here!" Although Amanda was laughing, she was seriously interested in this idea. "If we get right on it, we'll probably have enough warm days left to open the windows in each room as he paints it. And who knows? That might be a career for him to consider."

"It would get Dat off his case, too," Vera said with a laugh.

As the day passed while she was doing more laundry and deep cleaning, Amanda became more determined to spruce up these neglected rooms. Yet it seemed like a bad time to bring up the subject of painting this house when Wyman's place needed so much more time and money spent on it—especially if they were to get the main structure and the roof repaired so that the house was enclosed before winter. And because it took more than an hour in each direction for the drive, Wyman was putting in some long days.

At supper, Amanda could see how tired her husband looked, and how preoccupied. She set aside her big ideas about painting this place . . . after all, they wouldn't be living here for long. Jerome didn't seem to mind that the walls weren't fresh—especially now that all the furnishings were back in their original spots.

After their evening meal was cleaned up, Wyman called them together for the evening's devotions. Amanda enjoyed hearing her husband read God's word aloud in this cozy front room by the lamplight, just as Atlee had done years ago.

"Each day as we've worked lately, I've been thinking about what the Lord had in mind when he sent the storm that destroyed our home," he said as he flipped through the big Bible's pages. "And these words from the prophet Isaiah keep coming back to me. 'Remember ye not the former things, neither consider the things of old,'" he read. "'Behold, I will do a new thing; now it shall spring forth; shall ye not know it? I will even make a way in the wilderness, and rivers in the desert.'"

Wyman gazed at them all, his face alight with emotions Amanda wasn't sure how to interpret. "I believe God is telling us to move ahead with our lives, even as He leads us in directions we hadn't anticipated before the storm," he said earnestly. "So let's bow for a word with Him, asking for His blessing and insights as to how each of us is to follow His plan in the coming days."

As Amanda closed her eyes, her thoughts felt anything but prayerful. *What on earth is Wyman thinking to do? Will he just keep hinting about his new ideas, or will he reveal his thoughts to us? I'm not so sure I can handle yet another move in another direction . . . another new thing.*

The kids looked curious, too, but as they headed to their rooms, they murmured among themselves rather than asking their dat to explain his remarks. Amanda tucked the twins and Alice Ann into their beds. Simon was so tired from the day's work that he didn't demand a story before his head hit the pillow. After she wished the four older kids good night, she started downstairs to assist Jemima, and met Jerome going to his room.

"And what do you know about Wyman's mysterious frame of mind?" she asked. "You look like the cat that ate the canary."

"Me?" her nephew teased. "What would *I* know about anything?"

"Puh! You've been working with him these past few days—"

"And I respect a man's right to keep his own counsel until he's gut and ready to say what's on his mind, too." Jerome squeezed her shoulder. "Patience is a virtue, Aunt."

"Jah, you're a fine one to talk of patience. Gut night, you," she murmured as she swatted his backside.

"Denki for those hot dinners you've been sending with us," he added. "The food stays plenty warm, the way you pack the pans into the cooler with towels. I've never thought of doing that."

"You're welcome, dear." Jerome's compliment was his way of ducking the subject of Wyman's plans, but she appreciated it anyway. Amanda suspected her nephew had enjoyed living without two women bossing him, yet he seemed genuinely pleased to have the Brubaker bunch with him for a while.

As Amanda emerged from Jemima's dawdi haus apartment, the silence of the main house enfolded her. Only the ticking of the mantel clock and the whistle of the wind filled the shadowy front room. She noticed the lamp was still lit in the kitchen, and found Wyman there at the table, stirring two mugs of cocoa.

"Tired as you looked at dinner, I thought you'd be turning in early," Amanda remarked as she sat down beside him. "But it's gut to spend some quiet time with you after our busy day."

Wyman gazed at her over the rim of his mug. "What would I do without you, sweet wife?" he murmured. "You take such gut care of me, I've forgotten all about the emptiness that followed Viola's death . . . the way I worked like a man possessed to forget my loneliness. We have a lot to talk about, Amanda."

Her heart stood still. Was he going to discuss the Lord's new direction, or was something else bothering him? "All right. I'm listening," she whispered.

"Ah, but I need your opinion." His words came out in a rush as he grasped her hand. "These past few days, my mind has been whirling like those winds that plucked up our trees and dropped them on the house. I want to run some ideas past you before I mention them to another soul. And I might just burst if I don't talk about them *right now*."

Amanda's eyes widened. Wyman was getting very excited, yet he appeared apprehensive—*driven* to make her understand. He had saved his ideas to share with her first, and she felt honored. "And this is about the new thing the Lord has been prodding you with?"

"Jah, I— What would you think if I sold my house and my land? To the Fishers!"

Amanda's mug thunked against the tabletop and her cocoa sloshed out. "Wyman, what are you— Why would you do such a thing?" she asked in a hushed voice. Her heart was beating like a frightened rabbit's, yet her man's enthusiasm was contagious.

"Hear me out," he insisted. "Tell me if my logic's cock-eyed, or if you think I'm barking up the wrong tree altogether. I believe God's telling me to move on—and to move *here* for a fresh start. *Think* about it," he urged her.

Amanda stared at him in the flickering lamplight. His handsome face was alight with energy, and he looked anything but weary now. "I'm listening," she repeated. "I'm amazed and—and I'm shaking, too, but I want to know how you came to this decision. You're not a man who jumps to half-baked conclusions."

He exhaled loudly, composing his thoughts. "I suppose this idea took root when Trevor asked about renting the pasture for his dairy herd," he explained. "He and Ray went to the auction today to buy those other cows, and— Well, Trev's so excited about getting established—"

"Sally says he's taking his instruction to join their church. Which means he's got a girl in mind to marry, most likely."

"—and I couldn't help thinking that if the Fishers bought my farm, they could all keep living along the same road, and—" Wyman paused to slow himself down. "I recall being that excited about life when I was Trevor's age, and I want to feel that way with *you*, Amanda. But the bishop's ruined it for me. Twice I've been stung by his sanctimonious commands, and I've had enough."

Amanda's breath caught in her throat. "You'd sell out because of Uriah?"

"I'm selling out for *you*, my love." His whispered words shimmered in the stillness of the kitchen. "Don't you see it? We'll never satisfy that man. And I can't believe, in my heart of hearts, that the Lord expects me to sacrifice my peace of mind—and my family's happiness—just to remain in Uriah's district."

Wyman grasped her hands, entreating her with his bottomless brown eyes. "When I came home from your church service yesterday, it hit me like a ton of bricks. We have no reason to remain in Clearwater, being miserable, when we can live right here. Is that all right with you, Amanda?"

Her mouth dropped open but no sound came out. She wanted to laugh and cry at the same time, and her heart began dancing so fast she could barely breathe. "Of course it's all right, Wyman! But—but what about your elevator? We talked before about how your business would keep us in Clearwater—"

"When Jerome showed me around your farm, he pointed out that the same railroad tracks—the same trains—cross your property half an hour before they reach mine," he explained. "If I sell my farm, I'll have more than enough money to build a new grain elevator. Bloomingdale's a gut place for one, too."

Amanda stared at him, trying to harness the questions that raced through her mind. "But what about your partnership with Ray? I can't think he'll want to buy out your share of—"

"He won't have to. We can remain partners and expand our business!" Wyman gushed. "Instead of one facility, we'll have two. I can still work close to home, and he and Tyler can remain in Clearwater, so—"

"But how will you justify getting the electricity? And how will you install the computers that keep you up to date on grain market transactions?" she asked cautiously. "Lamar Lapp allowed me to make pottery to support my family, but he's dead set against modern technology."

Wyman smiled. He'd obviously thought about all these angles. "We can share Tyler between the two elevators, and if he has a laptop, it's not like we'll have his computer on the premises all the time. He'll enjoy setting up the new system and—"

"But what if Ray and his boys say no?" Amanda murmured. "What if they can't afford to buy your farm . . . or they don't want to?"

Wyman's breath left him like the air leaking from a balloon. "Jah, a lot depends on them saying yes," he admitted. "But I'm prepared to sell my land at less than its current market value if his family wants it. Ray's more than my partner. He's been my best friend all my life. And in many ways, he's a better businessman than I."

A grin twitched on Wyman's lips then, as though he'd been saving the punch line of the best joke he'd ever heard. "And can't you just imagine the look on Uriah's face when he learns we've sold out to *Mennonites*?"

Amanda laughed so loudly she clapped her hands over her mouth to keep from waking the children. "Oh, but, Wyman, you're pinning your hopes on a mighty big yes," she pointed out. "And you know Uriah will rant and rail against you. He'll accuse you of running from your responsibilities to your district—and to God."

Her husband's expression grew serious again. "There was a time I would've followed that logic—that absolute black-and-white Uriah demands of the faithful," he said somberly. "But we have every right to live on your land, in your district, Amanda.

"And truth be told," he continued, leaning closer to her, "when Eddie told me he didn't want to join the church because of Uriah's attitude, that's all I needed to hear. I don't want to lose my son because the bishop has turned him against the Old Order faith. And Pete would be jumping the fence right behind him."

"Jah, I can see that happening." Amanda sipped her cocoa, wondering what other stumbling blocks she should point up, even as she felt ecstatic about Wyman's ideas. Who could have believed he would leave the land that had belonged to his family for so many generations? "So . . . if the Fishers don't want your farm, what will you do?"

"Well, since Ray owns the parcel the elevator's on, I'll give him the opportunity to buy the pasture for Trevor's cows—and whatever else he might want, since it adjoins his property," he reasoned aloud. "Then I'll put the rest of the place up for sale at full value—which is very high, considering the rise in real estate prices these past few years. And if English buy it, so be it. God is still at work in all our lives."

In her mind, Amanda had been accounting for each section of Brubaker property as he'd mentioned it. "But what about the house? It's going to cost a pretty penny for the repairs—"

"Those Coblentz fellows from Cedar Creek are to come out tomorrow afternoon, to work up a bid. I wanted you to be there for that, Amanda—to have your say about the kitchen, especially," he explained as he clasped her hands. "But then it hit me: what if the Fishers *did* buy the place? Trevor and his bride might have a different idea of what they want in a house, so why shouldn't they decide about the remodeling? I'd lower the price of the place to allow for their additional expense."

"Oh, my," Amanda murmured. "I've never had the chance to choose kitchen cabinets or—and—and I don't need to! I love the kitchen here just as it is," she blurted. "Maybe letting Trevor—or whoever buys your farm—decide on the remodeling would sweeten the deal for them. I think that's a gut idea on your part."

As Wyman studied her in the lamplight, Amanda wished she'd thought before she'd spoken so hastily. It sounded selfish to point out that she'd never had a say about how her rooms were arranged. How many women did she know who *had* remodeled their homes?

Yet her husband kept hold of her hands, smiling gently. "You, dear wife, deserve far more than new cabinets. Every time I pass through this house, I see improvements I want to make for you—and if we stay here, I *will*. But let's deal with one situation at a time."

"Jah, you've got a lot on your plate right now." Amanda gazed at the large, work-worn hands that enveloped hers, grateful that Wyman was so patient. Come to think of it, hadn't he changed his entire mind-set? There was a time when he would never have allowed Brubaker land to pass into other hands—he would have been more likely to insist they sell *her* farm. This unexpected conversation was indeed turning up fresh soil, like a horse-drawn plow tilling the land to ready it for planting new seed.

Amanda closed her eyes, settling her thoughts. "So what's your plan for tomorrow? If you want me to go along, I will."

"I married such a wise, accommodating woman. Best thing I've ever done, too." Wyman thought for a moment. "How about if I talk with Ray and Trevor first thing? They'll need to put pencil to paper and pray on such a major decision—but I want Amos and his son to look the place over so they can put *their* pencils to paper, too. No matter who buys the place, I'll either need to complete the rebuilding or figure that cost into my selling price. Does that make sense?"

"Jah. And I think you should deal with the Fishers and the carpenters man-to-man," she said. "Your discussions will be freer that way. Less complicated."

Wyman raised her hands to his lips and kissed them tenderly. "You're probably right, Amanda. Never let me forget that, will you?"

Chapter 31

When Wyman sat down to breakfast Tuesday morning, he felt like a new man. He hadn't gotten much rest, and his muscles still ached from cleaning up storm debris, yet sharing his thoughts with Amanda had changed his life. Far into the night, they had whispered ideas and shared opinions as they cuddled in bed . . .

Yet as he watched his wife turn the bacon that crackled in the cast-iron skillet, Wyman grinned over a fresh secret. Was there no end to the surprises that fell into place, once he'd decided to sell his land—for her, mostly? He felt joyful and boyish, as though springs of hope and fresh enthusiasm were bubbling to the surface after being submerged for most of his life.

While Jemima and Vera placed bowls of hash browns, simmered peppers and onions, cheese sauce, and other makings for breakfast haystacks on the table, the rest of the kids and Jerome took their seats. Wyman winked at Vera, and she smiled back.

Simon's eyes widened as he surveyed the table. "Wow, this is a feast!"

Wyman ruffled his boy's thick brown hair. "You're right, son. We're lucky to be living with women who're such gut cooks. So let's say grace before it gets cold."

As he bowed his head, Wyman asked God for good timing and the right words. He and Amanda weren't telling anyone of their decision to stay in Bloomingdale until the Fishers responded to his offer. But that didn't mean he couldn't have some fun making other changes.

"I'll be heading to Clearwater by myself today," he announced as he spread a layer of hash browns on his plate. "What with cleaning up all the debris, I'd forgotten that Ray and I have a grain shipment going out this morning. So, while I tend to elevator business, you get a break from working at the house."

"My prayers are answered," Eddie murmured. Then he looked up from the biscuits that would make the base of his haystack. "No disrespect intended, understand."

"And none taken. You've worked mighty hard these past few days, son." Wyman fought a grin as he spooned peppers and onions over his potatoes. "A little bird tells me, however, that your mamm would like the inside of this house painted before winter. I thought you might be interested in doing that instead of any more work in Clearwater."

Eddie's eyebrows shot up, but not nearly as high as his wife's did.

"Oh, but that would be a wonderful-gut—" Amanda looked down the table. "I don't suppose *you* were that little bird, Vera?"

Their eldest daughter chuckled, and beside her, Lizzie's face lit up. "And now *my* prayers are answered," she said. "What do you think, Vera? Yellow for our room again, or cream? Or how about pale blue?"

"I want leapfrog green!" Simon declared.

"Pink!" Cora cried out.

"Pink like our favorite dresses," Dora agreed.

"Pink! Pink! *Pink!*" Alice Ann crowed as she kicked in her high chair.

The kitchen rang with an amazed silence as everyone gazed at the littlest Brubaker. Amanda let out an excited sob. "And what did you just say, missy?" she whispered as she rose to lift Alice Ann to her shoulder.

Wyman sat speechless. Never mind that Amish folks tended toward white or pale yellow walls to lighten their homes. If Alice Ann was talking at last, he would paint her room any color she wanted as a way to celebrate this long-awaited event. "My prayers are answered, too," he murmured. "Thanks be to God."

Alice Ann, aware she was the center of attention, giggled as she wrapped her chubby arms around Amanda's arms. "Pink," she repeated in the sweetest little voice. "I wuv pink. And I wuv you, too, Mamma."

Wyman didn't bother to blink back his tears as he drank in the sight of his precious toddler clinging to his new wife. He stood to place a hand on her tiny back, awash in the giddy wonder that—for whatever reason—Alice Ann had finally found words. The shock of losing her birth mother had apparently lifted, like fog from a pond. Was it because they had moved into a house she didn't associate with Viola?

"Well, now," Jemima said as she swiped at her eyes. "Not even half-finished with our breakfast and we've witnessed a miracle. It's been quite a day already."

As the meal resumed, the other kids took turns talking to Alice Ann until she had said every one of their names. Her sudden speech defied logic . . . and suggested that she'd been practicing words when no one could hear. To Wyman it was yet another sign that God was at work in their lives—and that He was favoring them here, in this home, for a reason.

And Wyman knew better than to ignore such a gift. After a few moments, he turned to Eddie again. "Well, son, your littlest sister stole our thunder—"

"Girls are gut at that," Pete remarked. He piled scrambled eggs on his hash browns and then drowned them with cheese sauce.

"—but what do you think about painting for us?" Wyman continued. "You did a fine job at the other house. And if you want helpers—"

"I'm a mess with paint, but I'm real gut at moving furniture," Jerome volunteered. "What if we went to the mercantile today for the paint, and I'll get the feed supplement I'm needing for my mules?"

Eddie was trying not to seem excited about this new job. "Long as I don't have to paint Pete's and my room pink, I'm gut with doing it."

"Denki, son. The Lord loves a cheerful giver." Wyman glanced at Amanda, delighted that he'd surprised her—even if Alice Ann had eclipsed him. "Ask your mamm about her color preferences, and which rooms she wants you to start with. Jerome can show you what ladders and drop cloths might already be here, and you can pick up everything else you need at Sam's store."

"Too bad I've got school," Pete murmured.

"Jah, too bad," Eddie echoed smugly. "You'll grow out of it."

"I can help, though!" Simon piped up. "I'm close to the floor, so I can paint down low."

When Eddie looked ready to object, Jerome beat him to the punch. "You and I can find plenty of ways to help out, little buddy. After all, when the furniture's been moved out of Eddie's way, the donkeys and horses and mules will still need to be fed and exercised. And you know those mares I showed you, with their sides sticking out?"

Simon nodded eagerly, his forkful of eggs suspended over his plate.

"They'll have their babies any day now," Jerome said,

his excitement rising. "And if you're around when those mules are born, they'll bond with your scent and your voice. And come time to work with them, they'll already trust you, Simon. That'll be mighty special, ain't so?"

Wyman considered Jerome's way with Simon yet another blessing, a sign that his family was meant to be here on this farm.

Sure enough, Wyman's talk with Ray and Trevor went well. He would wait patiently for the Fishers' response, for they had many things to consider before buying his land.

He was impressed with Amos and Owen Coblentz, too. And when they presented their bid by week's end, he would share it with Ray and Trevor.

Wyman then stopped by the bank to arrange for a survey of his family's farm, as a necessary part of selling it. Tyler had pointed out that they could find basic legal forms online and at the bank, since they wouldn't be going through a realtor—and meanwhile, Ray's younger son had helped Wyman find some surprises for Amanda, as well. Computers and the Internet amazed him, even if he didn't want to get personally involved with them.

On his way home, he stopped by the Cedar Creek Mercantile to pay for Eddie's paint. He chuckled at the sight of James Graber leaning on the checkout counter as he gazed at Abby. At the jingle of the bell over the door, they sprang apart, laughing.

"So have you lovebirds set your wedding date?" It tickled Wyman that instead of envying James his romantic notions, he was full of them himself. He hadn't felt this young in a long, long time.

"Matter of fact, we have!" Abby chirped. "And you'd better come celebrate with us on Thursday, the nineteenth of this month, too."

"Wouldn't miss it. Congratulations." Wyman pulled out

his wallet. "I've come to settle up for the paint and supplies Eddie bought, and whatever else Amanda might've had him fetch. And . . . was some of that paint pink?"

Abby laughed, clapping her hands together. "Jah, and when Gail and I heard about Alice Ann talking, we jumped up and down. Wyman, this is such gut news!"

"I can't explain it, except to say that with God, all things are possible." Wyman itched to share the other major developments he and Amanda were setting into motion, but such announcements would be shared with his family first. Perhaps by Sunday, when the Grabers and the Lambrights were coming out to the house . . .

"But you're too late with your money," Abby stated matter-of-factly. "The bill's been paid in full."

Wyman frowned. "Sam will *not* cover the expense for all that paint."

"Nope, he won't," Abby replied. "But when my brother saw how organized Eddie was about choosing his tools, and how eager he was to get started at your place, Sam hired him to paint the inside of the mercantile."

Wyman gazed around the huge two-story store. "That might take a while, because Eddie prefers to work by himself and—"

"Sam said he didn't care how long Eddie took, he just wanted a gut job." Abby's brown eyes sparkled. "He's tickled to be giving a young fellow work he doesn't want to do himself, you see."

"Seems to me your boy might be starting up a trade," James remarked. "The folks who see Eddie painting while they shop will recommend him to their neighbors. And come to think of it," he said as he winked at Abby, "our house across the road could use fresh walls, too. So see there? He'll have to get a calendar to keep track of his jobs."

Wyman shook his head. "First Alice Ann and now Eddie—two miracles in one day," he murmured. "But who paid for the paint?"

Abby's smile grew even wider. "Eddie asked Sam if he would consider the paint and supplies as an advance on his wages for painting the store, and Sam thought that was a fine idea. They started up an account in Eddie's name, and he's gut to go. I'd say you have an exceptional son there, Wyman. I was mighty proud of him when he and Jerome left here."

"Who could've seen *that* coming?" Wyman was so pleased he slapped the countertop. "I'd better head home to congratulate my son, the painter. He must take after his mamm, eh? Both of them."

Wyman clucked to the horse and headed into Bloomingdale. First he stopped at Lamar Lapp's home to consult with the bishop about a couple of things. Then, as the buggy rolled down the unpaved lane toward Amanda's old white farmhouse, he couldn't stop grinning. Had there ever been a day like this one? Even though awaiting the final decision from the Fishers—and the bid from Amos Coblentz— might keep him awake for the next night or two, he was the happiest man alive. He had the dearest wife on the face of the earth, and his kids were getting beyond their grief, growing again as they meshed with Amanda's girls. Life just didn't get any better.

When Abby saw Wyman's buggy pull onto the blacktop, she leaned across the counter to grasp James's sturdy hands. These moments without anyone else in the store were rare, and she enjoyed finding unexpected times and places to express her affection. "I love you," she whispered.

"Do you, now?" James gripped her fingers. "You just wait, Abby. Come November nineteenth, I'm going to show you a whole new meaning of love—and excitement, too. Are you ready for that, bride of mine?"

Oh, but she got a shimmery feeling when James talked that way. "For sure and for certain I am," she replied. "And speaking of excitement—is it just me, or was Wyman a man afire today? I've not seen him looking so happy, even on his wedding day."

"Just goes to show you that love improves with age, even if it's only been about a month since he hitched up with Amanda," James remarked. "Didn't we know she'd be gut for him?"

"Jah, but what's going on if they're painting the house in Bloomingdale?" she asked in a speculative tone. "That man's keeping secrets behind those handsome brown eyes, mark my word."

James placed his hand on his chest and let out a play-fully dramatic sigh. "Ah, maybe someday you'll say that about me and my eyes, Abby—and I'll keep you guessing about *my* secrets, too. Every one of them will be something wonderful involving you, after all."

While she loved their teasing chitchat, Abby had been hoping to discuss something more important before Wyman had interrupted them, and this seemed like an opportune moment. She focused on James, choosing her words care-fully. "And after we marry, how will you feel about me working here in the store? And continuing with my Stitch in Time business?"

James's brows rose at the change in her mood. "Honey-girl, I want you to be happy—"

"But you *know* Sam will insist that I stay home and start our family," Abby said in a rising voice. "I've seen how Barbara's and Amanda's jobs have caused them problems, so you and I need to figure out how we'll handle this issue."

James looked down at their entwined hands. "The way you've expressed your question tells me *your* answer to it," he said with a little laugh. "But your heart's in the right place, Abby, and so are your priorities. When the time comes for you to stay home—with our babies, or with my parents—you'll do that. I've never doubted it."

Abby blinked. While she hadn't figured James would

raise his voice or put his foot down, his rock-solid faith in her touched something deep in her heart. "Well, *that* simplifies things," she murmured. "This matter's been on my mind a lot lately—"

"So it's gut that you've come to me with your concerns," he replied. "We should make such major decisions together, ain't so?"

Abby smiled. Why had she thought this would be such a difficult conversation? "I suspect Sam will fire me if I don't quit working at the store of my own free will," she mused aloud. "But it wouldn't be that hard to do my sewing from home . . ."

"Rosemary bakes pies in her kitchen for Lois Yutzy, after all," James remarked, "and I don't see Matt or Katie suffering for it. Your Stitch in Time business is just one more way you connect with folks—and *help* them, Abby," he insisted. "And that's important to you."

"Jah, you said that just right. It's never been so much for the money as for the satisfaction of doing what I love."

James's smile teased at Abby, yet it was a sure sign of how much he respected her, too. "Watching Wyman and Amanda deal with this very same matter has taught me a few things," he said lightly. "I'd be foolish to ignore your needs, Abby, just for the sake of being a husband who ruled his roost."

And didn't that clarify this whole matter? A satisfying marriage was more likely when both partners could express their needs and exert some control—and this wise, patient man was allowing her to do that. "You make a gut mirror, James," she said softly. "When I stand before you, I see myself more clearly."

"And when I stand before you, Abby, I see the most beautiful, wonderful woman in the world," he replied in a dreamlike voice. "I thank my lucky stars—and God—that you'll soon be mine. And then, honey-girl," he added with a mischievous twinkle in his eye, "there will be no end to the kissing and the caressing and the loving. *Because I said so!*"

James blew her a kiss as he walked toward the door. "Meanwhile, I'm back to work. The fellows must wonder if I've eloped during my afternoon break."

As the bell jingled, Abby laughed. James had just told her in no uncertain terms how their marriage was going to be. And now, November nineteenth couldn't come soon enough.

Chapter 32

Saturday morning, Amanda was on pins and needles as Wyman kissed her good-bye and left for Clearwater. "Remember," he whispered. "You're keeping all of this business about our move to Bloomingdale under your kapp. Maybe tonight at supper I'll have an announcement."

Yesterday Amos Coblentz had presented the bid for repairing the Brubaker house, and her husband had passed it along to Ray and Trevor. And while Wyman had hardly slept for his excitement, Amanda had lain awake for a different reason.

"Sixty-five thousand dollars?" she had murmured over and over. "What if the Fishers won't want the farm, with that extra expense tacked on? And what if other buyers won't consider the property, either, unless we first make the repairs? And how will we come up with the money to—"

Wyman had shushed her with gentle kisses. "Have faith, Amanda. I have a gut feeling about this whole transaction," he'd murmured. "When the bank's assessor told me the going rate for that eighty-acre tract was six thousand per acre, my eyeballs nearly fell from their sockets. So when I told Ray and Trevor I'd sell it to them for forty-five hundred an acre—three hundred sixty thousand dollars instead of the four hundred eighty thousand it's worth—that made the house repairs seem pretty reasonable."

Amanda's brain was still swimming with such incredible figures. It boggled her mind, what farmland was selling for these days—but she set aside such calculations. No matter what the Fishers decided, Wyman had made up his mind. They would be living here at her farm permanently— because it made her happy. And *that* amazed her more than any of his other decisions.

He was such a good man, her husband. Wyman had changed lately: he seemed freer, more serene, as though a great weight had been lifted from his shoulders when he'd decided to leave the Clearwater district. And wasn't that worth more than any amount of money?

Amanda continued kneading the bread she was making for tomorrow's dinner with the Lambrights and the Grabers. Across the kitchen, Lizzie and Vera raced to see who could fill her baking sheet with spoonfuls of oatmeal cookie dough first. The three youngest girls were cutting out sugar cookies under Jemima's watchful eye, while Eddie was painting the front room. Jerome, Pete, and Simon were assisting one of the mares with birthing her mule foal. Everyone had a task, and all were working together today . . . one big happy family.

Such a blessing that was.

"Mamm! Mamm, there's a big ole truck comin' up the lane!" Simon's voice rang out in the yard. "Come and see!"

Cora and Dora ran to the door, floury hands and all, followed by a toddling Alice Ann. As Amanda wiped her hands, she peered out the window, past the broadfall trousers that flapped on the clothesline. "That fellow must surely be lost," she murmured. She slipped into her shawl and stepped out to the porch.

Up the lane trundled a delivery truck, and as Simon ran out to greet it, Wags circled the boy, barking loudly. Amanda strode into the yard, hoping to redirect the driver before he got all the way up to the house. "What can I do for you?" she called out as the driver's window lowered. "You must've turned in at the wrong farm."

The fellow replied, "If your name's Amanda Brubaker, we're right where we're supposed to be."

"Jah, that's me, but—" What was going on here?

The driver pulled forward until he was closer to the house, then shut off his engine. As he and another fellow hopped out of the cab, he waved toward the barn. "You guys are just in time to help us unload, if you care to," he hollered to Jerome and Pete. "Your backs are a lot younger than ours."

Then he held out a square box with a plastic screen that displayed some writing. "If you'll just sign your name here, Mrs. Brubaker—"

"But I have no idea— What are you bringing us?" she asked in a flustered voice.

"Says here we've got an oak bedroom set, a potter's wheel, and a kiln," he replied as he made the lines of tiny print move up and down on the screen.

Amanda gasped. "But I didn't order— Who could have—"

"You related to a Wyman Brubaker?" the driver asked. "His name's here at the top of the order. So if you'll sign off, we can get your stuff unloaded and be out of your hair."

"It's okay, Amanda," Jerome assured her with sparkling eyes. "Wyman told me to watch for a delivery, and it's arrived sooner than we thought."

Dumbfounded, Amanda took the thick plastic tool the driver handed her and wrote a signature that didn't resemble her penmanship in the least. It didn't seem to matter: his partner was already lowering a large wooden crate from the back of the truck on a motorized platform. The crate sat on a wheeled cart, which Jerome and Pete rolled toward the back kitchen door, where there were no steps to contend with. Simon followed at a jog while Wags bounded around all three of them, barking excitedly.

Amanda watched, agog, while the deliverymen lowered another crate with a picture of a potter's wheel on the side. It looked just like the kick wheel Uriah had destroyed . . . but what did this mean? She would have jumped up and down, clapping her hands, had it not been for the two fellows watching her.

"You okay, lady?" the driver asked. "Most folks don't seem so befuddled when we bring 'em stuff."

"You have no idea," Amanda gasped. "*I* have no idea— oh, my, but this is quite a surprise! And you have a bedroom set, too?"

"Yup, from an Oak Ridge Furniture shop in Jamesport," he replied. "Picked it up on our way. Nice folks there."

"My stars," she murmured, for she couldn't think of anything else to say. After the truck rumbled back down to the road, Amanda went inside—just in time to rescue two sheets of oatmeal cookies from the oven, because everyone else seemed to be in the other room, all talking at once.

"But why would Dat be buying her another kiln?" Vera asked.

"We dropped the other one, remember?" Pete replied.

"This wheel looks just like her other one—except newer, and not all busted up," Eddie remarked.

"And what'll we do when the Schmuckers find out?" Lizzie asked in a shrill whisper. "I was hoping Teacher Elsie wouldn't have any more reasons to pick on me!"

"And a whole new bedroom set for him and Amanda," Vera mused. "Something's going on here, and Dat's not been letting on. We'll have to pounce on him, soon as he gets home."

Amanda smiled, feeling giddy. For just a moment she lingered in the kitchen while the children speculated about these new items . . . ate a warm cookie as she stepped onto the porch. The boys had left the glossy oak bedstead, dresser, and night tables out here with the new mattress so they wouldn't bump Eddie's wet walls when they carried them through the front room.

Vera wasn't the only one who would quiz Wyman the moment he stepped through the door. Most likely he had ordered the bedroom pieces because her old mattress was too soft to suit him . . . and because Atlee had made the set in their bedroom. Another fresh start for them, this furniture— and it had cost a pretty penny, too. She'd nearly fainted at the prices for the kiln and the wheel on the invoice . . . and he'd purchased all these items before they knew if the Fishers were buying Wyman's land, too. And Wyman would soon be constructing a new grain elevator . . .

Does he think God's going to rain money on us? After years of scraping by following Atlee's death—and months of lying awake, wondering how they would pay their bills before that—Amanda hoped her generous new husband hadn't overextended himself in his excitement over leaving Clearwater.

Have faith, Amanda.

She let Wyman's earlier words soothe her as she went inside again. When Jemima sent her a questioning look from across the kitchen, where the kids were snatching fresh cookies from a plate, Amanda shrugged. She feigned innocence when they all pelted her with questions, too. "It's a mystery," she hedged. "Sometimes we must wait for all the reasons to be revealed, jah?"

"What's a *mystery*, Mamma?" Cora asked.

Dora sucked in her breath, excitement all over her face. "I know! Is a mystery like when we heard Eddie talking on the phone in the barn yesterday, like, to a *girl*?"

"And when we asked who it was," her twin continued, "he told us to *leave*—"

"Because it was none of our beeswax?" Dora finished with a giggle.

Eddie let out an exasperated sigh, grabbing another cookie. "I wasn't talking to a—"

"Oh, jah, you were! The twins are callin' it like they saw it," Pete countered mercilessly. "It was that blonde we met at church, ain't so? Fannie Lehman, the preacher's daughter."

"Fannie?" Simon piped up. "Isn't that another name for your *backside*?"

Amanda bit back a laugh, pleased that Eddie was already making new friends. It was a joy to watch her kids and Wyman's taking up for one another, having their fun even as they were undergoing such major changes. She slipped away as their animated discussion continued, to the little room where she'd previously made her ceramics.

Jerome was clearing away the boxes and crating. He had placed the wheel beside the windows, where she'd kept her old one, and he'd already hooked the kiln to the gas pipeline. With the pale yellow glow of the freshly painted walls reflecting the morning sunlight, Amanda yearned to be working in this cheerful room again. Her fingers itched to be covered with wet, pliant clay while she formed pitchers and bowls on the wheel.

"I'd say somebody loves you, Aunt Amanda," her nephew remarked. "And I'm guessing you know some things we don't, too."

"Maybe," she hedged as she spun the wheel with her fingertips. "But that's for Wyman to say, not me."

"Soon?" Jerome insisted.

Amanda laughed. "I hope so. This kiln and the wheel have *all* of us wondering what's going on. In God's gut time—and Wyman's—we'll have our answers."

As he drove up Uriah Schmucker's lane, Wyman inhaled deeply to steady his nerves—and needed no further reminder that the bishop was a pig farmer. Even on this brisk November day, the stench from the manure pits enveloped him as he approached the house. *Smells like money,* farm folks joked.

And money was the reason that—except for this final visit—Wyman felt as bubbly as a bottle of soda pop. Ray and Trevor had gotten approval for a loan, and they also wanted to take over the remodeling of the house. Tyler was excited about becoming a full partner and setting up the computer and automation systems for the new elevator in Bloomingdale, too. Wyman felt as if all his ducks were in a row for a wonderful future—but he couldn't leave Clearwater like a thief in the night.

Guide my thoughts, Lord, he mused as he knocked on the Schmuckers' door. It swung open as though Mildred had been watching him from behind her simple blue curtains.

"Jah?" she demanded.

Wyman blinked. Her jarring tone seemed yet another reason he and his family should no longer live here. "I've come to speak to Uriah, please."

"Fine."

Again Wyman was struck by this woman's lack of common courtesy, making him wait outside as though he were a stranger. Had the Schmuckers spread the word that he and his family had fled Clearwater rather than face up to Amanda's confession? If the bishop had gossiped this way, and the other members had believed him, well, that was just further proof that Wyman had made the right decision about selling his land.

Uriah appeared at the door, his eyes as hard as marbles. "Brubaker," he muttered. "What brings you here with your hat in your hand? Come to repent, did you?"

Wyman paused. He didn't intend to sink to this man's level, or to flare up in anger, for neither trait exemplified the Christ they both worshipped. Best to state his case and leave. "I've sold my land. We'll be living in Bloomingdale," he said. "I wanted you to hear it from me, firsthand."

The bishop looked startled, but then his eyes narrowed. "You can run but you can't hide, Wyman. Jesus said it best, asking what a man profits if he gains the world—or a big bunch of money, in your case—but loses his soul."

"I have entrusted my soul to God. I'm leaving the district because I prefer to follow His ways rather than yours, Uriah."

Wyman stepped into the doorframe to keep the bishop from shutting him out before he was finished. "You crossed the line when you destroyed Amanda's pottery—frightened our children with your violence—while she and I weren't at home," he said. "That's hardly the way Jesus taught us to behave."

"But Jesus overturned the tables of the money changers in the temple," Uriah countered in a rising voice. "He was chastising sin and dishonesty, as I have been chosen to do in the district I serve. You've forgotten how to accept constructive criticism and you're too enamored of your new wife, Wyman. Your adoration of Amanda has eclipsed your devotion to God."

Wyman's pulse pounded. This conversation was escalating into a heated exchange of Bible verses neither of them would win because they had already lost the trust and respect all servants of Christ should have for each other. "And you, Uriah, have lost your sense of humility, along with your *vision* for our district. Even my friends, the Fishers—"

"Puh. Mennonites."

"—have told us you've spoken out against Amanda and me," Wyman persisted. "And your lack of concern was blatantly obvious when you saw how the storm had damaged our home yet you didn't lift a finger to help us. That goes against all I've ever known about Plain ways."

"So you've sold out. Turned tail and run off rather than making Amanda face up to the confession I prescribed for her." Uriah widened his eyes, as he did during a dramatic moment of a sermon. "The wages of sin is *death*, you know."

302 | NAOMI KING

Wyman checked his urge to lash out. The bishop was like a dog who would never release this meaty bone of contention. So Wyman would be the one to let go.

"God is love," he said softly. As he stepped away, he wondered why he'd bothered to come in person when he could have written a note or left a message on the bishop's answering machine. Yet it had felt like the honorable way to—

"Never heard that your land was even up for sale, Brubaker," Uriah remarked. "Who'd you sell out to?"

Wyman bit back a grin. "Ray Fisher and his son."

"Mennonites? *Mennonites?* Of all the—"

Wham! The slamming of the door announced the end to his membership in the Clearwater church district, where generations of his family had followed their faith. Wyman regretted this deeply, yet he believed his father and grandfathers wouldn't have tolerated such treatment from the bishops of their day, either.

With his most difficult task behind him, Wyman climbed into his rig and clucked to his horse. He couldn't wait to get home to Amanda, to tell her and their family of the wonderful changes coming their way.

Chapter 33

Amanda caught herself looking out the window every five minutes as she helped the boys put the front room to rights after the cream-colored walls had dried. "The downstairs looks so pretty and clean, Eddie," she said as he was carrying his drop cloths to the porch. "Denki ever so much for helping this old house look its Sunday best again."

He shot her a lopsided smile. "It was tough seeing the other house in such a wreck, and finding our clothes and broken furniture in the mess we were hauling off," he admitted. "I'd lots rather be working here."

"I'm sorry you had that awful job," Amanda murmured. "But this, too, shall pass. We're all in it together."

At last a *clip-clop! clip-clop!* in the lane announced Wyman's arrival. Amanda hurried outside to greet him, but of course she was followed by the twins and Simon, all clamoring for their dat's explanation of today's delivery. She lifted Alice Ann to her shoulder, nuzzling the toddler's dewy cheek as she waited to catch her husband's eye.

And when Wyman looked at her from the huddle of the three little kids who had captured him at thigh level, her heart held still. That glimmer in his eyes could mean only one thing—and since his news was much more important than her curiosity about the kiln and the wheel, she merely returned his smile.

"Supper's nearly ready," she announced. "You girls can help Lizzie set the table, and, Simon, it's time to feed and water Wags. We'll give your dat a chance to catch his breath after a busy day, jah?"

As the children scattered to do their chores, Wyman slipped up to kiss Amanda's cheek and then Alice Ann's. "See there? Already they're listening to you and behaving so much better."

"And *you* need to behave, as well," she teased. "It seems we got a delivery today, and your name was on it, Wyman. And—and denki ever so much for the kiln and the wheel," she added in a voice that quavered. "But whatever were you thinking when you ordered them? What if Lamar Lapp sees no reason for me to take up my pottery again, now that my husband supplies all my needs? What about—"

"Do I, Amanda? That's gut to hear," he whispered. Then he grinned. "Consider them gifts. And Lamar sends you his blessings to make your dishes again, but perhaps with more . . . subdued colors."

A laugh escaped her. "You've spoken to him?"

"Just full of surprises, aren't I?" Wyman teased. "You'll have to wait for supper to hear the rest of the details. But they're gut, Amanda. It's all gut now, my love."

Somehow she contained her excitement as the older girls set on the bowls of creamed chicken, noodles, peas and carrots, and apples simmered with cinnamon Red Hots. After they prayed, Wyman held up his hand before the kids could start in with their questions.

"It's a historic day for the Brubaker family," he said in a resonating voice that filled the kitchen. "And while I tell you of things to come, please hear me out. Then you may ask your questions and express any doubts you have. But with God's guidance, and considering the entire family's welfare, I have made my decision. And I will not—cannot—change my mind."

Amanda's heart beat faster. The children's expressions bespoke the solemnity of this moment, yet their eyes were wide with eager curiosity. Bowls of food were being passed, but all eyes were on Wyman.

"After much prayer and soul-searching," he said, pausing to look at everyone around the table, "I have sold the farm in Clearwater to Ray and Trevor Fisher. Which means we will be living *here* now."

A tight silence filled the kitchen.

"Holy cow," Jerome murmured. "That's *huge*."

" 'Bless the Lord, oh my soul,' " Jemima intoned. "Yet another miracle this week."

"But—but what about our stuff at the other house?" Vera whispered.

"And what happens to all the hay we baled?" Pete asked. "There's not enough put by for the livestock here, what with Jerome's horses and mules—"

"That's all being worked out." As Wyman smiled, his rugged face glowed with the relief of sharing this news at last. "Trevor and his dat have been approved for their loan, and they'll take on the rebuilding of the house after we move out our belongings. Meanwhile, Ray and I will remain partners at the Clearwater elevator, and we'll build a new elevator here—down the road by the railroad tracks," he added in a rising voice. "We have a lot of work to do, but God has brought us this far, and He'll give us the strength to meet our obligations . . . and to deal with this major change."

After another moment of tense silence, pandemonium broke out around the table.

"We're *home*!" Lizzie crowed as she grabbed for Cora and Dora.

"So that's why you're having me paint these walls—"

"But, Dat, that's been our home *forever*!" Pete protested.

"And what about the pieces that belonged to Mamm? Where will we put them here in Amanda's house?"

"Pink! I want my woom pink *now*!"

"You knew this all along, Mamma! And you didn't tell *me*!"

When Simon's exclamation rang out above all those of his siblings, Amanda had to laugh. Bless his heart, he was calling her *Mamma* now, and his chocolate brown eyes bore into hers to demand her answer.

"Well, until just this minute, I didn't know how it would all turn out," she explained. "Your dat and I have talked and prayed all week long—"

"And, Simon, when you said no one would be happy unless your mamma was happy? You hit the nail on the head," Wyman said. "After those unfortunate incidents with the Schmuckers, it made perfect sense for this farm to be our new home. It was as though God dropped that answer into my head and brought all the pieces and players together, just like that." He snapped his fingers to illustrate his point, smiling at each of them.

"Uriah will be hopping mad when he hears about *this*," Pete remarked.

"Matter of fact, I spoke with the bishop this afternoon. And with all due *respect*," Wyman said emphatically, "I've not seen anyone do a better imitation of a whistling, overheated teakettle. When he found out I'd sold our place to Mennonites, well . . . he slammed the door in my face."

"Oh, Wyman," Amanda murmured, grabbing his hand. "I'm sorry."

"I wasn't happy about it, either," he admitted as he squeezed her fingers. "It's serious business to part ways with the bishop God chose for us . . . and, as Jesus taught us, we should pray for those who persecute us. As much as he's provoked us, Uriah needs our prayers."

When Wyman paused, Amanda saw how their children were listening intently . . . processing their father's wisdom. Even Alice Ann sat absolutely still in her high chair, as though she fully understood the magnitude of what her dat was sharing with them, and the higher road he was leading them on.

"I want you kids to know that first and foremost, I left our home district because I believe that if we are to follow God, we can no longer follow Uriah," Wyman stated. "He accused me of loving Amanda too much, to the point that I loved our Lord less than I should."

Wyman gazed intently at her. Amanda's heart beat steadily even as she held her breath, awaiting whatever her husband said next.

"But the way I see it," he continued earnestly, "if I love your mother and take gut care of her—love you kids and everyone under my roof—then I am in fact living out my faith, reflecting the heavenly Father's love. If I give my family my very best, am I not loving God with my whole heart at the same time?"

Amanda slowly let out the breath she'd been holding. Here in this clean, cozy kitchen, surrounded by those she loved most in this world, it seemed they were sharing a holy moment—the beginning of a whole new life as a family. The frustrations of her first weeks as a Brubaker faded away as she basked in the glow of her husband's love.

"You're such a gut man, Wyman. A fine example to us all," she murmured. "Truly, none of us could ask for more."

Acknowledgments

Again the thanks and praise go first to You, Lord. You continue to inspire me as I write and accomplish more than I ever dreamed possible.

Continued thanks and appreciation to my meticulous editor, Ellen Edwards, for your vision—and for sharing ideas to set me apart in the Amish romance genre. Many thanks as well to William Bauer for your enthusiasm and the concept behind the story.

And to Evan Marshall—what would I do without your continued support, expertise, and guidance? Thank you all for believing in my work and its potential reach.

My continuous gratitude goes to Jim Smith of Step Back in Time Tours in Jamesport, Missouri—the largest Old Order Amish settlement west of the Mississippi River. Your research assistance is invaluable, and I treasure your friendship, too!

If you enjoyed *Amanda Weds a Good Man*,
don't miss Naomi King's

Emma Blooms at Last

HOME AT CEDAR CREEK

Available from Berkley

This is what a Monday morning should look like, Amanda mused. Her kitchen was thrumming with activity as her family finished breakfast—and everyone looked happily intent on getting where they needed to go next. In the six weeks since she'd married Wyman Brubaker, they'd known some rough moments, yet it seemed that their eight kids and the four adults had finally figured out a morning routine that worked. Today they'd all been dressed and ready to eat on time, without any squabbling or drama. It was a minor miracle.

"What a wonderful-gut meal," Wyman said as he rose from his place at the head of the table. "The haystack casserole had all my favorite things in it. Lots of sausage and onions and green peppers—"

"And *cheese,*" five-year-old Simon piped up. "So much cheese the hash browns were really gooey and really, *really* gut."

"And what are you three fellows doing this morning?"

Wyman asked. He rumpled Simon's dark hair, looking from Eddie to Jerome. "Did I hear you say we might have baby mules by the end of the day?"

"That's my best guess," Jerome replied as he, too, stood up. "Eddie and Simon are going with me to get some feed supplement. Let's hit the road, boys, so we'll be back in time if the mammas need our help with their birthings."

"I'm already outta here!" Simon sprang from his chair and shot through the kitchen door, slamming it behind him.

Eddie, his fifteen-year-old brother, headed toward the jackets and hats that hung on wall pegs. "Well, there's the speed of light and the speed of sound—and the speed of Simon," he remarked as he grabbed his youngest brother's coat along with his own. "At this rate, we'll be to Cedar Creek and back before those mammas can turn twice in their stalls."

"Enthusiasm is a gut thing," Jerome replied as he came over to hug Amanda. "Anything you need from the mercantile, Aunt? Maybe a big bag of raisins for my favorite kind of pie?"

Amanda laughed as her nephew wagged his eyebrows at her. The money from Jerome's mule business had seen her through some tight times after her first husband had died, leaving her to raise three young daughters. Now that she'd remarried, Jerome was taking to Wyman's boys with a sense of fun and responsibility that was once again a big help to her. "Bring whatever you think will taste gut," she replied.

"Raisin-filled cookies," Wyman hinted wistfully. "And with that luscious thought, I'll head to the barn. Reece Weaver's supposed to call me with a progress report on my new grain elevator."

Amanda felt a rush of goose bumps when Wyman smiled at her. With his dark hair and a thick, silky beard framing his face, he was such a handsome man—and a wonderful provider for her and their children, as well. "Jemima and I plan to get some baking done today to stay ahead of you fellows with your bottomless stomachs," she said. "So it can't hurt to sweet-talk the cooks."

"I'm going to kiss this cook instead," Wyman murmured. He quickly brushed her lips with his and then waved Eddie and Jerome out the door ahead of him. "You ladies have a gut rest of your morning. Oh—and you, too, Pete!" he teased as he playfully clapped his middle son on the back. "See you and Lizzie after school."

As the three fellows left the kitchen, Amanda joined Pete and Lizzie at the counter, where they were closing the lids of their coolers. "Denki to you both for packing your lunches," she said as she slung an arm around each of them. "You've really smoothed out my morning doing that."

"And it's the easiest way to get exactly what we want to eat," Lizzie pointed out. She elbowed her new brother. "Pete made *three* ham sandwiches—"

"Well, I for sure didn't want any of your stinky tuna salad," he insisted. "The barn cats will probably follow us to school, yowling for your lunch."

As the two thirteen-year-olds donned their winter coats and hats, Amanda noted that they resembled each other enough to be twins, even though Pete was a Brubaker and her Lizzie was a Lambright. "Make it a gut day," she said as they started out the door, "and we'll see you this afternoon."

"Bye, Mamma," Lizzie replied while Pete gave her a wave.

As Amanda turned back toward the long kitchen table, she was pleased to see that Vera, Wyman's eldest, had been putting away the breakfast leftovers while Amanda's four-year-old twins, Cora and Dora, had scraped and stacked everyone's plates. "Well, now that it's just us girls, the real work can get done!" Amanda teased as she lifted Alice Ann from the wooden high chair.

"I be the helper!" the toddler crowed. "Me—Alice Ann!"

Amanda felt a surge of sweetness and love as the little

blonde hugged her. "Jah, and you're everyone's blessing, too, punkin," she murmured.

"We're going to start on the laundry," Vera joined in. At seventeen, she was tall and slender—and she'd become well versed on running a household after her mother had died. "Alice Ann's going to help me sort the clothes by colors, and then hand me the clothespins when we hang everything out to dry."

"A never-ending job, the laundry," Amanda remarked as she lowered the toddler to the floor. "And while you start the dough for the bread and pie crusts, Jemima, the twins and I will fetch the morning's eggs."

Her mother-in-law from her first marriage nodded as she ran hot dishwater into the sink. "Better you than me. These cold mornings make my legs ache, so I'm happy to stay inside."

"And when we come back from the henhouse, can we make cookies, Mamma?" Dora asked eagerly. "Chocolate chip ones?"

"And a pan of butterscotch brownies? *Please?*" Cora chimed in. "You know how we don't like raisin-filled cookies—"

"But we were too polite to say so when Dat asked for them," her twin finished the sentence.

Amanda laughed, hugging her look-alike daughters. How could she refuse them when they brightened her days—and had already started calling Wyman their dat? They were just at the age to wear their hair twisted into rolls and tucked into a bun . . . growing up so fast. "If you think you can do all the measuring—"

"Jah, we can do that!" they said together.

"—we can make your goodies *after* we redd up your room and Simon's," Amanda replied. "So let's get out to the henhouse. The sooner we finish our work, the sooner we can play."

As her girls scurried ahead of her to the low-slung building that adjoined the barn, Amanda felt a deep sense of satisfaction. A few weeks ago, her mornings at the Brubaker place had been chaotic and stressful, but when Wyman had decided they would move to her farm in Bloomingdale, everything had fallen into place, as though God had intended for them to be here all along. She marveled at how the first light of this fine autumn morning made the frost sparkle. The maple and sweet gum trees glistened with bursts of red, orange, and gold to form a glorious backdrop behind the white gambrel-roofed barn, and as the horses and mules in the corral whickered at the twins, she couldn't help but smile. Her life was so good now . . .

Wyman paused in the unlit barn, watching the wall phone's red message light blink. Had Reece called while he'd been outside seeing Jerome and the boys off? Or had someone else left a message? What with Jerome running his mule-breeding business here, it might be a good idea to get a new message machine that allowed callers to leave their voice mails for specific businesses and family members.

But then some districts' bishops spoke out against such an updated message system, saying it allowed for keeping secrets. In a lot of Amish towns, two or three families had shared a phone shanty alongside the road for generations. *You've gotten used to the phone being in your elevator office rather than in another fellow's barn,* Wyman realized. *This is just one more minor adjustment—like learning a new phone number after having the same one all your life.*

Wyman pushed the PLAY button. If the message was for Jerome, he would jot the phone number or the caller's name on the pad of paper Amanda kept on the wooden bench beneath the phone. "You have one new message," the voice on the recorder announced. "Monday, November sixteenth, at seven eighteen."

"Jah, Wyman, this is Reece Weaver, and we've gotta talk

about some more up-front money," the contractor said in a voice that rang around the barn's rafters. "Started digging your foundation, and we're gonna have to blast through solid bedrock, which jacks the price way up from what I quoted you last week. Got some issues with EPA and OSHA regulations that'll cost a lot more, too, so that seven hundred thousand we figured on won't nearly cover building your elevator now. Better gimme a call real quick-like." *Click*.

Wyman's heart thudded. He'd left Reece's written estimate in the house—not that it would answer any of the questions spinning in his mind. Wouldn't a commercial contractor know about environmental and safety regulations—and the possibility of hitting bedrock—before writing up an estimate? And why on earth had Reece left a message about monetary details instead of waiting for him to call back? As Wyman glanced around the shadowy barn, he was relieved that only the horses and mules had heard the contractor's news. The seven hundred thousand dollars he'd spoken of—money from the sale of the Brubaker family farm as well as from the Clearwater elevator's bank account—was all he could spend on a new facility. He'd kept money back to see his family of eleven through the coming year until his Bloomingdale elevator was bringing in some money . . . but Reece's strident words made it sound as though he intended to demand a significant price increase.

Wyman pressed the number pads on the phone, hoping he and Reece could settle this matter immediately rather than playing cat-and-mouse with each other's calls. After assuring Amanda that he could support her; her mother-in-law, Jemima; and their eight kids, he did *not* want any more messages about money left on the phone, where she might hear them and start to worry. Finally, on the fourth ring, someone picked up.

"Jah, Weaver Construction Company," a woman answered.

"Wyman Brubaker here, and I need to speak with Reece about—"

"He's out on a job. I'll take your message."

Wyman frowned. More than likely this was Reece's wife, because the company had been a small, family-owned business since Reece's dat had started it more than thirty years ago. "He just called me not five minutes ago, asking me to call right back," Wyman replied. "I'd rather not discuss the details of my elevator with—"

"Oh, you're *that* Wyman Brubaker," the woman interrupted. "I'll page him and he'll call you back as soon as he can." *Click.*

And what did she mean by snipping and snapping at him that way, as though he were an inconvenience rather than a customer? Wyman's stomach tightened around his breakfast as he hung up. There was nothing to do but wait for Reece to call back, even as every passing moment allowed him to think of things that didn't set right about this situation—

The phone rang and he grabbed it. "Jah? This is Wyman."

"Reece Weaver. So you see where I'm coming from, far as your job costing more?" he asked. "How about if I stop by, say, around noon? Another hundred thousand should cover the blasting and the—"

"A hundred thousand dollars?" Wyman closed his eyes and curled in around the phone, hoping his voice hadn't carried outside the barn. It took him a moment to corral his stampeding thoughts. "I don't understand why you didn't know—*before* you started digging—about that bedrock, and why you didn't call me—*before* you started digging—about maybe changing the location of the elevator," he said in a low voice. "That's a huge difference from the price you quoted in your estimate."

"Jah, well, the excavation crew I use is only available this week, before they've got jobs with other contractors," Reece replied. "Can't get them again until middle of January, see, so I didn't think you'd want to wait that long."

Middle of January? Nobody poured concrete then, so his facility would be delayed by months if he waited that long. Wyman drew in a deep breath, trying to compose himself. "It seems to me that bedrock would be the ideal foundation for an elevator anyway," he said. "It's not like I need a basement—or even a crawl space—under the silos or the office building."

"Oh, jah, the new EPA regulations are making us do a lotta things different these days," the contractor replied. "Nothing's as easy as it was when Pop put up your elevator in Clearwater. That *was* about twenty years ago, after all."

Wyman blinked. Norbert Weaver's friendly, reliable service had been the main reason he and his partner, Ray Fisher, had wanted Weaver Construction to build their new facility, but it seemed that some of the family's values had died with the company's founder. Wyman heard the hum of equipment in the background. Could it be that Reece was being so pushy because he was focused on what was happening on a work site? And perhaps had several big projects going on at once? The younger man had acted quite accommodating and professional last week, when they had discussed the plans for this new elevator . . . and Wyman realized that because he, too, was feeling pressured, he wasn't handling these details well over the phone.

"Tell you what, Reece," he said, trying to sound reasonable and relaxed. "I need to discuss this situation with my partner before we proceed. How about if I meet you at the elevator site tomorrow morning—"

"I'll be outta state on another big job. Won't be back around Bloomingdale until Friday."

Wyman caught himself scowling yet again. But he would not be pushed into paying out more money until he'd talked with Ray about this new development. "What time on Friday, then?"

"You really want to wait? My excavation crew'll most likely be gone by then, or they'll charge me double time for squeezing your job in over the weekend," the contractor replied. "You know what they say. Time is money."

No, time is TIME, and this is MY money we're talking about. Wyman let out the breath he'd been holding. "Three o'clock this afternoon, then. But don't come to the house," he insisted. "Meet me at the elevator site so we can talk about our options."

"See you then. With at least half of that hundred thousand bucks." *Click.*

Wyman sank onto the wooden bench near the phone. How had this opportunity for his future changed so radically? Just a few weeks ago, the details of his move to Bloomingdale had fallen effortlessly into place because, he believed, God was directing him to start a new life with his new blended family on Amanda's farm. He'd sold the Brubaker home place to the Fisher family for less than market value because he and Ray had been best friends since childhood, and so that Ray's son could have a place to expand his dairy operation when he got married.

The transaction had been seamless, on a handshake. Wyman had felt confident that he could afford a new facility—in addition to the elevator he and Ray had run since they'd been young and single—or he wouldn't have dreamed of stretching his family's finances. They had agreed that Weaver Construction would do the work because they wanted to support other Plain businesses in the area.

Had they made a mistake? Maybe they should've gotten a bid from another construction company . . . but it was too late for that now. They had already put down more than half the money up front.

Wyman punched in Ray's phone number, hoping his level-headed Mennonite partner would offer him some advice. Because Ray had already borrowed a large amount to buy the Brubaker place, Wyman had insisted on financing the new elevator with the money from the sale and the Clear-water account, without expecting Ray to kick in any more. Out of sheer Amish tradition and principle, Wyman refused to get a loan from an English bank to make this deal work—or to feed his family. Generations of Brubaker men had remained staunchly self-sufficient, supporting one another rather than going to outside sources for funding.

The phone clicked in his ear. "Hullo?"

"Jah, Ray. How was your weekend?" Wyman relaxed, knowing he could trust his partner's feedback, his sense of perspective. "I suppose you and Sally and the boys are gearing up for Trevor's wedding . . ."

On the other side of the barn wall, Amanda listened as her husband chatted with his partner. She and the twins had been gathering eggs in the adjoining chicken house, and when she'd heard Wyman holler, *"A hundred thousand dollars?"* she'd sent the girls outside to scatter feed. It wasn't Wyman's way to raise his voice. His calm demeanor and sensible approach to problems were two of the traits that had attracted her when they'd courted.

"Got a call from Reece Weaver this morning, and I don't know what to make of it," Wyman was saying into the phone. "He's telling me he needs another hundred thousand dollars—half of it *today*—because he ran into bedrock and some other unexpected issues . . . Jah, this is on top of the seven hundred thousand on his bid."

Amanda sucked in her breath at such a large amount of money. Wyman was a careful planner, a solid businessman, and his rising voice said it all: he was *upset* about this new development. And very concerned about where so much additional money would come from.

"When we were going over the items on his bid, didn't you think Reece had covered all the angles?" Wyman asked. "I can't have him coming by the house or leaving any more phone messages about needing money, so I'm meeting him at the elevator site this afternoon . . ."

Ah. So Wyman was protecting her from this situation, was he? Amanda understood that, because like any Amish husband, he believed it was his responsibility to support their family. But she knew firsthand about making the pennies stretch . . . about the fear that she might not be able to pay the propane bill or buy shoes for her three young daughters when she'd been their sole support for four years after their dat had died.

Wyman sold his home place, left everything he'd loved all his life, so you could be happy here in Bloomingdale, Amanda reminded herself. *You can't let him face this crisis alone . . . even if he won't tell you about it. He may be the head of this family, but YOU are in charge of keeping everyone fed and together, body and soul. Better get back to work!*

Amanda stepped away from the wall as the twins bustled into the henhouse with the empty feed bucket. In the cold air, the wisps of their breath framed their precious faces. "Let's take the eggs to the house, girls. Maybe Vera or Mammi will help you bake your cookies," she said gently as she stroked their pink cheeks. "Your mamma's going to start making her pottery again."

Ready to find
your next great read?

Let us help.

Visit prh.com/nextread

Penguin
Random
House